Copyright © 2025 Tina.R.Abbott

All rights reserved.
No part(s) of this publication may be stored, reproduced and/or transmitted in any form and/or by any means mechanical, electronic, photocopying, AI or otherwise without written permission from the author/publisher.

The right of Tina.R.Abbott to be identified as the author of this novel has been asserted by Tina.R.Abbott in accordance with the Copyright, Designs and Patents Act 1988

Independently Published
ISBN: 9798315951797

Please note that this novel is a work of fiction.Any names, incidents, locations, events, and/or places are either used fictitiously or products of the author's imagination. Any resemblance to actual persons, alive or deceased, is purely coincidental.

Trigger Warning: This book contains some scenes of sexually inappropriate advances that some may find upsetting.

Chapter One

"Oh, heavens, Audrey, that is … Well, it's… it's…"

Florence Braithwaite couldn't quite muster the correct words, it seemed, Audrey Whittemore mused as she stood before the young woman. An apparent sense of wonderment, evidently writhing beneath her friend's pale skin. Holding her breath, Audrey patiently bided her time as Florence fidgeted on the spot, the young lady's subtle movements revealing the somewhat mountainous effort it entailed for her to find the correct word – or perhaps words – to elaborate her opinion.

"Scandalous?" Audrey offered, quite unable to refrain from speaking any longer. It was as good a word as any, she thought, wondering whether perhaps that was indeed the word her best friend was searching for. She smiled wryly, then began to reattach her skirts to her bodice.

"Well, some may say so indeed, yet I myself wouldn't quite use those words, my dear." Flossie blushed a subtle shade of pink all the way to the roots of her hair as she attempted to suppress a grin. "But my mother certainly would," she whispered, emitting a breathy chuckle. Excitement glittered in her blue eyes. "Where, or should I say *who*, did all that for you? I don't know of any seamstress I could, *nor would*, trust with something like that."

Audrey sighed, relieved to note the lack of judgement in her friend's reaction. "Of course, you are correct, Floss, for I very much doubt there would be any seamstress one could trust to carry out such a task without gossip spreading like wildfire in its wake, yet there is one wonderful young lady who is rather a dab hand at needlework."

Florence Braithewaite looked fit to burst with questions, Audrey observed with a smile. "Ivy, my maid," she revealed, stepping to the side as a sharp blade of light pierced through the branches of the overhead trees and snapped the spring air in front of her eyes. She really could do without another nasty headache, Audrey grumbled silently. Raising her arm, she placed her hand just above her eyes to shield them. "It is she who has been helping me," Audrey continued, "and I trust her implicitly."

Both young ladies ambled forward towards the edge of the lake as they continued to chatter. Florence seemed quite lost in her own mental meanderings as she perused the scenery far off in the distance, all the while Audrey merely let her eyes wander only a few feet in front of them, observing the delicate beads of sunlight scattered over the glassy surface of the lake. Now that she had her new disguise, she would be able to wander down here alone whenever she pleased, Audrey considered with a serene smile tilting the corners of her mouth.

Audrey hauled her mind away from the water and back to their discussion. "We have been working on it together. Ivy has been a great help, and I am rather grateful, for I had the distinct feeling that it would have been far too risky to have allowed anyone else, other than you, of course, to be privy to our little project," she said, brushing down the front of her sage green skirts and giving her hips a gentle wiggle. The remaining folds tucked between the layers shimmied down the length of her legs until her skirts hung heavy in a fabric waterfall that splashed the leather boots concealing her feet. "There," she exclaimed matter-of-factly, "no one need ever know that the skirt is detachable. One would simply think this gown to be like any other. It is all rather perfect, even if I do say so myself."

Flossie stepped closer to her friend. "May I?" she enquired, her nimble finger stretching in a delicate point as she gestured to the floral button discreetly perched on the generous curve of Audrey's hip. Intrigue swam in the young woman's eyes. Their blue was almost dazzling against her curls, Audrey thought with affection as she watched the breeze sweep up Flossie's golden tresses and tousle them at the sides of the young woman's face.

"Yes, of course." Audrey shifted, twisting her body and raising her hip ever so slightly so her best friend could take a closer look at her newly altered clothing. It had been time-consuming, to say the least, to have altered most of her gowns, but with the freedom it would allow her in the coming days, weeks and, hopefully, months, she thought it would be rather worth it. It was not merely freedom she wished for, for it was time alone and space away from her home so that she could think or at least forget about everything – or to be more precise, her father and that awful Lord Gastrell.

"The stitchwork is impeccable, Audrey," Flossie breathed, interrupting her friend's thoughts and thus the decline of her mood. "One wouldn't know your gown had been altered unless you showed them what you have just shown me." Flossie's eyes widened with awe as she lightly touched the button. "So wonderfully clever," she whispered. "And how it merely looks part of the design as if it has absolutely no functionality at all is tremendous. Such a sly little button." Flossie grinned.

As far as appearances went, Audrey and Flossie were rather different, Audrey considered, for where Flossie was blonde and blue-eyed, she herself was a deep brunette with pale green eyes. It was much the same for their personalities, for, although Audrey's father would have liked very much for his daughter to be tame and submissive, thus making his current plans much more easily attainable, she was indeed secretly wild to a degree, and, if one were to dig a little deeper into the matter, she may even be deemed to be a little reckless, as it were, whereas Florence Braithewaite was every inch what society viewed as perfection. Of course, Flossie was not quite so demure when it was simply she and Audrey, for Audrey was quite sure she knew all of her best friend's scandalous thoughts, and thus, despite their differences, one could not have met two ladies who were as closely bonded as Audrey Whittemore and Florence Braithewaite. One may say they were more like sisters in public and as thick as thieves in private, but altogether it was true that they did indeed have an unbreakable bond.

Audrey giggled, giving her friend an affectionate smile. "It's only a gown with a few alterations, Floss."

"Why, yes, I know, but a gentleman would never think a lady would be capable of something so ingenious." Flossie lowered her bottom onto what appeared to be a rather neatly chopped tree stump and placed the basket she had been carrying to the side of her, its weight nestling into the slightly damp grass. "That's better," she mused, sighing as she stretched her legs out in front of her. "It is a beautiful day, is it not?"

"It is, indeed, Floss," Audrey replied, unrolling the blanket from beneath her arm, whipping it up in the air and bringing it back down until it settled at its full size at their feet. She gently fluffed out her skirts and lowered herself down onto the green plaid fabric, settling back on her elbows.

"Can you imagine if you were to make these for every lady?" Flossie wondered aloud. "There are so many that I am quite sure that you would earn more than enough money to be independent. Indeed, you would never have to marry."

"And can you imagine the scandal of offering such a service?" Audrey snorted at the very thought of the reaction of the other ladies of the *ton*. "Besides, I don't think my father would agree to me doing such a thing, Floss," she added. "That man is beyond adamant that I marry Lord Gastrell."

Both ladies shuddered simultaneously at the dreadful thought of such a union, the finger of disgust slithering down their spines. Audrey glanced secretively sideways at her friend. She shouldn't feel jealous of her; she knew she shouldn't, for none of it, not even a single iota of it, was Flossie's fault, but she found herself almost angry that her friend's response to her impending marriage, or perhaps one should refer to it as doom, did not even scrape the surface of how she was feeling.

Audrey let out a breath. In truth, she was glad that Flossie would not be facing such a despicable future. She would never want her to marry someone such as the festering beast of a man that was Lord Gastrell.

Florence Braithewaite's eyes flicked in Audrey's direction as though she had read her mind. "I'm sorry, Audrey," she muttered. "You don't deserve this. I wish with all my heart that there was a way that you could be excused from such a ghastly future. Although I may heave a little, or perhaps profusely, I would swap places with you simply so you would not be subjected to such a dreadful fate." Flossie's brow furrowed as she turned to face her friend.

The expression on Flossie's pretty face only echoed Audrey's own inner turmoil. She had been incorrect to assume that the young lady did not understand, Audrey realised as she offered a timid smile. She may have offered a deeper version, but it appeared that everything she had been trying to not so much as consider had rapidly descended into her stomach with the weight of a cannonball. Audrey was not particularly fond of moments such as these, for she found ignorance to be rather blissful with regard to the matter at hand and had spent most of her days avoiding the repulsive subject of the impending doom that she was indeed being hurtled towards. She wasn't sure whether she was trying to come to terms with her fate by dismissing every thought of it or whether she was simply waiting for the moment when a knight in shining armour would gallop into her life and save her, for that is what always happens to young ladies like her in rather similar situations, is it not?

Audrey sighed, then quickly replaced it with a forced giggle to cover her emotions. It would achieve absolutely nothing to wallow in them, and she certainly wasn't going to spoil the afternoon with her friend by pushing the subject further than what they had already, she mused, feeling quite sure that there could not be a lady alive who would wish to discuss their betrothal to a man forty years their senior. "Let us not dwell," she exclaimed quietly.

"Indeed, my dear," Flossie returned a little sheepishly. "But should you wish to speak of it or any other matter troubling you, Audrey, then you merely have to say."

"Thank you, Floss."

"I mean it, Audrey. I know you must feel terribly alone, especially considering that it is you who will have to face it, but you will never be completely alone when you have me. Perhaps we will think of a way for you to avoid this altogether."

Goodness, Audrey thought. How had she been so very fortunate to have such a wonderful friend? As Audrey gazed at the young woman at her side, she realised she couldn't love the sister she had in her any more than she did in that moment. Flossie desperately wanted to help her escape the burden her father had willingly pressed down on her shoulders, it seemed, yet she had lost count of the times they had sat in contemplation attempting to do just that. But alas, no matter how much or how often they had wracked their brains for an idea, they had always been abruptly met with the blasted barriers created merely by their gender. It was rather more than a little unfair, it has to be said.

In a world where ladies would have the opportunity to make their own decisions, Audrey would have gladly waited for the right moment to marry. She, Audrey Whittemore, would have been the one to decide whether she wished to marry a particular gentleman or any gentleman at all for that matter, and she certainly wouldn't have had it thrust upon her by her father. She rather thought that she would swiftly sidestep the opportunity to marry if she were given the choice, but then she could not help but wonder whether she merely thought that because the only marriage she was given to think about was that to Lord Gastrell. Indeed, a life alone seemed rather more appealing than one tied to the likes of Lord Lecherous, as she preferred to call him, for the man was positively vile in every sense of the word.

"I wish there was indeed a way, Floss," Audrey replied with another sigh. At this rate, she mused, the only thing she would achieve is blowing her friend off the tree stump she was currently perched on. "But you know how my father is," she continued. "He believes that Lord Lecherous is his key to a much higher status, other than the demise of my uncle, of course."

Flossie let out a breath. "It is all very

frustrating. Nothing would please me more than to help you, Audrey."

"Well, if you have brought them with you, then your brother's clothes would be a great help." Audrey forced her lips to curl into an enthusiastic smile. The air around them was becoming far too melancholy, so much so that she could feel the once subdued panic begin to crawl up her insides.

"Oh, yes. Silly me." Flossie reached across and retrieved a bundle from the picnic basket. "These are Francis's. Fabian's breeches would be rather too lacking in leg length on you, but I think these should fit you perfectly, and Francis is less likely, if at all, to notice anything is missing. My brother has more clothes than I do," she said, laughing softly as she passed Audrey her brother's garments.

"Thank you, Floss. These will do quite nicely, I am sure." Audrey rose to her feet and began to loosen her bodice. She needed something to distract her, she reminded herself as she fought to push away the dread that lurked in every shadow of her mind. Shock would be just the thing, and she was quite aware that what she was in the midst of doing would indeed shock Flossie. Audrey grinned at the sound of Flossie's sudden intake of breath. It was far too easy, Audrey thought, chuckling soundlessly as her smile deepened, but this was the distraction she had been looking for. She had always found her friend's reactions to such trivial matters rather amusing indeed.

"Audrey!" Flossie chided gently, turning away, a little pink-cheeked.

"We are well hidden, Floss, and anyway, don't be such a prude. All I am doing is concealing your brother's clothes beneath my gown. I can't have anyone questioning me about them, and they will do just that if I walk into my home with them clutched in my arms without a care for who sees them." Audrey inhaled as she pushed the fabric down beneath her bodice and corset, trying to keep them flat against her stomach. A curvaceous figure had its perks, she considered, for no one would be so audacious as to question her about why she may appear a little more voluptuous than what they were used to seeing. "Be a darling and help me fasten my corset, Floss, won't you?" she called to her friend's back. "I seem to be having a dashed time of it."

Flossie turned with an expression of playful chastisement on her face. "You will be the death of me, Audrey Whittemore," she teased, as she struggled to seal her friend back into her corset. "Perhaps next time you might consider sewing pockets beneath your petticoats. It might have been rather less conspicuous."

"Oh, Floss! That is a spectacular idea. Why did I not think of that? I could make enough to take all manner of items out with me without my father ever knowing."

Flossie rolled her eyes at her friend's

enthusiasm. "Perhaps you should simply leave it to the detachable skirts for now and see whether your plan to wander the lands as a gentleman will be as successful as you hope. Small steps, Audrey, please," she pleaded, "or I shall simply die of worry for you."

"Alright," Audrey relented with a grin. "But only for you, but I shan't dismiss it completely." Audrey tucked the bodice back beneath the waistline of the detached skirts, rendering both items as one to the eyes of others.

"I wouldn't expect you to. I know you far too well," Flossie groaned.

"However," Audrey added, eyeing the boots still sitting in the picnic basket. "They may need somewhere to go."

"Oh, you wouldn't? Audrey, you will rui-"

Flossie gasped as the whistle of ripping stitches zipped through the air. Audrey had lifted her skirt and torn a pocket into her petticoats. "Audrey!"

Walking over to the basket, Audrey picked up the boots and carefully lowered them into the large makeshift pocket she had created. "I shall call it the Flossie Pocket," she announced with mischief. "It rather beats trying to put those boots beneath my corset, do you not think?"

Flossie gulped. "I'd rather you didn't use my name, Audrey, but yes, I do see that *that*," she said, wiggling her finger at the now concealed pocket, "is rather more sensible."

"Indeed, my dear. Indeed, it is perfectly wonderful."

Audrey ambled rather awkwardly up the stone front steps of the Whittemore residence, cursing herself for not considering the wonderful idea of hidden pockets under her skirts a tad more carefully before she had ripped them so low in the layers of fabric. Had she not rushed so eagerly to make Flossie's spectacular idea a reality, she may have considered the weight of what she wished to fill them with before she had opted to place them directly in front of her poor shins. As she was finding out with every step, it would have been kinder to her legs if she had torn the makeshift pockets further up; perhaps, she mused, in front of her thighs, for as much as it pained her to admit it, even to herself, her legs were slightly more cushioned in that area, and she would not have felt the force of the gentlemen's boots bashing against them so painfully as she was currently experiencing. Then, of course, the discomfort of the male garments squeezed beneath her corset and scratching her flesh was not exactly helping matters either. She could only imagine how ridiculous she appeared as she shuffled toward the door.

Audrey inhaled, sucking in her stomach muscles to make a little more room for what felt like several buttons. They were digging curiously into her flesh, and one had decided to make itself at home inside her belly button. She gritted her teeth as a distraction, trying not to wriggle profusely in order to dislodge the blasted thing. "Please do not be home, Father," she whispered to herself. "Or at least, please do not greet me. I do not think I will be able to cope with you today."

"Miss Whittemore," the butler drawled, as the door creaked open, the sound of the rusting hinges grating through the foyer as he frowned briefly, then schooled his features.

Audrey wished she could simply tell the door to hush. She really did not want everyone to see her in such a predicament. Even the butler could not hide his confusion at her sudden change in deportment. Not that she could blame him, she thought as she strained to offer him what she hoped resembled a rather natural and friendly smile. "Bernard," she sang quietly, continuing past him towards the staircase.

She was wiggling. Audrey grimaced as the realisation struck her like a highly inconvenient and rather mortifying bolt of lightning. She never wiggled, did she? Oh, she hoped she didn't. The thought of behaving like one of those tittering twits that the gentlemen of the ton practically fell over themselves to dance with did not sit well with her. It was positively revolting. "That is why you have never married, Audrey," she berated herself in a whisper as she trudged up the stairs. Had she wiggled and been slightly more feline-esque in her movements, then she may not have found herself betrothed to a giant slug. Although, she mused, she doubted she would have had any luck anyway, for the wiggle that she now possessed was rather inelegant, to say the least.

"Miss Audrey."

"Yes, Bernard?" Audrey did not turn to face the butler. She was rather afraid that everything she was hiding would simply drop to her feet, so she merely stopped and waited for him to continue.

"Your father has requested you join him for dinner, miss," the butler informed her.

Audrey stiffened and exhaled a heavy, drawn-out breath of exasperation. She should have known that avoiding the man for one day would have been too much to ask for. "Thank you, Bernard," she replied kindly. "I shall freshen up a little first, and then I shall be down for dinner."

"Apologies, Miss Audrey," Bernard called quietly up to her.

"You have nothing to apologise for, Bernard."

Audrey's insides swirled; the recognition of dread in the butler's voice warned her that whatever reason her father had for wanting her to attend dinner in the main dining room with him would not be pleasant. Mind you, she thought, she could not think of a single moment when the man had ever been pleasant. However, these days, she knew that unpleasant had soured into downright dreadful, for the conversations between them—or rather, lectures from him—were always about Lord Lecherous. The servants knew it too. Gosh, Audrey's own mother knew it, yet even though Marjorie Whittemore knew of the nightmare unravelling for her daughter, the woman had not so much as uttered a word. She had simply taken to silence on the matter and an extended avoidance, which was usually spent in her bedchamber.

Blowing out a breath, Audrey continued climbing the remaining steps of the staircase, her mind fighting for something, anything, else to think of rather than what seemed to haunt her continuously in one way or another. She had hoped that the time she spent out of the house would have offered her respite from reality, but it seemed that as the days passed, venturing closer to what was now the inevitable, her troubles followed her, tarnishing every happy moment. However, there was no denying that upon her return, the truth of her predicament was somewhat more abrasive as the walls of her home closed her in with those who appeared not to care one whit for her happiness. Of course, it was probably for the best, she surmised as she reached the top step, shifting her skirt to the side so that those blasted boots did not hit her poor shins again, for it did not do one any favours to be so complacent when it seemed that one's life was being moulded and shaped by the hands of another. The anger it mustered was what drove her forward, she realised, building her up with a steely sense of determination. Audrey Whittemore was not standing at the altar yet, and if she had any say in the matter, then she was never going to be. She did not care what anyone thought of her anymore. Perhaps her freedom in the guise of a man would give her the time she needed to come up with a plan.

Audrey ambled silently and rather haphazardly towards her bedchamber, panic lacing itself between each rib bone as her mind raced. "Almost there," she mumbled quietly to herself, her words softening as they trailed into an exasperated sigh as she wrapped her dainty hand around the door handle and twisted it. Pushing her bedchamber door open, Audrey stepped inside.

The medley of buttons popping free of their fastenings and of laces being loosened spattered and whistled across the silence as Audrey hurriedly freed herself from her current self-inflicted torture. In her haste, she had not even so much as considered closing the door.

"Oh, good lord," she grumbled, kicking the door closed behind her, then yanked the top of her bodice away from her bosom and reached beneath it, where she grasped the fabric of Flossie's brother's attire and dragged it away from her skin.

An extremely rumpled jet-black jacket with matching breeches flew through the air, landing on her bed, followed by a brilliant white shirt and a blue silk cravat that matched the waistcoat she already had acquired.

"Oh, thank goodness," she exclaimed with a sigh of relief, picking up a fan off her dressing table and quickly wafting the air in front of her face. It was awfully hot, she mused as she placed the fan back down and began shifting and hitching up the fabric of her skirts, where she rummaged amongst the many layers until her hands settled upon the dratted pair of men's boots.

"Blast you," Audrey cursed quietly at the boots as she placed them on the bed. Rubbing at the sore spot they had made on her shins, she scowled at them. "I have no doubt my poor shins shall be covered with bruises," she grumbled, then hit the boots with the back of her hand in an act of petty revenge, adding a muffled snort for good measure.

The distant sound of approaching footsteps snapped Audrey from her rather murderous considerations towards the sturdy boots and sent her into somewhat of a panic. She could not afford to be discovered with such items, for her freedom would be snatched from her before she so much as tasted it. That would never do, she mused anxiously, setting about making herself look what she hoped would indeed be presentable as she tightened and fastened the dishevelled clothing on her body and tucked the fallen strands of glossy, rich, mahogany brown hair behind her ears and back into the updo that had originally been perfectly styled atop her head. The crumpled masculine clothes lay scattered across her mattress. It was a shame indeed that they were so terribly wrinkled, she considered as her lips pressed together thoughtfully. It seemed the heat of her own body had not only creased the fabric but practically ironed the unsightly folds into it. She would merely have to remedy that, she decided as she cursed herself for not considering such consequences of her methods.

Retrieving the masculine clothing with some speed, Audrey arranged them neatly on the spare hangers in her closet, placing them between her gowns as she glided her hand over each item to ensure that they would be as smooth as possible between the press of her dresses. It was not exactly an ideal solution, she thought, yet it seemed it was the only one she had had on such short notice. She was not inclined to put more work on her poor maid's shoulders, so she rather hoped that it would be sufficient to see the fabric right itself.

Feeling rather flushed from panic, Audrey stepped quickly toward the small window and opened it as she listened to the footsteps halt outside her bedchamber door. The cool air rushed in as she stared nonchalantly across the estate grounds.

How had her father managed to accrue such a vast, well-established estate? she wondered as the winds gently kissed her cheeks, quietly stealing the crimson glow that had nestled in them. She had never paid any heed to their obvious wealth before. She supposed she had merely taken it all for granted, but as she totted up all that her father owned, she could not help but be a little confused by it all. Audrey's brows crinkled in contemplation. Her uncle owning such a place, she could definitely understand, but he and her father were estranged, and, aware that Wallace Whittemore held no title, it all seemed rather odd now that she thought about it.

"There you are, Miss Audrey. Penny for them?" the maid sang.

"To be truthful, Ivy, I don't think I really want to know the answers to my mental ramblings, so much so that I am quite afraid to even utter them aloud." Audrey stepped away from the window to join the maid. "I have, though, procured some male clothing from Flossie. I have put them in the closet between my gowns in the hope that they will make them look a little less crumpled."

Ivy's eyes turned to the centre of the satin-covered mattress.

Audrey followed her gaze. "Oh," she mouthed, her skin beginning to glow again. "I believe I am rather glad you came in here, Ivy, for I doubt I would have noticed." Reaching over, Audrey retrieved the pair of gentleman's boots from the top of her bed and hid them beneath it. "I was in a bit of a panic when I heard you walking towards my chambers. I was worried that it was somebody else. It seems, had it not been you, I would have made a rather catastrophic error."

Ivy grinned as she moved around the room. "Were the clothes that Miss Florence gave you suitable for you, Miss Audrey?"

"I believe so," Audrey replied. "But I may have to wait a while."

The maid frowned with curiosity.

"The creases were rather magnificent," Audrey explained. "You know I never do things by halves, my dear, and they may take a bit of time before they look presentable enough to wear."

Ivy walked over to the closet and retrieved the items. "Don't you worry about that, Miss Audrey. I'll have them pressed in no time." The maid held the garments up in front of her face, her lips pursed in determination. "If anyone asks, I'll just say they belong to one of the footmen."

"That is indeed very kind, Ivy. Thank you." Audrey kicked the boots further beneath the bed, rearranging the satin coverlet so that it concealed her burgeoning secret in amongst the darkness. She was already making mistakes, she realised. Her plan was far too important to her to be acting so carefree about it all.

"Perhaps you might like these?" Ivy enquired, holding up a bundle of tweed fabric.

"Where did you get those?" Audrey queried, her eyes wide with surprise and intrigue. It was rather impressive what one could hide in Ivy's basket, it seemed.

"They were my brothers… But they are clean, miss, honestly. He takes pride in his appearance. He has high hopes, and I did ask him if I could have them. Of course, I didn't tell him about you, miss."

Audrey grinned. "It's perfectly alright, Ivy. I trust you implicitly. And I must say, I am terribly grateful for them. Thank you," she added, running her hands over the tweed garments. There were breeches, a fine waistcoat to match, and a soft off-white shirt. In truth, Audrey thought she rather preferred them to the others.

"You didn't mind me giving them to you, Miss Audrey?"

"Absolutely not, Ivy. This is extremely thoughtful of you. Indeed, I believe they will suit me rather better than the gentlemen's formal wear."

Something fell from the bottom of the pile as Audrey adjusted her hands around them.

"Oh, yes, I almost forgot," the maid announced, hurrying forward to fetch the item from the floor. "This is a gentleman's cap for you. I thought you could tuck your hair up in it when you go out."

"You have thought of everything, dear Ivy," Audrey exclaimed, her lips curling, matching the beginnings of the burgeoning excitement curling in her chest. "Thank you so much."

"You are very welcome, Miss Audrey. I'll just

prepare you a bath, and I shall leave you to it."

Audrey was feeling a little emotional at the maid's kindness. It was small deeds such as these and the kind words often offered that reminded her that when she married, she would not only be subjecting herself to the lecherous man, but she would also be risking Ivy. Lord Gastrell was not the sort of man who possessed any morals, and she highly doubted that would alter once they were married. She could only imagine how many of his maids he was currently tormenting. She shuddered. To force a life with Lord Lecherous on her was one thing, but to force one upon someone as lovely as Ivy was indeed another.

"I nearly forgot to say, Miss Audrey," Ivy announced as she stood at the bedchamber door, preparing to leave, "I think your father has invited Lord Gastrell to dinner, and I thought it best that I warn you."

It was as though the maid had been sifting through her thoughts, Audrey noted. "Ivy."

"Yes, Miss Audrey?"

"Do you wish to work for Lord Gastrell?"

The maid bit her bottom lip, her eyes averted as though she was summoning the right words. "Not particularly, miss, but I want to continue tending to you, so if that means I have to work for Lord Gastrell to do so, then I will. Wherever you go, Miss Audrey, I go."

"Thank you, Ivy," Audrey rasped with a nod. "That will be all."

Something twisted at the centre of Audrey's gut. She shouldn't have been so willing to have accepted her father's demand. It was all well and good to commit her life to the beast, but she was not quite so willing to allow Ivy to.

Chapter Two

"Sir, you have a caller."

"Who is it, Harmsworth?" came a low, rather disinterested rumble.

"The man says he is your father's legal representative," the butler quietly explained across the study.

Hunter Carlisle paused his quill and lifted his head. It seemed the very mention of his father had his butler scratching at the back of his neck with unease. He could hardly blame him, he thought, for Lord Carlisle had the ability to make any man come out in a rash. "My father?" he queried, ignoring the cold chill that washed through his veins as he straightened his spine. "I haven't heard from the man for *fifteen* years," he muttered incredulously. Hunter frowned. What in the devil did he want? He highly doubted it would be to invite him to a rather overdue family reunion.

"Indeed, sir," Harmsworth offered, pulling his hand away from his slowly crimsoning neck and straightening his posture. "The man says it is paramount that he speak with you, sir."

The butler's apprehensive demeanour as his eyes darted to the side and settled back on Hunter again was not only pointless, Hunter thought irritably, but it seemed only to hinder Hunter's ability to make a simple decision. The feeling of being hurried to decide whether to speak with the caller was irksome, to say the least, especially when Hunter's mind had suddenly filled with a whirlwind of the past and the present. Hunter ground his teeth together and narrowed his eyes, then let out a breath of resignation. He had no right to be rude to Harmsworth, for he suspected that the butler's nervous behaviour was more to do with the fact that the household staff were all too aware of the bad blood between Hunter and his family. He supposed he might have been nervous if he too had been in the same situation. "Yes, of course, show him in, please, Harmsworth. I shall speak with him here."

As the butler turned his back, the centre of Hunter's brow pinched into a V. Solicitors rarely ever offered joyous news, Hunter mused, ignoring the sudden onset of nausea roiling in his stomach. And if the man had travelled this far, then Hunter did not think that what the solicitor would have to say to him would be anything he would find particularly merry. The intrusion, it seemed, had Hunter curious, unsettled, and indeed peeved simultaneously.

"Good morning, Lord Carlisle. My name is Mr Baldry." A man with golden hair that matched the rim of his spectacles cleared his throat and nodded his head. "Thank you for allowing me to speak with you," he continued, brushing down the thick black fabric of his coat as it hung heavily over his arm.

"I am not a lord, sir, but simply Mr Carlisle," Hunter corrected, the furrow in his brow deepening at the use of his father's title.

"Ah, I see," Mr Baldry muttered, walking over to the chair opposite Hunter and seating himself without invitation.

Hunter's brows rose. He was being petty, he knew it, but he was beginning to feel rather like a caged animal about to be informed that it was to be slaughtered.

Thankfully, the solicitor did not appear to notice, for he simply continued. "It seems I have arrived prior to your mother's letter, which means that this is a little more awkward than I had anticipated." The solicitor swallowed, his eyes roaming the room as though he was simply unable to focus on anything other than his ability to fidget with apparent discomfort.

Hunter Carlisle placed his elbows on the desk, anger rolling over his broad, muscular shoulders as he leaned forward, fingers laced together in a tight clasp that resembled a rock, albeit with a fleshy tone and evident muscle, beneath his chin. He wished the man would bloody well spit it out. "Mr Baldry, your reluctance to elaborate is concerning to me. Perhaps it would be best if you simply start at the beginning and tell me what it is my mother was supposed to have informed me of in the letter you mentioned."

The solicitor fidgeted momentarily on the seat, then quickly stood, placing his hands behind his back as he began the rather annoying habit of pacing. "Very well," he offered, "for I must seem rather unprofessional. I apologise, *my lord,* for my behaviour. It is merely that it is a rather sensitive matter, but as you say, it does indeed need to be said. Therefore, it is with considerable regret that I must advise that both your elder brother and your father have passed." Mr Baldry inhaled and quickly lowered himself back into the seat, lowering his eyes to his lap as he did so.

Hunter was quite relieved that the man was not staring at him. His skin felt thick and cold, yet he was perspiring. "My father *and* my brother?" he enquired in a faint rumble. One of the two gentlemen popping off the mortal coil would have seemed almost realistic, yet two simply seemed as though it was rather unlikely. If he had not been reeling slightly from the news, Hunter would have corrected himself, for the view that two people could not pass at the same time was utter nonsense. Indeed, it would have been rare but certainly not impossible.

"I am afraid so, my lord. Your mother has

requested that you return to the estate, where you will take up your new role."

Hunter had never expected to be given a title. The role of his father's heir had always been placed upon his brother. The non-transferable position of baron between brothers had been drummed into them both, so there was no questioning whom it belonged to. In some ways, Hunter had been relieved, yet in others it had left him out in the cold, even at a very young age. Argyle had been the apple of his parents' eyes, and Hunter was simply the *other* Carlisle son. It was the very reason he had been determined to make a life for himself, to be self-sufficient in trade, which in turn had been the blade that had severed the ties between him and his family, for the first utterance of his new venture saw to it that they promptly disowned him. They were convinced that the news of his chosen way of life would see them as the laughingstock of the ton. Yet despite all the bitter blood that had passed between the three gentlemen, the news of his father's and his brother's passing felt like a heavy punch to Hunter's gut. "What happened?"

Mr Baldry's eyes met Hunter's with a certain air of discomfort. Hunter had unknowingly asked the man something he was clearly not wanting to answer. "I think I should allow your mother to inform you of that, my lord." The solicitor began to examine the contents of his briefcase, his fingers flicking through the sheets of parchment as though he was searching for something terribly important, yet Hunter knew that no one could interpret the contents at that speed.

"I would prefer it, Mr Baldry, if you told me now," Hunter snapped, agitated as the minutes seemed to drag with the weight of the news. Having to probe for answers was rather irritating when the solicitor could have quite easily told him everything to begin with. Of course, the man had assumed that Lady Carlisle would have already informed him of everything, Hunter considered, scoffing at the very idea of obtaining the truth from his mother, for he knew that her version would have been twisted, dramatised, and exaggerated merely to soften and manipulate as she sought to garner sympathy from him. Conversing with the woman was not appealing in the slightest, Hunter thought bitterly, and returning to her was even less so. No, he could not and certainly would not ask Lady Carlisle. He wanted the truth prior to facing her.

"Very well, my lord. It appears there was some disagreement over money, and they were shot."

The solicitor was chewing the inside of his cheek as his eyes roved over the bookcase behind Hunter, avoiding meeting the man's gaze. There was something he wasn't saying, Hunter thought suspiciously. "Did they catch the man who did this?" he asked, fixing his eyes on Mr Baldry's forever-altering expression as he watched for any signs of deception.

"Men, my lord, and yes, I suppose they did," the man mumbled sheepishly.

"How can you merely *suppose* that the criminals responsible have been apprehended, Mr Baldry? They either have or they haven't. Surely, it is not that difficult to ascertain?" Frustration at the man's refusal to speak plainly simmered beneath Hunter's skin. He no longer felt the heavy boot of shock in his stomach but a rolling rage that was beginning to grow.

"There is no easy way to say this, my lord, but your father and your brother appear to have shot each other. Some sort of duel that went terribly wrong." The solicitor pinched his lips together as his eyes rounded.

Tipping his head back, Hunter couldn't help the roar of laughter that burst from the back of his throat, all the while feeling the heat of the solicitor's eyes as the poor man simply stared in confusion. It wasn't amusing, yet, then again, it was, Hunter thought as he wiped a tear away from the corner of his eye. It was terribly strange to be finding amusement in the death of one's own brother and father, but there he was, laughing as though he had been told the funniest thing he had ever heard. It appeared that neither his father nor his brother had altered an iota from the men he remembered. Perhaps they had gotten worse to have gone to the extreme of a duel, he considered. He didn't think his mother could have changed much either. Suddenly, realisation that Hunter may have literally dodged a bullet dawned on him, for had he not left fifteen years ago, one of those bullets could very well have been intended for him.

"My lord, are you quite alright?" the solicitor queried. "I don't believe I have ever had such a… a…an unusual response to the news of a loved one parting this world."

Hunter knew he should have felt sorry for the man, but he couldn't quite bring himself to feel anything above the range of emotions that had suddenly gripped his entire being. The ridiculousness of his father's and brother's deaths was utterly ironic and far too ludicrous for him to school his face into a more sombre look. He could, at least, try, though, he supposed.

Hunter cleared his throat, then closed his eyes, taking a slow, deep breath that filled his lungs and faded the images in his imagination. "I apologise, Mr Baldry," he began. "I know I must seem terribly uncaring, but you see, I have not seen hide nor hair of my father, brother, or mother for the past fifteen years. It was their ways that sent me far from them and into a life of trade, which they very much disapproved of. I know my reaction was not at all normal, per se, but the news had indeed caught me off guard, and the irony of it all was what had amused me, not their actual deaths."

The solicitor nodded. "Ah, I see," he mumbled.

"No, I don't think you do, sir. My family disowned me. I was a disgrace to them because I wanted to make a life for myself and not have to rely on my father's money. Yet here you are telling me that they killed each other for the very thing that they would have gladly seen me use without having to work a day in my life. If I had agreed to their terms and expectations of what a gentleman should be, there could have been a third deceased Carlisle male, or I could have switched places with one of them. It seems to me that if my brother had worked for his own money and my father had not deemed it necessary to try and prevent us from attempting to do so, you, my dear man, would not be sitting opposite me with the news of their demise. In fact, it is extremely likely that you would not be sitting opposite me at all."

The solicitor remained speechless, his mind evidently absorbing Hunter's words. "Yes, it does seem rather ironic, doesn't it?" he mused aloud, understanding of Hunter's explanation animating his features as his eyebrows rose.

"Indeed, Mr Baldry, it does. However, I assume you have some news for me other than their passing," Hunter enquired. The solicitor seemed like a decent man, he thought. He would listen to what was bequeathed to him, and any issues he had with his mother, he would then take them up with her. After all, the gentleman in front of him was merely the messenger and not to blame for any of it.

"Oh, yes, of course. I believe I got quite distracted. I apologise."

"No need, my good man. Please continue."

Hunter listened as the solicitor reeled off the contents of the estate under his new title. The shackles of his past had come to drag him back to where it all began, but the worst of it all was that they had come to drag him back to the woman who had stood idly by as he was demanded to leave.

"Very well, I shall return, Mr Baldry," Hunter began. "But I shall not return for another month. I have matters here to attend to. I cannot simply drop everything when my mother tells me to jump," Hunter stated with a positive air, yet inside he was not quite as certain of his decision as he had liked to seem.

"I-"

Hunter eyed the solicitor, arching his eyebrow as he waited for him to put forward a case that could override his responsibilities in London.

It seemed that the poor man could not muster a single one, or perhaps he was too afraid to. "Very good, my lord. I shall inform Lady Carlisle that you shall return in a month," Mr Baldry replied, relenting as his face crimsoned. "I do not think she will be best pleased. Your mother is…" The solicitor's voice dwindled into silence, dragging the rest of the sentence with it, thus leaving it unfinished as he had intended.

"My mother is what?" Hunter enquired, feeling rather amused. He was intrigued whether the woman had revealed a part of herself that he had never seen her use on those outside of the family home before.

"It is nothing, my lord." Mr Baldry blushed from misplaced guilt, believing he had spoken out of turn.

"My mother is demanding, Mr Baldry," Hunter said, offering the man a sense of camaraderie. "She always has been, and she always will be. Do not worry, for you need not return to her and deliver the news. I shall send word to her myself, which I have no doubt will arrive before you do. You, my good man, may return to your somewhat easier clients and consider your work here done." Hunter smiled and rose from his seat.

"Very good, my lord. And I thank you," the solicitor offered, looking rather less flushed.

"Think nothing of it. After all, you are in my employ now, are you not?"

"Indeed, my lord, for if that is what you wish, then I am."

"Harmsworth!" Hunter bellowed as soon as the front door clicked shut. "Harmsworth!" Where on earth was the man? he grumbled silently to himself, feeling a little aggrieved at the upheaval of the situation afoot.

The butler arrived at the study door, appearing rather breathless and out of sorts. "Yes, sir?"

Perhaps he should have curbed his temper, Hunter considered, noticing the high rise of red in the man's skin and the glimmer of fear in his eyes. He was handling it all wrong, he thought, for it wasn't the fault of the people who had served him loyally for so long. Slowly, Hunter inhaled, then let out a long, calming breath. "Have I received any correspondence recently?" he enquired gently.

"Yes, sir. Every day I put them over there." Harmsworth pointed to a silver tray. His shoulders had lowered with the change in his employer's tone. The look of fear in his eyes had dissipated, leaving only a subtle confused expression. Harmsworth had always assumed that his employer knew exactly where he placed his correspondence. It was a routine that he had adhered to religiously on a daily basis over the years and he had never been queried on the matter before. It was rather strange indeed.

Hunter stared at the pile of unopened letters. "So, you have, Harmsworth. It appears I have been busier than I thought. Thank you."

"Is there anything else, sir?" the butler asked, straightening his jacket.

Although Hunter noted the return of a healthy glow to Harmsworth's face and felt rather relieved that he had quickly vanquished any fear the man had had of him, he wondered whether he should correct him by mentioning his new, ridiculous title. Mulling it over, he realised with a scoff that it would be far too pretentious. Besides, it wasn't as if he actually cared for the blasted thing anyway, and the butler did not need to be feasing unnecessarily over a damned change to his name. No, it did not matter a jot about the title, and it certainly wasn't worth making the butler think of him as he had his father – as the devil incarnate. "That will be all, thank you, Harmsworth."

Lord Hunter Carlisle pinched the pile of letters between his thick fingers and settled back into his padded and rather comfortable leather-upholstered wingback chair. He couldn't quite describe the emotions going through him as grief, but they were indeed rather odd. Had it been the absence of fifteen years that had cushioned the forceful blow that one expected from such news as the death of a family member, or, in this particular case, two? Hunter could hardly decipher. In truth, he had never considered such a day to arrive. It all seemed as though it was something he would never have had to face. Yet there he was with such information and not knowing what it was he should do with it nor how he was supposed to react. He certainly couldn't go around laughing maniacally like he had in front of Mr Baldry, for he could only imagine what people would say. Indeed, he would be bound for Bedlam before he had the chance to explain himself.

"Invitation, invitation, Lady Howell's Orphanage... Ah!" Hunter held the familiar penmanship up before him. His mother always did take peculiar pleasure in elongating the curls and loops of letters such as the C in their surname. It was as though she had always believed herself on par with the monarch, he thought, and even after all the time that had passed, it was evident that she had not changed in that regard.

As he tore through the envelope with the silver letter opener, the scent of lavender tickled his nostrils. "Still wearing that fragrance then, I see, Mother," his voice rumbled into the silent room. One was supposed to find joy and comfort in the familiar fragrance of one's mother, but that was far from the truth for Hunter, for it only served to remind him of the moments when it had wafted through the air as she had turned on her heel and left him scolded by his father's tongue. Once it had made him sad, but now it merely made him angry. No, perhaps the word angry would have been how he'd felt in his younger days, but after so many years, the depth of his animosity was bordering upon parchment-thin, so perhaps the words disgruntled or peeved were better terms to use, he considered, yet either way, it was not pleasant. Lavender, it seemed, was rather repugnant to him.

Lady Agatha Carlisle's words were almost poetic, he thought with a wry smile and a brief roll of his eyes as he studied the contents of the woman's correspondence. Her words practically sang off the parchment in the most poetic, false description of a relationship between mother and son he had ever read. Had he missed something? Did they once have all that she had professed? He thought not. As far as he had been aware, he had, for the past fifteen years, been donning the crown of being the disappointment of the Carlisle family, an invisible, gleaming circlet of gold that he had been forced to wear. It had been embellished with the finest of jewels that had been born from disapproval and faceted by the sharp-bladed glint of disgust that flickered in the eyes of society and especially in those of his closest family. The way the woman wrote of their past had made it sound as though they had spent wondrous days running through rosy gardens, giggling in the sunshine together—a perfectly happy and contented family. Yet, the past that Hunter remembered had been filled with harsh words, strict rules, and sullen faces. They were the exact words he would have used to sum up the first eighteen years of his life.

Even before he had had the opportunity to deliver the news of what he intended for his own life, he had always felt as though he had been somewhat lingering at the furthest border of the family unit—an inconsequential addition, as it were —for every action and word, or perhaps life in general, had always evolved around the family name and thus the heir, his older brother.

At the time, when he had confessed to his parents about his plans, Hunter had braced himself for some form of confrontation. Although he hadn't known exactly what to expect, he certainly knew he had not expected a reaction to the extent that his mother and father had bestowed upon him. Of course, that is not to say that he was not aware that it was deemed beneath one to be in trade, for his family had drummed it into both he and his brother often. So, let it be known that there had been no mistake in the matter, but Hunter could not keep away from what his mind and fingers itched to delve into. He wished to be self-sufficient and to not have to rely upon his father the way his older brother had seemed to do quite easily. To Hunter, it was utterly degrading to seek his father out whenever he needed financial aid for this or for that. For lack of other words, Hunter craved independence, and it seemed that the declaration of his decision triggered the beginning of said independence in abundance.

Hunter shook his head. "Look where that got you both," he muttered under his breath as the image of his father and brother emerged out from beneath his barrage of thoughts. If he and his brother had just been allowed to go out into the world freely with their parents' blessing, it may have been so very different. Hunter was indeed proof of the security that independence had brought him. He was the master of his own fate, yet now that the letter burned his fingers, he wondered how much control he could maintain over his life. His mother would want to have her say in every decision like she always had. It was one of the reasons he considered having a month to prepare. Perhaps he did not have to face three Carlisle relatives, but he still had to face one.

Hunter rose from his seat, dropping the fairytale-filled letter onto his desk, then poured himself a whisky to dull the rush of angst flooding his veins. Would his nerves stand to wait a month? he wondered.

"Harmsworth!" he bellowed, ushering the poor butler through the door at tremendous speed for the umpteenth time that morning.

"Yes, sir?"

"See to it that my belongings are packed. Enough for a month, and would you please ask Thomas to prepare the carriage? I will be away for a while." Hunter Carlisle didn't have it in him to wait, he realised. He had learned over the years that it was better to face matters such as these head-on. The month he had initially intended to wait indeed had its perks, one of which was merely to annoy his mother, but in turn it would only annoy him. There was nothing else for it, he decided, he would simply have to face her sooner rather than later.

Having decided on the next course of action, Hunter allowed himself to think about what would happen post his arrival at the Carlisle Estate. It all looked pretty bleak, he thought, sighing inwardly. First he would claim the manor, he decided as he began to pace, but his mother could not live there with him... Oh, no! Certainly not! There would be no ifs or buts on the matter, for it would be utterly disastrous for them to share a home. However, he would not do to her what she and his father had done to him. Perhaps one of the other properties he knew his father to have possessed. Preferably one that was far away. Yes, that sounded rather ideal, he pondered positively, for he rarely, if at all, would have to cross paths with the woman if she was miles away.

Hunter began to whistle. The action always seemed to help him think. The solicitor made no mention of any clause or clauses regarding his mother's position in the home. Although, he considered, that didn't surprise him in the least, for it was rather apt for his father to metaphorically slap his lifelong ally in the face in the event of his demise. However, he hardly imagined it was negligence on his father's part nor even deliberate but simply that her well-being did not so much as occur to him. Indeed, he almost felt sorry for his mother. *Almost.*

He shook his head, shaking off the lack of words he could muster at the kind of man the late baron had been. The only one he could think of was *despicable*. But in being *despicable*, the late Lord

Carlisle had inadvertently given Hunter free rein, and he knew that had the man been alive, he would be spluttering and turning purple in outrage at the news that his disappointment of a son could send his widowed wife to live anywhere he deemed fit, and that was exactly what Hunter intended to do.

Chapter Three

Audrey inhaled as she lowered herself deeper into the bath, willing the warm, soothing water to wash away her rather unwelcome emotions. Her mind, it seemed, was quite determined to subject her to scenario after scenario of what her life would look like as the future Lady Gastrell, and of course, one would think it rather unnecessary to mention that none of her imaginings could possibly reveal so much as a morsel of happiness. Indeed, they consisted of long and bleak, intermittent nightmares that would stretch out as she remained by the lecherous toad's side year after year after year.

Groaning in frustration, Audrey lowered her head beneath the water, allowing the tears that sprang to the corners of her eyes to flow freely into the gentle ripples of her movements. Each salty droplet of despair, mingling and morphing with the sweet scent of orange blossoms. She did not want anyone to even so much as guess as to how very frightened she was. Yes, that was it. The thought of marrying Lord Gastrell *frightened* her. Of course, it disgusted her too, for the very thought of having to lie beneath him as he mauled her into carrying his heir was beyond hideous. There simply was nothing for her to gain from marrying the man, yet every time she tried to conjure a plan to escape him, it was as though she was trapped tightly within an unforgiving box with absolutely no way out.

"Mmmorbry! Mmmorbry!"

Audrey pulled on the sides of the bath, lifting her head out from beneath the water at the loud mumbles that met her ears. She gasped as the air hit her lungs.

"Miss Audrey," the maid exclaimed. "You gave me a right turn. I thought you'd drowned!"

Wiping fingers gently over the closed lids of her eyes, Audrey brushed away the remaining droplets of water, then turned her temporarily blurred gaze to the woman standing over her. The poor maid's eyes were wide with concern. "I apologise, Ivy. I didn't mean to startle you. I was merely relaxing." She coughed as water ran down the back of her nose and hit her throat. "Perhaps I was under for a little too long," she remarked, offering the rather pale young lady a wry smile.

As Ivy's gaze softened, Audrey wondered whether the maid had a rather remarkable talent for reading one's thoughts and knowing one's heart, for there was a glimmer of sadness in her searching eyes.

"Let's get you dried and dressed, shall we, Miss

Audrey? You know how the master can be if you are late," she suggested softly. "I've got all your clothes ready and waiting. I chose the blue gown with the high neck and long sleeves," Ivy added with a small nod of understanding.

"Thank you, Ivy." Audrey smiled, determinedly ignoring the heaviness in her chest. It was paramount, she reminded herself, that she did not weaken, even in the presence of those she knew understood her predicament perfectly well.

The gown was one of those that Audrey had had altered specifically. After meeting the lecherous lord for the first time, she knew that her usual pretty gowns and elegant day dresses simply wouldn't do. An apparent and rather dire need for attire that would cover as much of her skin as was indeed possible had overtaken any sense of vanity. One might say that their introduction was *loathe at first sight* for her. As for the man's first impression of her, Audrey hadn't cared one whit. Well, at least, not until her father revealed his sordid little plan for her anyway. The way in which Lord Gastrell had run his eyes up and down the length of her, Audrey remembered with a shudder, was as though he had been undressing her in front of everyone, and it had made her feel positively grotesque. The trail of his perusal had marked her skin with his filth as though he had trailed his sweaty fingers over her exposed flesh and even beneath her modest gown. And as ridiculous as she knew it to be, she had bathed profusely after meeting him, merely in the desperate hope that the water would wash away the remnants of his intrusive gaze. She supposed that may have been why she had almost swooned with fear when her father had given her the news of her betrothal.

"Extra petticoats again, Miss Audrey?" Ivy offered.

"Absolutely. Thank you, Ivy."

Audrey's skirts ballooned out around her legs, each layer of fabric over and under the crinoline adding an extra layer between her and Lord Gastrell. It didn't matter what she wore, she thought, for she knew he would take every opportunity to be inappropriate towards her, yet if layer after layer of additional fabric would mean that she would not have to endure quite as much of his wandering hands, then she would indeed grasp it with both of hers. Ivy had already wrapped swathes of fabric around Audrey's bosom in an attempt to ward off temptation. It was ridiculous, Audrey grumbled silently, that she had to go to such lengths to flatten and reshape her female parts simply to keep the disrespectful advances of a man, who at his age should know better, at bay. However, it seemed that it was imperative that she adhere to her new routine, for it was rather apparent that she had been reduced to nothing more than a piece of meat to be fondled by whoever was so inclined.

"There you go, Miss Audrey. If that man is

going to fondle, then let him fondle fabric, I say," the maid announced as she brushed down the back of Audrey's skirt.

"Indeed, Ivy. You know, I don't think I shall marry him," Audrey announced, straightening her spine as she stood in a regal stance. "I may not have thought of a way out for us both yet, but I shall, dear Ivy. Indeed, I shall."

Ivy grinned, her eyes twinkling. "That's more like the Miss Audrey I know," she beamed. "You deserve much better than the likes of him. You, miss, deserve happiness."

"As do you, Ivy. As do you."

"Ah, Miss Whittemore," Lord Gastrell drawled as his eyes trailed the length of Audrey's well-concealed body. A lascivious hunger glistened at their centres as he searched for the slightest glimpse of skin beneath her gown, only then for his unwanted gaze to settle upon her flattened breasts.

As the man's gaze turned rapidly into a glare, Audrey took comfort in his displeasure, wiggling her fingers as she delighted in the fact that she had not so much as even offered her hands for him to look upon, for they too were neatly concealed by the caress of fine white satin. "My lord," she replied, curtsying as she hid a sly smirk of satisfaction. "This is an unexpected visit, is it not?" Audrey smiled as she willed her polite expression to remain whilst fighting the sudden urge to grimace.

"Forgive my daughter, Lord Gastrell. It appears she has misplaced her manners."

Wallace Whittemore's head turned sharply, his eyes filled with malice as he shot Audrey a silent warning, one that would have indeed reprimanded a thousand soldiers. Yet Audrey was not a thousand soldiers, she mused, nor was she even one, and she was getting rather peeved with her father, for the more she thought of how he did not even care so much as to ask her what she wanted in life, the deeper the anger towards him settled in her stomach. She often wondered whether she did indeed *hate* the man.

Ignoring the visual animosity between the two Whittemore family members, Lord Gastrell ambled brazenly closer towards Audrey. He looked very much the beast that she thought he was as his eyes darkened dangerously. Beads of sweat trickled in the deep furrows of his brow as his licentious thoughts and inclinations vibrated energetically within the trembling folds of his face and in the jiggling of his jowls. Audrey turned her eyes down to the faceted glass tumbler slowly sliding out from between his perspiring fingers. "Be careful, Lord Gastrell," she sniffed. "You are going to drop your drink."

Her words snapped the lecherous lord from his obvious perverse thoughts and drew his attention towards his nearly empty drinking vessel.

"Ah, yes, you are quite right, Miss Whittemore," he replied.

Lord Gastrell's tongue flicked out between his thick, wet lips as his eyes dropped to her breasts.

'A serpent and a fish, all in one foul form,' Audrey thought, narrowing her eyes and swallowing in an attempt to suppress the vomit slowly crawling up her insides. *How could a beast, such as he, truly believe that she would want him?* The man was positively deluded.

Audrey promptly schooled her features into a placid expression, ignoring the sudden urge to clench her jaw and wrinkle her nose merely at the sight of him. No indeed, it wouldn't do to give too much away, and she certainly had no intention of forgetting what she had promised Ivy only moments ago, she reminded herself. She wanted to be released from this agreement that he and her father had with her in mind as the prize, but she knew she would have to be clever about it. If they ever discovered that she was contemplating an escape, then she was quite certain, they would not allow her to simply walk away unscathed.

Lord Gastrell grabbed at her gloved hand like a slow yet possessed animal, curling his fingers around her digits as he bent slightly at the waist to deliver a kiss upon her knuckles. He grunted with satisfaction as his lips lingered.

Audrey could not stop the downturn at the

corners of her mouth as the repulsion she had tried to ignore deepened, travelling through every inch of her body. There was spittle bubbling from the man's lips, leaving a moist trail on the fabric of her gloves. Without further ado, she whipped her hand away. "Oh, dear me," she tittered, feigning a blush. "You are such a gentleman," she lied as she gritted her teeth. She could feel the moisture from his mouth seeping through the satin, accompanied by an unquenchable desire to tear her glove from her hand. However, if she took such drastic measures as to remove her now soiled glove, the kiss he would force upon her next would press against her skin, she realised with a shudder. It seemed she would have to simply put up with the ghastly sensation. At least until she could make her excuses to leave and return to her bedchamber.

"I thought I would visit to surprise my betrothed," Lord Gastrell breathed, totally unaware of Audrey's feelings towards him.

Putrid vapours seemed to fill every orifice of Audrey's face as Lord Gastrell's words travelled upon his hot, pungent breath directly towards her. The humid, acrid smell was rather intense, she thought, pressing her hand to her stomach to still the rumblings of persistent nausea within. "How kind," she replied. What Audrey had actually wanted to say to the man was that he would not find anyone who wanted to marry him anywhere in the vicinity and that he had most probably misread the address, but she knew that would only lead to more trouble for her.

"My lady's maid advised that you will be staying for dinner. Is that correct, my lord?" she added, steering herself away from the dreadful thoughts she was having.

Stepping out of Lord Gastrell's looming shadow and flower-wilting breath, Audrey turned her gaze upon her father. "Is Mother joining us for dinner, Father?" she enquired. She already knew the answer, but she supposed it was merely hope that the woman would be there to offer her some form of support.

"Your mother has a migraine, Audrey, and she is hardly needed here this evening," Wallace Whittemore replied curtly. "Come, let us eat."

Audrey lingered behind the two so-called gentlemen as they strolled towards the dining room. It was a well-planned tactic simply to avoid Lord Gastrell's eyes lingering on her from behind. As they guffawed, bragged and boasted, she noted how thoroughly caught up they were in their plans for her future. Perhaps, she mused, she might simply slip away and up the staircase to her bedchamber. After all, they did not seem to require any input or even her permission for anything to do with her life, and she highly doubted that they would even notice her absence.

As Audrey slowly dragged her eyes away from

the invisible scorch marks she had bestowed upon her father's back, the maid caught her attention with a subtle wave of her hand. Ivy was shuffling on her feet whilst trying to convey some sort of secret message, yet, no matter what she did, Audrey simply could not hear nor decipher what the message was supposed to be. She frowned with confusion, humour curling her lips as she observed Ivy partaking in what seemed to be a rather peculiar dance.

"I'll fetch you in an hour," Ivy repeated with exhaustion, her voice a little louder than a whisper.

Wallace Whittemore and Lord Gastrell had slipped into the dining room, quite oblivious to the maid's antics, thus leaving both ladies alone in the quiet of the abandoned hallway. Audrey's grin deepened at their secrecy as she nodded profusely. Ivy's words had been like music to her ears. "Thank you," she mouthed, then quickly disappeared through the door of the dining room to face the two men she despised the most.

Audrey had spent most of the meal with her eyes firmly fixed in any direction other than at Lord Gastrell. The sight of the man shovelling food into the cavernous pit that was his mouth as though he had not eaten for an entire week was rather revolting, to say the least. The lecherous buffoon did not even appear to attempt to so much as chew, nor did he swallow the contents before he opened his mouth to speak. Later, when the monstrous performance came to its conclusion, allowing Audrey's gag reflex to stand down, they retired to the drawing room where she might attempt to regain some normal hue to her complexion. Grey was not the colour she had been looking for. Of course, it would have been a tad easier if the end of the meal had signified Lord Gastrell's departure, for Audrey would have taken much comfort from it, but she was not to be rid of the lecherous lord quite yet.

Audrey watched the clock, wondering where Ivy had gotten to. Surely, it had been an hour already, she thought, terrified as she observed Lord Gastrell begin to move towards her. His rather obvious attempt to appear as though he were merely trying to get past failed magnificently, for, despite there being plenty of room on either side of her, he acted as though they had been squeezed between the walls of a very narrow alleyway, the pressure of his hand lingering on the back of her thigh.

"I beg your pardon, my lord," Audrey snapped, quickly softening her tone with a smile to mask her acidic hatred of him. "I did not mean to get in your way." She stepped forward toward the centre of the room, leaving a generous gap between them, one that would not permit him to reach for her again.

"Don't concern yourself, Miss Whittemore," he crooned, "for it was no trouble at all."

Suddenly, Lord Gastrell was in front of her, his vast body backing her up slowly towards the wall until she felt the thud of her spine impact against the stone surface that had been lovingly decorated in lilac by her mother. Audrey peered over the man's shoulder, terrified, as she tried to catch her father's eye. *Surely, a father would not permit any man to be so utterly improper towards his daughter?* she considered. Audrey's breathing gathered speed as fear clawed at her. Panic soared and rumbled through her veins.

Lord Gastrell watched her with a smirk. "Oh, your father won't stop me," he whispered, running his finger over the skirts of her gown and up her thigh. She could feel the pressure of his touch as though he had burned her through every layer of fabric. "Exquisite with clothes on, yet it has to be said that I imagine you so often without," he slurred, bringing his lips to her ear.

Audrey clenched her teeth as she shuddered in disgust.

"Does that excite you?" he asked, smirking as though it were true.

Shaking, Audrey brusquely turned her head away from him, closing her eyes to hide the tears that were threatening to fall. Her body was wedged between the devil and the walls of her home whilst the man who was supposed to protect her had merely lowered himself into his usual chair and had casually lit a pipe.

"I shall have fun with you, my dear," the lecherous lord continued as he ran his hand up her bodice and rested it upon her flattened breast. "So young and tender, exactly what a man needs to keep the blood pumping.

"Not long now, girl, and the entirety of London will know how lovely you are," he added, moving to her other ear as he walked around her, his hands directing her to move forward as she tensed at his touch. Lord Gastrell pressed his body up against her back as his hands slid over her bottom.

The lecherous lord had paralysed her with the most dreadful fear, Audrey realised, for as she tried to step away, her legs would not move no matter how much she willed them to.

Why wasn't her father helping her?

"Please, my lord, this is highly improper," Audrey rasped. "I am not your wife yet."

"Ah, but you will be. Your father has all but sold you to me. I shall touch whatever I please," he groaned, pressing his fingers just below her bottom and nudging them between her legs. She silently thanked the thick fabric of her skirts that stood between her skin and his, but it was not enough to silence the panicked cry of her mind and body as her heart pounded beneath her ribcage.

Audrey's limbs began to tremble as the fear that was coursing through her veins loosened its grasp on her. She stumbled forward in a desperate attempt to get away from him, her attention darting back and forth from the disgusting man to her father in swift and rapid movements.

Lord Gastrell grinned, highlighting his obvious pleasure at her father's supposed ignorance of his antics.

"Father," Audrey pleaded.

"Don't whine like that, Audrey. It is most unbecoming. Lord Gastrell does not want to marry a female that wails." Mr Whittemore rose from his seat, then turned on his heel to face his daughter, his gaze finally settling on the other man in the room. "Is everything to your satisfaction, Gastrell?"

Audrey's eyes widened in horror. Her father had planned it. He knew what that dreadful man was going to do to her, she realised, reeling from the revelation. Ivy or no, she simply could not remain in the room any longer.

Discarding her fear of her father's reprisal, Audrey backed towards the door. Her breath was shaking along with every inch of her muscles; she had to get away from the monstrous men. She certainly could not even begin to entertain the idea of sitting quietly whilst trying to be pleasant to them. The very notion was both preposterous and hideous. "Please excuse me, for I have a terrible headache," she muttered briskly, then quickly turned and fled from the room and up the stairs to her bedchamber.

"Oh, Miss Audrey, I was just about to come and get you," the maid offered quietly, her eyes searching

Audrey's face.

Audrey's heart crashed against her ribcage as she threw herself down onto the bed and sobbed. The man who was supposed to love and protect her in her life was selling her as though she were merely meat from the butchers. Could the emotional pain from such knowledge, not to mention humiliation, be any more excruciating? she wondered.

The gentle touch of Ivy's skin closed around Audrey's hand. "I'm sorry, Miss Audrey. I should have come for you earlier. I didn't know they would upset you like this," she whispered.

Audrey wiped her eyes, brushing the hair back off her face as she turned to look at the maid. "You have nothing to be sorry for, Ivy. My father could have stopped him," she sniffed as her voice croaked around another sob. "Yet he simply watched. In fact, they had planned Lord Gastrell's ex...ex-" Audrey could not speak beyond the sudden onset of shame.

"You can tell me, Miss Audrey. I shan't tell another soul, I promise." Ivy handed her a fresh, clean handkerchief to wipe away the continual flow of her tears.

"He examined me," Audrey rasped, accepting the handkerchief. She really couldn't think of any other way to word what he had done to her.

The maid gasped. "Oh, Miss Audrey," she whimpered. She knew it was not the way for a maid to behave, but she threw her arms around her mistress in an embrace.

"It would have been far more harrowing if you hadn't helped me with my layers, but it was awful, Ivy. Simply awful." Audrey leaned into the embrace, glad of the comfort of someone she considered a dear friend. If it hadn't been for Ivy and Flossie, she did not think she would have coped over the last few months in particular.

"I'm going to help you in any way I can," Ivy announced, pulling away from Audrey as she held her shoulders to look directly in her eyes. "Anything you want me to do to help you, you just tell me, and I will do it. I don't care what anyone says, and that miserable ol' git downstairs can dismiss me if he likes, and I'll simply say good riddance to the ol' bugger!"

Audrey chuckled. She had never seen such passion bubble up from her lady's maid.

"I mean it," the maid added, grinning as she observed the change in Audrey's emotions.

"I know you do. I am not laughing at you, Ivy, I promise. I am laughing from happiness at having such wonderful friends in you and Flossie."

"And you shall always have us. Now, you need to put that lecherous old goat out of your mind and start thinking of ways we can get away from it all. I'll have a think too, but I know you will think of something before I ever do. Perhaps write a list, and we can go through it together. Miss Florence will help too. I know she will."

"Well, I know I cannot marry him. I do not care whether my father wants a higher status or even if it will ruin his reputation; I cannot spend my life with a man like Lord Gastrell. The things he said, Ivy!" Audrey shuddered. "I would rather spend my life alone than with him."

Sitting up, Audrey brushed her face with the back of her hand and wiped the last tear away. The sadness within her eyes had begun to wane as she forced herself to think. "I simply wish I knew what I could do."

"Well, don't try and force the ideas to come, Miss Audrey, or you will end up panicking and not be able to think of anything. My best ideas come to me when I'm not thinking of anything in particular at all."

"Yes, I think you may be right, Ivy. Perhaps that is why I have been so unsuccessful so far." Audrey stood. "Please, would you help me out of all this?" she queried, gesturing to the gown that bore the invisible stain of Lord Gastrell's touch. She did not want it anywhere near her. In fact, if she had not needed it for a while longer, she would have seen to it that the blasted thing was burned to cinders. Once the lecherous lord had departed from her world, only then would she watch it burn. "Please, can you wash these clothes twice, Ivy? I know it might sound ridiculous, but –"

"I understand," the maid offered with a gentle nod as she began to unfasten the gown and all the layers cocooning her mistress's body. "I will make sure that there is no trace of the man."

"Thank you, Ivy."

"Shall I run another bath for you?" Ivy whispered kindly. "Might make you feel a bit better."

"Would you mind?"

"Not at all, Miss Audrey."

"Thank you. I would love a bath. Even if I cannot wash the pressure of that ghastly man's touch off me, I can at least try and wash away some of the memories of it." Audrey closed her eyes as she felt more tears prick at the back of them, all the while her throat seemed to tighten with anguish.

"It's alright, Miss Audrey. Remember, you are not alone. Even if I have to hide you at my ma's, you are not going to marry that old scoundrel."

Audrey placed her hand over her maid's as Ivy squeezed her shoulder. "Thank you, Ivy. Thank you so much," she rasped.

Chapter Four

The leatherbound book lay open in the cradle of Hunter's hand as his free fingers leafed through its delicate pages. His deceptive portrayal that he was simply reading seemed rather pointless if he had indeed intended it to be a deception, for there were no others anywhere near him to witness it. Of course, he had not intended nor wished to deceive anyone, and it was not as though he had not been trying to absorb the contents of the pages, but what his eyes caressed, his mind thoroughly ignored. The persistent chatter of his thoughts about facing *her* again seemed to deny entry to anything else as it tumbled around quite vociferously inside his skull. A grown man could not be afraid of his mother, Hunter assured himself, yet he could not deny that returning to the estate to set eyes on the lady was not precisely something he had ever wished to participate in, nor could he deny that he found the prospect rather unsettling. Lady Carlisle was practically a stranger to him, and what he could remember of her did not exactly inspire warmth and fuzzy feelings within him. Their reunion would be nothing but fraught indeed.

Hunter thumped the inside of the carriage

box. "Take me to the next inn, if you would, please, Tyler," he bellowed.

The sky appeared to be greying dramatically, and no doubt it would be dark soon enough, Hunter considered. If he was being honest, he had no qualms about taking his sweet time to venture back towards his past. Indeed, something warm to eat, something exceedingly strong—and perhaps mentally numbing—to drink, and somewhere to sleep sounded rather appealing. Initially, he had sought to get the deed of returning to the estate over and done with, merely in the hope to make a swift departure, but the further the carriage travelled in the direction of his mother, the less determined he found himself.

"She can wait," Hunter rumbled softly, careful not to rattle his brain, as his fingers proceeded to make small, clockwise rotating circles delicately over his temples. The stress of the blasted expedition had left him with a pounding headache, and he still had another day, at least, of travel remaining.

As the carriage rolled to a stop at the inn, Hunter stepped down from the vehicle, making light of the distance between the bone-shaking contraption and the entrance of the quaint and rather humble-looking establishment.

Entering the property, he identified which of the many men was the innkeeper. "A room for the night, sir, if you please?" Hunter requested boldly but kindly.

"Are you certain you wish to stay here, sir?" the landlord questioned sheepishly. "We don't get many like you here."

"Like me?" Hunter queried, his lips twitching as the man fumbled, trying to find his next words.

"I don't mean any offence, sir. I just mean that this place ain't exactly posh."

"No offence taken, I assure you. However, are you able to offer this weary traveller a warm meal, the use of a bath and a bed?" Hunter enquired, one eyebrow quirked in amusement.

"Yes, sir. We definitely can offer you those, but the room'll be much smaller than you may be used to." The landlord smiled apologetically.

"My good man, as long as I can have what I have mentioned, I would not mind if you said it was no bigger than a carriage box." Hunter smiled.

"Well, if you're sure, sir, then I'll show you to your room."

"Yes, indeed, and thank you. Perhaps you may find another for my driver. One that may be close to the stables?" Hunter requested.

The landlord observed Hunter with a respectful gaze. "You really ain't like the others at all." The man nodded with what Hunter thought was approval. "Of course, we will be happy to find a room for your driver," the innkeeper continued. "If you'd like to follow me, gents, I will see you to your rooms."

Hunter settled on the mattress of the small bed, welcoming its softness as he allowed every inch of his spine to relax into it. His shoulders and back had become noticeably taut with tension. Of course, it was of his own doing, he reminded himself, for he had allowed that woman to taunt him again in a matter of less than a day, and he was quite aware that the tension seizing his posture as though he was about to engage in battle would only increase when he eventually had the misfortune to lay his eyes upon her. Distance had indeed created a sturdy barrier between his present life and that of the past, and thus between him and the family he had left behind. He supposed that over the years his memories of them may have softened somewhat, yet not quite entirely, but that served only to make him rather more concerned. Although he was no longer the young man who they had turned their back on, he struggled to ascertain how he would feel when once again standing merely a few feet from the woman who raised him. Would he become a fool in her presence again, one who was ridiculous enough to believe that she had changed? Or had he truly been victorious in the battle that had been raging for so very many years?

Hunter could almost taste the acid upon his tongue as his unwanted thoughts soured his mood and intensified the persistent throbbing pain in his head. He had hoped the decent meal that had been delivered to his room would have appeased the tension clawing his insides, for he had assumed that it had been merely a lack of sustenance over an extended period of time, but alas it remained in full force like the repeated knock of a hammer to his skull. Although, he had to admit, he was not entirely surprised, for it did not take a genius to know what or who it was that made him feel so ghastly. Abruptly turning onto his side, Hunter bunched the pillow beneath his head as he screwed his eyes shut against the pain. "If she expects me to behave as *he* did, she'll have another think coming," he muttered bitterly into the quiet of the room. "If I have no choice but to become the new baron, then things will be very different indeed."

"Mr Carlisle. Mr Carlisle," a voice called through the thin wooden chamber door.

"Come in," Hunter replied. "I haven't locked it."

A young maid entered the room. "I've got the last pail of water for your bath, sir," she panted.

"Good heavens," Hunter exclaimed quietly so as not to frighten the poor woman. She was looking rather flushed with exhaustion, he thought as he rushed to his feet and strode to her side. "Let me take that from you," he offered kindly.

With a nod of acceptance from the maid, Hunter relieved her white knuckled hands of the large heavy pail. "What happened to the young man who bought the others?" he queried. If he had known the landlord would expect this woman to carry the water, he would have preferred to have seen to it himself.

"The boss said he had to see to something else," she replied with a smile. "It's no bother, Mr Carlisle."

"Thank you," Hunter replied. "I won't need any more than this, though."

Slipping the maid a couple of shillings, he walked her to the door.

"Oh, thank you, sir," she said, blushing as she stared down at the coins in her hand.

Hunter smiled. "Thank you too."

Bathed and feeling somewhat more relaxed than he had been an hour ago, Hunter snuffed out the candle and dove beneath the thin coverlet of his bed. The bath had been pleasantly warm, and the time immersed in the water had restored him to feeling some way towards being his usual self, albeit with the exhaustion that was continually creeping up and over his body. Perhaps he would look at it all in a new light in the morning, he considered briefly as sleep finally silenced his mind.

They had made good time, Hunter noted, trying to maintain a light and pleasant attitude as the carriage rolled through the wrought iron gates of Carlisle estate. His arrival bore a sense of unease as the moment crashed through the thin, brittle veil that had once stood defiantly between the present and the past. He had left behind the life he had become accustomed to in exchange for the one he had tried to forget. Even with the stretch of time and distance of miles paved out between them, the memories paid no heed to his unspoken objections, insisting upon making tiny, irritating abrasions over his soul as a reminder that he would never really be permitted to forget what had happened. His own mind, the one that was quite aware that he would rather not think of such things, was apparently rather keen on tormenting him and riling him up in some twisted hope, much like his mother's, that he would eventually become a *true Carlisle.* Hunter scoffed, for the very thought of becoming as bitter and emboldened, outwardly rude and selfish as his late father was the furthest from his list of ideals as was indeed possible. Hunter was not so naïve as to believe that he did not possess some of the man's traits, but, as far as he was concerned, the only people that deserved that side of him were the Carlisles themselves or anyone of a similar nature. He could not imagine nor ever wish to believe that he would behave anything like the late baron toward any other soul.

    The manor was still as grand and pretentious as he remembered, and no matter the beat of the sun through the carriage window as he narrowed his eyes to stare at the monstrosity, the chill of the familiar surroundings sent an eerie shiver up his spine. He could not bear the thought of having to live in it permanently. The idea of residing in the same property as Lady Carlisle was thoroughly atrocious. If his mother did manage to forcibly affix herself to the property like the leech he knew her to be, then he would simply leave her to her own devices. Of course, it would be expected of him to visit on occasion to ensure all was in order. He highly doubted he would be able to sidestep that responsibility, he considered, practically snarling at the revolting probability.

Hunter inhaled. Perhaps he didn't have to do any of this. He could feign ignorance and simply instruct the driver to turn tail and get them the hell out of there. But if someone was watching from a window, that particular action would look rather weak, and one did not show weakness in the presence of a Carlisle, not unless they wanted to be crushed beneath one of their boots. Cursing, Hunter berated himself for being far too impatient. He had told Mr Baldry that he would not be arriving until a month had passed, yet there he was, four weeks early like an impetuous fool, about to make the biggest mistake of his life before he even had to. Hunter slowly shook his head at his own ridiculousness. *What did it matter?* He was quite aware the month would not have been anywhere near as peaceful as he was trying to convince himself, for Lady Carlisle did not possess a patient bone in her entire body, and she would certainly not have been content to wait for a month for his arrival. No indeed. He had not forgotten that irritating trait of his mother's. Mr Baldry would have been a gibbering wreck by the time she would have finished harassing the poor fellow, and he, he rather imagined, would have been wading through an ocean of correspondence and the unpleasant familiar fragrance of lavender.

Feeling a little more determined – or perhaps one should say *resigned to the facts of the matter at hand* – Hunter thumped his fist on the inside of the carriage box. He couldn't bear the idea of alighting the vehicle directly in front of the steps to the main entrance. He needed to distance himself, perhaps have the opportunity to get a few breaths of fresh air in the hope that that and a minute or two of quiet would aid his sudden and rather sensible desire to strengthen his composure. "Carry on to the stables, Tyler," he instructed. "I wish to walk a little."

Without another word, the carriage wheels rolled away from the front of the manor and towards the stables.

The country air was wonderfully crisp and refreshing. It was a far cry from the smog-filled London air that he could never quite get used to. However, as he inhaled deeply, he noted that its caress was not quite on par with the promised breeze that never failed to greet him as he stood upon the shores of Whitstable. Such a simple reminder had Hunter wishing he could merely blink to be transported to his small home by the sea. Had he been back in London, he could have opted to travel by rail to take him there. It was not quite as rapid as blinking, but it was indeed considerably faster than a carriage, he mused.

A sense of longing for the bustle of the busy harbour and the freedom it offered to simply step onto a vessel anytime he wished to, engulfed him. It was one of the perks of owning a fleet of ships, he reminded himself, smiling proudly. What had once been one rather well-beaten vessel and a few hard-working men had gradually grown into a rather profitable business exporting hops and grain. Such a simple venture had thrived until he had found himself living perhaps better than many of the ton claimed to do. Of course, he did not talk of such things openly, for he was a private man where matters of wealth were concerned. He had seen firsthand the likes of those who would worm their way into a man's life merely because they deemed him worthy by the weight of his purse. He preferred the company of those he chose carefully – many of whom he employed, if he were being truthful. They were honest, decent men that indeed embodied the phrase *'salt of the earth'*.

Feeling the hold Whitstable had on him, Hunter acknowledged the gentle tug at the centre of his chest that pulled him towards its shores. The memory of the salty, clean air tickled his nose, and he inhaled as though he were there. There was something about the ocean that was indeed freeing; perhaps one might refer to it as soothing, he thought as he exhaled.

Hunter hadn't returned to the small seaside town for quite some time, for he had many other matters that had needed addressing and still needed to be addressed. He wondered whether the Carlisle estate would spare him the time so that he may return or whether it would be yet another distraction. He wasn't worried about his business, for he knew it was in the extremely capable hands of Thomas Rigden, yet he hoped that he would see the humble town again soon. Dusting down his somewhat crumpled heavy coat, Hunter pulled back his shoulders and pushed aside his longing for that which he could not so much as entertain at such an important time.

With his bare knuckles, Hunter rapped loudly upon the large and rather daunting wooden door. The very sound made him shudder, every thud seeming to summon link after link – the final links of the invisible shackles that had dragged him back to his childhood home. There was no way but forward now, he reminded himself as he held his breath at the sound of the door creaking open.

A familiar tall figure in midnight blue and gold livery stood looking thoroughly miserable in the doorway. Hunter recognised him immediately, yet he could not remember the man being terribly thin or indeed looking quite so thoroughly deflated. As the man raised his eyes to Hunter, his features seemed to melt. His jaw slackened to leave his mouth agape, and with eyes as wide as tuppences, the poor fellow looked as though he had seen a ghost. He was positively pale from what very much appeared to be fright.

"Elkins, who is it?" a lady, one that Hunter didn't recognise, enquired as she ambled up beside the butler to see him for herself, only for her to then let out a bloodcurdling scream that seemed to pierce the very centre of Hunter's ears. He would have been surprised if the entirety of Britain had not heard her cry. "He's alive!" she whimpered, then proceeded to crumple in the direction of the floor in a faint.

Hunter stepped forward past the butler, attempting to grab the chit before she hit her head upon the solid marble floor. However, as gallant as that may sound, it was not executed in the most dignified of manners, for she seemed to arch in his grip, her nose pressed to the centre of his chest as she proceeded to slide down the front of him, twisting her nose at the most awkward and inelegant angle he had ever seen.

"Elkins, a little help here, if you please," Hunter ground out.

"Yes, of course, Master Argyle… I mean, my lord," the man stuttered.

Ah, so that was who they assumed he was. Hunter wasn't entirely certain whether he should be flattered by such an assumption or whether he should be as irked as he was beginning to feel. Instantaneous irritation at having been mistaken for one of the men he despised crawled beneath his skin as he tried to stifle any telltale signs that may appear on his face. Perhaps he would find it amusing later, he thought, but the weight of the woman whom Elkins was trying to manoeuvre out of his grasp was sucking any humour out of him. "I'm going to lower her," Hunter ground out as the woman slid further down. Thankfully, she was now nowhere near his body, but he couldn't work out how he was supposed to stop her face from getting a close-up of the marble flooring.

Elkins shifted so that he stood at the unconscious woman's side, placing one of his hands under her arm and the other on her hip. The man was blushing, Hunter noted, trying to curb the corner of his mouth as it flicked up into a smirk. It seemed that the butler was rather aware of the intimacy of where his hands touched the woman's body. *Sly ol' dog*, Hunter mused. He could not help but chuckle silently to himself, and indeed it was that simple moment that alleviated his bad mood.

"Is everything alright, my lord?" Elkins enquired. The butler's voice was rather strained as he struggled to maintain his grip on the woman being dragged down with the persistent force of gravity.

"My apologies, Elkins. I seem to have gotten lost in my own thoughts. Shall we?" he queried, nodding at the limp form of the evidently skittish chit.

Elkins nodded profusely.

"She is at a rather unfortunate angle, so we will need to turn her so that her back meets the floor. Are you ready?"

Elkins nodded again. A bead of sweat was slowly trickling down the centre of his forehead. Had the man been holding anything else, Hunter thought he may have had a mind to have simply dropped it, whether it smashed or no.

Slowly lowering the woman to the ground, the men turned her body and, finally, when at a safe distance from the floor to do so, they released her gently onto her back. Hunter let out a breath. "Does she always do that?" he asked, wiping the sweat from his own brow. Hunter knew he was quite capable of carrying a person, but he had not been expecting a lady to have swooned quite so promptly upon his arrival. He had been caught rather off guard.

The butler glanced at him curiously. "You're not Master Argyle, are you?"

"No. I am not my brother, Elkins." Hunter pretended to peruse his jacket to hide his involuntary scowl. It was not the butler's fault, but he had rather hoped that he bore hardly any resemblance to the Carlisle men.

"Master Hunter?"

"Yes, the very same," Hunter retorted, covering his thoughts with a smile.

"Oh, thank the lord," Elkins proclaimed. "None of us were told what happened to you. We simply assumed that…"

"I had died?" Hunter interjected.

"Well, yes, sir… I mean, my lord. Your father wouldn't say anything about it. It was as though you had never even existed," Elkins said, his face apologetic.

"It's alright, Elkins. It was what I had expected." Hunter had indeed expected it, yet he had never quite put his expectations into exact words. He realised that being aware that there had been truth in his mental meanderings stung like the devil.

"I do apologise, my lord."

"No apology needed, and I suppose I shall have to get used to my new title, won't I?" Hunter grinned as he tried to shrug off the sudden sense of awkwardness. He would not treat Elkins nor any other member of staff the way his father or any other member of the Carlisle family once had. Their similarities extended only to his outward appearance, and that was all there ever would be that linked them together other than the blasted name, of course.

The lady on the floor began to stir. "Elkins, I thought I saw the strangest thing," she whispered conspiratorially, her fingers scrunching around the lapels of the butler's jacket as he crouched down to hear her better. "I saw Master Argyle's ghost."

"I think you better stay where you are, Gertie," Elkins replied gently as he prised her fingers from his attire.

Hunter stepped forward. "Gertie, my name is Hunter Carlisle. I can assure you that I am not a spectre of my late brother," he offered in way of explanation. "However, for my sins," he added quietly, "I am the new lord here on the Carlisle estate."

"Oh," Gertie rasped, her face flushing with a sudden onset of embarrassment. "I'm terribly sorry, my lord. You must think me a right nincompoop. *Oh, how mortifying.*" The poor woman was rambling. "I do beg your pardon, my lord, for I, honest to God, didn't know there was another Carlisle gentleman in the family."

Hunter assisted Gertie to her feet. "It is quite alright, young lady."

"Young lady? Oh, how kind, my lord," Gertie tittered, as her blush deepened into a natural rouge.

Hunter couldn't help but grin. "I wonder whether you will be able to show me to my bedchamber, Elkins. I am not quite ready to face the lady of the house," he requested.

"Yes, of course, my lord. Please step this way," Elkins replied grandly. "It is rather lovely to have you home, you know."

"Thank you, Elkins. Unfortunately, I am not so certain as to whether I am quite as enthused as you seem to be," Hunter remarked, following the tall, slender gentleman up the stairs towards a large mahogany door. The decor of the house hadn't changed at all other than the carpets. Where they had once been a faded green, they were now a dangerous hue of deep blood-red. It seemed rather fitting, Hunter thought sardonically.

Turning his gaze towards the butler, who looked a little taken aback by his admission, Hunter smiled kindly. "I do not mean I am not glad to see you, Elkins. It is just that returning here has begun to restitch the ties that I had once tried, and rather successfully, severed."

The butler nodded.

"Still," Hunter beamed, trying to lighten the mood, "I am the owner of these properties now, so perhaps I can work out a way we can all be happy."

"I am sure you can. You were always the best of the Carlisle men. I hope you don't mind me saying, but it is quite true, my lord." Elkins opened the bedchamber door, hiding his face from Hunter with uncertainty as to how his new employer would react to such a statement. "Here we are, my lord. The master's bedchamber."

Hunter wanted to turn around and seek out an alternative room, one that did not remind him of his father at every angle. The room positively reeked of the previous Lord Carlisle.

"Would you prefer another chamber, my lord?" Elkins enquired worriedly. The man was indeed rather perceptive.

"No, this will do, Elkins, but thank you, and thank you for what you said earlier. It is lovely to hear." Hunter stepped further into his new bedchamber. He didn't want to be Lord Carlisle, and he certainly didn't want to sleep amongst the lingering fragrance of his deceased father and his memory, but he was determined that if he had to take the title, then he would take control. Any sign of weakness to his mother, and she would sink her teeth into him and his life. He would not allow her to, for she relinquished that right years ago.

Chapter Five

Audrey lay wide awake, staring at the canopy over her four-poster bed. The light in the room was non-existent, albeit the dying flames in the hearth. Yet sleep, it seemed, was doing all it could to evade her, for even though her mind stirred rather relentlessly, leaving her thoroughly exhausted, it simply refused to relent to slumber's persistent pull. Desperation to think of something —anything—to escape the marriage she had no intention of going through with was all she cared about, and even though she had not technically given her body and brain permission to remain awake, she quite agreed with them.

Pulling back the coverlet, Audrey rose from her bed and wandered towards her escritoire, where she lit the wick of a new candle. The flickering, enthusiastic flame threw a vibrant flush of light into the room that lingered curiously, illuminating the surface of the delicate piece of furniture. Miniature sketches of flowers and wildlife were scattered over the highly polished mahogany wood. It seemed she had quite the collection, she mused. Audrey rather enjoyed doodling in her quiet moments, most of which she spent out of doors, but as she lowered herself into the small seat beside her escritoire and lifted the delicate quill between her poised fingers, she knew she did not have time for such leisurely activities, for the precious minutes could indeed be put to much better use.

Audrey slid a piece of parchment across the surface of her desk until it sat neatly in front of her, then proceeded to dip the quill into a pot of ink. "Think, Audrey," she whispered as she stared out of the window. With the night creating a solid, deep, dark blue – almost black – canvas, denying her the details of the world outside, she was greeted with her own reflection and that of the illuminated contents of her chamber. After a moment or two of pure frustration due to her mind simply refusing to conform to the task, she wondered whether she should perhaps give up and return to bed. It was as Ivy had said: one hardly ever thought of any plans when one pushed one's mind beyond one's limits. However, it seemed a terrible waste of time to simply lie back beneath the coverlet of her bed and continue to stare into oblivion. Shaking her head, Audrey shifted in her seat and straightened her spine. There was still time, and she might very well think of something, she thought optimistically, or at least conjure the beginnings of a plan. Whatever she would achieve in the remaining hours of the night, it had to be better than nothing at all.

"Oh, heavens," she breathed as she stared

down at the blank parchment. Thoroughly lost in her mental meanderings, Audrey had not noticed the ink drip from the tip of her quill onto it, thus spoiling it completely. Audrey crumpled the paper and threw it into the hearth, watching the dying flames feed off the offering. "Perhaps not such a waste, after all," she mumbled, wiggling her bare toes as the brush of warmth from the growing flames kissed her feet.

Selecting a clean sheet of parchment, Audrey dipped the quill in the ink pot for the second time and set to work. As the hours passed, the morning sun rose in the distance. Its golden hue washed over the fields, houses, and trees, gently revealing them through the window as it erased the night, offering Audrey the most wonderful view of the only home she had ever known. She wondered, if she simply stared at it long enough, whether everything else would disappear, including Lord Gastrell. Audrey sighed. How wonderfully marvellous that would have been.

Audrey's eyes roved over the parchment, admiring her neat but tiny formed letters. The size of each one was indeed quite deliberate, for should anyone she did not trust come across her list, whether through her carelessness or through a tendency to snoop, then she had no intention of allowing them to decipher its contents. As a matter of fact, Audrey was rather proud of herself, for she had finally managed to muster a few ideas.

However, the very first one, it has to be said, she did not particularly agree with, for a lady would rather not trap a gentleman into marriage. The thought of dragging her husband-to-be down the aisle, the man silently and begrudgingly kicking and screaming in protest simply because he had had no choice but to marry her due to having been caught in a compromising position, did not bode well for their future nor for either party's egos. Not to mention that – other than forcing a woman to marry a man forty years her senior – trapping a gentleman into marriage had to be at the top of her list of cruel acts. One then has to wonder why she had bothered writing down such a preposterous idea at all, yet feeling how she did about her future prospects, Audrey thought it rather obvious, for she could not see how the temptation to discard her morals merely to avoid such a fate as marrying the lecherous lord would not be deemed understandable. Had any other lady had to face such a fate, Audrey was quite certain that they would have considered the option quite pleasant in comparison.

Audrey let out a breath, her stomach roiling with guilt at an act she had not committed but merely considered. There were other ideas, she reminded herself. One of which was running away or taking Ivy up on her offer to stay with her family. However, if she ran away, she would be leaving her poor maid to face her father's wrath. Wallace

Whittemore would want to apportion blame onto someone, and she was quite sure that that someone would be Ivy. Needless to say, there was still the option of accepting Ivy's kind offer to live with her and her family. That would certainly put a stop to her father's unwarranted confrontation, but even that knowledge did not detract from the fact that Ivy's family would be down one income as well as having an extra mouth to feed. Audrey sighed. The battle wasn't over yet, she reminded herself. *There would be time. There had to be.*

Audrey gazed down at her desk. She had made rather a mess, she realised, noting the array of crumpled scraps of parchment. "Oh dear," she muttered. There were some rather unsightly blobs of black ink dribbled over her desk. It appeared that, at some point or another, she had somewhat lost herself in her thoughts, and had become quite oblivious to the free flow of ink, for it had evidently dripped onto the furniture. Disorganisation and chaos seemed to be her forte, Audrey thought to herself as her eyes flitted from drop to drip and from splash to splatter. It was rather a similar sight to that of her paint palettes and utensils. Indeed, one would think, simply by looking at the mess, that she had dropped everything onto her escritoire from a considerable height and merely watched whilst it had exploded. "Never mind," she breathed. She could only hope that, as messy as it looked, her plan would follow a similar path to that of her art, for the journey towards her desired piece always was a little chaotic, yet the end result never failed to turn out rather spectacular. She very much hoped that that would indeed be the case.

One by one, Audrey tossed the spoiled parchment into the hearth, destroying all and any evidence of her nighttime endeavours bar one. She had absolutely no intention of losing her list to the ravenous flames.

Exhausted, yet still clinging to the remaining threads of hope that she would eventually conjure the perfect escape plan, Audrey yawned. It was pointless returning to her bed and trying to squeeze in a few hours of sleep, she thought, although she had to admit the sight of the soft pillows and cold cotton sheets was indeed rather inviting. Besides, she was quite aware that, in all likeliness, the second her head hit the pillow, her brain would start chattering fervently all over again. Perhaps she would take a ride out over the fields, she considered. After all, it would give her the opportunity to test out her new masculine attire, would it not? And she was rather thrilled at the prospect of a little deceit where her father was concerned.

Audrey's hands were a mixture of pale skin and blue-black inky patches. She could only imagine what her face must look like. She was not naïve as to how many times she had brought her hand to her face to push back the usual offending wayward mahogany lock of her hair. It was a most persistent curl indeed, one that she had threatened with scissors on many an occasion for simply being an utter pest and getting in her way.

Dear Ivy had run her a bath. The maid had not so much as mentioned the terrible state that Audrey knew herself to be in, and she was rather thankful to the young lady for her discretion. However, it is true that they both could not help the subtle giggle as Ivy caught her eye. One would have had to have been devoid of sight to not have noticed Audrey's ink-splattered appearance. It was quite the picture, she thought, quickly glancing at herself in the looking glass before settling into the welcoming heat of the warm, summer-scented water.

Audrey lathered her body with her favourite soap. The wonderful infusion of orange blossoms drifted upward amongst soft curls of steam as she created a continuous cloud of bubbles upon her skin. She simply could not get enough of the delightful fragrance, she realised, breathing it in. Once she had tended to her ablutions and all and any signs of ink had been erased, she quickly dried herself and dressed in her clean undergarments, tweed breeches, gentleman's shirt, bodice, and skirt. It was indeed rather peculiar to put one's familiar gown on in two parts, not to mention over even more clothes than she was used to. Between she and Ivy, the gown had been altered so it would not bear any differences to its original appearance, for the fastening of the bodice at the front had been cleverly disguised beneath a ruse of ruffles that simply tucked into her detachable skirt. And should one wish to look even closer, then one would note that the intended fastenings of laces and grommets at the back of the gown remained—it was all a rather spectacular illusion.

Tugging at the high neck of the gown, Audrey tried to stifle the grating scream of frustration brewing at the back of her throat. Unfortunately, there was no escaping the need to cover the entirety of the gentleman's shirt no matter how terribly uncomfortable it was. Taking a deep breath to cool the heat of vexation blossoming in her cheeks and chest, she reminded herself that it really was a very small price to pay for the freedom she so desperately craved.

"Your missive has been sent, Miss Audrey," Ivy announced as she returned to the room.

"Thank you, Ivy. I do hope she will meet me. I would like to tell her what I have decided to do. Perhaps she may give me some ideas."

"I am sure she will try, Miss Audrey. If not Lady Florence, then perhaps the fresh air and open space will be your inspiration." Ivy scooped Audrey's hair back with her gentle hands. "Shall I arrange your hair so you will be able to hide it neatly under your cap, Miss Audrey?"

"Yes, please, Ivy," Audrey beamed. "Do you know, I am rather excited about this."

The maid returned her grin. "It is lovely to see you happy, Miss Audrey, and I cannot wait to hear what you have planned."

"I shall keep you fully informed, I promise. You know, Ivy, I have a very good feeling that, this time next year, we will all be laughing at Lord Gastrell's and my father's foolishness. Perhaps I will become the mistress of my own fate. Wouldn't that be wonderful?"

Audrey swung her leg over the saddle, dismounting Athena quickly. The makeshift feminine ensemble had previously been discarded and hidden behind the bales of hay in the stable, where Audrey had then mounted her horse in merely breeches and a shirt and set off across the fields towards their arranged point of rendezvous. As her feet hit the earth, Audrey lifted her head, finally allowing her friend to witness her face beneath the tilted cap. "Thank you for meeting me here."

"Audrey?"

Audrey grinned. "Did you not recognise your best friend?"

"I thought I was about to be compromised," Flossie gasped. "Your disguise is incredible."

"My maid gave these to me. They were her brother's." Audrey gestured to her attire. "I thought they would be less conspicuous than formal clothing for a quick gallop over the land. If anyone should see me, they will simply think that I am one of the tenants or a stable hand, or at least that is the plan."

"Yes. That is good thinking indeed."

Audrey gently patted her horse as she slowly walked away from her, leaving the gentle mare nibbling on the grass by the lake. "I hope I didn't upset any of your plans, Floss."

"Well, I had been planning to sit in the window of the library," Flossie replied, sighing dramatically as though everything was such a terrible burden. "I was hoping I may have been able to tend to my usual bout of staring out of it whilst intermittently gazing down at a book that I have read *at least* fifty times before. You know I was quite looking forward to the repetition of book to window, window to book, etcetera, etcetera, for I thought it may be rather jolly and liven things up." Flossie attempted to deadpan yet the tug of a wry smile at the corners of her mouth betrayed her.

"Oh, that does sound awfully exciting, Floss," Audrey retorted sarcastically, her eyes twinkling with amusement.

"Terribly so. One has to contain oneself, though, for fear of swooning."

Both ladies giggled, the sound of their laughter drifting into the peaceful ambience of the morning as they continued their walk along the edge of the water. The scene was rather glorious, Audrey noted, yet it did not seem to detract from the persistent troubles that followed her around. "I've been thinking, Floss," she rasped, seeming to struggle to find the confidence to actually voice her decision.

"That sounds intriguing. Do tell."

"I won't marry Lord Gastrell." Audrey's announcement bit the air with gusto.

"I should think not," Floss replied, looking rather relieved that her friend had finally mustered the determination to seize control of her own life. "So, what do you need me to do to help you?" she queried.

Audrey was quite surprised to observe how clear and bright her friend's eyes became at the news of her decision. She had not realised just how much her own troubles affected Flossie, yet the young lady did not hesitate to offer her assistance. She had said it as though she were merely taking another breath, never fully understanding how such words affected Audrey nor feeling how they had caressed her heart with a warm, golden rush of gratitude. "What would I do without you, Floss?" Audrey sniffed daintily. She would never have guessed that an offer so simple yet so incredibly kind would affect her so, but alas, there she was, scrabbling to keep herself from blubbing all over her new tweed waistcoat.

"If it were me in this predicament, you would

have seen to it by now that Lord Gastrell was on the other side of the earth, where he could not touch me. I feel I have not done enough, Audrey," Flossie replied as her lower lip trembled. "If I had even half the amount of courage you have, Audrey, perhaps you would have been rid of this mess months ago."

Wrapping her slender arms around her friend, Audrey pulled her in. "You are a wonderful friend to me, Flossie. Please don't ever doubt that. And you are here now offering help, are you not?"

Flossie nodded.

"Well then." Audrey smiled, giving her friend a gentle, playful nudge. "I can promise you that you have nothing to be so glum about."

The two young ladies ambled slowly side by side, occasionally pausing to skim stones over the languorously calm surface of the lake. "You are not married yet," Flossie breathed thoughtfully. Her words lingered as she paused, deciphering whether what she was thinking was indeed a good idea.

"No, I am not," Audrey interjected, drawing out her sentence in slow, stretched syllables as she wondered whether her friend would elaborate further.

"Yes," Flossie gasped with clarity.

Audrey growled gently. *What was she talking about?* "This is agony, Floss," she ground out with impatience. "Please tell me what it is you are thinking."

"All we need to do is find you another match, Audrey. It is really so very obvious."

"Indeed it is, but you must know that my father has forbidden my attendance at any soiree or social event. It was one of the clauses of the agreement he has with Lord Lecherous." Audrey's shoulders slumped with disappointment.

"Yes, it was the agreement *he* had with the scoundrel, but I don't recall *you* agreeing with any of it." Flossie was practically bouncing with glee.

Audrey watched as the excitement bubbled up inside of her friend, the young lady's golden curls bouncing with every movement.

"There is to be a masquerade ball on Friday. Tell your father, should he ask, that you will be spending the evening with me, and I shall ensure that you can attend the ball with us," Flossie announced.

"Oh, I don't know, Flossie. What if I am recognised?"

"What if you are not?"

Audrey pinched her lips together. When would she get another chance like this? she considered. The situation was far too dire to let such an opportunity slip through her fingers. "Alright, I will do it," she exclaimed, forcing an optimistic smile in an attempt to outwit her doubt and hesitation.

"Wonderful! Meet me at mine in an hour. We need to find you something fabulous to wear."

Audrey silently sent up a prayer for everything to work out in the end as she watched Flossie hurry away.

An elaborately crested Braithewaite carriage conveyed the two young ladies rather swiftly into the heart of town, and Audrey could not have been happier, she thought as she nestled her body deeper into the luxuriously padded seat of the vehicle. The freedom of her morning expedition, whilst dressed as a gentleman, had left her in high and somewhat hopeful spirits.

"Something subtle, yet noticeable," Flossie mumbled, tapping her slender gloved finger against her chin as she perused the scenery outside the carriage window. "One that is elegant," she continued thoughtfully, "but perhaps a little on the risqué side. One might as well, after all."

Audrey quirked an eyebrow at her friend in a wordless request for her to elaborate as to what it was, exactly, that she was wittering about.

"Oh." Flossie's cheeks flushed. Giggling prettily, she offered Audrey a mischievous grin. "I was simply considering what sort of gown we should have the modiste create for you," she explained.

"Risqué, Floss? Tsk, tsk, tsk," Audrey teased. "It is usually I that makes such suggestions. Where is my friend Flossie? Tell me, what have you done with her?" Audrey giggled.

"It appears that I have learned from the very best," Flossie retorted. "Although, I must say, I do not think that, if this were about me, I would be quite so forward in my suggestions."

"Of course not, Floss, because it would be I who would be the one suggesting it and I who would be conspiring to corrupt you instead."

Audrey and Flossie erupted into laughter. Their bursts of mischief and joy, intermittently interrupted as new ideas of what the perfect gown should be spilled from them in excited chatter. Audrey had not felt so incredibly happy in quite some time, she considered. In fact, if she were honest, it felt like years. It was indeed rather marvellous to feel such a simple yet wonderful emotion again.

"Oh, Audrey," Flossie gasped, "would you look at this silk? It is utterly divine." The light of the shop lamps glistened in the young lady's captivated gaze as she perused the fabric longingly. "Sage green always looks so splendid on you."

Audrey considered her friend's suggestion carefully. After all, she was expected to wear pastel colours, yet, she surmised, one did not get noticed when one was merely blending in with the other ladies of the *haut ton*. No indeed, Audrey had swiftly concluded that if she was to be successful in finding herself a husband, then she would have to be a little more daring than even Flossie believed her to be. "This one," she breathed, running her fingers over a swathe of shimmering velvet the colour of rubies. The fabric and colour together were exquisite.

"*Oh my.*"

A squeak scratched the back of Audrey's throat as her body leapt in time with her heart. "Goodness, Flossie, you startled me," she gasped, placing her hand over the centre of her chest. She had not realised her friend was quite so close. Flossie's head was practically perched on Audrey's shoulder as the young lady leaned over and admired the velvet.

Flossie merely grinned. "Never mind that," she replied breathlessly. "That colour will look divine on you. And very risqué too. I approve."

"Indeed," Audrey agreed, biting her lower lip. "Yet I do not believe it is quite risqué enough yet, do you?"

Mischief shimmered across the blue of Flossie's eyes and crinkled their corners. "I believe that is where the modiste comes into play," she offered. "I have heard she is the very best. Shall we?"

Brimming with excitement, Audrey lapped up the warmth of the coffee house. As she and Flossie settled into their seats at a table in the far corner of the establishment, they were quickly greeted with two coffees and a plate of biscuits. "May we have a pot of tea as well, please?" Audrey requested, smiling kindly at the young man.

"Right away, miss."

"Thank you." Audrey sighed as the strong coffee slipped over her tongue, her eyes focusing solely on the bowl of delightfully invigorating brew as they waited for the tea to arrive. The alternate beverage was merely a precaution, for one never knew if tea may be preferred to coffee. However, she could not quite understand how one person could find something that she supposed one might refer to as being so very tart, for lack of other words, when others, much like herself, found it rather pleasurable. Indeed, it seemed that Audrey may have forgotten to mention that fact to Lady Florence Braithewaite. An unintended and rather unfortunate mistake, Audrey thought, keeping her eyes down. As Flossie took her first sip of coffee, the slight tremor of the wooden table had been duly noted. Audrey pressed her lips together, attempting to suppress the rising bubbles of laughter at the back of her throat. The aforementioned tremor had mirrored the unexpected shudder that had gripped Flossie's entire being at the touch of coffee upon her innocent tongue.

"Good grief, Audrey," Flossie exclaimed. The young lady's eyes narrowed and her mouth curled down at the corners in a rather definitive grimace. "I don't know how anyone can possibly drink this vicious liquid."

Slowly, so as not to spill it, Audrey placed the bowl of coffee on the table in front of her. Raising her gaze to look upon her dearest friend, she could not keep the glint of playful devilry from twinkling in her light green eyes. "It is a good thing that I ordered tea, then, Flossie, is it not?" Audrey grinned, unable to stifle her amusement at her friend's lingering disgust. As a way of an apology, she poured Flossie a cup of tea, passed it to her, then waited. "Better?"

Flossie pursed her lips. "You really are mean to me, Audrey Whittemore," she announced, trying desperately not to answer Audrey's cheeky smile with one of her own. "You told me it was rather lovely, but it most definitely is not!" she protested. "I can still taste it above my second sip of tea."

Audrey snorted, then quickly placed her hand delicately over her mouth. "Oh, I am sorry, Floss. I, honestly, did think you would like it. You can see that I do, so I simply assumed. But, in hindsight, I can see that perhaps it is indeed an acquired taste."

"Yes, indeed." Flossie playfully scowled and took another sip of her tea. "I think I shall opt only for tea from now on, Audrey," Flossie remarked, finally giving in to the broad smile she had been suppressing. "Although, one must admit, you do look brighter now that you have had some of that foul brew. You looked quite exhausted this morning."

"I feel brighter, my dear. I hardly slept at all last night. I was awake writing lists."

"Lists?" Flossie enquired, raising her eyebrows inquisitively.

"Yes, indeed. I thought I would write a list of what one might do to escape one's father's ridiculous demands and conveniently opt out of marrying an overgrown slimy toad of a lord."

"All hypothetical, of course," Flossie teased.

"Absolutely, Floss. Could you imagine if it were real?" Audrey's smiled kindly. The full force of the gesture dampened by her unforgettable reality. "Perhaps you might take a look?"

"If you would like me to, Audrey, then I would be very happy to."

Audrey slid the folded piece of parchment across the table. "I would like you to be brutally honest with me, Floss. Anything you think I should or should not do, you must tell me."

Flossie nodded, then carefully unfolded the concealed list. "Your writing is huge," she commented, her tone thick with sarcasm.

"Very droll, Floss."

"Jesting aside, Audrey, I do not believe I have ever seen writing quite so tiny in my entire life." Flossie laughed, squinting as she tried to read it.

"Rather convenient though, don't you think? If my father finds himself nosey enough to pry, he most probably won't be able to read it, what with the penmanship being that small and his eyesight being not quite what it once was," Audrey offered, looking rather pleased with herself.

"Yes, I would agree with you, but perhaps you should destroy it when you are done with it, for if your father is desperate enough, he will find a way. The man must possess a magnifying glass, after all, Audrey. Every gentleman does, do they not?" Flossie commented.

Audrey gazed in wonder at her friend. "Oh, Flossie, you are quite amazing. I've been rather silly indeed, for I had not thought of that. Thank you, I shall have to find a very safe place to hide it from him."

Flossie's cheeks flushed pink, pleased with both the compliment and her ability to have thought of something that Audrey had not. "You are most welcome, Audrey," Flossie replied, shrugging off the slight awkwardness that always seemed to follow any compliments that were offered in her direction. "But you know," she added, "I don't believe you will be needing that list after Friday. I have a very good feeling that you will meet a gentleman who will make the aforementioned slimy toad of a lord very much a thing of the past."

"I do hope you are right, Floss. That would be rather wonderful. I do worry, though, that there will be complications, what with me being promised to Lord Gastrell."

Flossie laughed. "Dear Audrey, once you are wearing that gown, no gentleman will accept that he cannot have you. And I, for one, cannot wait."

Chapter Six

Hunter bathed and dressed for dinner, dismissing the valet early so he could dress in private. All the unnecessary faff of being primped and preened by another could sometimes be rather intolerable, especially when he was more than capable of seeing to such matters all by his three-and-thirty-year-old self, he thought with an inaudible scoff whilst studying his rather admirable handiwork in the looking glass. Thankfully, his own valet was quite used to his reluctance to be pandered to and took no offence when ordered to simply see to merely the essentials, such as fetching a bowl of hot water, a towel, and any shaving equipment. However, there were the odd occasions when Hunter had the sudden urge to be generous. It was then, and only then, he might request assistance with the odd fancy cravat if the occasion called for it.

The late baron's valet, it seemed, did things the late baron's way, which certainly was not Hunter's, and, although it was not the valet's fault, it left Hunter biting back his words simply so he would not snap at the poor man out of pure frustration. Indeed, he would be glad when Stanhope eventually arrived. Usually, the man would have travelled with him, but with it being such short notice, Hunter had requested that Stanhope remain in London to tend to a few matters first. In truth, Stanhope was more of a personal assistant with regard to business matters rather than those of Hunter's appearance. Although, he reminded himself, the man did press his suits to perfection.

As tempting, albeit somewhat cowardly, as it was to have dinner in his chamber, Hunter realised that he had little choice other than to take his meal in the dining room and stare across the table at his mother's sour visage. If he didn't, he considered bitterly, she would insist on darkening the door of his personal space with the ridiculous excuse of merely visiting him. Lady Carlisle would then proceed to thoroughly torture him with whatever it was she would wish to say. Of course, he was quite certain that she would do the same in the dining room, but there he would be able to simply remove himself from her company. Being trapped in one's private chambers, having to endure her fake and loathsome nonsense, was not something he particularly relished the idea of. Unless, of course, he wondered, should she and her flouncy attire indeed fit, there was the rather delightful possibility that he could simply push her out of the window. Hunter smirked as he witnessed her descend from a great height, the scene encased within the safe seclusion of his imagination.

Introductions to the household staff had been carried out quite efficiently by Elkins with the unrequested—albeit welcome and somewhat amusing—commentary from Gertie as she latched on to them, ready and willing to offer any additional information she thought necessary. Most of the staff were very new, Hunter noted, offering them a warm smile as he silently guessed their ages. Indeed, it was not a surprise to note that most of them were young in years, for the younger they were, the easier it would have been for his parents to manipulate and, dare he say it or so much as think it, *bully*. There were a few that he thought looked rather familiar, and they certainly remembered a younger version of himself, but Hunter found himself tiptoeing carefully around the conversation to avoid admitting to them that he could not quite recall their names.

The wariness that oozed from most, if not all, of the servants initially was troublesome, Hunter mused. It seemed they did not expect another Carlisle to behave any differently from the ones they had already endured. *Especially the late baron*, he thought angrily. Augustus Carlisle had had the tongue of a viper but the roar of a vicious lion, and, even fifteen years later, Hunter could recall the severity of the man's bellows as they had echoed through the manor and rattled beneath doors. He, too, as a child, had been on the receiving end of them on many an occasion and knew all too well how each barb could penetrate a person's soul. Indeed, it was rather unsurprising that they were a nervous bunch. But to observe their unease in his presence was rather disheartening. It seemed that he would need to be a tad softer with them to begin with. There was nothing to be gained by confirming their beliefs. Of course, Hunter was nothing like the late Lord Carlisle, but he was not entirely a pushover either. He, like every other human on the planet, had the ability to snap or grumble, and perhaps he could be a little Carlisle-esque when in a foul mood, he reluctantly admitted to himself, for he had snapped at poor Harmsworth only once, and the man was still jittery ten years later.

Descending the staircase, Hunter looked toward the closed door of the dining room, wondering whether time alone with his mother at dinner would be anywhere near as amiable as the time he had spent meeting with the servants. He sniggered at such a ridiculous thought as he adjusted the starchy cuffs of his shirt sleeves and admired the golden flicker of his cufflinks. She would, no doubt, be enraged by his rather obvious effort to avoid her since his arrival. He even wondered whether she would be expecting an apology. "Do not hold your breath, Mother," he mumbled quietly.

"I beg your pardon, my lord?" A footman stepped forward.

"Apologies, Brent. I was merely muttering

to myself." Hunter drew back his broad shoulders, allowing his hands their last attempt to ensure that he looked respectable, then smiled.

"Very good." Brent nodded. "If you would like to follow me, my lord," he added, ushering Hunter towards the dining room. "I have been informed that Lady Carlisle will be down shortly."

So that was how she was going to play it, Hunter noted, his teeth grinding briefly before releasing the building tension amongst an exasperated sigh. He was quite aware that the woman would play games, but it was thoroughly unnatural that a mother would wish to do so with her son, whom she hadn't set eyes on in fifteen years. Hunter massaged his aching jaw and softly closed his eyes for the space of a single beat of his heart. "Thank you, Brent," he responded kindly, then stepped into the grand dining room.

Elaborate was putting it somewhat mildly. Hunter's lip curled with repulsion as his eyes scanned the room inquisitively. Indeed, elaborate was not at all the word he would have used to describe what his eyes would not be able to forget for quite a while, if ever. In fact, Hunter thought the word *ghastly* was far more apt, for he was beginning to wish one could simply wash one's eyeballs and scrub the vision away with soap and water. The wallpaper was a horrendous, eye-searing crimson. Hunter wondered whether his father had been trying to disguise that fact with the numerous paintings hiding some of the unforgivable shade, but if that had been the man's attempt to make the walls seem more pleasing to the eye, he had failed magnificently, for the images upon the canvases were hideous. Hunter thought he could have given his horse a brush and some paints and the gelding would have painted much better pictures. In truth, he was quite certain that Galileo's artwork, with all the sloppy hoofprints and globules of equine saliva included, would have been far more exquisite in comparison. Cautiously turning a fraction to examine what other horrors may lie to the right of him, Hunter caught sight of his reflection in the looking glass over the fireplace. It appeared that his thoughts had scribed themselves upon his face in a horrified expression. Schooling his features, he returned to his perusal of the room.

One did not have to be the most observant gentleman to have noticed the overzealous amount of silver on every shelf and scattered across both sideboards, nor the odious statues that were enough to put a man off his meal, propped in every corner. The sight of his father's *trinkets* was on par with being punched in the face, detestation knocking him off kilter. And if his father's unspoken declaration of wealth and bad taste in décor was not repugnant enough, then one only had to look at the ludicrous size of the gilded mahogany table that ran down the centre of the room. Good lord! Had that beast always been there? he pondered, narrowing his eyes at the offending item. At least he could keep his distance from Lady Carlisle, he thought optimistically as he seated himself at the head of the table and waited.

Fire danced in the hearth, the crackle of the writhing flames chipping into the silence above the sound of tension tightening Hunter's breaths. He was probably anxious merely because he was sitting in a dining room that Lucifer would have been thoroughly proud of, he told himself as he began to drum his fingers over the solid surface of the table, trying to ignore the prospect of having to keep a civil tongue with his mother. He would have much preferred to have been in London in his cosy drawing room with a good book and a bottle of whisky, for there he would not have been subjected to such a detestable notion. *There* he would have been miles away from Carlisle House, miles away from *her*, and that was exactly how he preferred it.

Servants lined up along the wall, their spines rigid as though they were standing to attention, an army of soldiers ready to face whatever was about to be thrown at them. Hunter couldn't bear the anguish on their faces. He wondered how they managed to stand at all. It was ridiculous that anybody could find pleasure in diminishing a person, or people, to such a state.

"You are dismissed," he offered, his eyes roving over the younger members, practically quivering with nerves. "Go to the kitchen and find something to eat, then rest for a little while," he ordered gently. "Lady Carlisle and I are quite capable of tending to our own needs. You all do far too much already," he added with a slight smile and a nod.

"Are you certain you do not wish for us to stay?" Elkins enquired, frowning with concern. "We would be happy to assist."

"Please, you must leave before I change my mind," he teased, offering the younger ones a grin. "Go, go," he added, interrupting as they looked to one another to confirm that they had heard him correctly.

As each servant filed out of the dining room one by one, Hunter savoured the softening of the atmosphere as they whispered with excited speculation, every morsel of tension dissipating as their voices faded into the distance. Carlisle House was evidently fraught with fear. It was a sorry situation indeed.

Left alone, Hunter's ears plucked the ticking of the clock on the mantelpiece from the air. A pendulum echoed it with a duller beat as it swung rhythmically inside the tall grandfather clock that seemed to eye him ominously from the dark corner at the far end of the room. Any other time, perhaps Hunter would have appreciated the simple sounds dripping into the silence, however, on this particular occasion, the ticking merely drew his eyes towards the time. Lady Carlisle was late.

Agitation at the woman's deliberate tardiness

slithered under Hunter's skin. "I refuse to play your silly games, Mother," he grumbled to himself as he proceeded to fill his plate with the delicious food that had been prepared by the cook. Lady Carlisle, it seemed, did not even care who it actually was she was disrespecting, and her despicable behaviour, he assumed, was purely so that she could enact some kind of petty revenge on him. Hunter snorted. *Revenge for what exactly?* He had no idea. The woman was clearly insane. Pouring himself a generous amount of wine, Hunter lowered himself into the chair which was the furthest away from the door, then began to eat.

Hunter had not seen nor tasted a meal quite so sumptuous for many years. Back in London and in Whitstable, he had never seen the point of such overindulgence, for a man only needed to prepare what a man needed to eat. Anything else was merely a waste of food and of blunt. Gazing at the frivolous display of the cook's efforts, Hunter could not help but wonder where the wasted food would end up after he and Lady Carlisle had had what they'd needed to appease their appetites. He could only hope that the servants had the sense to either make use of it themselves or perhaps offer it to those who may be in need of it. Hunter exhaled. Perhaps he would make a point of asking them or even suggesting it if they had not done so already. He had seen many a family with nothing, he thought, shaking his head, and all the while *this* was happening. It was outrageous that one man could have everything when another had nothing. Now that the estate was his, Hunter wouldn't have it, he decided. The tenants and servants deserved better than what they had known.

A light cough disturbed Hunter's mental meanderings and promptly halted the singular journey that the morsel of rich beef in gravy was taking as it sat poised upon the tines of his fork.

"Hunter."

Hunter closed his eyes and lowered the now not-so-appetising bite of beef. He did not even need to look in the direction of the door to know who the voice belonged to. "Mother," he replied curtly. "I see you finally found the time to join me for dinner."

Fifteen minutes late. One minute for every year since he had been cut off from the Carlisle family. The woman was trying to make a point, it seemed, Hunter mused irritably. It was not a thought he particularly took pleasure in, yet he was quite certain that it would not have been a mere coincidence. The absence of Lady Carlisle in his life had not served to erase the memory of her, unfortunately. The sharpness of her desire for punctuality was carved into his brain, for the woman despised the tardiness of others, but even more so, she despised being tardy. This was, without doubt, deliberate. Indeed, it seemed that she had used the number fifteen as a weapon, one she wielded spitefully, jabbing at the fraught relationship they now possessed between them. No doubt a subtle hint that she did not want him there despite her ridiculous drivel in the correspondence she had sent him. The woman was no more pleased than he was to be reunited. Hunter scoffed silently as his eyes lifted to burn her with his gaze. It appeared that Lady Carlisle had just made her removal from the property a tad easier than he had anticipated.

The baroness lifted her chin in defiance and sashayed further into the room, briefly glowering at her son as she noted where he was sitting. Lips pinched, skin pale, and cheeks hollowed by the tension in her face, the woman revealed exactly what Hunter had expected her to, and if hatred alone was a weapon, Hunter thought he may very well have met an early demise right there at the table. Lady Carlisle portrayed not a single jot of joy at seeing her estranged son. Not that he had expected her to, of course, but he could not help but notice that the temperature of the room had seemed to plummet dramatically to match the warmth, or lack thereof, that she evidently harboured for him. Hunter had only ever once felt so unwelcome, and strangely enough, it had been right there in the same room.

His mother had aged more than what perhaps one would have considered normal, Hunter observed as he studied her face from a distance. It seemed that anger and bitterness had drained years from her, dragging with it any beauty she may have once possessed. A generous stroke of grey threaded through her hair in fine, brittle strands amongst the deep mahogany as though the ice in her glare had spread upward and tangled amongst the rich hue, draining it as it bled across her scalp.

"Help yourself to food, Mother," he offered. Hunter's words were short and perhaps a little sharp, but it was all he could manage as a knot of anger coiled and settled in a burning ball in his chest.

Watching the flicker of aggravation spasm over one side of his mother's face, whilst her left eyelid did a peculiar little dance, Hunter pressed his lips together to stifle his amusement, for the woman was searching the room for the usual array of servants. He wondered whether perhaps she had lost the plot entirely and thought he had locked them in the cupboards, for no one needed to look very far to understand that the servants were not there at all. "I dismissed them for the evening, Mother. They are overworked, and we are quite able to see to our own meals, are we not?"

Hunter gave in to the smirk he had been suppressing as Lady Carlisle's nostrils flared in disgust at the news. A white line formed around her thin lips as they puckered further in frustration. "Please sit down, Mother."

"This is ridiculous," she muttered quietly to herself as she sniffed with disdain. "Overworked indeed."

"I beg your pardon, Mother. Did you say something?" Hunter had heard exactly what she had said, but he wanted to see whether she would be bold enough as to repeat it for him.

Lady Carlisle's lips curled against the tug of a snarl. "I was merely saying that this meal looks wonderful," she lied. One would have thought she was sucking on the juice of a lemon with the way her face suddenly shuddered with the unusual effort of being pleasant towards her son.

"Indeed, it is. It is quite elaborate for two people, is it not? Perhaps it would be best if we only arrange something like this if *I* am entertaining." Hunter paused, waiting to see whether his mother noticed the deliberate use of *I* instead of *we*. If she did, she certainly was not ready to question it, for she simply nodded and clenched her jaw.

Hunter was surprised that the woman had held her tongue. Perhaps it was because it was merely her and him now, and she no longer had the other two Carlisle men to stand behind her and strengthen her words. Oh, yes indeed, the Carlisle men, who had passed, and his mother were like a pack of wolves. They had stood together at all times, even when they were quite aware that one of them was in the wrong. Lady Carlisle would need to stand her ground on her own this time, which suited Hunter perfectly. Although, it has to be said, he certainly was not the young man that had left so long ago, and she would, in time, come to learn that he would not be controlled with her temper nor by her deception.

Lady Carlisle tucked her skirts beneath her and lowered her body into the chair at the opposite end of the table. It was the tiniest rebellion, one Hunter could only smirk at. He rather preferred her there, but he did not say as much for fear of conflict. She hadn't even mellowed a smidge, Hunter considered as he recollected his younger years. Alas, he would allow her her moment of satisfaction, for it would be short-lived indeed. Hunter had every intention of finding a wife to replace her as lady of the house. It would displease his mother immensely, but that was not something that needed to concern him, he decided. He had been forced into the role of baron, and he would adhere, but it would be on his terms and his terms only. He was not willing to relinquish the independence and success he had fought for and achieved without his family's help, and he would not permit any interference from the woman opposite him simply because they were now reacquainted. Besides, if everything worked out accordingly, he would not have to lay eyes upon her for much longer anyway. Lady Carlisle would not like the news of relocating, but if Hunter was to be who he was expected to be, he could not do it with the woman scowling at him from every dark corner. She had to go.

"I have been pondering matters with regards

to my new role, Mother," Hunter began as he sat lazily back in his chair, curling his fingers around his glass of wine. He lifted it and swished the red liquid, admiring the viscosity of its hue as it lingered up the edges of the glass. There was no point allowing her the illusion that she would remain in the house, he thought, and was it not better to let her know now so she would have a little time to get used to the idea? Hunter certainly thought so.

Lady Carlisle's chest rose and fell, her jaw clenched as she schooled her features.

"So full of animosity, Mother," Hunter drawled as though it were merely a passing comment. "You have not heard what I have to say yet."

"I don't know what you mean," she replied snippily. "I am merely listening to what you have to say, Hunter. Did you not get my letter?"

"Yes, yes, I did indeed get your letter, Mother. Rather pretty words, but they are just words, are they not?"

Lady Carlisle sniffed and pulled back her shoulders. It seemed that she could not bring herself to even pretend that she had meant what she'd written.

"That is precisely what I thought, and it is the very reason that there will be changes. Your role as lady of this house will cease once I have found you somewhere else to reside. One of the other properties, I am certain, will be suitable for you and your taste." Hunter eyed the room and its revolting décor, then opened his mouth to continue. However, as he did so, Lady Carlisle slammed her fists down on the table, abruptly cutting him off.

"This is my home!" she spat furiously as her fingers curled around her napkin. Hunter watched the thick fabric crumple as she squeezed it with the ferocious bite of her nails, turning her knuckles white.

"Correction, Mother dearest, this is *my* home. You and I both know that we cannot live together." Hunter kept his expression placid. He wasn't particularly fond of the woman, but he was not a man who thrived on confrontation either. He found that such tête-à-têtes simply gave him a terrible headache.

Lady Carlisle's cheeks hollowed as she pursed her lips, her skin stretching over and accentuating the jutting of her sharp cheekbones. The woman looked rather gaunt indeed. "You have not lived here nor stepped on the estate for *fifteen years*, Hunter, and now you come into *my* home and demand that I live somewhere else. No doubt you intend to replace me with another lady, I assume?" she seethed.

Crimson rose and deepened into a rather angry purple upon her face. The intensity of Lady Carlisle's rage seemed to stretch her skin further, emboldening the veins that crawled up the sides of her neck like ivy up the stone wall of a building.

Although, one had to say, such a description may seem rather a terrible insult to nature, Hunter considered, for ivy could be quite quaint and charming upon the walls of a pretty cottage. However, in this instance, his mother was not a cottage, it was not really ivy, and she certainly was not very pretty with her malice on display for him to see.

Hunter lifted his eyes to meet hers, something relatively close to fury licking at the edges of his vision. The audacity of the woman to suggest that his absence had been his decision. It was a lie, and if there was one trait Hunter despised the most, it was indeed lying. "Do we really want to discuss what actually happened fifteen years ago, Lady Carlisle?" he queried sardonically. "Of course, if that is what you wish, then I shall happily recall every detail of it. It is all stored rather neatly up here," he said, pointing at the side of his head. "And very vivid too, I might add," he intoned. It was not a lie, for merely being in the room with her had flooded his brain with every unwanted memory along with every unwanted detail they contained.

Lady Carlisle took a deep breath, a faint growl rumbling at the back of her throat. She tried in vain to disguise it, but Hunter did not fail to hear her displeasure.

"It was your father's decision," she retorted waspishly.

"And yet you did not utter a word of protest

when your son was marched off the property," Hunter replied calmly. "I fail to see how the action of the late baron and your response to it differ, for they both conjured the same result."

"We should not be discussing this in front of the s—," Lady Carlisle began.

"Servants? Perhaps you are in need of spectacles, for I do not see anybody else here," Hunter drawled, raising his eyebrows as he waited for her to speak. It seemed she had forgotten that it was simply the two of them.

Lady Carlisle harrumphed, clasping her hands together, her fingers nervously intertwining with one another. For the first time, it seemed that she had no one to offer her an escape, and indeed there was nowhere for her to run, unless, of course, she wished to leave the house, in which case Hunter would personally see to packing her luggage for her.

"Besides," Hunter continued, "I am quite certain that by now they have the measure of you and are quite aware of exactly what you are like, so none of this discussion would have caused them any shock, even if they were here. Why don't you simply sit and finally face the truth of what actually happened rather than the lie that seems to appease your conscience?"

Lady Carlisle scoffed. "Truth," she mocked, her eyes and posture not quite as certain as her words. She refused to sit.

"Indeed, the truth, Lady Carlisle. As much as it is a rarity to you, I can assure you that it very much still exists. Let's try a little of it, shall we?" Hunter cleared his throat. "Do you remember how you turned your head abruptly away from me when I tried to catch your eye as the late baron ordered me to leave? I was eighteen years of age, Mother, and, as far as you were aware, I had nothing to my name." Air burst from Hunter's lips scornfully. "You know, it is much the same as you are doing now."

Lady Carlisle sniffed disdainfully.

Hunter inhaled, trying to cool his temper. "It's interesting," he continued, "for I believe only those who have something to hide cannot look another in the eye. You refuse to look at me now because you know your own wrongdoing, just like you refused to look at me fifteen years ago when you knew that I had nowhere to go. For all you and the late baron knew, I could have ended up homeless or perhaps I even did, but neither of you cared in the slightest then and you, Mother, certainly do not care now."

Hunter was wasting his breath, he realised, for the exercise of trying to engage in a conversation with his mother appeared futile. The woman had doubled down on her stance, continuing to refuse to look at him. It mattered not, he thought, for he was quite aware that she would deny her part in the past beyond her dying breath, and he certainly wasn't going to waste any more time or effort on her. Indeed, it was dangerous for him to continue, not for her but for him. Hunter had buried everything, and the more he tried to speak of it, subconsciously hoping that there may be something good in the woman who had given him life, the wider the wounds of his past seemed to rip open. There was no salvaging any jot of a mother-and-son relationship, he noted, for Lady Carlisle was and would only ever be merely a spectre of bad memories.

Hunter rose from his seat. "I think I shall retire to the parlour," he announced. "I do not wish for you to follow me, Lady Carlisle, but I will say this to you: I am not you, nor the previous Lord Carlisle, nor am I Argyle. Therefore, I will not see you without decent dwellings and the luxuries to which you are accustomed. I am not a cruel man, but I have made my life on my own, and I cannot risk scuppering all of that by allowing you back into it. If you wish to discuss it further, then you may seek me out tomorrow, but I really do not see what more I can say on the matter other than you will leave this house, and yes, Mother, I will be looking for a wife, a lady of this house that will be far kinder and fairer than the previous."

Hunter nodded towards her back as she turned away from him. "I shall see you tomorrow. Goodnight, Lady Carlisle."

Chapter Seven

Slipping her skirts and the top half of her gown behind the hay bales, Audrey turned to her mare, swinging up into the saddle rather scandalously as perhaps a gentleman would, then pulled the peak of her cap lower over her eyes until all one could see of her was her mouth and dainty chin. Even her rich mahogany tresses were tucked neatly beneath the hat to conceal them.

How freeing it felt, she mused, savouring the sensation of the thin fabric on her legs and the soft, supple ripple of the cotton of her shirt against her bosom and back. The difference between what a gentleman wore and what a lady was expected to wear was rather stark indeed, for she almost felt as though she had wandered out in her shift. Audrey grinned at the thrill of it. "Audrey Whittemore, you are shameless, an absolute Jezebel," she breathed, her teeth scraping over her lower lip as she quietly squealed with excitement at her secret identity. Pressing her thighs gently into the side of her horse, willing the mare into a trot, her grin widened with pure elation.

The gentle blue of the sky softened the vibrant tones of nature as Audrey set off over the open land, travelling toward the invisible, outstretched fingers of the wind. They explored her body, caressing her form through the delicate fabric of her attire, all the while a mere breeze trickled through the branches of trees and timidly brushed through the grass.

Perfection raised its head as the morning, yet there was one particular thought that marred its beauty. The reality of her impending and rather disturbing marriage to Lord Gastrell simply would not leave her alone. It seemed she was not allowed to be free of the fact for more than a few seconds, for every time she tried to forget it, it would always come crashing into her brain unannounced like a spoilt child having a tantrum. Yet, Audrey noted, it was she who had the overwhelming desire to kick and scream.

Audrey shook her head as though the sudden movement would dislodge every nasty thought, eradicating reality with the rattle of her brain. If it didn't erase that particular thought entirely, then perhaps she would simply settle for it being lodged further back in her mind. Closing her eyes briefly and with a quick intake of breath, Audrey encouraged the horse beneath her to charge forward in a gallop. This morning when she had awoken, she hadn't intended to ride quite so close to the breakfast hour. She thought that it may arouse suspicion in her father, but with her mother still abed and the brief mention of a new neighbour by Lady Florence Braithewaite in a rushed missive, Audrey found she simply could not resist the open air.

The Whittemore family hadn't known the late baron and his son very well, but their demise had been noted as a double murder, and apparently, according to the paper, the offending criminal had already been apprehended. One had to wonder whether it was a disgruntled member of the ton, for they were not known to be the most pleasant of men. Some had mentioned that there were those who simply could not understand how a mere baron could exude such pomposity and wealth, so perhaps the lives of the Carlisle men were taken in a fit of jealousy. However, she rather thought that they may have angered someone, for she had always assumed them to have been like her father, hell-bent on status and ready to do any number of untold things to achieve their wealth. Whatever the reason, whether jealousy or the result of underhandedness, they had indeed been murdered for it, and it only proved that the root of all evil was indeed money.

Audrey growled, the sound scratching the back of her throat. Thinking of men like her father and then thinking of the man himself, whether briefly or not, only brought her back to the subject of her future. She really did have to be careful when trying to divert her mind, for she always seemed to end up back in the place where she had started, and the subject of her grotesque impending marriage was beginning to give her terrible nausea.

Suppressing the rising bubbles of fear that always seemed to want to be freed, Audrey slowed her horse into a gentle canter; the slow pace carrying her towards the farther side of her father's land, where she knew it met that of the Carlisle estate.

Not wanting to be seen when in the pursuit of being incredibly inquisitive, Audrey swung out of the saddle and slipped down the side of her equine friend to the floor. Leading the horse behind some trees to graze on the grass, Audrey permitted herself the freedom to clamber up into the tree as she had used to do as a child. She knew she would get a much better view from up high, and as she perched her bottom on a sturdy branch, she silently congratulated herself for being wonderfully correct, for she had a rather perfect view of the neighbouring property.

Surprised and intrigued by her impeccable timing, Audrey gasped with glee as Lady Carlisle stormed from the front of the manor. If dark clouds above one's head were truly a thing, the lady would indeed have been wearing one, Audrey considered, noting the pinched lips and furrowed brow as the woman bestowed a steely glare upon the path before her. Audrey couldn't help but wonder who or what had put her in such a beastly mood. As if sensing her question, Lady Carlisle turned her head, her eyes honing in on someone in the distance.

Audrey's eyes widened as she followed the woman's line of sight, her focus settling on a tall, dark, masculine figure. *Another Carlisle?* Surely not, Audrey ruminated. Although distant cousins were not exactly unheard of, she reminded herself. Was it not the way of things that the lady of the house would lose everything to someone they hardly knew or perhaps even someone they had never met at all? It would not have surprised Audrey in the slightest if Lady Carlisle had been forced to live with a virtual stranger simply because she was female. "Another ridiculous rule," Audrey grumbled, yet still quite unable to muster any sympathy for the woman. Had Lady Carlisle had the ability to burn a person with a simple look of disdain, Audrey quite believed that she would have been turned into a pile of ash by now.

Audrey could not see the gentleman very well from such a distance, but the way in which he moved in his dark, mysterious attire sent a thrill coiling up her spine. The brim of his hat was angled over his eyes, while his long black coat casually flapped open in the breeze, seductively revealing a broad, well-dressed physique that seemed to steal the air from her lungs and make her heartbeat intensify beneath her ribs. So lost in this mysterious gentleman, Audrey did not realise that she was leaning forward a little too far, becoming rather unsteady indeed. "No, no, no, no, no," she whispered hurriedly as she grappled for purchase, pulling herself back up into position. Trembling, Audrey pressed her spine against the trunk of the tree and tucked herself further away. She had made quite a commotion, what with the shaking of the branches and perhaps the odd frightened squeal, and it was that that had her muttering a rather rapid prayer. Indeed, she was relieved that Lady Carlisle had boarded a carriage earlier, but Audrey's entire being was far too aware of the well-chiselled form of her new neighbour. She had hoped that he had been completely oblivious, yet the sudden turn of his head and the narrowing of his eyes in her direction made her wonder whether she was merely asking a bit too much, for it was rather evident that she had not been as inconspicuous as she had hoped.

Audrey remained still, careful not to make any sudden or swift movements to cause any further suspicion. By the expression on the gentleman's face and the shrug of his shoulders, he seemed to have dismissed the notion that some ridiculous person was sitting in a tree spying on him. Audrey blushed, all too aware that *she* was the ridiculous person sitting in a tree, spying on him. "Beyond ridiculous, Audrey Whittemore," she berated herself. Scrambling down to the ground and swinging back onto her horse, Audrey headed towards her home before she could make an even bigger fool of herself than she had secretly done already.

"Miss Audrey, your mother is asking to see you," Ivy announced as she bundled into Audrey's bedchamber and gathered up the gentleman's clothing to be washed and pressed. "I'll freshen these up," she added, lifting the garments briefly to show Audrey.

"Oh, thank you, Ivy. That would be marvellous. I may have made them a little grubby today, what with climbing the tree." Audrey flushed, realising she had mentioned the one thing that seemed to have caused a lingering sense of embarrassment despite her being quite aware that no one would have known about her antics if she had simply kept quiet about them. Except that is, of course, she reluctantly reminded herself, for perhaps one person. One very handsome person. There was something about the mysterious figure that seemed to lend her an air of inexplicable insecurity, one that ignited... well, it wasn't exactly a sense of shame but more of a burning embarrassment that nestled between her stomach and her chest. If she could have merely managed to gather her scrambled wits, she would have perhaps been able to extinguish the dreadfully uncomfortable heat with her own advice. After all, he could not possibly know it was her, for he had yet to discover that she even existed.

Ivy's eyes widened. "Tree, Miss Audrey?"

"Oh, I think I may have said too much." Audrey began to fumble with her hands. She had never done that before, at least as far as she was aware anyway. It was the stress of her wedding, she assumed, which could have also been the reason she was feeling so frightfully vulnerable.

"You don't have to tell me, but you know I won't say anything if you do, Miss Audrey." Ivy looked at her mistress with a measure of concern. "I don't think I have ever seen you looking quite so lost, if you don't mind me saying."

"I am a little off-kilter, I have to admit, but I shall simply put it down to all the stress, Ivy, for I cannot think what else it could possibly be. And it would explain why something which really is nothing at all to be embarrassed about has… well… it has left me feeling extremely embarrassed indeed."

The maid nodded.

Audrey bit the inside of her cheek thoughtfully, then flomped down with an exasperated sigh onto the bed. "I think I shall tell you," she exclaimed, staring up at the underside of the canopy before quickly sitting up again. "After all, if I were thinking straight, I would know there is no real shame in what I was doing, unless perhaps if I were caught doing it."

Ivy's eyebrows shot up until they almost met

her hairline. The young maid's expression served only to make Audrey chuckle. "Nothing like that," she giggled. "I was being rather nosy, if truth be told. Flossie said that we had a new neighbour, and I wanted to know who they were, so instead of having to explain my gentleman's attire or perhaps having to pretend to be a gentleman, I hid amongst the branches and simply watched."

Ivy clucked and shook her head playfully. "I thought you were going to say something scandalous, Miss Audrey," she replied with a grin. "You had me wondering how we were going to keep it from the master."

"No, nothing so exciting, Ivy. Although I did nearly cause a scandal when I almost fell out of the tree." Audrey grinned at the look of shock on the maid's face. "Don't concern yourself so, Ivy. I don't think he saw me. Besides, I really could be anyone. He will be looking for a gentleman or a boy anyway, for he certainly would not suspect a trouser-wearing female of spying on him."

There she had said it, Audrey thought with a sigh as the burning heat of unwarranted embarrassment subsided. She had spilled out everything that had happened, making sense of it along the way, and it really was not as bad as her mind had led her to believe. *Thank heavens for Ivy,* she mused.

A burst of air escaped the maid's lips as she exhaled with relief. "These clothes have come in more 'andy than we gave them credit for," she muttered, walking towards the door. As she went to leave, she turned. "Will you be alright, miss?"

"Now that I have spoken to you, I shall be. Thank you for listening, Ivy."

"My pleasure, Miss Audrey. Oh, and don't forget to pop in to see your mother as soon as you can, for she seems quite desperate to speak with you."

"I shall, and thank you again, Ivy," Audrey called after her as she disappeared onto the landing.

"Hello, Mama," Audrey whispered, squeezing through the gap in the door and offering her mother a warm smile. "Ivy said you wished to see me."

"That's right, my darling. Please, won't you sit with me? I've ordered some sandwiches and tea to be brought here so that we may have a late luncheon together."

"Oh, that sounds wonderful, Mama. It has been quite some time since you and I dined together." Audrey was pleasantly astounded by her mother's effort to spend time with her. She had thought that the woman had simply abandoned her.

"I have rather neglected you, haven't I, dear?" her mother queried, trying to capture Audrey's attention.

Audrey kept her gaze upon her slender hands. She did not know how to admit that she had felt abandoned when it was plain to see that the woman whom she loved so deeply had indeed been poorly. It had been selfish of her to have only thought that she would be the one affected by her betrothal, for it was evident that the news had taken its toll on her mother as well. "Not at all, Mama. You have been unwell," Audrey rasped.

"That may be so," Marjorie Whittemore replied, "but I am well aware of what your father has been up to, and I have been rather selfish, allowing my upset to get the better of me and thus leaving you to fend for yourself with that dreadful man. I am rather ashamed, my dear."

Audrey did not think that her mother quite realised the extent of what Wallace Whittemore had gone to to secure the *sale* of his daughter, but she did not want to tell her for fear of upsetting her and making her migraines even worse than they had been. Besides, there was nothing she could say or do to reverse the days and hours so that she could prevent it from happening in the first place, she thought. Men, it seemed, could do what they liked to a lady they deemed their property, and there was not even a constable who would have intervened on her behalf. No, indeed. If her mother knew, she would most probably confront her father, and the only thing it would achieve would be her father taking matters out on her mother and perhaps a precipitous rush towards the wedding itself. "It's really alright, Mama. You have nothing to be ashamed about," Audrey replied kindly.

Marjorie Whittemore patted the seat beside the bed. "Please take a seat, my sweet girl."

The muscles in Audrey's throat spasmed around the lump she was trying to swallow. The softness of her mother's voice had sparked an uprising of emotion that was currently strangling her and pricking the back of her eyes.

"You do not want to marry Lord Gastrell, do you?"

Audrey shook her head. She was afraid that if she tried to speak, her tears would begin to flow, and she really had no idea whatsoever as to how she would manage to stop them.

"I see. Well, I know it would not be as simple as telling your unreasonable father that you won't marry that man, so perhaps there is a way that we may be a little devious, Audrey." Marjorie Whittemore pressed her lips together as she drank in the surprise on her daughter's face. "Did you really think that I agree with everything that buffoon has to say?" she queried.

Audrey did not know whether this was some sort of trick, yet she also knew that there was no love between her mother and father, for just as she was doomed to a marriage of convenience, her mother had had to face the same fate with Wallace

Whittemore. The whole fiasco with Lord Gastrell had only deepened her sympathy for the woman in the bed at her side. Slowly, she shook her head in reply.

"No, indeed. I may have had to marry the devil, but that does not mean I want the same for my daughter. Of course, for you to avoid marriage with that ghastly old prune of a lord, you will have to marry another without your father knowing." Marjorie pursed her lips as her eyes stared off into the distance. "We need to get you out into society," she mused aloud. "The right gown, the right people, and with that beautiful visage of yours, you will have offers in no time."

Audrey did not know what to say. The concentration on her mother's face was all she needed to witness to know it was not merely a trick. Besides, she was quite certain that her mother would never do something so cruel to her. "Mama."

"Yes, darling?"

"I may have a plan already," she began. Audrey's stomach tightened around the danger of revealing what she and Flossie were planning, but really, what harm could it do to reveal something that may give her mother some hope?

"Oh, do tell," her mother encouraged, her eyes alight with mischief and excitement for her daughter.

Audrey's heart swelled to see such life in the

woman as she regaled all that she and Flossie had discussed. The small group of three that consisted of Flossie, Ivy, and herself had now grown to four, and Audrey could not have hoped for anyone other than her mother as her ally.

Chapter Eight

The morning sun, although somewhat hidden behind the warped, lacy, white clouds, was a welcome sight. The subtle warmth upon the side of Hunter's face lifted his spirits as his feet picked up the pace of what had meant to be a peaceful walk across the dewy grass. He had attempted to slip out early for the sake of pure avoidance. The very idea of having to interact with Lady Carlisle so early in the day made one lose one's appetite, Hunter thought to himself with a shudder. It had all been carefully orchestrated, and he had even taken with him a small, neatly wrapped parcel of bread and cheese so he would not have to face the woman over the damned breakfast table. Despite it being a rather reasonable plan, and one would think a plan that would not fail, the familiar and harrowing tap of carriage boots had morphed his leisurely walk into more of a brisk and somewhat hurried stride. "Damn woman," he muttered. If he could just get far enough away, then his understandable endeavour to escape his mother may very well succeed. Yet the ghastly sounds behind him had warned him that he was on the brink of failing magnificently.

How a woman could clear her throat quite so audibly, Hunter was uncertain, but at the sound of Lady Carlisle trying to catch his attention, he feigned utter ignorance and continued walking, gaining more distance between them. The last thing he intended to do was explain himself, nor was he willing to acknowledge the filthy glare that was currently burning his back. The sooner she was gone, the better, he thought irritably. Hunter rolled his shoulders to ease the tension in his muscles as he listened to the rumble of the carriage fade into the distance. For now, he supposed, a carriage dragging the woman away for a few hours would simply have to do.

Safe in the knowledge that the carriage had disappeared off to somewhere that was bound to freeze over as soon as his mother arrived, Hunter stood perfectly still and simply listened to the subtle breeze and the song of the birds. It was a sound one hardly noticed or had the opportunity to notice in London, and he could not help but be rather mesmerised by it. It, perhaps, would have captured him in a splendid state of awe had the sudden squeak and tremendous ruffle of leaves not crashed into the ambience of the morning. Hunter turned his gaze just in time to see a pair of legs dangling in the tree. Perhaps a child, he wondered, narrowing his eyes in the hope he would be able to see them more clearly, but before he could focus, the suspected child had pulled himself out of view.

"Interesting," Hunter whispered, smiling to himself. He quickly and quite visibly shrugged so that his audience of one would assume that they had concealed themselves from him rather admirably. Of course, the child shouldn't have been there, apparently spying on him, but he was not about to scold them for being curious. In fact, he could remember doing much the same when he had been just a boy. If he recalled correctly, he had spent many hours spying on that dreadful man who had owned the estate next door. *Peculiar*, he thought, for he had almost forgotten about Whittemore and his wife. Perhaps he would pay him a visit. After all, it would not hurt to reintroduce himself, and, of course, it would slake his sudden bout of curiosity. Perhaps the child had something to do with Whittemore, he mused.

Hunter rather hoped the man had changed, for he could remember, quite vividly, Whittemore's abhorrent manners towards his wife. Even at such a young age, he had begun to question whether that was indeed how a gentleman was meant to treat their wives. What with his father and the beast next door, he really did not have any idea how a real gentleman behaved, yet there was something within him that simply knew it was unkind and certainly uncalled for. Now it seemed such an utterly ridiculous thing to even consider, for the men he had met since venturing out on his own had opened his eyes to so much more than the small, fractured bubble he had considered his entire world. Indeed, they had opened his eyes to the very sad truth of it.

"Good mornin', my lord!"

Hunter pulled his hat forward, shielding his eyes further as he gazed in the direction of a rather deep voice, softened with a gentle northern accent. The man grinned kindly at him, his eyes twinkling with amusement, putting Hunter at ease. "Good morning," Hunter replied.

Removing the flat cap from atop his head, the man proffered his hand in greeting. "You've chosen a fine day, my lord, to be out on't land. I trust that you're my new boss?"

Hunter took the man's proffered hand and shook it heartily. "I am indeed. It is a pleasure to meet you, sir. Apologies for not introducing myself sooner. I'm afraid that my relocating to this place is going to take quite some adjustment." Hunter laughed, attempting to hide just how terribly uncomfortable it was for him to be back amongst his old, unpleasantly familiar haunts. "Perhaps I could start by saying that there really is no need to call me '*my lord*', for I would much prefer it if you would refer to me as Carlisle. It is less formal, do you not think?"

"If that's what you prefer, then Carlisle it is. The name is Frederick Knowles, but Fred is just fine. I'm your reliable groundskeeper," Fred added, drawing back his hand and placing his cap back upon the top of his head.

"Reliable, eh?" Hunter teased, noting the way the man dipped in and out of his accent. It seemed the easy northern lilt had slightly receded over time. It made him wonder exactly how long Mr Knowles had worked for his father.

"Well, I like to think so, Carlisle," the groundskeeper returned with an easy smile. "Perhaps I best show you around, then you'll be able to familiarise yonself with the place."

"That would be incredible. Thank you, Fred. I do remember most of it, but I haven't been here for fifteen years."

"Oh, well then, there've been a few changes, I should imagine," Fred replied, pulling his shoulders back proudly. "I've been working 'ere ten years, so I hope you like what you see."

"I am sure I shall, Fred. There is quite a lot of land, far more than I remembered, in fact, so I rather appreciate the offer of a tour. After all, as you say, I should familiarise myself with it all."

Fred tugged briefly on the peak of his flat cap. "Off we go then."

Hunter allowed the groundskeeper to lead the way, falling in beside him as they leisurely strolled further away from the manor.

"If I'm being honest, Carlisle," Fred began, "I had no clue that there was another Carlisle gentleman in't immediate family, which I assume you are by how much you look like Master Argyle. I had wondered whether all this," he added, stretching his arms out to gesture to the land, "would go to a distant relative, perhaps a cousin."

The groundskeeper was tall, Hunter considered, swerving subtly to refrain from receiving a rather unwelcome elbow to his perfectly straight nose. Hunter was quite sure that he did not want it altered in any way. "Yes, you are not alone in thinking that I am quite similar to my brother," Hunter replied as though nothing had happened at all. Keeping his eyes ahead, he continued. "As I mentioned earlier, it has been fifteen years since I stepped foot on the Carlisle estate. My father and I did not part on good terms, and if I am being honest, I rather thought he would have seen to it that this estate and everything entailed would have bypassed me to another relative, yet alas, for my sins, here I am." Hunter turned his face further away from Fred merely to hide the ill feelings he knew his expression revealed.

"Well, Carlisle, whatever reason brings you here, 'tis good to finally meet you, I reckon. I've heard nothing but compliments from the servants, and you know how they love to gossip." Fred grinned, his eyes crinkling gently at the corners.

The groundskeeper's skin was gently bronzed from the sun. No doubt the man spent most, if not all, of his days out in all manner of weather,

Hunter thought kindly. In fact, he rather envied the man's freedom to do so. Perhaps the outdoors would be where he would find some respite, Hunter considered. It was certainly tempting. "I do not believe I have ever had the pleasure of seeing somewhere quite as lovely," Hunter offered, taking in the view. "It is indeed much easier on the eye than that of the interior of Carlisle House."

Fred chortled. "That bad?"

"Horrific does not even come close to explaining it, my good man," Hunter drawled sardonically. "It seems that the late Lord Carlisle had accrued far more wealth than one expects for one who held the mere title of baron." Hunter raised his eyebrows, wondering how precisely the man had achieved it and, to be more exact, who he had blackmailed or swindled. "Yet with all that wealth and money," he continued wryly, "it appears that no matter how rich a man may become, he will never be able to purchase good taste if he does not already possess it. And believe me, my father had none."

Hunter sighed. "That will all change, though, Fred, for there will be many amendments around here. Of course, I shall begin by ridding the place of the monstrous décor." Hunter smiled wickedly to himself as he silently included his mother in that plan. "But I would also like to ensure that there will be a rise in pay and fairer hours for all of you," he added. "I have no doubt you would all like more time with your families, and I will not be responsible for taking advantage of your need for employment."

Fred nodded, appearing quite impressed.

Hunter wanted to prove to them that he was nothing like the late baron, yet he did not wish to be presumptive by offering further details that were indeed very uncertain, for he had yet to assess the estate's accounts. Deceiving his employees with a random figure plucked from the air would not be a very good start. "Shall we?" he suggested instead, gesturing to the path ahead, then began to walk forward.

"Aye," Fred muttered, hurrying after him. The man, so lost in his thoughts, had unknowingly traded places with his employer and found himself hurrying to catch up.

Although Hunter adored the seaside, it seemed that both the country and the sea were indeed on par with each other despite being so very different. He hadn't appreciated the outdoors much as a child, for most of his days were spent in the schoolroom or being stifled by the formalities of the aristocratic ways his mother and father adhered to. He could not understand why they had even bothered with including him in any such nonsense, for they hardly took him anywhere, and when they did, or if they had visitors, they had always insisted that he keep quiet and, whenever possible, simply disappear into the backdrop of every scene.

"What are your duties here, Fred?" Hunter

enquired, pushing his mental meanderings aside for another day.

"I wouldn't know where to begin," the groundskeeper replied warily.

"By that remark, I assume that you are severely understaffed. Am I correct?" Hunter drawled.

"We manage, Carlisle."

"I don't wish for you to merely manage, Fred. That is unfair to you. I would like to know exactly what is needed to assist you." Hunter was curious as to what lengths, precisely, his father had gone to to remain within the bounds he had created for himself. Augustus Carlisle had always been tightfisted, which, as one would expect, was always at the expense of others. Forcing the work of ten men onto three or four had always been the man's way, yet not once did he so much as contemplate paying the wages of said ten. *'Never spend more than you have to, Argyle, my boy!'* Hunter had once overheard him tell his brother. *'Employ those who are simply grateful for work for as little as you can offer them.'* That attitude no longer belonged on the estate, Hunter decided. He did not treat his employees like that in either London or Whitstable, and he certainly wasn't going to now simply because his father had. Hunter inhaled furiously, his teeth clamped together, imprisoning the frustration he felt towards the late baron, for what could one possibly achieve by bellowing into the breeze when the man was no longer present to hear his son's opinion of him?

"Perhaps you would be so kind as to tell me how many men are employed under you?"

Fred's shoulders lifted as he inhaled, and then abruptly dropped as he blew out a heavy sigh. "There are a few, but if I am being honest, I must confess that there are not nearly as many as we need."

Hunter caught the look of hesitation on the groundskeeper's face. "Go on. Please," he encouraged.

Fred took a moment as he contemplated his next words. "I am sorry to say that four men, including myself, can barely manage an estate this size, and it is even more troublesome when I'm required to travel back and forth to your brother's grand house. Some days it leaves only three."

"I see," Hunter mumbled. "What about the land on my brother's estate?"

"That's a little bit smaller, but there are only three there, and, again, that's including me. I don't touch any other property you may have, though."

Hunter chewed the inside of his cheek as he considered the information. "How many men do you think we will need to cover both estates comfortably? And that is without any of you having to travel from one estate to the other? Actually," Hunter quickly added, "you do not need to answer that. If you are in agreement, and considering it is you who will have to work with these men, I would like for you to hire as many as you need for both estates."

"Aye, that's marvellous, thank you. I will get on with it right away. I have a few lads in mind already."

Hunter smiled. It seemed he had found an ally in the kindly groundskeeper. "Things will improve for every employee here from now on. I am not a pushover by all means, but I am fair, I can promise you that, Fred."

Fred removed the cap from his head and continued to lead Hunter further across the land. "Aye, that you are, Carlisle, and I will have some happy men, I can tell you that now."

"It is the very least I can do, Fred. However, there is one thing you can do for me, if you will."

"Anything, sir," Fred replied, twisting the soft fabric of his cap in his hands.

"This estate of my brother's, is it vacant?"

"Yes, it is."

"That is good news indeed. And I assume it is habitable?"

"Aye. Your brother kept a fine home." Fred looked at him curiously. "May I ask why?"

Hunter clasped his hands behind his back. "I do not mind returning to this estate, yet I am afraid that it is not wise for my mother and I to reside at the same property."

"I think I understand," Fred offered with a hint of sympathy. "I would think Lady Carlisle would be quite happy there, should you convince her, as it is rather a grand property. Almost as grand as this one."

"Thank you, Fred. Let me know when you are next heading that way, and I shall accompany you. Not a word to anyone, though, if you please. I think this is something I will inform my mother of when I know for certain."

"Mum's the word, Carlisle, if you'll pardon the pun. Your secret is safe with me."

Hunter winced at the sound of voices drifting from the parlour as he strode into the foyer of Carlisle House. The simple yet rather harrowing tone of his mother's voice never failed to sour his temperament. He had hoped, of course, that he might have maintained the pleasant mood that the out of doors had instilled in him, yet with the other feminine voice responding to Lady Carlisle beyond the door, Hunter did not particularly like his chances.

"Oh, Hunter is terribly handsome," Lady Carlisle declared enthusiastically to her guest.

The very sound of his name on the woman's sharp tongue at any time made Hunter suspicious and this time was no different. Her tone was cold and calculating, a thin lacquered layer of sugar smoothed its edges attempting yet failing to sweeten it. The hairs on the back of his neck lifted with suspicion. *'What are you up to, Mother?'* he mused, pausing outside the door. *'Meddling again, no doubt.'* It was dangerous indeed to risk being seen and hauled into the room, but he was all too aware of what Lady Carlisle could do, and after he mentioned finding a wife, this was all a little too coincidental for his liking, to say the least.

"You know, you and he would be rather well suited," she continued.

And there it was! Hunter was beginning to regret his curiosity. If that woman thought for one moment that she could dictate or have anything whatsoever to do with the choosing of the future Lady Carlisle, then she was sorely mistaken. Hunter shook himself, trying to dismiss the ominous dark clouds rolling in, smothering his mood and tinging it with anger.

A high-pitched roar of laughter rattled through the door.

Wonderful, Hunter thought, his blasted mother wanted to matchmake him with a hyena in a gown.

"Oh, wouldn't it be wonderful," the hyena replied. "You would be my mother-in-law."

"Precisely, my dear, and you will be able to

keep me informed should he wish to make any adjustments to the estate and any other matters."

Hunter narrowed his eyes. Lady Carlisle was intending to ingratiate herself with his future wife to keep herself tightly woven into the very fabric of the Carlisle estate and of him. Although he was only slightly disturbed by the woman's audacity, for he was quite certain that he would never marry any lady that his mother approved of, he knew he would have to have his wits about him. The very idea of marrying the satin-swathed beast sipping tea with Lady Carlisle was not his idea of a happy union. No indeed, and one could not afford to run the risk of being lured into the shackles of wedlock with links created by the oldest trick in the book... *a marriage born of compromise.*

Angling his head perfectly, Hunter peered through the gap in the door. Alright, so the hyena was not in fact a hyena, it seemed, and for those who would have been enamoured by the clichéd blonde, blue-eyed, lithe debutante, she would have been perfect for them, yet for Hunter, his bodily response to the lady was similar to that of when he stared at parchment. Although his mother certainly did not pull any punches, he thought, laughing wryly to himself, she did not know him at all. "You can try, Lady Carlisle," he muttered to himself, "you can certainly try."

"My lord?"

Blast! Hunter jumped in time with the

sudden, single thump of his heart as it slammed against his ribcage. He had been so enthralled in what his mother was doing that he hadn't seen Elkins approach. "How can I help, Elkins?" he queried, trying to slow his pulse.

The butler's eyes shifted to the parlour door, then back to Hunter with an apologetic look.

"Oh, don't worry about that, Elkins. She won't be here for much longer. A week at the most, if all goes well."

"Very good, my lord, but you may need to brace yourself for this." Elkins handed Hunter a card.

It was an invitation, Hunter realised as he admired the penmanship and the gilded emblem. "Has Lady Carlisle been informed of the invitation?" he enquired. Her name was certainly there, but the very thought of attending a soiree with his mother left nothing but a rather horrid sensation in his stomach. Not nerves, but simply disgust.

"No, my lord. I thought it would be best for you to, if you were so inclined."

The butler was an astute fellow, Hunter mused as he offered the man a grateful smile and a nod. "Much appreciated. I would prefer if we kept this between you and I, Elkins, if you please."

"Absolutely, my lord."

Once within the safe confines of his study, Hunter took one last look at the invitation, etching the details into his memory, then threw the fancy parchment into the jaws of the hearth. It was wiser to destroy it than to keep it somewhere Lady Carlisle may discover it, he thought. Besides, they may have had the same surname, and he may have grown up with her under the guise that she was his mother, but that mask came off years ago, and he would not allow her to play pretend any longer. No doubt she would play the victim instead, and in doing so, he would appear the villain, but it was a small price to pay, Hunter considered. After all, those who took the time to know him would soon learn that he was nothing of the sort.

Hunter watched the flames devour the invitation. It seemed almost symbolic, he ruminated, observing the way in which the paper curled and blackened, charring and crumbling the names of mother and son to ash as though putting an end to the ties between them. Perhaps then he too, he wondered, would indeed rise from the ashes just as the phoenix once had. The pages of a new chapter of his life were turning, and within them he had the opportunity to make new memories in the exact place where it had all started.

A light knock on the door disturbed his thoughts. He had not even realised that he had poured himself a whisky, yet as he lifted it to his lips, he frowned at the revelation of the half-filled glass, then sighed. "Come in," he called.

As though he had conjured her with his silent

cursing, Lady Carlisle stood in the doorway.

"Oh, it's you. What is it that you want, Lady Carlisle?" he replied curtly. "I am rather busy, as you can see," he added, gesturing to the paperwork spread out on the desk. He was rather glad he hadn't bothered to put it away when he had first noticed it, for she would not know that he hadn't so much as glanced at the mess of parchment, wax, pencils and books since he had entered the room. The truth was that his father had left the study in such a state that he simply didn't know where to start in order to make sense of it all.

"Oh, I do wish you would call me Mama or Mother as you used to do," she tittered.

"And why would I wish to do that?" Hunter queried, pinching the bridge of his nose.

"Because I am your mother," she answered innocently. "It is the way of things, is it not?"

Hunter inhaled. He was rather tired of the woman already, and he had not been there even a week. "Was there anything you particularly required, Lady Carlisle?"

Lady Carlisle pinched her lips, her jaw twitching as she ground her teeth together. "We have been invited to—"

Hunter peered at the burning hearth and wondered whether she knew of the dinner invitation.

"—a ball this Friday."

Blast it! It seems that Elkins did not quite manage to keep every invitation from her.

"I am sure the invitation is solely yours, Lady Carlisle, for I have not been here very long, and as far as I am aware, no one knows that I exist."

"Nonsense," she chirped, feigning an affectionate smile. "I would talk about you often," she lied. "Besides, news of your arrival has travelled far, it seems, for you are most certainly named on the invitation." Lady Carlisle proffered the fancy folded parchment to her son. "See. It says Lord Hunter Carlisle. It would be most impolite if you do not attend."

Hunter let out a long breath of frustration. "Very well, but, Lady Carlisle, please do not forget that you and I will be leading very separate lives again soon enough. In fact, I shall be visiting a perfectly respectable property within the coming days, which I have been told by a very reliable source will be to your liking."

Lady Carlisle's smile did not echo the malice in her eyes as she tried in vain to appear amenable. "Of course," she replied, "I understand, for I do not want to be a burden to you."

Coldness slithered into Hunter's gaze as his mind absorbed her words. "If you play these little games with me, Lady Carlisle, you and I will be parting company sooner than I had intended. Do not toy with me. Your ridiculous attempts to make me feel sympathy for you do not fool me in the slightest, for I am more than aware of your love of manipulating those around you to do as you wish. Is that understood?"

Crimson crept up the woman's neck as she vibrated with poorly concealed anger. "I shall leave you to it," she spat. "Enjoy *my* home, but know this..."

"Know what, Lady Carlisle?" Hunter dared, his eyes growing darker.

Lady Carlisle pressed her tongue to the roof of her mouth to still the words that wished to spill off it.

"Very wise, or you shall be out of this house tomorrow. Then, Lady Carlisle, what would you tell your friends when you attend the ball alone? They will want to know where I am and you shall have to explain as to why I do not wish to be seen in your company," Hunter seethed. Curling his hands into fists as they trembled, he turned his back on her. If she had been a man, he would have picked her up off her feet and physically thrown her from the room. "I think you should leave before I say something I might regret. Good day, Lady Carlisle."

Chapter Nine

Audrey lifted her skirts above her ankles, revealing her carriage boots, as she hurried up the staircase. Her gloved hand, gliding over the smooth wood of the railing as she made her way towards her mother's bedchamber, where she gently knocked on the door.

"Come in." Marjorie Whittemore lowered her book and lifted her eyes to the door expectantly, sighing with relief when it slowly opened to reveal her daughter.

"I shall take my leave in a few minutes, Mama. Flossie is expecting me, and I am far too nervous to wait any longer," Audrey explained quietly to avoid alerting her father to her imminent departure.

"But you are not wearing your new gown, my darling," Marjorie exclaimed. "I did so want to see you wearing it. And please do tell me that your nerves have nothing to do with a change of heart and are merely because you are still attending the ball."

"Of course, Mama. I have every intention of

attending, and I can assure you that my nerves do indeed have everything to do with the ball," she responded with an affectionate smile. Closing the door quietly behind her, Audrey walked further into her mother's bedchamber and settled herself down on the edge of the bed. "If I prepare for the ball here, Mama, then I shall run the risk of making Father very suspicious. It is safer for me to do all that is needed at Flossie's house, for if he does find out what I am up to, then he will be sure to stop me or, worse still, drag me from the ball in front of everyone, and it shall be mortifying, Mama. I do not think I could cope with any more humiliation."

"Yes indeed, my darling. I fear you are quite correct. I do so wish I could have given you a better father. I am so sorry." Marjorie Whittemore's fingers curled around her handkerchief as she held her hand over her heart.

Audrey gazed softly at her mother. There was so much regret and sadness in the woman's eyes that it simply took Audrey's breath away. "It is not your fault, Mama," Audrey offered soothingly, hoping to bring comfort to her mother as she reached out to take her hand. "It is not as though we ladies are given much of a choice with regards to anything, is it? Although I know I have no experience of marriage as you do, *I am* currently staring down the barrel of a pistol that my father is happily wielding with the lecherous Lord Gastrell as the ball. Therefore, I think I can say that I am not entirely devoid of sight as to the power Father wields over this household, not merely the servants but also you and I. Correct me if I am wrong, but I highly doubt that your marriage to Wallace Whittemore was a love match, Mama."

Marjorie shook her head gently. "No, my darling, you are not wrong. It was an arrangement my father made for me."

Audrey clasped her mother's hand gently and kissed her on the cheek. "Then you must stop blaming yourself, Mama. Do you promise me that you will stop?"

Marjorie Whittemore smiled. "You are a good girl, Audrey. I do love you so very much."

Audrey swallowed against the sudden ache in her throat. Her mother looked so forlorn that she was reluctant to leave her. "Will you be alright, Mama, if I take my leave?"

Marjorie's eyes met her daughter's. She could not quite ascertain whether her daughter was merely suggesting her departure in the following minutes or whether she was enquiring about some other time in the future that may be a little more permanent. "As long as you are happy, my darling, so too will I be." She hoped that was enough to let her daughter know that she must do what she needed to do to escape the clutches of that dreadful Lord Gastrell.

A look of understanding passed between the

ladies.

"I love you, Mama," Audrey sniffed, wrapping her arms tenderly around her mother. "Wherever I go, I promise to always let you know where I am, and I shall never ever be that far away from you."

Kissing Marjorie on the cheek for the second time since she had entered the woman's bedchamber, Audrey released her and made her way towards the door. "I will see you tomorrow, Mama," she whispered with a wistful smile. "And I shall be sure to tell you everything," she added, her eyes brightening and her smile broadening as she anticipated the possibilities that the evening may hold for her.

"Be safe, my darling. I shall see you tomorrow."

"Ah, Miss Whittemore," the tall, kindly butler offered in greeting. "Miss Florence is expecting you."

"Hello, Albert, and thank you." Audrey stepped into the Braithewaite family home, quite expecting to have to muster some patience in order to wait quietly whilst Flossie tended to whatever it was that she had been in the midst of doing. It was sadly true that Flossie rarely hurried to greet Audrey on occasions like this particular one, what with her usual preening and primping in preparation for the upcoming soiree, but today, it seemed, much to

Audrey's pleasant surprise, that it was not entirely impossible for such an occurrence. Audrey's right eyebrow elevated as a sudden flurry of fabric rushed down the staircase to greet her. She wondered whether her friend's undergarments were on fire, what with the speed the young lady's feet were carrying her, but the squeals of excitement could not fail to quash her theory rather rapidly.

"Oh, Audrey, you are finally here," Florence Braithewaite exclaimed breathlessly. "Quickly. You must come with me, for I cannot bear to wait any longer to see how splendid you will look in that gown."

Audrey giggled at Flossie's enthusiasm, watching as her friend descended the last step and curled her nimble fingers gently around her wrist. Audrey gasped as the young lady then turned on her heel and practically hauled her up the staircase.

"Everything has been prepared," Flossie informed Audrey, "and my maid will help you with your hair. Oh, tonight is going to be fabulous, Audrey. I simply know it will be."

Audrey listened whilst Flossie continued to bombard her ears with excited chatter, all the while biting her lower lip to refrain from interrupting.

"Oh, you are going to look spectacular, Audrey," Flossie continued, practically bursting at the seams. "You are certain to be the belle of the ball."

As they reached the bedchamber door, Flossie hurried Audrey in. Audrey could not help but grin at her friend's well-intended bossiness. "How can I be the belle of the ball, Floss, when it will be you who will hold that title?" she queried, trying to offer her friend an affectionate glance over her shoulder.

Audrey turned as Flossie closed the door behind them. "Oh pfft, what utter nonsense. Tonight is about you, Audrey. I have the most wonderful feeling that tonight your future will change for the better."

"You will look wonderful, Flossie," Audrey offered, feeling rather uncertain as to what it was exactly that she was meant to say.

"Of course I shall." Flossie grinned mischievously. "One cannot attend as a vagabond, so one should always intend to look her best, yet, no matter what you say, Audrey Whittemore, I simply know you will outshine us all. Now." Flossie turned her attention to the array of tiny bottles on her dressing table. "I must smell exquisite," she breathed thoughtfully. "What fragrance shall I wear?" Picking up one of the small bottles, Flossie pulled the stopper from the top of it. "Mmmm, lemon," she crooned, closing her eyes and savouring the aroma. "Definitely lemon."

Audrey gazed around her friend's bedchamber. She didn't know whether it was because her friend was not doomed to be the wife of a revolting man and so Flossie's future was not as bleak as hers, but Flossie's room seemed rather more uplifting than her own. In truth, the entire house was rather more joyful to be in. She supposed that was only to be expected when one did not live an overcast life under the tyranny of a greedy, selfish father.

"I decided upon my usual orange blossom perfume. It comforts me," Audrey replied, willing herself back into the conversation.

"Oh, I have more here if you would like to add a little extra before we leave?" Flossie suggested, as she practically smothered the entirety of the underside of her wrist with the summer-kissed lemony fragrance.

"Thank you, Floss, that would be most appreciated."

Time had passed rather swiftly, Audrey mused as she glanced at the clock on the mantelpiece. It appeared that Flossie's welcome, endless chatter about the eligible men she had heard of had made two hours seem like merely ten minutes. The young lady was quite enthused as she informed Audrey about how she had subtly made enquiries when in casual conversation with her eldest brother, Finley. Finley had always been rather a closed sort of gentleman, so Audrey was surprised to hear that he had been so willing to divulge such information.

"Oh, it was easy, Audrey," Flossie explained. "All I had to do was enquire as to who was best to avoid."

Audrey frowned. "But surely then your list would be of those that one should not address?"

Flossie giggled. "If you should know anything about Finley, it is that he will never give you a straight answer. If I had asked him who he thought was eligible and a decent fellow, he would have given me a list of those he deemed unpleasant and thus a list of those to avoid, which would have left us without any names at all as well as an evening in which we would have to deduce for ourselves as to who was not on my brother's list. In my opinion, to have done it in that way would have been an absolute waste of one's time, especially when there is fun to be had."

Audrey's nose wrinkled as she frowned with confusion at the rather odd way that Finley appeared to answer his sister's queries.

"I know, Audrey. I'm afraid Finley can be considered a tad peculiar, what with the way he responds in the most indirect fashion known to mankind, but he is rather knowledgeable, I must say, and fortunately for us, I know him quite well and have extracted the actual details we shall require rather than the ones we do not."

"Yes, indeed."

Audrey turned toward the looking glass for

one last glimpse of herself. The modiste's superb skills had created the most stunning velvet gown that fit her in all the right places. She could not deny that she felt far more confident in her new attire than she had ever felt in anything else she owned. The rich ruby velvet flowed over her body, the lustrous fabric shimmering decadently over her feminine curves, drawing the eye to what her usual garments would hide.

The air whistled through Audrey's teeth as a horrid thought struck her.

"What is it, Audrey?" Flossie enquired, her expression one of utmost concern. "Are you unwell?"

All colour had drained from Audrey's usual complexion. She was trembling, she noted, as she clasped her hands together with as much strength as she could muster simply to refrain from shaking any more than she was already. "What if Lord Gastrell is at the ball?" she rasped, unable to divert her mind from the dreadful thought of him seeing her in her splendid and somewhat revealing gown. She couldn't bear the thought of being in the same room as him, especially when she knew he would not stay away from her, nor would he refrain from his indecent behaviour.

Flossie placed her hand comfortingly over her friend's. "You mustn't panic, Audrey. After all, you shall be wearing a mask. I very much doubt that Lord Lecherous could recognise himself in one, let alone anyone else. Besides, I have no doubt he will be in his cups by the time we arrive, if he does attend. Then, of course, it has to be said that all the while I am with you, the wretch will not be able to get within even a mile of us."

Audrey threw a questioning look in Flossie's direction.

"Indeed, never fear, my dear," Flossie crooned, lifting the hem of her pale blue gown to reveal her matching boots, "for I have decided to wear these tonight, and it just so happens that I have been known to crush a toe or two before with these heels," she added wryly.

A burst of laughter bubbled up from Audrey's throat. "You are simply the best friend a lady can have, Floss," she replied with a joyful smile. "Do you know, I think I may wear my boots as well."

"Always be prepared, Audrey." Flossie grinned. "But I must warn you that should you feel the need to crush a man's toe, always feign the utmost innocence and surprise directly after the event, for one demure glance followed by a gentle sniff of shame and all will be forgiven, I can assure you."

Feeling a tad better than she had a moment ago, Audrey lowered herself into a chair and slipped off her satin slippers, replacing them with her highly polished carriage boots. She happily noted how the gown concealed her footwear as the skirts cascaded down over her shapely legs. No one would ever know, she mused with satisfaction. "There," she exclaimed. "I believe I am quite ready for this little adventure."

"You look ravishing, Audrey. We shall be shooing the gentlemen away," Flossie assured her as they linked arms.

"As do you, my dear Flossie." Audrey gently squeezed her friend's arm. "You know, I think you look so much more than splendid in pale blue. The hue simply belongs on you."

Flossie blushed. It was true, Audrey thought as they descended the staircase. If neither lady found suitors at the ball, then she did not know what on earth they would have to do to stand a chance of finding a husband. Indeed, Audrey was rather hopeful for what the evening would bring.

"Fabian," Flossie warned, elevating her perfectly arched brows at her brother. "Didn't Mama tell you that it is quite rude to stare at a lady?"

"Don't be mean, Floss. I am quite sure that Fabian was simply lost in his own thoughts and looking right through me, weren't you, Fabian?"

It was no secret that Fabian was rather infatuated with Audrey, but she did not see the need to embarrass the poor thirteen-year-old up-and-coming gentleman.

Fabian nodded profusely, then cleared his throat. "Indeed," he replied. "You know I do not like having to visit Aunt Caroline. She treats me like a baby, and I am a gentleman," he exclaimed as heat burned his cheeks.

Audrey admired the way in which the boy had thought so very quickly to cover his tracks. "That is also what I deduced," Audrey added to the conversation in her way of support and then winked at him, sending the colour of his cheeks from raspberry pink to that of scarlet. Audrey supposed she should not have teased him, but she viewed him very much like a brother. With ten years and a few months between them, she still remembered the sweet little bundle he had been when he was merely a baby.

Flossie elbowed her in the ribs. "You would say that," she replied with a giggle. "You two are as thick as thieves."

The sound of laughter from all three parties shooed away the tension in the carriage. "Fabian knows that I will always protect him, and I believe he will always protect me. Isn't that correct, Fabian?" Audrey queried, smiling kindly at the boy.

Fabian simply nodded, unable to control the rush of crimson from his cheeks to the roots of his hair. However, the smile on his face and the innocent twinkle in his eyes as he alighted the carriage to spend the evening with his aunt assured Audrey that he had been grateful for her support.

The ballroom was awash with guests. Flossie had been correct, for hardly anyone had been recognisable with masks upon their faces. Audrey readjusted the glittering lace fabric of her own as it caressed and concealed the upper half of her face, giving her a mysterious air. As the lower edge of the delicate mask kissed the very top of the apples of her cheeks, Audrey lifted her shawl, revealing her bare shoulders, then handed it to the awaiting servant. "Thank you," she offered kindly. She should have been afraid in such a daring gown, she mused, yet she had come to realise that disguises, whether masks or gentlemen's clothing, always seemed to ignite a flare of courage that burned right through her.

Audrey sashayed through the throng of guests, noting the air and the heavy-lidded gazes of gentlemen tickling the exposed, sensitive skin of her décolletage. Keen eyes whispered over the soft curves of her breasts where her bodice pushed up and held her bosom enticingly in place. Her father would have had an apoplexy if he could have seen her, she thought with a sly giggle as she bathed in the sense of power conjured from the attention garnered. Indeed, she felt thoroughly wicked and perhaps a little wanton. "Oh, this is wonderful, Floss," she whispered loudly, drawing her friend closer to her side. "I have never seen such extravagance."

"Lady Chilcott is known for her love of fine things. I do not think I have ever attended one of her soirees where I have not been awestruck at the decadence of it all," Flossie replied, squeezing Audrey's arm gently. "Shall we?"

As Flossie and Audrey paused at the refreshments table, Audrey allowed her eyes to rove over the guests. The light from the chandeliers rained over them in tiny drops of light as though she were gazing into the imaginings of a child reading a fairy tale for the first time. None of them appeared to be anyone that she knew, she noted, and she had to admit to herself that she was rather grateful for that fact, especially when she was quite sure that had Lord Gastrell been there, she would have easily recognised the sweaty, festering mess that he was.

Florence Braithewaite felt the breath leave Audrey's lungs as her friend relaxed with relief at her side. Flossie was quite certain she knew the reason, for she too had been scanning the crowd for Lord Gastrell. "Wretched, filthy little man," she grumbled quietly to herself. Flossie crossed her fingers, hoping that the beast would not make a late appearance and upset Audrey. However, she did not believe that he and Lady Chilcott were acquainted. The woman had more taste than to associate with the likes of the lecherous ogre. "You must forget about him, Audrey," she offered kindly. "Tonight, you must concentrate on enjoying yourself. You needn't worry about *you-know-who*, for I shall remain vigilant on your behalf, and should I have the misfortune to lay my eyes upon him, then my boots and I will make sure that he doesn't step within a mile of you. This is your night," she reminded her.

"Thank you, Flossie. Although I do not think I can tell one gentleman from the next."

Flossie snorted. "There is no mistaking that lech," she scoffed. "However, if you are referring to those you may wish to dance with, simply keep hold of your dance card, and I shall check them against my list to see whether they are a scoundrel. Oh, look." Flossie handed Audrey a glass of lemonade. "Actually, don't look. Simply pretend you are rather nonplussed."

Audrey frowned but did as her friend instructed.

"Good evening, ladies."

A rather handsome gentleman with golden hair stood before them, his eyes twinkling under the overhead lights. He was slim yet rather broad-shouldered and thoroughly vibrating with a warm energy. "I wonder whether you would care to dance?"

"Oh, she would love to," Flossie declared.

"I do believe the gentleman is asking you, Flossie," Audrey corrected as she smiled at the way the gentleman blushed awkwardly, seemingly embarrassed by the confusion of the situation.

"Me?"

"Indeed," the gentleman replied, "if you have a space on your dance card?"

A blush crept out from beneath Flossie's mask. "I believe you are the first to ask, sir."

"Well, in that case, perhaps you would do me the honour of dancing with me now?"

"I would be delighted."

Audrey watched as Flossie stepped onto the dance floor with the gentleman. It appeared as though they were quite well suited, she considered as she observed her friend talk animatedly with him. Flossie only ever spoke like that when she was comfortable with someone, Audrey noted. Unless, of course, someone had added something to the lemonade. Audrey sniffed the offending drink. No, it was simply lemonade. Nothing more, thank heavens, for she quite liked the possibility that Flossie may have found her suitor within the first few minutes of her arrival.

The spaces, albeit one, on Audrey's dance card took less than fifteen minutes to fill. She had opted to save the last waltz of the night in the hope that perhaps the perfect gentleman for her would wish to be her partner. She supposed it may have been pointless, for she was, in effect, diminishing one of the few chances she had to find her future husband, yet she could not help but hope. It was all she had, after all, she realised. And was it really all too much for a lady to wish for love in a marriage? She certainly hoped not.

"So, Miss... err... err." The gentleman who had opted to partner Audrey for her first dance stepped rather out of time as he insisted on admiring his own reflection whilst glancing in the scattered mirrors about the ballroom.

Audrey watched as he wiggled his hips randomly then flicked his long hair back as though it was all part of the dance. Had he not been so amusing, she might have been embarrassed, but he was rather interesting to watch in an odd sort of way, she thought, pitying the young lady who found herself betrothed to him. "Jones," Audrey offered. Of course, it probably wouldn't have hurt for him to know her surname was actually Whittemore, but she was rather afraid her father would hear of her escapade or that the fun yet rather conceited, fellow would call on her at her home. It dawned on her then that she would not be able to give any of the gentlemen she danced with her real name. She sighed. How would she ever court anyone if he would not have the option of calling on her? *Good heavens!* Would she really have to be a little more forward than what propriety deemed appropriate? she wondered. Her cheeks heated at the thought.

"You are blushing, Miss Jones," the gentleman teased as he puffed out his chest. "It has to be said that you are not the first beautiful chit that I have had that effect on. One simply cannot help it when one is as dashing as I." The gentleman flashed a grin in the closest looking glass and then aimed it at Audrey.

Audrey swallowed the laughter crawling up her throat for fear of offending him. "Indeed, sir. However, I do not have your name, and I was merely blushing because I had forgotten to ask," she lied, offering him a sweet smile.

"It is Lord Williams. William Williams," he sniffed, raising an eyebrow at her as he waited for her to comment on the double name.

Audrey pressed her lips together. She supposed she may have laughed, but it did not surprise her that he would be the type of gentleman to have such a name, and in all honesty, his rather humorous name suited his humorous personality. "It is a pleasure to meet you, Lord Williams, and I thank you for the dance," she added as she extricated her hand from his. "If you'll excuse me," she said, lowering into a perfect curtsy.

"Help," Audrey mouthed, chuckling inaudibly, as she headed towards her friend.

Flossie grinned and handed her a lemonade. "You shall have to tell me all about it," she encouraged. "From what I could see, he looked rather eccentric."

"Absolutely, yet who knew a conceited gentleman could be so entertaining? I can't say that he has captured my heart, though, Floss. Indeed, I think he may have captured his own a long time ago, for he was rather enamoured with his own reflection," Audrey replied with a smirk.

"Oh dear." Flossie giggled but was then swiftly twirled away by another gentleman.

Flossie's absence left Audrey feeling rather vulnerable, so much so that she rather liked the idea of running from the ballroom, especially when she spied the next gentleman heading directly towards her. As much as she may have wished to slip away discreetly, the possessive look in his eyes informed her it was too late.

Audrey sighed. Wretched dance cards, she cursed. They were simply tiny little contracts that every lady found herself having to adhere to, merely for the sake of etiquette. Half of the gentlemen on them she would rather have ignored, she realised, for she certainly didn't feel inclined to engage in small talk with them.

This one resembled a bull, Audrey considered. She had never seen quite so much determination on a gentleman's face. Indeed, had she been a debutante, she thought she would have been terrified of him. *'One cannot be picky, Audrey,'* she reminded herself. After all, if one had to choose between a bull and the lecherous lord, she was more than certain that she would find herself at the altar about to marry a gentleman closely related to the bovine species.

Chapter Ten

"Just so that you and I understand each other," Hunter drawled begrudgingly, his voice sharp and demanding as it cut through the silence, "this is the one and only ball I shall ever attend with you, Lady Carlisle." Closing the carriage door behind him, Hunter seated himself in the farthest corner of the vehicle, creating as much distance as was possible between himself and his mother in such close confines. "Of course, that does not mean that I will be attending any other form of soiree you may feel the desire to manipulate me into attending with you either. If you should attempt any further subterfuge where my life is concerned, you shall find yourself extremely disappointed."

Lady Carlisle sniffed haughtily as she turned her head to stare out into the dark. "I really do not know why you do not like me, Hunter. It is unnatural for a son to treat their mother this way."

Hunter let out a breath, forcing some of the burning anger from his chest. It billowed out from between his lips and plumed into the cold evening air. He couldn't remember a time when he had felt quite so harassed, for it appeared that no matter what he said to his mother or how many times he said it, she did not want to accept her role in their estrangement, nor did she want to understand that she could not meddle in his life like she so clearly wished to. Had she seemed regretful for the right reasons at any point since his return, he thought he might have even tried to rebuild their relationship, but the evidence that she was as devious and manipulative as she ever was was indeed unignorable. "Enough," Hunter warned. "I am not going to keep repeating myself, Lady Carlisle. Neither of us suffers from amnesia, yet you insist on asking the same questions over and over again. However, there is one more thing I had forgotten to mention, and that is that you may not presume to introduce me to your acquaintances. I do not intend to do anything beyond escorting you to the ball. Once we are there, we will go our separate ways. Is that clear?"

Lady Carlisle turned abruptly. The light from the carriage lamp glinted off the needle-sharp malice festering in her eyes as she glared directly at her son. Gone was the feigned pleasant smile, and in its place was the woman that Hunter remembered. "Do not fret, Hunter," she hissed. "I believe the ton are quite aware of your downfall with regard to entering into trade, so I highly doubt they would wish to make your acquaintance. In truth, I would rather you disassociate yourself from me anyway. You are not exactly the son that any mother could be proud of."

Hunter smirked, feeling rather pleased that she had allowed her sickeningly fake mask to drop. It was better that way, for they both knew where they stood with each other. Indeed, Lady Carlisle had unwittingly proven his point, thus replenishing his animosity towards her. "I am glad we understand each other."

"Of course," she added, staring down at her hands, then out of the window. "I cannot help it if certain young ladies require an introduction, for you are quite like your brother in appearance even if you are not as agreeable in reputation. It would be considered rude for me not to introduce you to them."

Hunter snorted. It seemed his mother was subtly insisting on continuing her convenient matchmaking scheme. "Argyle was in no way agreeable, Lady Carlisle. The man was intimidating," Hunter retorted, leaning back lazily in the seat. "If he had ever found a lady who had agreed to marry him, then I doubt she would have actually wished for such a union, for it would either have been a marriage of convenience or the poor defenceless chit would have been scared what would happen to her reputation if she had refused."

"Utter nonsense; Argyle was highly sought after, I will have you know!"

"Assuming you are correct, and I being quite

aware as to what Argyle was truly like, I can only assume that it was his money they were after. After all, isn't that what marriage is amongst the aristocracy – simply *trade?*" Hunter let the word 'trade' linger in the air. His mother thought it an offensive word, and it was utterly delicious to taste it upon his tongue as he placed it directly in reference to his late brother and their acquaintances.

He was met with nothing but taut silence, and so he continued. "Should any of your acquaintances wish to be introduced to me—"

"They won't!" she snapped.

"*If* they do, Lady Carlisle," Hunter continued, drawing out the words, "then I am quite certain that it will either be merely because I have inherited the title meant for Argyle as well as the Carlisle wealth, not to mention having acquired even more blunt from *trade, or* you have been meddling again." Hunter arched his left eyebrow at the woman, indicating that he was all too aware of her current plan for him.

"You are merely a baron. You are not that enticing," Lady Carlisle retorted bitterly.

"Perhaps you are correct," Hunter began, feigning consideration of his position as baron. "Yet I did mention wealth, and I am quite certain that many ladies overlook a title when financial gain is taken into consideration, do they not? One cannot believe that your interest in the late baron was born of anything else other than his bulging..." Hunter paused merely to watch the horror building on his mother's face as she presumed to know what he would say, then smirked. "...wallet, Lady Carlisle. I should imagine that the mere tinkle of coins had you quite smitten with the man."

Lady Carlisle's face burned as bright as a furnace, her body vibrating as she sucked in her cheeks and pinched her lips. Hunter wondered whether he should snuff out the lamp and allow her to light the carriage instead of the nifty little contraption. In fact, the woman could have lit up the entire road. He had never seen her so positively crimson with rage.

"You... you... you," Lady Carlisle began, yet as a screech of frustration ripped from the back of her throat and whistled through her clenched teeth, she refused to say any more.

Hunter took no pleasure in seeing the woman react like that. Perhaps he had taken it a little too far, he considered, yet maybe he had needed to in order for her to cease her antics entirely. He certainly hoped that his words would be an end to it all. Of course, time would indeed tell, but if they had been, he would not need to confront her about her little tête-à-tête with the young lady in the parlour.

Lady Carlisle sighed. "I don't know why you won't allow me to help you. If you wish to find a wife, Hunter, you will need to mingle amongst the ton. Surely, you would require my assistance there," she offered feebly.

"Please let us not go over it again, Lady Carlisle." Hunter pinched the bridge of his nose. He was exhausted. "Trust me when I say that I know perfectly well why you wish to assist me. And, with that in mind, I must decline your offer and inform you that I will marry for no less than love."

Lady Carlisle let out a condescending cackle. "Such a simpleton," she scoffed.

Hunter's muscles tensed as he pulled his shoulders back and narrowed his eyes at the woman. "I wonder, Mother," he mused aloud, his lips curling at the corners as he kept his voice low, "how much did Father bequeath to you with regard to an allowance upon his demise?" *Dear lord,* he was so tired of the back-and-forth, repetitive battle with the woman, yet if she wanted to play, he would indeed play. "The amount is on the tip of my tongue," he continued, tapping his finger thoughtfully against his chin.

Lady Carlisle's spine stiffened as her eyes widened, then narrowed. The evident pleasure she had garnered at mocking her only living son evaporated instantly.

Hunter locked eyes with her, his gaze stone-cold. "Ah, yes, that is correct. It was zero. Not a single shilling. I suppose that is the way of a loveless marriage, is it not? I mean, what would one care of what became of their spouse if they did not love them?"

Silence lingered in the wake of his words, the lack of sound expanding and filling the carriage.

"Nothing to say, Mother dearest?"

Nothing.

"Wonderful. However, I want you out of Carlisle House by Sunday. That is *this* Sunday. I shall arrange for your belongings to be moved to your other son's dwellings. It puts quite a splendid distance between us, which I believe will be rather fortunate for us both."

"But—"

"Lady Carlisle," Hunter interrupted, "you are indeed fortunate that I am offering anything at all to you after what you allowed Father to do to me. I will not see you without dwellings, and I will ensure that you have a generous allowance. You may think little of me, but I have made my way in life and have been very successful. Indeed, my success is the very reason I can afford to keep you in the life in which you are accustomed. And, I might add, that is without destroying others' lives as the late baron evidently insisted upon doing. Your allowance will not dwindle and, although I have not seen the property in which you shall be residing, I have been assured that it will be to your taste," he added, abruptly pushing open the carriage door.

With all the words having been somewhat

heatedly exchanged, the journey had been considerably quick. Hunter was rather grateful, for it meant that he did not have to confine himself to such a small space with the woman any longer. "Now, let us not talk of it anymore." Hunter offered her his arm, taking the first and last entrance he would ever take with his mother into Lady Chilcott's or any other person's home. "Best foot forward, Lady Carlisle. We do not wish to make a scene now, do we?"

Agatha Carlisle sniffed, lifting her chin as her jaw clenched around her venomous words, keeping them tightly locked behind the grinding cage of her teeth. At least she had learned something, Hunter considered, noting the way she swallowed the temptation to offer a vicious retort. Her sharp features twisted with the tug of her lips as she plastered a strained smile upon her face. "Very wise, Lady Carlisle. Very wise," he whispered.

Uncurling his mother's claws that were spitefully digging into his arm as he had escorted her into Lord and Lady Chilcott's home, Hunter grasped the moment to step away and become thoroughly lost amongst the throng of guests. It was exhilarating to be free of her. Nevertheless, whilst Lady Carlisle was anywhere in the same building as he was, no matter the distance between them, Hunter was certain he would have to keep his wits about him. After the incessant verbal battle in the carriage ride, he had no doubt that he had not convinced her of anything, and she would simply continue with whatever it was she wished to.

Hunter wandered around the edge of the ballroom, ignoring the tittering of young ladies as their eyes followed him from over the tops of their fans. There seemed to be no happy medium in which one would find a woman to be a harmonious combination of a gently bred lady and one who seemed somewhat sane. It has to be said that there were also a few gentlemen who were a smidge or two less than sound of mind, he thought, catching sight of the sudden flailing of arms and the wriggling of hips as a gentleman attempted to impress his partner on the dance floor. Trying to dodge between the man's rapid movements to capture the expected look of dismay on the young lady's face, Hunter could only grin, for the chit, it appeared, was thoroughly amused. *Interesting*. Surely a gently bred young lady would be mortified at such a performance? Or, at least, that was what he assumed as he narrowed his eyes in her direction to get a better glimpse of her. For a while as the dance came to a close, he wondered whether he had been mistaken, yet as he watched the young lady curtsy then turn away from the man to venture back to her friend, all the while his own feet travelled around the edge of the room at a rather brisk pace to keep her face in his sights, the amusement and mischief emanating from her alarmingly stunning features assured him that he had not been mistaken at all.

"Hunter, I would like you to meet someone. This is-"

Blast!

Hunter swivelled on the heels of his hessian boots and stared at his mother. A warning heating his eyes and scorching her skin as he ground his teeth together. Knowing it was not the fault of the lady at the woman's side, Hunter smiled. Hope, it seemed, was rather futile, yet he kept dipping in and out of it where his mother was concerned. He had *hoped* that merely being out of Agatha Carlisle's company for a few hours would have offered him some form of respite from the interfering woman. After all, he had warned her, had he not? However, it appeared the woman suffered from a rather worrying case of selective hearing, for she was in the throes of foisting an unrequested introduction upon him when he had specifically told her not to.

Despite manners dictating that he be polite, and indeed Hunter was the absolute epitome of politeness, he was no fool, for he recognised the chit from his parlour. "Lady Carlisle," he drawled, his voice deepening with a level of annoyance that only she would understand. He wanted this to be over and done with so he could escape her once more. Hunter glanced behind him, but the mischievous little minx he had spied earlier was nowhere to be seen. *Damn!*

"Hunter, this is Lady Vanessa. Lady Vanessa,

my son, Hunter," Lady Carlisle announced, trying to pull Hunter's attention back towards them.

Lady Vanessa offered a low curtsy, offering Hunter a better view of her low neckline before she rose to greet him with a flutter of her lashes.

Careful so as not to roll his eyes at her attempt to seduce him, Hunter nodded his head. "Lady Vanessa," he intoned. "It is a pleasure to meet you, but if you will excuse me, I am needed elsewhere."

Lady Vanessa faltered, looking to her partner in crime, yet Agatha Carlisle failed to notice, for she was scowling at her son's back as he simply walked away.

Air. That was what he needed, Hunter reassured himself, listening to the gasps and rapid onset of gossip on the dance floor as he strode through an array of flouncing fabric. *Air and plenty of space*, for that woman was going to drive him to an early demise with her constant pestering, Hunter grumbled as he reached the edge of the ballroom and headed directly for the doors to the garden. It was damn well difficult enough simply having to deal with the hustle and bustle of pompous, ill-behaved guests, what with their gossiping in corners, behind uplifted hands and stretched-out fans, yet now *she* had rattled his temper again. Having his mother back in his life was rather suffocating indeed.

Hunter leaned against the wrought iron balustrades, removing the mask from his face and allowing the cool night air to wash over him as he inhaled deeply. Tucking the mask into the inside pocket of his jacket, he wondered, had he not worn the disguise, whether anyone would have commented on the visual similarities between he and his late brother. Hunter shuddered. Of course, he was sure that Lady Carlisle had spread the news of who he was by now, but for them to have been given the opportunity to comment on the unmistakable Carlisle facial features would have been as effective as allowing them to strip away at his sense of individuality. If Argyle had been a decent man, Hunter supposed he may have been flattered, but where the three members of his family with the initial A were concerned – Agatha, Augustus, and Argyle – one did not believe that any reference to either one of them in relation to him was flattering in the slightest.

Light whispered around the edges of the moon, blurring its perfect shape. Its ethereal glow laced the night sky and illuminated the earth below. The celestial white light crept through the branches of trees and atop the hedgerows as Hunter gazed out, allowing the silence to soothe him.

"*I can't marry him.* No. It's not that I can't, for I simply will not. Of all the men he could have chosen."

Hunter narrowed his eyes, searching the garden as he listened to the soft, feminine, exasperated rant. The chit was apparently rather passionate about not marrying a particular gentleman, it seemed. Whoever he was, Hunter assumed he was either lacking a title or had very little money. He could not think why a young lady who mingled amongst the ton would otherwise be so against the idea of a marriage. Hunter shook his head. It was none of his business. He required fresh air, that was all. He certainly had not wished to listen to a chit's tantrum.

Resigned to the idea that he simply would not find peace anywhere, Hunter pushed away from the balustrades and began to walk back towards the doors.

"Bastard!"

"I beg your pardon?" Now that was not the sound of a gently bred young lady, he considered with intrigue.

"Oh, blast," she muttered. "Apologies, sir. I was not referring to you."

Hunter descended the steps onto the narrow garden path, following the soft whispers of further curses pouring vehemently from the young lady's mouth. Most of them were merely because she had been discovered, yet there were a few regarding her father and some lord who was apparently lecherous, Hunter noted with a grin.

Approaching the chit, Hunter had hoped to have been somewhat discreet, yet the snap of the rather inconvenient twig beneath his hessian boot sounded rather more like a ball being shot from a pistol than a simple snap, the sound shattering the breathless silence. *Damn it!*

"Do not scream, please," he rumbled. "I come in peace. Your reputation is safe with me, and, from what I could hear earlier, I believe you and I are out here for similar reasons."

The young lady's breath fogged the air, bursts of clouds stretching into the night before her, revealing her position marvellously as they trailed out from behind the statue of a rather brazen gentleman. "May I approach?" Hunter queried.

"Yes, but I am armed."

Hunter chuckled, yet he wasn't certain whether it was a nervous one because of her apparent weapon or an amused one because she seemed to have more wits about her than the entirety of the other ladies in attendance. "I shall be very good, I assure you," he drawled.

Hands in the air, Hunter stepped out of the shadows and stood before the masked young lady. "It's you," he commented, his lips curling into a lopsided grin. *Dear lord,* she was much more beautiful up close. He didn't need for her to remove her mask to realise that.

"Well, that is a rather silly thing to say," she retorted, swinging her reticule around haphazardly. Hunter wondered whether that was what she had referred to as her weapon. "You could have said the same sentence to any one of the people here tonight, and you would have been correct, for who else would I be if not myself?" she added.

"Beautiful, forthright, and intelligent."

The young lady's soft lips quivered, battling against an involuntary smile. Whether Hunter was a danger to her person or perhaps a potential friend were two possibilities apparently at war within her mind.

Hunter lowered his hands, then seated himself on the bench at his side. "What is it that you do not like about your intended?" he enquired, keeping his gaze ahead.

"You heard that?" she rasped, stepping closer to him. Her hands were twiddling nervously with the small reticule now freely dangling from her dainty wrist. The reticule, it seemed, had been demoted from weapon to mere fashion accessory once more.

Hunter nodded. "That and a few choice words," he replied, grinning wolfishly as he faced her to witness her dismay. "Do not panic," he offered. "I will not suddenly expire simply because you felt the need to curse, Miss…"

"Miss Whittemore," she offered quickly, followed by a sudden onset of regret and self-chastisement crumpling her features.

"Do not worry, Miss Whittemore. I shall not repeat your name to anyone else," he promised, making a mental note of her kissable lips and the way in which her gown hugged her womanly curves.

"Thank you. And may I ask you your name?" she queried, snapping him out of his slow perusal of her.

"Hunter."

"Hunter," Miss Whittemore repeated, gesturing for him to move further along the bench so she could sit.

Hunter watched as she settled herself close beside him, amazed at how quickly she had relaxed in his presence. It had only been a few moments prior that he had wondered how he might be able to protect himself from any forthcoming reticule-induced bruises. "Although I am quite aware that you are not attempting to steal my virtue, Miss Whittemore," Hunter teased, "you do realise that it is improper for a young lady to be out here and quite unchaperoned, especially with a gentleman as handsome as I, do you not?" he questioned with a wicked grin.

Audrey's gaze travelled from the tips of his polished hessian boots, up his legs, over his evidently toned thighs beneath breeches, and as she twisted her body towards him, her eyes continued the long perusal upward, savouring his defined torso, broad shoulders, and every inch of him all the way to his splendid features. "Handsome?" Audrey cleared her throat, blushing profusely. "Perhaps," she continued. "As for unchaperoned, yes indeed, and I am fully aware, thank you. Yet you must understand, I was alone without the need for one until you walked out here and insisted on conversing with me." *'Good heavens,'* Audrey mused, the man was indeed quite beautiful. Her heart thumped and fluttered in agreement. She wondered if Hunter could hear it.

"Ah, I cannot deny that fact, Miss Whittemore, yet the desire to escape a certain person was rather too strong for me to ignore. I apologise for the intrusion." Hunter stretched out his long legs and crossed his ankles, leaning back slightly against the cold, wooden slats of the bench.

The man was doing it on purpose, Audrey thought, pulling her gaze away from his magnificent physique. *Why couldn't this man have been Lord Gastrell instead of that lecherous muttonhead?* She groaned.

"Is there something the matter, Miss Whittemore? Would you like me to leave?"

The man's eyes glittered with stifled laughter, which only deepened the hue of mortification spreading over Audrey's face. "No," she replied, a little too quickly. She didn't know why, but she rather liked his company. "There is no need for you to leave. We are both adults, are we not?"

Hunter nodded, looking rather impressed with her response.

"And with regards to your other question, you needn't worry, for it is my problem. I will not burden anyone else with it."

"You know, Miss Whittemore," Hunter replied thoughtfully, releasing a sigh as though he had the weight of the world on his shoulders. "Sometimes it is better to speak of your problems than to keep them all tucked up inside of you, for there, all they are capable of doing is festering and seeming to expand until they appear to be ten thousand times worse than what they actually are."

"I do not think they could be any worse," she retorted with an exasperated sigh as she sat forward.

Audrey's bare shoulders rose, luring Hunter's eyes towards her soft, milky skin and the loose dark curl coiled down the back of her neck. Hunter cleared his throat, denying his urge to brush her hair aside and replace it with the caress of his lips. His hands itched to glide across her shoulders and to pull her closer towards him. "Perhaps," Hunter began, trying to distract himself from his growing need, "if I tell you why I needed to escape the ballroom, then you may feel more comfortable telling me what it is that you detest about your betrothed so much that it has you fleeing to Lady Chilcott's gardens at this hour."

Audrey straightened her spine and shuffled further backward into the seat of the bench until the wood almost touched the fabric caressing her spine. She nodded. "You can certainly try," she responded kindly. "I cannot deny it will be a welcomed distraction, if nothing else."

Hearing her curse as she had, along with the tone of utter desperation amongst her grumbles, Hunter wondered whether he could indeed distract her. Her struggle between defeat and fight was rather evident, he realised as she turned to face him, but there was something else, something he recognised, for, as of late, he had seen it often whenever he caught sight of himself in the looking glass. It seemed Miss Whittemore felt quite *trapped*. "Well," he began, hoping to put the young lady a tad more at ease now that the conversation had become uneasy, for, of course, one does not like to discuss that which one wishes to forget. "I suppose I should start by saying that *I* am avoiding my mother."

"Your mother?" Audrey couldn't imagine avoiding her own mother. Her father? Yes, but her mother? Never. "Just your mother and not your father?"

"Yes, but if my father were alive, I am quite certain I would be avoiding him too."

"Oh, I see."

"Perhaps you do, perhaps you don't," Hunter muttered dismissively, "but in my defence, I have to tell you that I have not seen the woman for fifteen years. Apparently, I am a disgrace." Hunter smiled sardonically.

"But you are here now."

"Not by choice, Miss Whittemore, believe me. It seems that when one's father and brother decide to blow each other's heads off –"

Audrey gasped, to which Hunter merely grinned, a breath of air escaping his lips in a short burst of laughter.

"–the Carlisle family require the attention of the only heir waiting in the wings, as it were," he continued. "And I quite agree, Miss Whittemore, for, although I found it somewhat ironic, the fact that two men killed one another behaving like fools over money is utterly ridiculous and indeed worthy of a gasp or two."

"I am sorry for your loss, Hunter."

"Dear Miss Whittemore, you should only feel sorry for me for having to put up with my mother again and for being forced to become a baron, certainly not because my previous dictator of a father and idiot of a brother are currently residing with the devil. The loss is only felt when I think of where I had been before I was summoned back to my old haunts. I was quite happy where I was, and now, unfortunately, I am here, and that woman in there," Hunter declared, pointing in the direction of the ballroom with a wiggling, accusatory finger, "is trying to matchmake me with some chit of her choice."

"Perhaps I should have thought to have escaped like you had, for my father has already decided who I shall marry," Audrey offered with a defeated smile. "My fate is sealed, as it were."

Guilt stirred beneath the tight muscles of Hunter's abdomen. "Yes, I forget how much more difficult it is for young ladies than it is for gentlemen. I feel rather fortunate in comparison."

"Oh, please. You must not feel as though your problems are less, my lord."

Hunter ignored the stir in his loins as she had addressed him with his title. That was a first, he thought, shifting slightly on the bench and making a mental note to ponder the reaction to her a little later. Miss Whittemore seemed quite alone in her troubles, and if she needed to tell him about them, then the least he could do was listen. "I thank you, but the difference between you and I is that I can avoid the fate my mother desires for me, whereas you, Miss Whittemore, and any lady of the ton for that matter, are not able to simply say no to the men who believe they possess the right to control your futures."

Audrey softly stared into Hunter's eyes. It was the first time she had ever heard a gentleman actually grasp the truth of some of what a lady has to endure. "I must say you are quite insightful, my lord."

"Please, just Hunter will do, Miss

Whittemore." Hunter rasped, repositioning his hips at an angle as he pulled his jacket closer around him. If she didn't stop referring to him with that blasted title, his manhood beneath the fabric of his breeches would make it impossible for him to hide his attraction to her.

Audrey's soft, sensuous lips curled. "Very well, Hunter."

"Who is it that your father has promised you to?" Hunter pressed his lips together. "Of course, you do not have to tell me, Miss Whittemore," he quickly added, cursing his relentless curiosity.

"It is quite alright. My father has not merely promised me, for he has practically sold me to a man named Lord Gastrell."

"I do not believe I have ever met him."

"Then consider yourself rather fortunate, for he is not a nice man, and he certainly does not respect women."

Hunter observed Audrey's lips purse into a gentle pout, the muscles in her jaw flexing occasionally as she clenched her teeth together and inhaled deeply through her nose. Afraid to discourage her from unburdening her fears and troubles, he remained silent and waited for her to continue.

"The man is four-and-sixty years of age," she explained, a subtle quiver in the tone of her voice. "That is forty years my senior." Audrey clasped her hands to still the tremble in her fingers. "He is crude, disrespectful, and highly inappropriate."

Sitting so close to Hunter, the warmth of his body radiating outward towards her and delightfully licking her exposed skin, Audrey couldn't help but wonder whether she would have shuddered so vehemently if *he* had laid his hands on her rather than Lord Gastrell. Of course, if he had been as disrespectful as the lecherous lord, then she was sure she would have, but somehow, she knew that if Hunter had touched her, it would have been with her consent, and she would have welcomed it.

"Miss Whittemore?"

"Apologies, Hunter. Where was I? Oh, yes, crude and inappropriate. As I was saying..."

Listening to the young lady intently, Hunter noted how she would occasionally drift off, her eyes resting on him as the air vibrated between them. Her luscious lips parted, softening her delicious pout, and her breathing deepened. His body hummed in response. Had they not been discussing her woes, he would have perhaps leaned in to kiss her, but *that* would have been inappropriate. He certainly would not seduce a woman when she was at a low ebb. "What will you do, Miss Whittemore?"

"That is the problem," Audrey rasped, wondering why the man was so interested in her life when he had problems of his own. "I do not know what to do. I had intended to perhaps change my life here tonight."

Hunter raised an eyebrow inquisitively.

"Oh, no, nothing so bold, merely attracting the attention of another gentleman. Of course, I cannot say that the alternative had not crossed my mind, after all, desperate times and all that," she replied as she closed her eyes, savouring the slight breeze drifting over her delicate features. Audrey's chest rose and fell as she pushed back the sadness pressing a terrible ache at the centre of her chest. "Yet, I am simply not that kind of lady, Hunter. My conscience is too loud to trap a gentleman into marriage. I shall simply have to find another way."

Hunter soaked up the ambience of the midnight-swathed garden and the sight of the beautiful Miss Whittemore before him. Reaching out, he smoothed his thumb over her soft cheek to wipe away a single, escaped tear before it dropped down and disappeared into the velvet of her gown. "You know, Miss Whittemore, I do not think that any gentleman would ever consider himself unfairly treated were he to be compromised by a lady such as yourself, but that may very well be not only because you are indeed very beautiful but also because you are the type of young miss who would never intentionally do such a thing. You are a rarity in a rather wonderful way."

Forgetting herself, Audrey leaned into his touch. "Thank you, for I think that is the kindest thing any gentleman has ever said to me." She smiled warmly.

Hunter reached into his pocket and withdrew a calling card. "Take this, please," he said, placing the card into her hand and curling her fingers around it. "If you need to escape or merely to talk things over, then you will find me here," he advised, pointing to the address on the back. "There is no pressure, of course, but I want you to have other options, Miss Whittemore. Fifteen years ago, I walked away from my family without any more than what was in my pocket. I would have loved to have had someone to call upon in my hour of need after my departure, but more than that, I would have loved to have had that person to call upon before I did leave. Perhaps I can be that someone for you."

Audrey swallowed. She had wondered whether he was the new baron. The name and the fact that he had returned after fifteen years made sense, but to see the address on the card only confirmed it. "Thank you." She'd wanted to tell him that they were neighbours, yet she wanted this – *him* – for herself. If he knew where she lived, then he would possibly call on her, and her father would see to it that she never laid eyes upon him again.

"If you are afraid of being confronted by or gossiped about by my mother," he offered, misreading her thoughts, "then may I suggest you wait until Sunday, for she will be gone by then, and I would have had enough time to smother the hellish flames she so often trails in her wake." Hunter smirked.

Audrey giggled. "Perhaps I shall see you Sunday then, Hunter," she whispered, rising to her feet. "And thank you, truly. You have been very kind, indeed."

Chapter Eleven

With one last backward glance at her home, Audrey encouraged the mare beneath her into a gallop. Athena's hooves flicked up the grass and scattered the grit as she carried Audrey away from the house and further towards the borders of the estate. With each day as her impending marriage crept closer, Audrey found it harder and harder to be around her father. She needed to be as far away from him as she could possibly be, merely for her own sanity and for the simple fact that she wondered how much longer she would be able to hold her tongue. She was angry, she realised. *So very angry.* Yet to scream her objections would be a waste of breath. Such a sharp reaction would only ever lead to her being forced towards the altar earlier than her father had informed her she would be.

Informed her. A growl of frustration scraped the back of her throat at the selfishly malicious audacity of it all. Closing her eyes and mind to the tangle of pain in her chest, Audrey held her breath, then exhaled, her ribcage shuddering around the effort of such a simple task. Somehow everything felt so much more prominent today. Everything had darker and gloomier hues, except for the moments when she could not help but recall the time she had spent with Hunter. Perhaps it was the contrast between the splash of colour he had brought into her life in one mere conversation with that of the life she had no choice other than to return to. Indeed, perhaps that was what had made reality morph into something much more dismal. It would certainly make sense, for even after only a few moments with her new neighbour, her repetitive nightmare of facing Lord Gastrell at the altar had mellowed into a wonderful dream, for the lecherous lord had vanished and, in his place, gazing down at her, was Hunter. She was being silly, she told herself. She hardly knew the man, and as far as she was concerned, every man could be charming until they didn't get their own way. Experience had taught her that when a man was confronted with the word *'no'*, he became anything but wonderful.

    She could quite easily keep going forward, she considered, for in men's clothing she could simply gallop out through the gates and never look back. Who was there to stop her? she mused, turning Athena back to face her home in the distance. "Easy, my darling," she whispered breathlessly, patting the mare gently to soothe her. The idea of fleeing was far more than enticing than ever before, for she felt as though her soul was being torn from her body and dragged in the direction of the road. However, her heart, although fractured, tugged towards her mother, her friend, and her maid. "This is as far as we go, Athena. I can't leave Mother or Ivy behind, and Flossie would be most disappointed in me if I simply ran away."

"You!"

Audrey inhaled sharply. The simple breath pulled at her body like marionette strings, lifting her posture and straightening her spine. The brittle ice scraping the edges of the man's voice froze her into position. "Yes," she replied, deepening her voice as she slowly lifted her hand to the peak of her cap, tugging it lower over her eyes.

"What are you doing on my land?"

Lord Carlisle's voice was dark and irritable, stirring the most terrible nausea into a whirlpool within Audrey's stomach. He hadn't sounded like that in Lady Chilcott's garden, she thought with an inaudible gulp. "Apologies, my lord. I was not aware that I had left my f—" Audrey cleared her throat, halting her words, then deepened her voice again. "I meant my master's estate. I shall remove myself at once."

Keeping her back to Hunter so as not to be recognised, Audrey encouraged Athena to sidestep. The mare was having none of it, Audrey realised, as the horse began to whinny with apparent distress. It seemed that Audrey had no choice but to turn a fraction towards the man, baring the side of her disguised form to him, but she was not about to allow the gentleman the opportunity to second guess her gender. He wasn't the Hunter she had met the night before. This version of him set her nerves jangling. She had no choice but to make a hurried departure.

Athena set off at a gallop. "Good girl," Audrey whispered in the horse's ear as she leaned forward to thank her. "That was indeed rather close." The wind whipped up around them as Audrey kept one hand on the reins and the other holding her hat still upon her head. The rapid, forceful current of air fought her with all its might to relieve her of her tweed cap and reveal to the world her true identity. She wouldn't allow it, for she was not entirely certain as to whether she was still in Hunter's sight. He had caught her rather off guard, and now with her need to deceive him - although perhaps merely temporarily - mingling with the memory of their conversation the previous night, she felt almost as though she had betrayed him. It was rather ludicrous, she thought, to feel such a way, yet she believed there to be a beginning of a bond between them that she simply could not ignore.

Arriving back at the stable, Audrey dismounted and then retrieved her makeshift gown from behind the bales of hay. Shaking with the rush of emotions surging vehemently through her veins, she could not believe how very close she had come to being discovered. She only hoped that her disguise had indeed fooled him, for it was the first time she had been seen in it by anyone other than those who knew of her ruse, and it had been the first time she had had to withhold the truth of who she was.

Audrey blew out a breath, flomping down onto a bale of hay. From a distance, she was quite sure Hunter would have believed that she was a man, but he had gotten closer than she would have liked, and it made her uneasy. If he had recognised her, surely, he would have mentioned it, she considered, rising to her feet.

As Audrey contemplated the possible outcomes of her encounter with her new neighbour, visions of the brooding baron rippled across her mind, sending a slow, simmering heat over her skin. Absently, she buttoned the skirts at her hip. His temper may have made her nervous, she considered quietly, but he had believed her to be a man trespassing on his land. She was sure that if he had known it was her, then he would have been as kind and considerate as he had been at the ball. "No, he wouldn't have, Audrey," she hissed into the silence of the stable as she tucked the frill of the bodice in at the front of her skirts. "He would have been utterly horrified that a lady was wearing men's clothes."

Audrey patted her hair, wondering whether it looked as dishevelled as it felt. The cap was indeed a rather genius addition to the ensemble of menswear, but it did nothing to ensure a graceful appearance for her when she took it off again. If anyone, especially her father, asked why she looked like she had been dragged through several bushes backwards, she would have to simply inform them that it had been the wild winds that did it. "Perhaps bring a bonnet next time, Audrey," she admonished herself. With that being said, she rather thought she would expire from shock if her father even noticed, for the man had never so much as shown an iota of concern for her as a person, let alone for her appearance.

"Where have you been?" Wallace Whittemore seethed as he curled his strong, spindly fingers around her upper arm.

"Father, you are hurting me," Audrey protested, attempting to extricate her arm from his menacing grip. "I went for a walk, is all."

"And last night?" he queried. "Where were you then?"

Audrey was startled by her father's expression. She knew of his anger, for she had witnessed it many times, but never had his eyes looked so terribly dark. They were practically onyx, and there was an unmistakable level of distrust in them, she noted as she observed the lingering glimmer of suspicion. "I was with Florence Braithewaite," she explained. "I did mention it."

Audrey had indeed told her father of her whereabouts the previous evening, although rather nonchalantly and perhaps a little low in volume so that he may not have heard her at all. She was hardly going to shout it from the rooftops so that he had the opportunity to forbid her to go.

Audrey rolled her eyes.

"You told me no such thing, you wretched girl. Are you trying to ruin everything?" Her father seethed. Anger deepened the creases in his brow as the storm continued to brew at the centres of his eyes. "You will not go anywhere without Lord Gastrell or I to accompany you. Or better yet, you will remain on the estate until you are married. Is that clear, girl?"

Audrey simply stared at the stranger who was bruising her with his unrelenting grip as though she were nothing more than a rag doll. Pain was searing up her arm beneath her flesh in waves as she suppressed the cry of anguish ripping through her chest, her eyes silently pleading with him to release her.

"Is that clear?" Wallace Whittemore repeated, his words snapping the air of the vast, hollow foyer.

"I do not think you could make yourself any clearer, Father," she replied. Audrey tensed her body and snatched her arm away from him with every ounce of strength she could muster.

Tumbling slightly as he ceased to maintain a hold on his daughter, the corners of Wallace Whittemore's mouth curled into a snide smile, sharpening every crease in the man's face. It was enough to curdle milk, Audrey thought as she scowled at him.

"I am pleased we have an understanding, Audrey," her father drawled. "And while we are on the subject of what is expected of you, you shall make yourself available for dinner tomorrow night, for we are expecting guests."

"May l enquire as to who we are expecting?" Audrey queried, every syllable perfectly enunciated in a strained attempt to maintain her claim of power between them. She had wanted to scream at the man, but that may have taken it a little too far. The situation was already rather fraught, and so, if she so much as put a foot wrong – or should one say *'was caught putting a foot wrong'* – her father would take great pleasure in opening the floodgates of hell especially for her, and she was quite certain that the lecherous lord would be the one standing behind them awaiting her.

"You may not!" Wallace Whittemore spat. "But you should know that your betrothed will be in attendance, and with that in mind, I expect you to look your best. I have witnessed your attempts at sabotaging your future with Gastrell, and I will not have you wearing any of those ridiculously high-collared gowns any longer. In essence, daughter, you will consider Lord Gastrell your husband from this very minute onwards, and that means you will dress and behave as is expected, You will willingly permit him to peruse a little of what he will be purchasing."

Mouth devoid of moisture, Audrey tried to swallow. It didn't matter how many times her father proved to her how despicable he was, he never failed to shock her. Nor did his actions and/or words fail to place another scar over her already bruised, beaten, and considerably fatigued heart, she thought as she placed her fingers over her breastbone, trying to soothe the pain stretching in tight ribbons across her chest.

"This is so very wrong," she muttered quietly. She was four and twenty. Surely, one would not need to endure such cruelty from one's father as he had been subjecting her to. Indeed, it was sufficiently abhorrent that the selfish man was ordering her to marry someone she loathed; he had practically reduced her to fodder. There had to be a point where she would have the right to draw a line and refuse. Audrey quite thought that this was it.

"What did you say to me?" he barked. "If you are going to be insolent, then speak up, girl."

"I said." Audrey inhaled, closing her eyes gently, then opened them again to stare her father directly in the eyes. She refused to cower in front of him. If he tried anything, then she would simply have to run, she decided quickly as he pushed her closer towards her wit's end. "I said," she repeated, "I shall not reduce myself to reveal more than is necessary." Audrey lifted her chin in defiance.

Wallace Whittemore circled his daughter, prowling predatorially in the hope that she would back down and break under his glare. Stopping behind her, he stepped forward so that only she would hear him. "You will do as I say, girl. If you wish for a fight, then let me assure you that you have met your match. However, it would serve you well to remember that I can do whatever I wish with you, child. Marriage, a poorhouse, and even an asylum. One might wisely suggest that you should adhere to my wishes. On that note, there are to be no high-collared gowns, Audrey. Do I make myself clear?"

Heart hammering, Audrey nodded, then turned and fled up the stairs.

"Miss Audrey," Ivy sang sweetly as she curled the upper half of her body around the door. Wariness whispered into the room as the maid simply stood there, unsure as to whether she should enter.

Audrey groaned. "What is it, Ivy?" she asked, her throat aching as her emotions tightened their fingers around it with the strength of her misery and frustration. It did not matter that she had been able to walk away from her father, for the damage he had caused clung to her like a thousand leeches, a thousand loyal, unwanted companions that she simply could not shake off.

"Apologies, miss, but your mother would like to see you."

"Would you please tell her that I shall visit her in another hour, Ivy? I do not think it would be fair for her to see me like this," Audrey explained, wiping a single tear away from the corner of her eye.

"I think that is why your mother wants to see you, Miss Audrey. She's quite worried about you. We all are." The maid stepped further into the bedchamber. "Might you visit her, Miss Audrey? I do not think I have ever seen her quite so afraid for you."

Sitting up on her bed, Audrey swung her legs over the side and slipped her feet into her satin slippers. "Very well, Ivy. I do not want Mama to be sad. Perhaps we can cheer each other up," she added with a delicate smile, trying to feign anything that wasn't what she was feeling.

Ivy smiled warmly, giving a slight nod as she slipped back out of the room with Audrey following closely behind her.

"Is Father still downstairs?" Audrey enquired as she kept in time with the maid. She had no desire to bump into the man, especially after their little *discussion.*

"I believe he went out after he spoke with you, Miss Audrey." The maid shuddered. "Brrr. That man looked like the devil ran through him. I don't think I have ever seen him that unhappy before," she muttered darkly. "If malevolence had a form, well, I think he might just be that man. *Oh*." Ivy halted and turned, her lips pressed tightly together as she grimaced apologetically. "Apologies, Miss Audrey. I'm afraid my mouth and my brain don't always work in unison. You just ignore the ramblings of this woman, for I'm sure he will be much happier when he gets back, and everything will be bang up to the elephant."

Unable to prevent the grin at her maid's rambling and rather loose tongue that seemed to tangle further with every word, Audrey patted her affectionately on the arm. "Please do not give it another thought, Ivy. I am quite aware of my father's ill temper, and I assure you that I have no intention of worrying about it, until I have to, which I believe will be at dinner when I shall have to endure his presence again," she offered, wishing her words were true. Although she had been and was still trying to forget everything about him, her mind would simply not allow her to forget. "Besides, I am quite sure that he is far more of a tyrant with the staff than he is with Mama and I."

The maid shot Audrey a look that pierced the centre of her heart. It seemed that Wallace Whittemore took greater pleasure in controlling his wife and daughter than he did the servants. "Not quite," Ivy whispered, confirming Audrey's assumption.

"Come, Ivy. Let us not dwell for now." Audrey

encouraged, picking up the pace towards her mother's bedchamber. "You and I will end up with unwanted lines on our faces from our incessant frowning, and you are far too pretty for me to allow you to get them because of me. If you feel a little glum about it all, then you must remember that one day all of this will merely be a memory for us both." Audrey was quite aware that her words were an attempt to console herself as well as her faithful maid, but she took pleasure from witnessing Ivy's expression soften. "Yes, indeed, Ivy," she added kindly, "for you and I both know that I shall not simply walk down the aisle to the altar of my own free will. We have time, my dear, and I will do all that is in my power to ensure that come the morning of my so-called wedding, Wallace Whittemore will not have so much as a clue as to where to find us."

"Whatever you need, Miss Audrey, just let me know, and I will help anyway I can," the maid offered eagerly.

"Thank you, Ivy. I may indeed call on you again. Oh, that reminds me," she breathed, her eyes sparkling with a sprinkle of mischief. "Will you please come to my bedchamber in an hour? For I believe my father needs to understand that, although I may compromise, I will never simply relent."

"Ooh, I'm intrigued," Ivy cooed. "Will I need a needle and thread?"

Audrey chuckled. "Of course."

"I thought as much," Ivy replied, tittering happily to herself as she walked away.

"You wanted to see me, Mama?"

Audrey stepped into her mother's bedchamber, hurrying towards her bed, where she quickly settled on the edge of the mattress. Her mother, she realised, was indeed a comfort to her. It was, in truth, something which she had never expected, for the lady had made herself rather scarce after the announcement of her father's plans for Audrey. Audrey, although she had not wanted to, had believed Marjorie Whittemore had washed her hands clean of anything to do with it, including her only daughter.

"Yes, my darling. How are you?" Marjorie pressed her lips tightly together as her chin wobbled with unspent despair. "It is a ridiculous question, I know," she rasped.

"I am alright, Mama. Please do not fret so," Audrey soothed. "In fact, I have some news that may offer a little hope," Audrey added. She had not forgotten the kind offer from Hunter. She only hoped that she had not spoiled it all with her deceit. The memory of his words and enticing, rumbling voice appeared to bat away her father's venomous chastisements and demands that so very often crashed, uninvited, ricocheting haphazardly around her brain, smashing anything so much as a tiny bit wonderful in its path. How long Hunter could keep the noise of her father away, she did not know. Perhaps, she mused, by voicing hers and Lord Carlisle's conversation to her mother, she could make Hunter's words louder, more real, and thus make her more hopeful that the gentleman would indeed be able to help her.

"You say he is our neighbour?" Marjorie Whittemore questioned after hearing her daughter's news. "Lord Carlisle?"

"Yes, Mama."

"Oh." Marjorie's gaze flicked to the other side of her bedchamber, concern etched in the taut lines on her face.

Audrey's brow furrowed. Whatever her mother was thinking, it certainly did not look remotely comforting. "You do not sound as pleased as I thought you may be, Mama. Whatever is the matter?"

"Oh, ignore me, my dear, for I am simply being silly," Marjorie tittered, batting the air in front of her face. "After all, I am quite certain he is nothing like the previous baron or his other son. No one could be as brutish as those two," she added.

"He seemed rather kind, Mama, although perhaps a little dark and mysterious, I suppose. But he did not think much of the ton and certainly did not appear to think very kindly of his family. However, he only ever mentioned his father and brother briefly. It was Lady Carlisle whom he spoke of more. She s—"

"Hmmph!"

Marjorie Whittemore's face had never looked so unforgiving, Audrey thought as she waited for her to explain the burst of indignant air that puffed from her lips. "What is it, Mama?"

"Lady Carlisle is a dreadful woman. If indeed he does think very little of her, as you say, then I believe he may be the only Carlisle that I shall ever like."

Audrey chuckled. "That is very high praise indeed, Mama," she replied with a wry smile. "I shall be sure to tell him."

Marjorie's face paled, and her lips pinched into a playful pucker. "You will do no such thing, my girl. I do not want that vile woman knocking on my door."

"Do not concern yourself, Mama. Your secret is safe with me," Audrey assured her mother, unable to contain her giggle. "Besides, Lord Carlisle has suggested that I pay him a visit on Sunday, or perhaps after, simply because of her. He thinks it would be best to avoid her, so even if I did say something, which I shall not, I do not believe for one second that he would hold it against you."

"Perhaps you are right," her mother agreed. "But, remember, one may moan about one's own family, but you will always find that they may not be quite so thrilled as one may think should any other wish to add their criticisms. The human race is rather funny that way."

"I promise he will not hear a word of criticism towards his family from me, Mama. Now tell me, what have you been up to while I have been away?"

Both ladies settled into a light-hearted conversation. The easy flow of chatter scooped them up in its warm embrace and carried them far away from Wallace Whittemore for an hour. Audrey watched as the colour returned to her mother's cheeks and the sparkle reignited in her eyes. She welcomed the sight, for it helped to dull the blade that her father incessantly wielded.

Wallace Whittemore paced the drawing room of Lord Gastrell's home, whilst the man himself casually poured them both a brandy.

"I do wish you would stop pacing, Whittemore," Gastrell snapped, slowly growing irritable with his guest. "Once you have this drink in your hand, you can explain to me why it is that you have taken it upon yourself to darken my door."

Wallace Whittemore practically snatched the copper liquid-filled snifter from the man's hand, then drained the contents before Lord Gastrell could even so much as blink. "She is too strong-willed," he blustered, flomping down into the deep brown leather wingback chair.

"I assume you are referring to Miss Audrey Whittemore?" Lord Gastrell raised the brandy to his lips as he smirked. Of course, he wanted what Wallace Whittemore had promised him, but he quite enjoyed witnessing the man sweat a little, for it made his bride-to-be so much more in the way of a prize.

Wallace Whittemore nodded, his skin a fiery red as he clenched his jaw with anger.

"Are you trying to rescind your offer of your daughter? You know it would be awfully irritating if that is why you have spoiled a perfectly good afternoon."

"Perhaps I could offer you something else in exchange for what I wish for, something I can guarantee," Wallace snivelled.

"Something you can guarantee?" Gastrell's eyebrows rose in question as he sipped his brandy. "Now, now, Whittemore, you promised me your only daughter. You must think me void of sight as well as an utter buffoon, for I would have to be both to have failed to notice that the young lady has a certain allure, what with that curvaceous figure of hers. She is perfect for what we have planned. So, in response to your suggestion, I shall decline, for there is not anything you can offer me that would entice me to remain bound to our agreement other than her." Gastrell tipped his head back to drain the last dregs of his brandy. "I believe, Whittemore," he continued, pouring himself another, "that you may be forgetting how handsomely you will be rewarded. Her marriage to me will see you elevated in wealth and free from the debts you have foolishly accrued, not to mention the matter of your partnership in my little business. Of course, if you are happy to lose all of that as well as everything else," Lord Gastrell drawled.

"Of course, I am not," Whittemore snapped. "I was simply venting my frustration. It was foolish of me to suggest anything else."

"Very wise, for I very much doubt that you would be able to cope with debtors' prison, Whittemore. Gentlemen such as yourself simply rot there, driving themselves to utter despair and madness." Lord Gastrell smiled spitefully. "Do we have an agreement then? I shall marry the chit and do as we intend with her, whilst you and I shall reap the rewards of our rather beneficial exchange."

"Agreed."

"Oh, and Whittemore, do try to remember that you will also be receiving an additional ten thousand pounds for your troubles."

Wallace Whittemore's lips began to twitch at the corners. The very mention of the blunt sparked a renewed energy that would ensure he would indeed see to it that Lord Gastrell would marry Audrey. "You are quite correct," he replied. "I fear she has simply irked me today. It is nothing I cannot handle, and rest assured you shall have your bride."

Lord Gastrell leaned back in his chair. "That is good to hear, *I hope*. Forgive me if I am not entirely reassured by your words, Whittemore, but I believe it is paramount that you do not misunderstand me when I say that if you do not adhere to the agreement, I may find myself having a quiet word with a few gentlemen, and you, my dear fellow, will find yourself in rather a dilemma. As I mentioned before, there is debtors' prison, and I hear it can be rather dreary and cold this or any other time of year."

"Now see here!" Wallace cut in, enraged at the threat.

"Please refrain while I am speaking, Whittemore, for I haven't finished, and I do not know of anyone who finds it thrilling to be interrupted. Do you?" Gastrell eyed Whittemore, his gaze scratching at the air between them with irritation. "I'm glad we agree," he offered, noting Whittemore's silence. "Now, as I was saying before I was so rudely interrupted... Debtors' prison is cold and dreary, and of course, whilst you are residing in said debtor's prison, Whittemore," Lord Gastrell continued as though the man currently turning all shades of red was entirely irrelevant in the grand scheme of things, "perhaps I will claim your entire estate on the pretence that you owe me as well. It is not entirely untrue when you would have let me down absurdly. A cold bed and empty pockets can make a man rather sour, so perhaps I will even take your wife. Admittedly, she is not as pert in certain areas as your daughter evidently is, but one cannot be fussy."

Wallace Whittemore rose to his feet as though someone had propelled him from it, his mouth poised as though he was about to speak, but before he could, Lord Gastrell merely stood and towered over him. "So, Whittemore, it is you that needs to *see here*. You either hand over your delightful daughter or I will ruin you."

Wallace Whittemore paled.

"Now if you will excuse me, I have a perfectly good afternoon to enjoy. I do not expect to see you nor hear from you until tomorrow evening, as we have planned."

Wallace Whittemore excused himself in a hurry, scurrying enthusiastically from Lord Gastrell's home. Audrey was going to destroy everything if he could not control her, he realised. If she did not adhere to his demands, he would have to take drastic measures, for there was far too much at stake.

Chapter Twelve

Hunter had never meant to sound quite so harsh, nor had he intended to frighten the figure on the horse, he considered quietly, although his accusation of trespassing could not really have been interpreted as friendly whether he had barked it at them or merely whispered. Initially, he had assumed that the rider was a young man, but on closer observation, as they had been forced to reveal the profile of their body to him, the soft feminine curves in the gentleman's clothes disclosed the young lady's secret. That, in itself, filled him with regret at having spoken to her in such a manner, for had he known, he would have approached her a little more cautiously.

A sliver of admiration curled in his chest at the memory of the chit's disguise. He couldn't believe she had found the courage and drive to be so bold as to even consider embarking on such deceit. Yet she had, he mused with a grin, recalling how she had attempted to deepen her voice despite her form and those soft lips fervently denying her claim of masculinity. *Those lips were rather familiar.* He had memorised them from the evening before when the young lady had said her name was Whittemore. Then, he hadn't really considered any connection, yet, as his mind pondered her delicate, luscious lips and arousing curves, she had him rather curious indeed.

"Hunter, where have you been?" Lady Carlisle crooned from the parlour.

Hunter rolled his eyes, shooting a look of utter despair at the butler.

Elkins kept his guilty eyes averted.

"Tomorrow," he whispered, reminding them both of his mother's promised departure.

Pushing open the door with some force, Hunter stepped into the parlour. "Lady Carlisle?"

"Oh, heavens. Surely, he does not address you so formally, Lady Agatha," the blonde chit exclaimed, placing closed, gloved fingers daintily over her mouth as she proceeded to titter.

The feigned laughter was irritating, Hunter noted, scowling, yet it was not quite the assault on his ears as her hyena-esque laughter had been when he had previously overheard their conversation.

"Do not fret, Lady Vanessa, for Hunter is merely jesting. Aren't you, my dear?" Lady Carlisle tilted her head in a manipulative questioning manner at her son.

The look of admonishment in her eyes served only to amuse him. "Am I, Lady Carlisle?" he responded with ease.

Agatha Carlisle swallowed, then guffawed dramatically. "You see how he is," she exclaimed, whilst pressing her hand to her chest. "Such an amusing young man. I have no doubt you will come to enjoy this side of him as you get to know him better," she said, offering the simpering lady a hopeful smile.

"Oh, I would very much like that," Lady Vanessa crooned, her eyes fluttering flirtatiously at Hunter.

"Lady Vanessa is quite the talk of the ton. She is always inundated with gentlemen vying for her attention, aren't you, dear?" Lady Carlisle began in her attempt to encourage Hunter's attention and desire for the woman.

Lady Vanessa nodded profusely. "I am indeed."

"We have already been introduced, have we not? So, with that in mind, I must wish Lady Vanessa the best of luck when choosing one of her many suitors and both of you a good day, for I have important matters to tend to." Hunter bowed curtly, hiding the glare of burning anger towards his mother and the wealth-seeking wench opposite her. He could not escape them quickly enough, he thought, making his way towards the door as every muscle in his face grew taut with the tension of being in their company.

"Hunter! Hunter!"

Hunter sighed dramatically, his entire body suddenly statuesque as he came to an abrupt stop. It seemed that he had not made himself quite as clear as he had hoped, for Lady Carlisle's meddling in matters that did not, nor ever would, concern her was rather apparent once more. "What is it?" he snapped, keeping his back to her as he tried to dampen the rage heating his insides.

"You are being extremely rude," she replied with a haughty sniff.

Lady Carlisle had evidently chosen to ignore every word he had uttered in warning, he inwardly fumed as he turned to face her, for the way in which she verbally poked the flames of his anger as she stood defiantly did indeed inform him as much. "Lady Carlisle," Hunter began, lowering the volume of his voice to a dangerous purr, "I thought that you and I had an understanding. One would think that you did not want a regular and rather generous allowance nor dwellings similar to this. It is almost as though you are deliberately pushing me towards the thin ends of my tether, simply so they will snap and I will be forced to rescind the generous offer and leave you destitute." Bringing his voice back up to a calm and more audible volume, Hunter continued. "Of course, that would be a rather foolish notion, would it not? For I cannot believe that there would be a person alive who would be so ridiculous as to wish for such an outcome." Locking eyes with the woman, a warning festered in Hunter's glare. "Or is there, Lady Carlisle?"

Agatha Carlisle inhaled. Hunter had not known that it was possible to inhale haughtily, but she had achieved it quite magnificently, he thought as her nose thinned and jaw muscles twitched. Her bravery in the single breath did not extend any further, for her eyes darted in every direction but towards her son. As tension laced the silence, she finally relented with a small shake of her head before turning abruptly on her heel and disappearing once again beyond the parlour door.

"Elkins, see to it that Lady Carlisle's belongings are packed into trunks right away," Hunter ordered.

The butler's face paled as his brow knitted in confusion. "Are you certain that you wish me to touch her ladyship's things, my lord? It seems rather improper, if you do not mind me saying."

"Perhaps, Elkins, but you are the only one I trust here at this present time. Gertie," he quickly added. "I trust Gertie also. Request that she assist you, as I know you both shall do as I ask and not what Lady Carlisle requests, should she attempt to interfere."

Elkins offered an unsure smile and nodded.

Hunter could not help but feel a little sympathy for the man, for he had served the Carlisle family for decades. It could not be comfortable to be immersed in such a tense atmosphere.

"Perhaps if Gertie tends to the more personal items and you to those that are less, it will ease your turmoil, Elkins?"

"Oh, yes, my lord. It would indeed. We shall do that." The butler's shoulders lowered considerably. "Thank you."

"No, thank *you*, Elkins, for I know this is not something you are terribly comfortable with, and it is a lot of me to ask of you. However, there is one more thing I need you to do for me."

Elkins gazed inquisitively at his employer.

"Please request that a carriage be readied for four o'clock. All her ladyship's trunks and valises are to be loaded onto it. Let it be known, I want Lady Carlisle out of this house today."

"Of course, my lord. We shall do as you wish."

"Thank you."

Elkins bowed and turned swiftly in the direction of the servants' quarters. He must seem terribly unkind, Hunter thought as he mulled over the orders he had just given, yet surely they must understand to a degree since every one of them had been privy to the Lady of the house's behaviour. Shrugging, Hunter dismissed his concerns and continued his journey up the staircase.

Running his hands through his thick, dark hair as he leaned against the mantelpiece, Hunter softly gazed at the flames flickering in the hearth. Where the thoughts of his mother and her attempts at interference had once been, now lingered another woman entirely. Hunter was practically salivating, he realised, as he recalled the image of the beautiful and rather mysterious Miss Whittemore on horseback, her legs astride in the most improper way. The way in which the chit's delectable derrière pressed against the saddle almost had him longing to be the lifeless equine garment. A breeches-clad version of the young lady only intensified the stir of something rather lustful within him, something she had unintentionally lured from him not even twenty-four hours prior.

A knock on his bedchamber door pulled Hunter from his somewhat private mental meanderings.

"My lord, I have come to inform you that her ladyship's belongings have been packed as requested. The trunks are currently being removed from the house and placed onto the awaiting carriages. I am afraid her ladyship had rather a lot, my lord, so there is an additional carriage."

"Splendid. Thank you, Elkins. You have been a marvellous help indeed."

Elkins remained quite still in the doorway.

"Is there something else, Elkins?" Hunter queried.

"Yes, my lord, there is." Peering behind him

briefly to ascertain whether they were quite alone, Elkins dipped his hand into the pocket of his jacket and produced a small white piece of folded parchment. "You have an invitation, my lord," he announced quietly, proffering the invite as he extended his arm. "I thought it best that I inform you when we were alone."

Hunter relieved the butler of the invitation, turning it over as he unfolded it and inspected the penmanship. "Whittemore." Hunter coughed abruptly as his abdomen tightened with the flash of the young woman in his mind. "I am assuming this is the Whittemores next to us?" Hunter queried, trying not to sound too keen on the prospect of spending the evening with Miss Whittemore.

"There is only one Whittemore family in these parts, my lord," Elkins offered. "The gentleman's name is Mr Wallace Whittemore. There is also his wife, Mrs Marjorie Whittemore, of course. Unfortunately, her ladyship and Mrs Whittemore do not see eye to eye," he added.

"In that case, I believe I already like this Mrs Whittemore despite never having met her," Hunter said, grinning. "Astuteness is an admirable quality indeed, Elkins, for it is rather apparent that the lady has seen something in Lady Carlisle which many do not. And are there any other Whittemores?"

"They have a daughter. Miss Audrey. She is a lovely young lady, my lord." Elkins shuffled nervously on his feet.

Narrowing his eyes, Hunter observed the fluctuation of the butler's expression from nonchalance to the intermittent pinch of an obvious wince at his thoughts. "There is something you want to tell me, is there not, Elkins?"

"Oh, no. It is not my place, my lord," Elkins said, refuting the possibility of offering advice.

"Nonsense, Elkins. We are both men, and as far as I am concerned, you are entitled to speak your mind and give your opinion. I believe I would be very glad of it."

"Very well, my lord, but please forgive me if what I am about to say is not my place."

Hunter nodded his head. "You need not fear anything from me, Elkins. Please continue."

The butler lifted his eyes to meet his employers. "It is my belief that Wallace Whittemore is a very unpleasant man. He is not like his wife or his daughter. I merely wish to give you this advice so that you are equipped with a little insight, for he is a despicable character, my lord, and only seeks to befriend those who are financially beneficial to him." Elkins lowered his gaze towards his feet.

The man had more to tell him, Hunter assumed. "Please go on, Elkins," Hunter encouraged.

"Wallace Whittemore is in considerable debt, or so I have been told, my lord. In fact, quite worryingly so. Might I suggest that you be cautious around him?"

"Thank you for telling me, Elkins. Information like that is most helpful indeed. And if you ever wish to be so open with me about such matters, please feel free to find me. Consider me your friend as well as your employer."

Elkins beamed with relief and pride as he pulled his shoulders back, standing at his full height. "Thank you. I am glad to have been of help, my lord."

Hunter grinned.

"How dare you do this to me, boy!" Lady Carlisle screeched as she flapped her hand at the footman attempting to relieve her of her hand luggage, only for it to be prised from her fingers within seconds and carried towards the awaiting vehicle.

Hunter's heart was pounding as the last scrap of affection he had for his mother battled with his brain, willing him not to relent. "It is better this way, Lady Carlisle, for both of us," he returned, then clamped his teeth tightly together to prevent any further comment. He was afraid that if he continued to speak, she would remain on the estate, where she would continue to try to control his life and all those in it. He needed his freedom, and the servants needed peace from the tyranny they had long endured. *It was time.*

"Better for you perhaps, but this is my home, Hunter," Lady Carlisle retorted bitterly, her hands clasped in front of her as her knuckles turned alabaster white.

"Correction, Lady Carlisle—this *was* your home, much like it was my home fifteen years ago until you and the late baron sought to remove me from it," he rumbled, reminding her and himself of what had passed between them, "but here we are, and it appears to belong to me. Only this time it is I who does not wish to share it with you." Hunter stared down at the woman he once thought the world of and noted how his heart had ceased to pound with indecision and a sense of unwarranted guilt. It seemed he could no longer muster even a crumb of remorse. He knew that, despite the threats to leave her desolate as perhaps she deserved, he would never have gone through with it, but the removal of her from the estate was something he had no hesitation to adhere to. "Who knows, Lady Carlisle, one day this may be yours again," he added with sarcasm. "But for now, whilst I reside here, you shall not. We are both in great need of our independence."

"What do you mean when you say that one day it may be mine?" Lady Carlisle's eyes were bright with intrigue and optimism.

"I was merely being sarcastic, so please do not get yourself into such a dither with any hope of it," he drawled. "Now, I believe your carriage awaits." Hunter gestured to the door as he lightly placed his hand at his mother's elbow.

"Get your hands off me," Lady Carlisle hissed, turning on him, her grey gown flouncing around her thin frame. "Oh, how glad I was when your father had the sense to force you from this house and out of our lives. You were, and have always been, an utter embarrassment to the Carlisle family name."

Hunter gazed at her, considerable boredom dripping from his features.

"Removing you from the family was probably the best thing that ridiculous old fool ever did, and then he went and got himself shot, only to leave me to deal with *you* again!" She sniffed as her lips puckered with spite.

A little bit more of a pucker and her face would have caved in, Hunter mused with a smirk. Once upon a time, Lady Carlisle's words would have, most likely, cut him to the core, he thought calmly, but it appeared that all those years of freedom had bestowed upon him a level of wisdom that he never knew could exist. It was what hardship had offered him as one of its rewards, and he was extremely glad of it. "Well, as you are leaving, it appears that you shall not have to deal with me ever again, Lady Carlisle."

Agatha Carlisle huffed and then stomped her foot. Aware that she would not change her son's mind, she stepped out of the front door and onto the stone steps, intermittently glancing backward with the assumption that Hunter would wish to escort her to the carriage. He had considered it, yet it seemed that her behaviour had changed his mind, for as she turned back to him, Hunter simply slammed the door in her face.

Lady Carlisle trembled with rage at the finality of the scraping and clanging of bolts and locks —the sounds continually ringing in her ears as she left the Carlisle estate alone.

The Whittemore residence was rather an ostentatious affair, Hunter considered as his eyes lifted from the buttons of his great coat and roved over the interior décor. With no possession of a title prior to the man's name and having no detailed history of the host, one may have believed that Whittemore dabbled in trade. The lavish art on the walls and the fine pieces of china, gold trinkets, porcelain figurines, and exquisite furniture certainly suggested he did and that he was very successful indeed. However, Hunter had been quite well informed that Wallace Whittemore had not worked a single day in his life. From what he had gathered from his conversation with Elkins and a little prior research, Hunter highly suspected the man would not even be able to contemplate what hard work was, nor did he have so much as a shilling to his name.

"If you would like to follow me, my lord," the butler offered stiffly. The tall, lean servant was considerably starchier in his attitude than Elkins. In fact, the Whittemore butler was probably starchier than all of Elkin's neatly pressed collars combined. Although, Hunter had to admit, Elkins hadn't always possessed such a comfortable demeanour, and the kindly butler, prior to Hunter's return, had most likely seemed very standoffish to most. Of course, Hunter quite understood all three reasons why Elkins had been that way, and perhaps, he mused, Whittemore treated his butler in a similar manner as the three previous Carlisles had treated Elkins.

Hunter shook his head, wondering how one would cope being so emotionally suffocated by the cruel hand and tongue of an employer. Indeed, witnessing merely a fraction of proof as to what Whittemore could be, such as the flashes of Miss Whittemore's troubled expressions as she had briefly touched upon her fate at the man's hands, had not spoken of a gentleman that Hunter wished to associate with. In truth, the only association Hunter felt inclined to engage in with the scoundrel was a brawl.

"Here you are, my lord," the butler announced, ushering Hunter into the drawing room. "Lord Carlisle, sir," he drawled before bowing and making a swift and rather desperate exit.

"Ah, Lord Carlisle. It is an honour to make your acquaintance," Wallace Whittemore declared as he leaned casually with one elbow on the mantelpiece, his eyes belying his words as they wandered the length of his guest with needle-sharp scrutiny.

Hunter was not particularly disturbed by the feather-light touch of hostility. In fact, he found it rather amusing as he returned the gesture. If Whittemore was short on blunt and had accrued debts, then he certainly concealed it well, Hunter considered, for the man's suit was one of the finest Hunter had ever seen, and he did not believe he had ever observed so many rings on a gentleman's hands. Hunter curled his fingers then stretched them as though he was shaking the sensation of the gentleman's jewellery from his own hands that wore nothing but the well-earned signs of hard labour.

"The honour is mine, sir," Hunter replied, drawing the man's gaze back up to his face. "I have to confess, I had never expected such a generous invitation so soon after my arrival."

"Nonsense, my lord, we are glad to have you, and we do so like to make people feel welcome here.

"Won't you have a drink with us? We have brandy, or perhaps you prefer whisky?" Whittemore crooned, his body rocking back and forth briefly on his heels. An amiable mask had slipped over the gentleman's face as the usual pleasantries dripped off his tongue, all the while failing magnificently at hiding the obvious plotting behind his brittle eyes.

"A whisky would be most welcome indeed. Thank you."

Wallace Whittemore's lips curled into a somewhat sickly smile as he handed Hunter the whisky-filled snifter, then stepped back into his original position as though it were a position of power.

"Oh, I do beg your pardon," Whittemore drawled. "Where are my manners?" A short burst of laughter fired from the back of his throat and flicked the air. "I believe I have failed to introduce you two gentlemen."

Standing proudly with one arm behind his back and the other resting on his paunch with a glass of brandy grasped in his fingers was a gentleman of a somewhat senior age, who, Hunter mused, apparently preferred to squeeze into his attire rather than perhaps alter it or purchase an alternative, for his pearl-white waistcoat appeared to be holding on for dear life. Hunter shifted slightly to the side, aware that he was in the firing line of the gentleman's straining brass buttons.

"Lord Carlisle, may I introduce Lord Gastrell, our dear friend. Lord Gastrell, may I introduce Lord Carlisle, our new neighbour."

"It is a pleasure to make your acquaintance, Lord Gastrell," Hunter lied, stifling the urge to grimace as he noted the glisten of perspiration above the man's top lip and the way in which his beady eyes peered over Hunter's shoulder to follow the maid around the room.

"Lord Gastrell is betrothed to my daughter," Whittemore announced as a not-so-subtle hint of warning laced his words. "She will be here in a moment with my wife."

Hunter's jaw slackened in horror and disbelief as he tried to understand how or why any father would wish such a fate for their daughter. The sympathy for Miss Whittemore and desire he had to aid the young lady in her escape had just amplified tenfold.

"Congratulations, Lord Gastrell," Hunter offered, keeping his voice steady as he swallowed the rising revulsion. *Dear lord*, the chit would be expected to produce his heir. Hunter gave his head a subtle shake. "I do not believe I have met Miss Whittemore nor Mrs Whittemore," he continued, "but I will be sure to offer my congratulations to them also."

"Why, thank you, young man. It is rather a fortuitous union, I must say," Gastrell replied as he lifted his chin and peered down the length of his bulbous nose. "Are you married, Carlisle?"

"No, but I do—"

The slow creak of the drawing room door diminished the remainder of Hunter's sentence as the exquisite beauty that was Miss Whittemore stepped into the room, an older version of herself at her side. Hunter's eyes lowered to Miss Whittemore's lips and then lifted to her pale green eyes. As their eyes met, a gasp whispered from the back of her kissable throat, then fluttered across the room, where it proceeded to run down his spine in a delightful trail of desire. Such a simple flick of one's eyes with the delicate sound of her surprise, and everything and everyone around them faded from Hunter's view. All he could see was her. A pleasant, thrilling heat simmered beneath his skin as he took his time appreciating the enticing fit of her modest gown. She was utterly breathtaking, he realised, and there was not a cat in hell's chance he would allow anyone else to have her but him.

Chapter Thirteen

Audrey twisted her hips from side to side, her skirts swishing and wrapping around her legs as they belatedly followed her movements. She grinned at her reflection, utterly elated at how Ivy had altered her gown in response to her father's demands. She certainly wouldn't be defying the man's wishes, nor could he argue that she was, for the high collar had indeed been eliminated as he had demanded rather unsubtly, yet the new neckline now stretched from one shoulder to the other and did not so much as reveal a crumb-sized portion of her skin on or below her shoulders. Now, it seemed that the only part of her that would indeed be on display to the lecherous lord was merely her neck and face. "Oh, you are a treasure, Ivy. Thank you. My father certainly cannot complain. One might even refer to the alterations as a compromise," she beamed triumphantly.

"As was my thinking, Miss Audrey." The maid winked playfully, stepping back to admire her work. "Will you be wanting these?" she added, proffering a pair of long, emerald green satin gloves to match Audrey's newly altered yet extremely modest gown.

"I certainly shall, thank you, Ivy. The very thought of that man's lips on my skin is unbearable," Audrey rasped, unable to stop the shudder of disgust running through her. "Having his beady eyes all over me is indeed dreadful enough."

Satin caressed Audrey's skin as she slipped her hands into the gloves, smoothing the fabric slowly up her arms until it kissed the cuff of her sleeves. With every inch of her slender upper limbs covered, she could argue that it was merely a coincidence in both the design of the gown and of the gloves themselves, but she knew quite well that it had been perfectly and utterly orchestrated by her. Her body was *hers*, Audrey fumed quietly, tilting her chin in defiance. *She* would be the one to decide what to wear and what to do with it, and she certainly wasn't going to be dictated to by a man who evidently cared not one jot for her. "There," she exclaimed, exhaling to rid herself of the last shred of frustration. "Not completely covered, which is what Father has requested, yet untouchable all the same just as I require."

"You look lovely, miss," Ivy offered as she observed the beginnings of dread flicker and darken Audrey's vulnerable gaze. The young lady's efforts to conceal her emotions by feigning a nonchalant perusal of herself in the looking glass had been rather futile.

"I will fetch Mama, and we shall face the guests together," Audrey exclaimed breathily.

"Perhaps we can offer each other a little courage." Pulling back her shoulders, Audrey gave a quick, stiff nod at herself in the looking glass, then turned away from her reflection to face the maid as she blew out a calming breath.

Ivy nodded. "I shall leave you to it, Miss Audrey, but if you should need me," she softly crooned, offering the young lady a discerning look, "then I shan't be far."

Savouring the contrast of the cool air against the deep rumble of dread burning in her veins, Audrey drew in another slow breath between her softly clenched teeth as she watched her maid take her leave. The acidity of her thoughts about the two men who awaited her in the drawing room seared into her flesh from the inside out, causing her to tremble with unspent rage. Tomorrow would be Sunday, and it was then that Hunter had told her to call on him, Audrey remembered, taking another deep breath and attempting to shrug off any doubts as to whether she would be bold enough to call on a gentleman. The very promise of his assistance was a precious gift of strength, so there really was no call for her to become a doubting Doris, she berated herself. Well, not right now anyway. She would leave all that nonsense until the morning.

Audrey was rather relieved to find herself in quite an animated chatter with her mother as they both reached the drawing room door. In her deep purple gown, Marjorie Whittemore not only looked very splendid as the hue complemented her silver hair, Audrey considered happily as she clasped the lady's hand, but she also appeared rather well.

"Shall we?" Marjorie enquired as they both stared at the closed door, afraid to so much as look beyond it. Observing the look of nausea wash over her daughter's face, Marjorie placed a soft kiss on the bridge of her nose. "You merely have to play along, for you still have time, my darling. And I will help you, remember that."

Audrey blew out a shaky breath and nodded as she curled and uncurled her trembling hands. "I can do this," she rasped.

"Yes, you can, Audrey. You are stronger than any man, no matter what they may have you believe." Marjorie laced her fingers with her daughter's, and then both ladies turned simultaneously towards the door, pushing it wide open.

The sight of Wallace Whittemore acting the doting husband and father tightened Marjorie's grip on Audrey. It was further evidence of what her mother had been through, Audrey thought as she squeezed her hand comfortingly. He had never bothered to act that way in front of Lord Gastrell, Audrey considered as she turned to face the guests, so why did he suddenly feel the need to now?

Audrey could not help the soft parting of her lips, nor the gasp that whispered over them as her eyes met with Hunter's. Her heart leapt with a burst of unexpected pleasure as a swarm of delicate butterflies took flight within her. Hunter Carlisle was far more magnificent under the light of the chandelier. She had thought him handsome in the low light of the ballroom, and although she had found herself wanting to drink him in, she hadn't dared to face him when she had encountered him earlier that day.

His blue gaze licked her, sending shivers up her spine and warmth flooding beneath her skin as it ignited a ripple of yearning that tugged at her core and in places she had never even so much as noticed any kind of response to a gentleman before. The depth of the blue of his jacket only served to brighten the cerulean hue of his eyes as they held hers in the most intimate gaze. His eyes sparkled with recognition, reciprocating her pleasure of seeing him again.

Wallace Whittemore cleared his throat. "Audrey, your betrothed is here. Are you not going to greet the man?" the man practically bellowed, then proceeded to chortle as though he had simply been teasing.

As difficult as it proved to be, Audrey tore her eyes away from Hunter, all the while basking in the heat of his gaze upon her as he refused to adhere to her father's rather obvious glare. It seemed that

Hunter was not about to be told what to do by the man.

"Lord Gastrell," she offered curtly.

Hunter leaned against the wall, his countenance cool and thoughtful as he seemed to closely observe the interaction between she and Lord Gastrell. The stark difference between the odious Lord Lecherous the First and the beautiful brooding baron was indeed profound, Audrey thought, unable to suppress the curling of her nose in disgust at her apparent betrothed. Feigning a dainty sneeze, she covered the evidence of repulsion. "Oh, I do beg your pardon, my lord, for I was caught rather unaware."

"It is perfectly alright, Miss Whittemore," Lord Gastrell replied, suspicion narrowing his eyes. "I do hope you are not under the weather."

"Indeed," she remarked, pinching her lips together as she struggled to ignore the low, sensuous rumble of laughter emitted from the man's antithesis. Hunter turned toward the window to hide his amusement. The pitch black outside the window blocked his view of the grounds as the light of the room on the glass offered him his own reflection and that of the drawing room. He was studying her, Audrey noted. The very inkling that he would be doing something so scandalous curled delightfully at her core, tugging at a tickle of excitement, making her breath stagger.

"Audrey," her mother whispered, gently squeezing her hand to pull Audrey's attention back toward the older gentlemen.

"Yes. Oh." Audrey blushed.

Marjorie Whittemore chuckled briefly, then turned her attention to her husband. "Wallace, darling," she sang, her voice now audible to everyone in the room. "Does our other guest have a name?" she enquired, noticing the malice burning in her husband's eyes as he glared at their daughter.

Wallace Whittemore inhaled, puffing out his chest. "Ah, yes. My apologies, my dear."

If looks could kill, Audrey rather thought she would have dropped there and then, for the look of disapproval emanating from beneath her father's untamed, bushy brows possessed the ability to slice through flesh and stir her insides with a generous dose of fear.

"This is Lord Carlisle, my dear," Wallace Whittemore offered in his wife's direction. "He is our new neighbour."

Hunter spun on his heels to, once again, meet the faces of the small gathering. His schooled expression was as tense as the muscles stretched across his broad shoulders as he pulled them back, making him appear taller as he came to a stop in front of the lady of the house.

She was gawking again, Audrey admonished herself, quickly averting her eyes before her father caught her admiring Hunter's fine physique.

As Hunter greeted her mother, his eyes glistened with a genuine kindness despite the feathering in the muscles of his jaw. His displeasure, it seemed, remained reserved for the men behind him. "It is wonderful to meet you, Mrs Whittemore," he began, lifting the lady's gloved hand to his lips, where he placed a delicate kiss upon her knuckles. Turning, he paused briefly, then lifted Audrey's hand. "It is quite wonderful to meet you too, Miss Whittemore," he drawled, never taking his eyes off her.

The caress of the baron's fingertips upon the underside of her wrist was hidden from view, yet Audrey felt every inch of it through the fabric. She had wanted to rip her glove from her hand and ask him to do it again upon her hungry skin, but she thought better of it, simply biting her lip instead in an attempt to prevent her knees from failing beneath her. How on earth she would explain her untimely collapse, she had no idea, she mused as a small, delighted spark flitted across her twinkling eyes - a spark that only Hunter had been privy to.

Wallace Whittemore cleared his throat. Twice.

So caught up in the moment and unwilling to shatter the thread of attraction between she and Hunter, Audrey bravely ignored her father, then proceeded to curtsy as her mother willed her with a gentle tug on her hand to pay closer attention. She knew it had been a risk, for she was proverbially prodding the man who could, and so often did, make her life hell.

The hell for her *insubordination*, as her father would have referred to her earlier behaviour as being, began the moment Audrey walked into the dining room, for the dreadful man had positioned her directly beside Lord Gastrell and his wandering hands. With her petticoats sat upon her knees and swathed around her calves, she had just about tolerated the vile lech's attempts to fondle her beneath the table. However, she found she simply could not eat. Her jaw had seized in response to the discomfort of his touch, clamping around the scream of frustration she knew she would have emitted if she so much as allowed herself to open her mouth even the tiniest fraction.

"Are you quite alright, Miss Whittemore?" a low rumbling voice enquired over her shoulder.

Audrey gasped, placing her hand over her heart. She had been thoroughly lost in her thoughts.

"I do beg your pardon. It was not my intention to startle you."

"It is quite alright, Lord Carlisle," Audrey replied. "I think I am simply a little tired, is all," she added calmly, ignoring how his presence made her heart pound and beat wildly with confusion. She was torn between whether she should be thrilled at the brush of his warm breath upon her exposed skin or terrified by the thoughts that plagued her, knowing that her future as Lord Gastrell's wife was just over the horizon.

"I believe it to be a little more than that, Miss Whittemore. Do not forget our little tête-à-tête at Lady Chilcott's ball."

Hunter abruptly straightened to his full height as Lord Gastrell and Mr Whittemore entered the room, followed closely behind by Mrs Whittemore, their presence abruptly severing the conversation as Hunter took several strides in the opposite direction to create distance between he and Audrey. Audrey shivered as cold air filled the chasm between them, the scent of warm spice twisting the uncomfortable sensation into something pleasant as it tingled over her skin. Hunter aroused something new from within her, she observed, noting the sense of longing tugging at her insides as she yearned to be close to him again.

"Ah, Miss Whittemore." Lord Gastrell pressed his paunch against her back with a subtle grunt. "You look rather fetching this evening," he added.

The sound of air rushing into Lord Gastrell's bulbous nose as he inhaled the scent of her hair made Audrey feel utterly bilious, not to mention the indecent, breathy groans emanating from the man as he tried in vain to put his hands upon her again, searching for the curves of her body through the layers of her gown. She couldn't bear it any longer. "If you will excuse me, my lord," she muttered, moving swiftly away from him, almost knocking the drink out from the grasp of his fingers. Audrey did not wait for an answer. She found herself not only disgusted but utterly livid that she was forced to be subjected to such indecency. Wallace Whittemore would not have the chance to object, she decided as she rushed towards the drawing room door. Thankfully, Audrey had mastered the art of thinking before she so much as attempted to speak, or, in this case, retaliate. After all, she had had plenty of practice as the daughter of Wallace Whittemore, had she not? It was for this very reason she knew it would be best for her if she made her escape to a position in the house as far away as was indeed possible from the lecherous lord before she said or did anything that might put her in a worse situation than she was in already.

Closing the door behind her, Audrey pressed her back to the cold wall, allowing herself a moment to breathe.

"I want you back in here within twenty minutes, my girl," Wallace Whittemore seethed, pulling the door open again and grabbing hold of her arm.

At the press of her father's fingers into her flesh, Audrey winced with the intensity of the pain. She should have simply kept walking, she realised as she tried to prise her upper limb from her father's grip. "You are hurting me, Father," she rasped. "I simply needed some air, is all."

"Pah!" Wallace Whittemore barked. "You must think me utterly naïve to your little games," he continued, keeping his voice to a bare minimum. "I will tell you now that I am not, and it does not matter the ridiculous displays you put on for others, child, for you will marry Lord Gastrell one way or the other."

The heat of her father's anger burned the side of Audrey's face as he leaned in a little closer.

"And, just in case you were considering defying me, you should be aware that your mother would never dare to take your side in all this. If that is what you believe, then I pity you. That woman does what I tell her to. Nothing more. Nothing less. And it is exactly as you will behave."

As she tugged at her arm to move away from her father, the man pulled her further back towards the door. "Please let go, Father," she hissed. "They can see us." An unwarranted sense of shame crashed over Audrey as her eyes caught with those of Hunter's. She was mortified that he had witnessed her at one of, what she deemed to be, her weakest moments.

Wallace Whittemore tightened his grip further.

Anger burned through her centre like a bolt of lightning as she turned her head away from the beautiful god-like man in the drawing room and locked eyes with her father. "*Let. Me. Go,*" she ground out through clenched teeth. Oh, yes indeed, Audrey Whittemore may have preferred to have trodden carefully where this particular matter was concerned, but she had also a rather incendiary spirit when pushed too far, and even though she was quite aware that she was treading upon dangerous ground as she wielded her temper close to the borders of carelessness, she could not help the venom towards her father from rising up from her chest and challenging him with a look that would have made any other simply wither on the spot. Indeed. Audrey Whittemore had reached her limit for one day.

Wallace Whittemore scowled at her, then with one last pinch of her flesh between his fingers, released her. "You are skating on thin ice, my girl. It is almost as though you wish for me to bring the wedding date forward. Is that why you are testing my patience?"

Cool air scuppered under the main entrance of the house and drifted down the hall. Very slowly, Audrey closed her eyes and inhaled, devouring the welcome chill as it filled her lungs. "Father, I am not trying to test your patience, nor do I wish to," she offered, trying to rein in the erratic pulse drumming in her chest. "I simply came out here to get some air, and then I had every intention of returning. You have created a scene for no reason at all," she added as her eyes lifted to meet the dark, alluring gaze of their new neighbour through the wide gap in the door. She could not decipher as to whether her father had forgotten himself in their guests' company or he simply didn't care what they witnessed of him.

"Look at him all you want," Wallace Whittemore growled, "but it will not be him you will marry."

"Look at who, Father?" Audrey, unable to prevent herself from doing so, turned to look at Hunter again. However, it seemed that Lord Gastrell had been in on her father's plans to threaten her, for the festering, pompous potato had placed himself directly between her and every other in the room.

"You know exactly who," her father snapped. "You are so deluded that you actually think Lord Carlisle will save you." The man chortled with what sounded very much like glee. "The boy disappeared for fifteen years, and you expect him to stay around for you? His own father detested him."

Audrey shook her head as she gazed at her father with a subtle expression of contempt. He was indeed a horrible man, she thought quietly. "You are mistaken, Father," she muttered. "I know my duty to the family, to you, and I shall fulfil it."

"I hope you do, Audrey," he hissed.

Audrey stepped away from him.

"I want you back here in twenty minutes, child," he grumbled. "Oh, and do not test my patience by being late." Wallace Whittemore turned his head in the direction of the open door. "And if you are late, do not think," he added, keeping his back to her, "that any of those in there will be enough to insist that I refrain from letting my feelings be known."

As Audrey fled from her father's side, she was quite certain he would do exactly as he had threatened to do if she was so much as a minute late. She was also quite certain that, should she offend the lecherous lord one more time, even if it meant simply escaping his indecent pawing of her person, hell would rain down on her in the form of her father's vicious tongue for all to witness. Her throat ached as she made her way along the narrow corridor, into the library, where she practically tumbled out of the door into the garden, her mind craving the peace and tranquillity of the outdoors as she consumed the air. A cool breeze kissed her damp cheeks. It seemed that tears had snaked from the corners of her eyes, unknowingly. Tears borne from a symphony of frustration and sadness.

"You're trembling, Miss Whittemore."

The resonating baritone of Hunter's voice warmed her as he approached. "I'm simply a little cold, is all," she lied, unable to look at him.

Warm spice coiled around her as he gently lowered his coat over her shoulders, his hard body brushing her back. "You know, Miss Whittemore, I would have thought that it was more likely that it was your father's detestable behaviour that has caused you to shake in such a manner."

The heat of Hunter's breath whispered enticingly down Audrey's neck, setting her body on fire. Now she was trembling for an entirely different reason, she realised, pressing her feet into the ground to cease the telltale sign of her attraction to the man. "Thank you, my l—"

"Hunter. My name is Hunter. I much prefer it to all this *my lord* nonsense. That makes me sound like my father," he offered with a smile.

"Yes, but you allow others to refer to you by your title. Why would you not wish me to do the same?"

"Because," he drawled, his lips brushing her ear, "they do not make me feel the way you do when you say it."

"Oh?"

Hunter moved around Audrey to face her, his eyebrows raised suggestively as his sensuous lips curled into a wolfish smile.

"*Ohh.*" Audrey blushed profusely. "I think I see." A giggle burst from her lips, and she quickly covered it with her hand. "Apologies, Hunter. I am a little lost for words, yet I suppose that oddly enough, I think I am a little flattered."

"Flattered?"

"Why, yes. I have never been thought of that way by a handsome man before," she quickly explained.

"Devilishly handsome, if you don't mind, Miss Whittemore."

"Apologies, I have never been thought of that way by a *devilishly handsome* man before."

"Much better. Although I can hardly believe that to be the case. I should imagine there may have been plenty, yet they did not suit your father's agenda, and so you never knew of them." Hunter stepped closer, tilting Audrey's chin up as he captured her lips.

Audrey curled her arms around his neck and leaned into the hungry touch of his mouth upon hers. As his tongue slipped between her lips teasingly, excitement fizzed in tidal waves through every inch of her body. It coiled and tightened, and, as she opened her mouth to him, she could not help the soft moan of pleasure that escaped amidst a sensual sigh.

Breathless, Hunter eventually broke the kiss. "You are exquisite, Miss Whittemore," he growled softly as he rested his forehead on hers. "You deserve better than that sweaty oaf in there."

Hunter's words were as effective as a bucket of cold water poured over her. For a minute she had allowed herself to be swept away in a dream of a life with someone such as he, yet his words had ripped her out of her imaginings and plunged her into her version of hell. Audrey exhaled.

"I have ruined the moment, I see, and for that I apologise, Miss Whittemore. That was not my intention."

"It is not you, Hunter. You have merely mentioned the truth. And, I have to say, your description of him is rather apt. I have yet to find a way out of this, but I am determined, if nothing else, when I put my mind to a matter."

Hunter slipped his hand further around Audrey's waist and pulled her closer. "Let me help you, Miss Whittemore."

"Audrey, please. If I am to call you by your given name, then it is only fair, do you not think?" she offered kindly.

"Audrey, it is then, but I think I will still refer to you as Miss Whittemore in front of your family to prevent any further upset for you," Hunter suggested, placing a kiss on top of her head.

"Yes, perhaps that would be wise. Thank you."

"Will you let me help you, Audrey?"

Audrey gazed into Hunter's eyes, noting the way they glittered, the moonlight caressing every wonderful angle of his handsome face. "Let me think about it, Hunter. This is my problem, and as much as I appreciate your kind offer, I don't want to involve you unless very necessary."

"Very well, Audrey. I understand, but if you should change your mind, then you know where I am." Hunter tenderly kissed the bridge of Audrey's nose. "Please remember, you are not alone."

Chapter Fourteen

"What do you know of Lord Gastrell?" Hunter enquired without so much as a greeting to the man still standing very much outside of the study.

Baldry's face crumpled at the obvious beginnings of what appeared to be an intense interrogation. The solicitor paused at the doorway, torn between offering a greeting of his own or simply diving headfirst into the matter that evidently was at hand.

"Apologies, Baldry. I realise you have only this minute arrived, but not knowing enough about the man plagues me somewhat." Hunter waved for his solicitor to step further into the room. "I met the man yesterday, and I have to say, he unsettles me, for he seems like a rather devious fellow, and if I should ever wish to do business with him as he suggested," he explained, distorting the truth to protect Audrey, "then I would like to know exactly who I am dealing with."

"May I?" Baldry gestured to the chair as he

made his way towards it, glad to be out of reach of the draught drifting down the corridor from the foyer.

"Yes, of course. Please make yourself comfortable, Baldry. Elkins!"

Elkins hurried into the study. "Yes, my lord?"

"Please, can you fetch us some tea and perhaps a spot of coffee too? We may be quite a while. I am sure Mr Baldry could do with a cup, and I have to admit I am quite exhausted this morning."

"Yes, of course, my lord."

"Thank you, Elkins. You are a treasure, sir," Hunter called after him as he watched him scurry away. The butler was indeed a blessing, so much so that Hunter no longer felt it necessary that Harmsworth make the journey to Carlisle estate. In fact, he had already sent word for the man to remain in London, where he had been instructed to see to the upkeep and maintenance of Hunter's dwellings there. He supposed someone would need to in his absence, after all.

"I cannot say that I have been privy to any information regarding the gentleman whom you have named, at least not that I am aware of, my lord, but I will be happy to look into the matter for you if you so wish," Baldry offered as he pushed his glasses back up the bridge of his nose, all the while fidgeting and looking rather ill at ease.

"You may relax, Baldry," Hunter encouraged.

"The only Carlisle here is me, and I can assure you that I am nothing like either parent or my late brother. You are quite safe."

"No Lady Carlisle, my lord?"

"Listen, Baldry," Hunter whispered, holding his hand to his ear whilst he smiled with pleasure. "Do you hear that?"

"Hear what, my lord?"

"Exactly, my good man. Lady Carlisle is no longer here. I have seen to it so that she is now residing at another property. Indeed, I am quite hopeful that I shall not see her for quite some time. That is, of course, if she has finally paid attention to what I have said to her."

Baldry's eyebrows collided with his hairline. He wasn't entirely convinced that Lady Carlisle would ever *pay attention* to anything that was not of some benefit to her. That woman wanted what she wanted, and he highly doubted she would simply retreat.

"You do not look like you are entirely convinced, Baldry." Hunter chuckled.

"No, my Lord. I apologise if I am speaking out of turn, but Lady Carlisle rarely ever relents on matters."

"Well, let us enjoy the peace while it lasts, then. I will deal with Lady Carlisle as and when she makes her presence known."

"Indeed, my lord," Baldry replied, shooting one last nervous glance towards the door.

"You were saying you could make enquiries with regard to Gastrell?"

"Yes, I can, my l—"

"Please refer to me as Carlisle, Baldry. I cannot bear the new title."

"Yes, of course, m—"

Hunter frowned.

"Carlisle," Baldry corrected, his cheeks turning a little pink, evidently embarrassed by the error. "I can certainly look into his reputation and the like. Is there anything in particular you would like to know?" Baldry retrieved a small notebook and an extremely small and well-sharpened pencil from his top pocket.

"I would like to know his financial and personal history. Anything from his past relationships or dalliances, including any rumours you feel may require further research."

Baldry scribbled notes haphazardly across the pages of his notebook. "Is there anything else you would like to know, sir?"

Hunter pressed his back to his chair as he steepled his fingers in front of his lips thoughtfully. "Yes, I would like to know of every detail of his dealings with a Wallace Whittemore. In fact, I would like you to get every scrap of information you can find on both gentlemen. Money is no object, so please feel free to hire anyone you wish to, but discretion is of the utmost importance. Perhaps for that purpose you might consider using an alias for me, should anyone wish to know my name."

The solicitor nodded.

"I don't mind if Whittemore and Gastrell think someone is on their heels digging into their past, for I believe I would quite enjoy watching them squirm, but I do not want them to know who it is that is so curious. I have plans for the information that I am quite sure they will not appreciate." Hunter smirked at the very notion of wiping the smile off their smug faces as well as the possibility that he could very well be the one to rescue Audrey. He couldn't stop thinking about her. The young lady had even filled his dreams and in the most improper ways. It was not exactly a surprise, he thought, especially after the kiss they had shared. Hunter had never felt so thoroughly bewitched by a woman before. His entire body burned with the memory of her.

"Carlisle?"

Hunter shook his head. Apparently, Miss Whittemore had more power over him than he had realised. "I beg your pardon, Baldry. What were you saying?"

"I was simply enquiring as to whether there is any particular reason you would need such information. Please do not misunderstand me, sir, for I do indeed trust you. However, as a legal representative, I cannot get involved in anything sinister." Baldry's cheeks flushed as he bravely put forward his misgivings on the matter at hand.

Hunter admired the man's honesty. "I assure you that I have nothing sinister in mind. In truth, I require information merely as a form of leverage."

"Blackmail, sir?" The solicitor's face drained of colour to reveal a chalk-white version of himself.

"No, Baldry." He grinned. "It will be used simply as encouragement. There is someone, I believe, who needs to be protected from them," Hunter admitted. It was not enough, he mused as he eyed the man, wondering whether he could trust him to keep it to himself. "If I tell you the details of my reason for wanting this, do you swear to keep it to yourself?"

"Of course. Everything we discuss is confidential, I assure you."

Hunter nodded. "Very well. Whittemore's daughter is being forced to marry Lord Gastrell. The man is old enough to be her grandfather." Anger flashed across Hunter's eyes. "I want to be in a position to help her should she need me to."

"That is indeed very noble, Carlisle," Baldry mused aloud. "And understandable. Now that I know, I am very happy to assist you."

Rising from his seat, Hunter helped himself to

coffee. "Would you like tea or coffee, Baldry?"

"Oh, just tea for me, please."

Handing the cup to the solicitor, Hunter lifted his own. "To uncovering secrets about Gastrell and Whittemore," he declared in a toast. "And to us, Baldry, for the beginnings of a great team."

Baldry pulled back his shoulders with immense pride. "Indeed, Carlisle," he replied, returning the gesture as he raised his cup, then took a large gulp of the liquid within. On the second gulp, the man drained the remaining dregs, gathered up his coat and notebook, and hurried to the door. "I shall leave you to it, sir."

Hunter looked rather perplexed. "In a hurry, Baldry? One would think your trousers were on fire with how quickly you wish to leave," he teased.

"Not at all, Carlisle. I simply believe there is no time like the present to make a start on your request." Baldry was brimming with enthusiasm as he held up his notebook briefly and gave it a little wiggle. "I do enjoy a bit of detective work. I am rather looking forward to this."

Hunter was both thrilled and amazed at the man's response to his request. This was important, and the solicitor's eager attitude offered him a sense of assurance that he had placed the matter in the right hands. "Then I look forward to hearing from you again very soon with all that you have discovered."

"Indeed you will, sir. Indeed you will," Baldry muttered, taking a quick bow before he hurried from the room.

Hunter smoothed his hand down the side of his horse, Galileo, in greeting, then promptly hoisted his large body up, swinging his muscular, breech-clad legs over the black gelding's back until he was sitting comfortably astride upon the magnificent beast. "Good morning, Galileo," he soothed. "Let's get you out of here." Pressing his thighs gently into the gelding's sides, Hunter encouraged him forward and headed toward the outskirts of Carlisle estate, his desired destination prompted by the mere fact that his land bordered Whittemore's. "Perhaps we may even come across a certain Miss Audrey Whittemore," he considered hopefully. Hunter could not think of any other way in which he might have the opportunity to see her again, unless, of course, she took him up on his offer and came calling. However, after their conversation last night, he was not particularly optimistic that Audrey was the type of young lady who liked to show weakness, even in the presence of her father, and perhaps it was a little too early for her to be seeking help outside of her home. Indeed, it appeared that Hunter would have to encourage fate and probability with a gentle nudge in the right direction. Attempting to accidentally-on-purpose come across her on his travels seemed like a rather good place to start.

Galileo trotted slowly forward as if he had all the time in the world. The gelding's calm attitude seeped into Hunter's limbs as his mind drifted – light green eyes, luscious lips and curls of mahogany hair. It would have been considerably easier all round if he could have simply called on Audrey, courted and wooed her like most gentlemen would have been permitted to, Hunter thought as his eyes scanned the grounds for any sight of her, yet Wallace Whittemore's obvious belief that his daughter was nothing more than a possession, one that he could trade and barter with, had placed an invisible barrier between them. It was a pesky barrier that Hunter needed to work out how he was going to get around. The thought of Audrey marrying Lord Gastrell, or any other man for that matter, Hunter considered, his teeth grinding around the bitter taste such a possibility left in his mouth, both concerned and infuriated him. He himself said he wished to find a wife, did he not? Then, if that was indeed the case, which it was, why should his wife not be Audrey? Of course, he would not force her hand into marriage, yet if she was amenable to the idea, then he would damn well ensure that Audrey Whittemore would become the next Lady Carlisle.

Willing Galileo into a canter, Hunter glanced across the Whittemore estate to spy nothing more than empty fields and silence. Audrey was either pent up in her home or perhaps further afield, he considered as the gelding increased his speed, galloping over the border and towards the lake. Hunter tried to tell himself that there would be other times that he may come across Audrey, and it really wasn't all that very important, yet as the breeze caressed his face and whipped his coat wide open, he could not quite decipher how her absence had become detrimental to his moods. It was indeed as though he craved her.

Hunter admired the light dappling over the lake, dazzling and, perhaps one might say, a tad mystical at the mere touch of the low spring sunshine upon its glassy surface. It seemed his efforts to locate the young lady had been rather futile, and so he decided to simply settle for a little silence and time alone to gather his thoughts.

Hunter dismounted Galileo, retrieved an apple from the saddlebag and, taking a bite from it first, offered the rest to the gelding. "What to do, Galileo?" he whispered, running his hands through his hair and then relieving himself of his coat. Placing the item of clothing on the dewy grass, he sat and began to whistle. There had to be other ways, he considered, yet the one aspect that was missing was that of a guarantee. He had not one iota of assurance that any of his ideas would be successful. There were soirees and balls to attend where he might see her, and perhaps out on the land on another day too, he mused, yet everything was all so indefinite.

Closing his eyes, Hunter lay back on his outstretched coat, allowing the sunshine to kiss the lids of his eyes as he listened to the ripple of the water. If he wasn't careful, he thought with a smile, he would drift off to sleep, for the tranquillity and pleasure of his current surroundings was rather calming indeed .

"This way, Athena... No. Oh, good heavens. You really are very disobedient. Any more of that and I shall eat your apples."

Hunter quirked a brow at the sound of gentle admonishment towards someone named Athena, then reluctantly opened one eye and turned his head to the side to see them. The world, it appeared, was not that easy to decipher at such an angle, and so he pushed his body upward until he was finally standing.

With his cap tilted low over his eyes and his legs positioned astride a young mare - who was apparently named Athena - a young man approached. The only sign he had spotted Hunter was the quick upward flip and then the downward tilt of the flat cap atop his head.

"Good morning," Hunter offered, grinning at the mare brazenly approaching Galileo.

The young man cleared his throat. "Good morning, sir," he rasped. "Apologies for the horse."

Hunter stepped closer, feigning the desire to pat the horse, but in truth, he was more intrigued by the rider. Very intrigued indeed, for hats cannot hide lips, nor, it seemed, could they hide wayward strands of mahogany hair, and they definitely could not hide the exquisite feminine form. A low involuntary growl of desire rumbled in the back of his throat momentarily before he reined it in with a cough. "I believe we met the other day, young man," Hunter offered, refusing to alert the young lady to his knowledge of her true identity. "I apologise if I startled you. It was not my intention. You simply caught me at a bad time. The name is Carlisle." Hunter proffered his hand.

"Aud...Aubrey," Audrey offered, placing her hand in his.

Clever girl, Hunter briefly thought, noting the slight alteration to her name. Had she been wearing a gown, he may have wondered why the change of name and the refusal to reveal who she really was, but by the gentlemen's tweed breeches and cap, shirt, and hessian boots, she would not have revealed her true identity to anyone for fear of reprisal. Hunter understood.

Lightning crackled down Hunter's spine as she placed her bare, delicate hand in his, offering him her strongest handshake. "A pleasure to meet you, Aubrey," Hunter replied. "Do you work on the Whittemore estate?"

Miss Whittemore opened her mouth to speak and then stopped as though she was carefully considering her next words.

"I only enquire as I am looking for a stable hand a few hours per day, and you seem to me like the kind of fellow who would be perfect for the position. It is rather evident that you have a way with horses." Hunter could not believe his good fortune, he mused, suppressing the sudden desire to pull her from her horse and take her into his arms. If Audrey agreed to tend to the horses, it would not only give him the opportunity to see her regularly, but, once he confessed to being aware of her secret, he would be able to court her, of sorts.

"Well, I—" Audrey began reluctantly.

"Of course, I am not trying to pilfer employees from Whittemore, Aubrey," Hunter interjected before she refused, "but I do believe that it should be the man who makes his own decisions and not the employer." He had wished to say that it should have been she who made her decisions and not her father, but he was quite certain that such a declaration would have been nothing but a blunder on his part.

Athena staggered beneath Audrey as the mare mimicked her rider's shock and indecisiveness. "That is indeed a very generous offer, sir," Audrey muttered, keeping her voice low and as deep as she could.

A lady did not work in stables, Audrey ruminated, averting her shielded gaze from Hunter's handsome and somewhat inquisitive face. In fact, a lady was not supposed to work at all unless she was a companion or a governess, perhaps, but certainly not as a stable hand. However, it did offer her an opportunity to accrue funds, and blunt meant that she would have more means of escape if it were ever necessary. Chances like these were indeed sparse, and it was extremely unlikely that she would ever get such an opportunity again in her lifetime, she reminded herself.

"Aubrey?"

"Apologies. Yes, I believe I would like to accept your offer, sir. May I enquire as to when you would wish me to start?" she asked. Her hands were still tingling from his touch, and she was perhaps gripping the reins a little too desperately, for her body wanted to fling itself off her horse and into his arms.

"Why don't you visit me tomorrow afternoon about two o'clock? Meet me at the stables, and I shall give you a tour. It will give you ample time to acquaint yourself with the horses and they with you."

"Thank you, H… Carlisle." Audrey blushed beneath her cap. "I shall see you tomorrow."

Chapter Fifteen

"Please say you will help me, Floss?"

Audrey stood with her hands clasped together in front of her rose-pink gown, feeling and looking nothing like the gentleman she had portrayed herself to be earlier in the day, her fingers lacing and unlacing with a medley of anxiety, hope, and disbelief. She still could not quite grasp how such a fortunate offer had freely tumbled from Hunter's lips, and she certainly did not expect he had any idea who Aubrey was. Indeed, she believed her disguise had hidden her identity quite well, despite the tickle of suspicion with regard to his reasons for such generosity. Audrey shook off the persistent doubt. No, there was no time to consider such a silly possibility of being recognised. She scoffed at the ridiculous notion, for Hunter had offered her the position on the understanding that she was a *he*. He certainly would not have offered a lady a position such as a stable hand, she reminded herself for further clarification and assurance.

"It all sounds rather improper, Audrey. What if you are discovered by your father? There is no telling what he would do to you," Flossie responded thoughtfully. Lines etched across Lady Florence Braithewaite's forehead and dipped between her brows. The fear of her friend being discovered and ruined was indeed rather obvious.

"What if I am not, though, Floss? This could be the answer to everything. My father has already sold me to Lord Gastrell, and there really isn't anything else he could do to me that could be considered worse than that." Audrey began to pace. "We no longer have the freedom of time to sit and contemplate when I have had a perfectly wonderful opportunity dangled in front of me." Audrey halted and dropped down into the chair.

Florence Braithewaite bit her lower lip as she gazed at Audrey with sympathy. "I apologise if I upset you, Audrey. It was not my intention. I think that I am so worried about you that I simply cannot think straight."

"None of this is your fault, Floss, and it certainly isn't you that has upset me. I apologise if I made you believe that I am cross with you in any way because that's simply not true." Audrey smiled kindly. "I am merely at my wit's end, yet now that Lord Carlisle has offered me employment, or should I say *Aubrey*, as his stable hand, I feel it is far too good an opportunity to dismiss. I shall be able to put those wages and my pin money together over the coming months, and that is sure to offer me a very generous start if I should feel the need to leave." Audrey closed her eyes softly and sighed.

"I hope you know that I will always help you, Audrey," Flossie offered after a moment of silence. "You need never concern yourself in that regard, but please promise me that you will be very careful."

"I promise, Floss. I won't do anything that will arouse suspicion, for the very thought of having to lie beneath that potato in order to give him an heir..." Audrey shuddered.

Flossie quirked a brow. "Potato? I do not believe I have ever heard a potato be so insulted before in my life." She sniffed, her lips twitching with amusement. "Fancy describing a perfectly good vegetable in such a manner."

"Apologies, all ye potatoes of the world," Audrey sang dramatically as she rested her hand over her heart and grinned.

"Perhaps you could broaden your horizons by considering a life upon the stage, Audrey." Flossie giggled, a blonde curl bouncing at the side of her face. "You certainly have a flair for it, it has to be said."

"Why, thank you." Audrey stood, offering a quick curtsy, and plunked herself down in the seat again, laughing. It was very good to laugh again, Audrey thought, for it seemed like an age since she had.

Pouring them both a cup of tea, Flossie proffered one of the filled floral vessels to Audrey. "When will *Aubrey* begin his position as a stable hand?" she enquired, glancing towards the door to ensure no one was eavesdropping. "And do you have everything you need, or should I raid Francis's closet again?" Flossie whispered with a smirk over the brim of her cup.

Audrey stood and walked to the door, peered out beyond the doorway, closed it, then returned to her rather comfortable seat. "There, that's better." She smiled. "And as for your question, I thank you, but that won't be necessary. I believe I have everything, albeit, of course, a sufficient number of excuses to be absent from the house. Without those, my father is very likely to gather that I am, indeed, up to something and he will want to know my whereabouts. And that, my dear friend, is where I shall need your help. If you have any suggestions, I would be rather glad of them." Audrey reached forward and delicately pinched her fingers around one of the Braithewaite cook's delicious shortbread biscuits and took a bite. As she sat back in the comfortable silence between she and her best friend, she realised just how exhausted she was with all that had transpired over the past few months. She was not physically tired, however, but emotionally and mentally, and the closer she got to the very day that she really did not wish to face, the harder it was becoming. The dread appeared to be thickening and cloying in her veins. Of course, now she had another person to consider.

Audrey placed her fingers to her lips. Hunter had surprised her with the kiss, but the heat of his desire upon her was not unwelcome. In fact, it had been the only thing that seemed to eradicate her mind of any concerns, even if it had only been for a few minutes. Yet, she reminded herself, he had not spoken of any affection for her, nor any intentions, and she was still feeling very much alone in it all. She simply could not place her future in the hands of a possibility that may never come to pass, no matter how much she may wish for her silly little dream to come to fruition.

"Audrey?"

"Hmmm?"

"I think I quite lost you there. Penny for them." Flossie placed her teacup back on the table and moved to sit beside Audrey. "I hope you know that you can talk to me, Audrey," she whispered, picking up Audrey's hands and clasping them gently. "I want to help you, but much more than that, I want you to be happy. In truth, your father is quite fortunate that I am not a man, for I would very much like to throttle the scoundrel. Of course, if that would please you, then just say the word, and lady or no, I shall certainly put my heart and soul into doing it. I can assure you, it would be my pleasure."

Audrey noted the feigned innocence in

Flossie's smile as though she hadn't just threatened a man's life in jest. "You are wicked," Audrey offered with a giggle. "Although I have to confess it had, indeed, crossed my mind once or twice." Audrey leaned sideways, gently bumping shoulders with her friend. "But unless you or I wish to find ourselves carted off by the constabulary, I believe we may need to find an alternative method."

"Spoilsport," Flossie chuckled, returning to sit opposite Audrey.

Eyes darting from side to side, Florence Braithewaite twisted and tilted her lips, her expression shifting and altering her features as she fell into deep consideration. "Hmm, perhaps," she mused quietly. "You know that could very well work. Or… Oh, no, that will never do. How about… No. Ah!"

Audrey let out a rather audible and somewhat exasperated groan as she followed her friend's one-way conversation. "I shall perspire if you do not tell me what it is you are thinking, Floss." Audrey positioned herself on the edge of the soft chair with a gentle jolt, her deep mahogany curls bouncing around her shoulders with all the drama the moment required.

"Now you mustn't be cross with me, Audrey," Flossie warned, part of her face hiding behind the teacup as she brought it to her lips. "But I was quite upset for you the last time I saw my aunt, and when she asked me what was wrong, I explained what you were going through." Flossie paused, her eyes roving over Audrey's face.

"I'm not angry, Floss," Audrey assured her, "but I must admit that your hesitance to divulge whatever it is you wish to say is causing me some concern. I beg of you to please put me out of my misery sooner rather than later."

Flossie smiled. "Well," she continued, the thrill of the story in hand settling as a rather distinct twinkle in her eye. "My aunt, Lady Esme, is quite aware of who Lord Gastrell is. In fact, they're quite well acquainted, and by all accounts, he has the ridiculous belief that they are allies. The ghastly man actually believes that it is simply not possible for him to take a single step out of line where my aunt is concerned." The young lady snorted, then rolled her eyes. "He is positively deluded. What on earth was your father thinking of when he agreed for you to marry him?" Flossie's cheeks flushed with annoyance.

"I should imagine it was the money he was thinking of, Floss, for he most certainly was not thinking of my happiness. His argument is that I am four and twenty, and so Lord Gastrell is the best I can hope for."

Flossie placed her hand to her mouth as she began to cough, her eyes rounding as she stared, pink-cheeked, at her friend. "I beg your pardon?"

"It is true. He even made remarks about my

figure."

"The very nerve of the man!"

Audrey could not remember a time when she had seen Flossie quite so enraged. In fact, she did not think she had ever seen Flossie enraged at all. "It is alright, Floss. I am quite aware that I am a little more curvaceous than most women, but I do not believe any daughter wishes to hear her father's opinion on something so personal."

"I believe your father is highly incorrect; that is what I believe, for you are absolutely stunning, Audrey Whittemore. What I would do to have a figure like yourself, you have no idea. You do not wear a gown; the gown wears you, for it is merely fabric before you show the world that it is decadent satin and silk that is meant to be worn just so. Do not ever let anybody tell you otherwise, my dear friend." Flossie nodded sharply to emphasise that she would not hear any argument on the subject. "Not desirable, indeed," she mumbled snippily. "Stupid, shrivelled-up, little weasel of a man."

Audrey laughed softly. "Do not fret so, Floss. But if you can provide me with the excuses that I require on the days I am to be *Aubrey,* it will certainly be an immense help," she said, gently encouraging her friend to return to the matter at hand.

"Oh, yes. Apologies, Audrey. Where was I?"

"You were saying that you spoke with your aunt, and Lord Gastrell believes they are allies,"

Audrey reminded her.

"Oh, yes. That was it… However, that simply is not the case, for my aunt utterly despises the lecherous old leech. They were her words, not mine, I might add, and indeed they were spoken rather angrily when she heard what he and your father expect of you."

Flossie took another sip of her tea, quickly followed by a nibble of biscuit, all the while Audrey remained patient as her eyes followed the young lady's every movement. If Flossie didn't get to the point of the story soon, Audrey thought she may very well expire with anticipation.

Flossie eyed her over the top of the teacup, a mischievous smile stifled upon her tightly pressed lips.

Audrey groaned. "I'm practically withering with anticipation here, Flossie. Not even your cook's wonderful biscuits will be able to save me if you do not tell me what else your aunt said."

"That is a tiny bit dramatic, Audrey, do you not think?" Flossie sighed with a teasing grin. "Alas, I suppose I should tell you, shouldn't I?"

"That would be lovely, Floss."

"Apologies, I shouldn't tease. Well," she continued, "the very crux of the conversation was that Aunt Esme has assured me that if there is anything she could do to help you, then we need only ask."

Audrey exhaled, relief flooding her body at finally hearing what Flossie had to say, but more so at the exceedingly kind offer from a lady she had yet to meet. "You are cruel, Lady Braithewaite, to have made me wait so long," she chided playfully, unable to be even a little bit peeved at the lady sitting across from her. "My only query is how?"

"How?"

"Yes. Please do not think I am ungrateful, but as relieved as I am at Lady Esme's kind offer, I am not quite sure what she can do."

"Well, that is easy," Flossie replied. "She and I will be your whereabouts on all the occasions when you need to leave your house."

"That is a lot for me to ask of you both," Audrey breathed.

"It never really occurred to me before now, but I believe my aunt reminds me a lot of you, for as you always seem to be very keen to help others, so too is my aunt. It appears, though, that this time, Audrey, it is your turn to be helped, and you do indeed need it, do you not?" Flossie brushed down the front of her deep blue gown.

"More than ever, Floss," she rasped, feeling choked with emotion.

"All will be well, Audrey," Flossie soothed, handing her friend a clean handkerchief in expectation that tears would soon follow. "I will send word to Aunt Esme today. Obviously, I shall refrain from including any particular details in case it falls into the wrong hands, but rest assured we shall call on you tomorrow afternoon, for she and I won't allow you to live the life your father has planned for you."

"Thank you, Flossie."

"There is no need to thank me, Audrey. This will all work out perfectly fine," Flossie offered. "Tomorrow, Wallace Whittemore will have the pleasure of coming face to face with the embodiment of adversity. Aunt Esme is rather formidable, and I have yet to meet a gentleman who has ever been able to win a battle when she is their opponent," she added, a confident and rather delighted grin brightening her features.

Leaning rather casually against the outer stable wall, Audrey attempted to feign what she hoped would be considered to be a carefree, masculine stance. Anxiety had accompanied her from the moment she had tumbled out of her bed, all the way through her sparse breakfast, and had indeed followed her across the land to where she was currently standing. Shifting slightly to place the sole of one boot against the wall, whilst keeping the other leg straight and boot flat to the earth, she tried to remember how one of the younger gentlemen had stood in the corridor of the Chilcott residence.

With a quick readjustment of the angle of her cap, she hoped that it would be sufficient to achieve it or perhaps something very similar.

Audrey did not think she could feel any more out of her depth, especially knowing it wasn't simply any gentleman she intended to meet, but indeed it was the devilishly handsome Lord Hunter Carlisle. The very same gentleman who had kissed her and whom she had kissed in return. Had she been meeting him so that they may continue in that very same sentiment, she was quite certain that she would have been rather thrilled. However, circumstance only permitted her to be Aubrey in this situation. She was no longer Audrey whilst on the Carlisle estate, and that, as well as having to endure the short walk from one stable to another, was a bitter pill indeed to swallow, *but*, she reminded herself, it was important that she did not lose sight of the reason for what she was doing. If she did, it could very well be disastrous.

Audrey blew out her breath as she brushed random stalks of hay from her tweed ensemble. It was another that belonged to Ivy's brother but in a shade or two darker this time. Between the maid's thoughtful donations and the secret rummage in her father's closet, Audrey had quite a selection of appropriate alternatives. She had never known a man to possess so many items of clothing. In fact, if hoarding attire was a sin, then Wallace Whittemore's closet would have been utterly scandalous.

A gentle breeze curled its finger in the coils of a stray, mahogany curl and lifted it into the air, drawing Audrey's attention to the feminine, traitorous hair that had escaped from inside her gentleman's cap. She supposed she should have been grateful for such an occurrence, for without it she would have been rather oblivious, and her secret would have been revealed to Hunter before she had so much as begun her role as stable hand. She could not afford to be so careless, she berated herself inwardly, especially when she had been so very fortunate as to have been offered such a position in the first place.

"Ah, young Aubrey!"

Audrey shifted uncomfortably as she peeked under her lashes at the magnificent specimen of a man striding towards her in his muscular, brooding form. She rubbed gently at her neck as though it would eradicate any evidence of her rapid pulse, yet nothing could soothe the unexpected pleasure the man's image induced, currently coiling in her midsection. It was rather peculiar, she thought, noting the darkening of Hunter's eyes as they settled on her, for Hunter oozed an air of danger, one that she should perhaps have run from, but the power he possessed was positively magnetic, so much so it seemed her body was being pulled toward him. The thrill trembling through her limbs and torso, elicited by a mere glance at him, was not one that a young lady was supposed to have. *Was it?* Audrey swallowed, trying to quench her suddenly dry throat and tongue.

Observing Audrey from afar, Hunter reminded himself that he was not to confess so soon that he was aware of her deception. That would indeed come later, but for now he would play along. The young lady had her reasons for the deceit, and he would not blunder straight in and frighten her away. The slight adjustments to her body as she attempted to appear masculine intrigued him as she tucked a wayward curl back into her cap, then finally settled her back against the stable wall, one leg bent and the other bearing her weight. Hunter wished he could press up against her, merely to lose himself in the luscious warmth of her lips and tongue as he stole another kiss. Even in her disguise she was more radiant than the sun, and he had no idea how he was to remain at a distance from her when she continued to warm every inch of him, without and within.

Keeping his gaze upon Audrey and ignoring the furnace of desire tightening his core, Hunter considered her predicament for the umpteenth time. He did not believe he had ever met a lady as courageous as she had revealed herself to be. After all, it took a brave young woman to don a gentleman's clothes and try to act the part, all the while knowing she ran the risk of being exposed, did it not? His eyes travelled the length of her appreciatively, wondering how she may have fared if another gentleman had offered her employment under such a pretence. If another man studied her physique the way in which he could not refrain from doing, he was, indeed, glad that he had been the one to offer her employment first. Hunter wanted to spend time with her, but more than that, he realised he had a rather strong desire to protect her.

"Carlisle."

Audrey teetered on the tips of her toes, caught between the beginnings of a curtsy and that of a bow. The twist of her body as she had corrected herself, desisting from attempting either, merely drew one's eyes to her bosom as the fabric of her clothes stretched taut across her chest.

"You are punctual, and that is a very good start, young man," Hunter insisted kindly. "I hope that your role here has not caused any upset for you."

Audrey cleared her throat. "None at all, sir," she returned, her soft lips parting as she gazed at Hunter from beneath the angled peak of her cap.

"I am very glad to hear that. Shall we?" Clearing his throat, Hunter gestured to the stable. Good Lord, what was the chit trying to do to him? Every inch of him stirred when she looked at him like that. He was starting to consider requesting that

Elkins deal with her, but he really did not want to miss whatever this was between them. Therefore, he would merely have to get a grip on himself and control his animalistic urges.

The dry scent of hay and damp wood engulfed them as Hunter strolled behind Audrey, eyes down or glancing to the side – whichever way necessary so that he could refrain from drinking her in. Though the new curl that had sprung free, teasing the long line of the nape of her neck, had not quite escaped his vision. As tempting as it was to reach out and offer her assistance with said curl, Hunter did not wish to highlight the revelation of her identity, so he merely locked his hands behind his back in a tight clasp. "You need not be nervous, Aubrey," Hunter offered instead as he sensed a note of hesitation in her gentle breaths.

"I'm not nervous as such," she replied cautiously, "only wishing to please you."

Hunter groaned inwardly. How was he to keep his hands to himself when she continued to say such things? He wanted to curl his arms around her, to comfort her. He wanted them both to acknowledge the truth. He didn't want to continue pretending that he wasn't gawping endlessly at her from a distance whilst they both continued the needless façade. "I am not expecting perfection, Aubrey, only that you try your best. Besides, you will only be expected to carry out light duties, which I am quite certain you will be able to do, and with your eyes closed, no less."

Walking around her, Hunter ventured further into the stable, hindered only by the very soft, yet not quite so subtle scent of orange blossoms that teased his senses and set his heartbeat galloping beneath his ribcage. With the disobedient curl and the feminine fragrance, Hunter wondered whether Audrey did indeed wish to remain undiscovered, for if he noticed, then he was quite certain that others may. "How much experience have you had with horses, Aubrey?" Hunter enquired, knowing she would not feel the need to lie to him.

"All my life," she replied. "Yet it is only recently that I decided to make their welfare the very thing that would earn me a wage."

Hunter was impressed. She had not exaggerated the truth but simply worded her answer diligently so that it adhered to her current identity. "Then I am certain you will settle in nicely," he rumbled quietly, unable to take his eyes off her mouth as she scraped her teeth over her lower lip.

"I do hope so," she whispered, then cleared her throat. "That is most definitely my wish, sir," she said in a deeper voice.

Galileo nuzzled into Hunter's hand as he proffered an apple. "This one here is Galileo," he announced. The gelding was a welcome distraction indeed, for if he kept allowing himself to gaze at Audrey, she would realise that her disguise was failing magnificently. *The curls. Good lord, the damned delicious curls.* He wished she would realise for herself that they were there, practically waving at him, for his fingers positively itched to tuck the most recent one behind her delicate ear.

Keeping busy was paramount, he told himself abruptly. He must make every effort to distract himself, as it were, for the more he glanced Audrey's way, the harder it was for him to hide his obvious attraction to her. Hunter took a deep breath, allowing his hand to glide up from Galileo's muzzle towards his forehead, where he briefly ruffled the horse's forelock. "He is not only my horse but also a good friend as well." Hunter grinned. "Aren't you, Galileo?"

The horse nudged Hunter's shoulder in response, momentarily putting him off balance. Hunter laughed, ruffling the horse's forelock once more. "You probably recognise him," he added, feeling less flustered as he turned his attention back to Audrey.

The short silence drew Audrey out from beneath the blanket of her reverie. She had been trying to pay particular attention to her new employer, but, she realised, she may have been paying him, his eyes, his hair, his hands, his chest and his thighs a little too much attention. She blushed, noting the subtle changes to the temperature of her body beneath her clothing. Her muscles contracted around a tug of exhilaration that bled down her centre and into her thighs. Of course, it had not helped matters when he had introduced her to Galileo. Audrey believed that such an open show of affection for one's horse, or any animal for that matter, spoke volumes as to a person's character. Hands wrapped gently around her rapidly beating heart and squeezed tenderly.

Very carefully, Audrey peeked at Hunter from beneath her hat. He was smiling at her, his eyes glittering with curiosity. "Is there something troubling you, my lord?" Audrey did not think it wise to refer to him as Carlisle when asking such a question, for perhaps it would have sounded as defensive as she knew it to be, and she most definitely could not afford to lose the generous position under his employment. She had been around her father long enough to know when to alter his name from father to papa or vice versa simply to avoid any reprisals that were likely to be forthcoming. Indeed, Hunter's correct title, she mused, demonstrated her respect for him when making such an enquiry.

"No, *Aubrey.* Should there be?"

The slight extension to her masculine name did not go unnoticed, for Audrey had the sudden urge to shift from one foot to the other, all the while trying to decipher why he had said her name that way or if indeed she had imagined it. "Not that I am aware of," she replied, deciding not to draw attention to it.

"Nor I."

As Hunter stepped back from the black gelding, Audrey shivered. A wild, sensual splash of goosebumps crashed deliciously over her skin at the mere brush of his arm through her thin shirt. Her breath caught. The continuation of his closeness seemed to set her body on fire as he moved to pass her from behind. The only barrier that stood between them was a sense of anticipation, simmering and fizzing in the thin fragrant ribbon of warm spice and coffee.

"My apologies, Aubrey," Hunter drawled, his voice whispering over the sensitive arc of her neck.

Surely, he did not know who she was? Audrey considered. Her toes curled in her boots, as though to deny the tremble in her legs as his breath fluttered over the edge of her collar, then crawled beneath the fabric of her shirt. Pleasure seeped beneath her flesh and into her muscles, but before she could allow herself to bathe in the sudden ecstasy, she sidestepped away from him. It seemed that Hunter Carlisle held the power to turn her into a wanton, she mused with a stifled sigh. It was a power she had never experienced before, and as much as she wanted to be dictated by it, she knew she could not allow such an outcome. "No, my Lord. The fault is all mine," she rasped.

"Would you like me to show you the rest of the horses?" Hunter drawled huskily.

"No," she snapped unintentionally, then cleared her throat. "Apologies, I must have had something in my throat, for what I meant to say was, 'No, thank you, sir.' I am certain I will be able to manage from here."

"Very good. I shall leave you to it."

Hunter began to turn away. It was better if he left, Audrey assured herself. After all, she was there to work, not gawp at him like a debutante, yet part of her did not want him to leave her alone. "I will take great care of them, Carlisle," Audrey called as he began to walk towards the door.

"Thank you, Aubrey, but I do not doubt that for a moment, for your good nature is indeed evident." Hunter smiled, his eyes softly assessing her, before he turned once more and left her alone.

As her thighs trembled, and her heart slammed with great fists within her chest, Audrey gazed down at the evidence of her desire peeking into traitorous buds beneath the thin fabric of her shirt. It seemed that Hunter Carlisle was making her endeavour to keep her gender secret rather more difficult than she had anticipated. "Think of Gastrell," she muttered to herself, the desire at her centre dissipating rapidly and descending into the most awful bout of nausea. "Eurrgh. Good grief, Audrey Whittemore," she groaned. "You took that too far. Perhaps we shall simply add a little extra padding over my traitorous body next time."

Chapter Sixteen

Lady Esme was a powerful force that was embodied in a feminine figure and thoroughly swathed in pearl grey satin and ivory lace, Audrey observed as she descended the staircase a minute or two after luncheon to greet the woman and her niece. With tall feathers quivering atop Flossie's aunt's head as the lady stood poised for confrontation and with Flossie sporting a lavender bonnet tied delicately beneath her chin, one could not deny that both ladies were rather contradictory to one another. The authority and strength emanating from Lady Esme thoroughly rendered Flossie's prim and proper demeanour to appear no more than merely timid. Yet, despite all that, Audrey was rather glad to see both ladies. To have two more people within the walls of her home whom she knew to be on her side was indeed rather welcome.

"I am here to see Wallace Whittemore," Lady Esme barked, pursing her lips at the butler. "Where is he?"

"I shall—" the butler began, his lips twitching at the corners as he evidently delighted in the fact that his scoundrel of an employer would have to come face to face with such a formidable lady.

Audrey glanced at the man, her eyes twinkling with mischievous and gleeful agreement.

"Who do you think you are to... *Oh*," Wallace Whittemore interjected loudly as he stormed into the foyer. "Lady Esme, it is a pleasure to—"

"Don't give me that rot, Whittemore," she replied abruptly, punctuating her displeasure with a sniff. "I am not here for polite chit-chat. I am here because I require a word with you."

Noting her own mouth hanging wide open, Audrey snapped it shut. Flossie's aunt was certainly not offering her father any means of escape, and Wallace Whittemore was slowly turning a deep shade of purple with indignation.

"Very well, Lady Esme," Whittemore grumbled. "But if you insist on barging into my home and demanding that I speak with you, then I insist that Lady Florence wait outside," he growled sulkily. "Audrey and she will do whatever chits do... embroider or something." Whittemore rolled his eyes. "If I really must hear what you have to say," he continued curtly, his eyes darkening with aggravation.

"Indeed, you must," she interjected forcefully.

Whittemore clenched his jaw. "Then follow me," he ground out, feeling utterly peeved by the woman's strength of character as he turned his back on the three ladies and one butler who were all watching him with keen curiosity.

Lady Esme was enjoying herself, Audrey noted as she witnessed the exchange. The woman's lips were tilting at the corners, a hint of glee and satisfaction gleaming in her eyes.

"Tea, Bernard. And be quick about it," Wallace Whitmore ordered abruptly. "Lady Esme will not be staying long."

The butler bowed, shooting their guest an apologetic glance, and then hurried off to the kitchen, only to return exactly four and a half minutes later with a pot of tea and two teacups. "Sir," he offered with a bow, placing the tray on the nearest table in the drawing room before making a rather swift exit.

"What is it you want, Lady Esme?" Whittemore snapped, ignoring the butler's announcement. "I have matters to tend to, and your arrival is an inconvenience."

"You always were the most charming of gentlemen, weren't you, Mr Whittemore? It is rather apparent that your daughter did not get her delightful traits from you, thank heavens. If my visit is such a burden to you, then perhaps I should relay your disapproval to Lord Gastrell."

Lady Esme lifted her chin in defiance as she remained standing. If Whittemore would stand, then so would she. She would not have the man towering over her in an attempt to intimidate. Although as she watched his face drain of colour, she believed that she was quite firmly in the winning position.

"You and Gastrell are acquainted?" he queried, his voice rising in pitch.

"Indeed, and I believe he would be very interested to know how you have treated one of his dearest friends," she crooned, absently running a finger over the shelf as though checking for signs of dust. "Your staff are to be commended, Whittemore, what with the amount of skin that snakes shed, one would have thought there would be remnants of you everywhere."

"I beg your pardon!" Wallace Whittemore's face crimsoned, utterly outraged at the lady's words.

"Temper, Whittemore. Just one word to Gastrell, that is all it would take, and I believe he would be mortified by the news of such ill-treatment. I should imagine that whatever it is you have concocted between you with regards to your daughter would soon be obliterated, and you, Whittemore, will find yourself back to square one."

Whittemore swallowed. "Let us not be too hasty, Lady Esme. Please accept my apologies, for my intent was not to offend you," he snivelled, reaching for the teapot and pouring them both a cup of tea. "I believe I am merely having a bad day."

"Apology accepted, Whittemore, but I do not

want that repugnant liquid. I will have some of that whisky over there, if you please."

Wallace's eyes followed the direction of her long, slender finger towards one of the finest bottles of whisky he owned. A wonderfully expensive bottle that he had been, and still was, exceedingly reluctant to open. He swallowed. "Yes, of course, Lady Esme. You have fine tastes, I see," he commented waspishly, bottling his rage at the audacity of the woman.

"Indeed, I do, and it is for that very reason that I shall be taking care of your daughter's wedding preparations." Lady Esme smiled wickedly as she watched him pause, noting the sudden tension in his back and the strengthening of his grasp as he held the bottle in his hand. With his back to her, it was a blasted pity she was denied the pleasure of witnessing the palpable horror in the man's face. She would rather have enjoyed that particular spectacle, she mused.

"I am afraid you are too late, Lady Esme," he replied, turning to face her with a hint of satisfaction laced in the twist of his lips, "for I am quite certain that Audrey has acquired everything she needs for her wedding." Wallace Whittemore coughed in an attempt to clear the rising rasp in his voice, all the while his knuckles whitened with the strength in which he kept hold of the bottle in his hand. His daughter's wedding was not supposed to drain him of his blunt, he seethed to himself. It was supposed to multiply it, amongst other personal perks to the agreement.

Lady Esme guffawed. "Nonsense! I have it on good authority that Audrey is quite unprepared. The poor girl does not even have a trousseau. *Oh the shame!*" Lady Esme brought the back of her hand to her forehead, feigning horror at such a thought. "How could you allow your poor daughter to be in such disarray, especially on her wedding night, Whittemore. No, it simply won't do, and I am quite certain that Lord Gastrell would be utterly appalled should you permit such a ghastly thing."

Wallace Whittemore placed the drinks on the table and practically fell back into his chair, silent and gaunt with shock at what he knew he would have to agree to, then simply nodded a quiet concession.

"Wonderful! I must make you aware, Whittemore, that I shall be spending every day with your daughter for the foreseeable future, for we will need to make all the necessary arrangements, and they will indeed take time. I will not have you interrupting our routine with any of your tantrums that I have, on occasion, borne witness to either. Is that understood?"

Wallace Whittemore nodded. The woman had him just where she wanted him, he reluctantly realised, and if he so much as refuted a single word, he knew she would be detrimental to everything he had planned with Gastrell.

"Excellent, my good man. Now, the money, if you please." Lady Esme extended her upturned hand expectantly. "And don't be miserly, for it is quite obvious by your home that you can indeed afford to be frivolous for your daughter's day. It is supposed to be the most magical day a lady will ever have." *Until she has to face the wedding night with that revolting man*, Lady Esme considered, swallowing the bile rising at the back of her throat.

Wallace Whittemore was as white as a spectre. The demand for him to hand over the blunt was evidently something he was struggling to come to terms with.

"Mr Whittemore, the money, if you would be so kind."

Rising and unlocking a drawer on the sideboard, Whittemore retrieved a heavy pouch. It appeared to contain a generous number of coins, and there were tips of notes poking out where the leather puckered with the tug and tie of the drawstring closure. "Will this be enough?" he enquired, dropping it into her hand.

"Very generous. Very generous indeed, Whittemore." Lady Esme scooped up one of the glasses of whisky from the table with her free hand, drained it of its contents, and then slammed the drinking vessel back onto the hard surface of the table. "Bloody good stuff, Whittemore," she announced, striding towards the door. "I will be back tomorrow morning to collect your daughter, and we shall begin all the necessary arrangements."

As the door closed behind Lady Esme, Wallace Whittemore began to burn with the heat of his anger. "A man being told what to do in his own home," he scoffed with disgust, then picked up the empty glass and hurled it at the wall. Trembling with rage, he gripped the arms of his chair and closed his eyes. His hands were metaphorically tied if it meant his cooperation would secure the deal with Gastrell, and despite not liking the current demands placed upon him by Lady Esme, he would simply have to endure.

Beyond the door, Lady Esme jumped, holding her breath momentarily at the sound of glass smashing against the wall. When silence followed in the aftermath, her breaths returned to a steady yet heavy pattern as relief at no longer having to converse with the dreadful man flooded her.

"Is everything alright, Lady Esme?" Audrey enquired as she hurried forward to offer support.

"Oh, yes, dear. Don't concern yourself with anything other than being ready and waiting for Flossie and I tomorrow at about eleven o'clock when our deception will be in full swing," she whispered. "Take this," she added. Between the join of their hands now sat a large pouch of money. "We do not need it, yet I have the distinct impression that you most probably will. Hide it well."

Glancing over her shoulder, Audrey witnessed the small nod of agreement from Bernard. The dear, stoic butler seemed quite aware of what they were up to and was willing to keep her secret close to his heart despite the risk to his position within the household. She would make sure that he would be alright, she assured herself as she returned his smile with one filled with gratitude and affection for the dear man. Indeed, it brought a tear to her eye. Turning back to face the ladies, she proceeded to wrap her trembling arms around Lady Esme. "Thank you," she muttered gratefully, reaching to the side to grab Flossie. As her fingers curled gently around the young lady's delicate wrist, she pulled her into the embrace.

"Oh," Flossie squeaked, the sound breaking into a soft giggle. "Time to make sure you have the future you deserve and want, Audrey," she whispered, nestling into the closeness of her aunt and best friend as she became part of the warm huddle of women.

"Yes, indeed," Lady Esme agreed. "Your father and *Ghastly Gastrell* won't know what has hit them."

"Ghastly Gastrell." Flossie chuckled. "You are naughty, Aunt Esme."

Tittering with excitement, the ladies untangled their arms. "Tomorrow, Audrey," Flossie sang as she hurried down the steps. "Don't be late!"

"I won't," she called after them, the smile on

her face increasing as a surge of hope—much the same size as the pouch of money in her hand—embedded itself at the centre of her chest.

"Elkins, what is she doing here?" Hunter Carlisle had not been absent more than an hour, yet it seemed that while he had been on his morning ride, only to have returned home feeling thoroughly disappointed at not having had the pleasure to have come across Audrey on his travels, Lady Carlisle had arrived with that dreadful tittering blonde again and had had the audacity to have made herself at home.

"I'm terribly sorry, my lord. I did tell her that you weren't at home, but she insisted she should wait in the drawing room." Elkins grimaced painfully, trying to turn his expression into a smile.

Hunter tugged at his jacket sleeves. "It's alright, Elkins. We all know how Lady Carlisle can be rather insistent. I shall simply freshen up and see to her and her guest in a moment." Hunter twisted in an awkward turn on his heels to face the butler again. "Perhaps you might refrain from mentioning my return. If the lady wished to wait, then who are we to argue?" He grinned. "I will see her when I am ready."

"Very good, my lord." Elkins nodded, a soft chortle shaking his shoulders. "I shall not breathe a word."

"Thank you, Elkins."

Ambling slowly up the staircase, Hunter wondered whether he might simply have to sell the Carlisle estate out from underneath the woman. She could not simply turn up unannounced if there were strangers residing in the property, and she certainly wasn't getting the hint with him living there. Nevertheless, it wasn't simply about him and her, for he had to consider the servants and what would happen to them, not to mention the young lady whose image tortured him with desire practically every moment of the day.

Upon entering his bedchamber, giving his valet a quick nod, Hunter considered that perhaps he would call at the stables again when he knew she would be working. After all, he was her employer, and had he not done the exact same thing over the past few days? Hunter's fingers paused on his buttons. He was not known for checking on his other members of staff, he realised, so perhaps it may begin to look a little strange. In fact, it probably already looked strange, he thought.

"They can think whatever they damned well please," Hunter grumbled, his voice low and deep as he tucked his clean shirt into his breeches. "What I do with my time and with whom is my business."

"Is everything alright, my lord?" Stanhope interjected.

Stanhope. The relief of the valet's arrival was

beginning to amplify with each passing day. The man reminded Hunter of his life before all of *this*. It had been the recollection that he had never known he needed.

"Lady Carlisle is in the drawing room," Hunter ground out, using the sour thought of her presence to cover his musings about Audrey, "and she thought to drag along a *friend*." Ripping the cravat from his neck, he suddenly stiffened and closed his eyes. "Not only can I not put up with that woman and her meddling, but it also appears I cannot do something as simple as tie my cravat."

Stanhope stepped forward. "May I?"

"I would be grateful. Thank you, Stanhope. And while you are there, if you have any solutions to be rid of that wretched woman, ones that will not see either of us hanged, please feel free to enlighten me."

Both men grinned. "I believe that Lady Carlisle, sir, is rather like a leech, for she will not leave until she has had her fill," Stanhope commented.

"Yes, indeed. I think you may be correct."

"There you go, sir. You look marvellous, even if I do say so myself."

Hunter quirked a brow. "You only did my cravat, Stanhope," he chided.

"That's the main part, Carlisle," he chuckled. "Is there anything else you may need?"

"Laudanum? Valium? A rock to the head? Anything to ease the agony of spending time with my mother?"

"I'm afraid I don't have any of that, Carlisle, but I do wish you luck," Stanhope replied with a playful quirk pinching at the corners of his lips.

"Thank you, Stanhope. I appreciate it. Luck and a little whisky will have to do."

"Lady Carlisle," Hunter intoned as he entered the room, "may I ask what brings you and your companion here?" Hunter clenched his teeth, then fixed her with a vacant stare.

"Why, you are my son, Hunter, are you not? Is a mother not permitted to call on her son?" Lady Carlisle tried to smile, yet the pinch of her lips held the corners of her mouth stubbornly still as she simply glared at him.

"Would you like me to enlighten Lady Vanessa as to why I may disagree with your sentiment, Lady Carlisle?"

Agatha Carlisle's nose thinned as she inhaled sharply. As her lips puckered further, Hunter wondered whether they would simply disappear into the vacuous layer of flesh that was her face.

She exhaled, then reattached her usual mask of pleasantry. "You see, Lady Vanessa," she cooed, "he remembers your name. I did tell you that you would catch his eye, did I not? My son has a gift for seeing those who will be good for him."

Hunter snorted with disbelief at the drivel spewing from her.

"Do you know we were sadly parted for fifteen years?" she continued.

Hunter found himself rather intrigued at what new story she had concocted for her avid, singular, dim-witted fan. The chit, wide-eyed and enthralled, simply shook her head and allowed the woman to continue.

"Oh, yes indeed. His father was a cruel man," Lady Carlisle offered, whimpering for effect. "He simply threw him out. I begged and pleaded for him to stay, but when I failed, I was beside myself, having to live fifteen years being afraid for my son and unaware of what had happened to him. You know, I even thought him dead." Lady Carlisle lifted an embroidered handkerchief to her eye and dabbed at an imaginary tear.

Shaking his head in disbelief, Hunter rolled his eyes. Good lord, the woman had an insatiable desire to twist and distort the truth, utterly embellishing the past that he already knew every factual detail of. He had to wonder whether she had convinced herself of her own lies. Whatever the case, Hunter knew she simply had to stop. "If you will excuse me," he exclaimed, turning on his heel, "I believe I have an appointment. Please see yourselves out." With that he simply slammed the drawing room door.

"If I am needed, Elkins, I shall be taking another ride over the estate," Hunter announced, stopping briefly in the foyer to take a breath.

"Very good, my lord. What shall I say to Lady Carlisle?"

"She will do what she wishes, Elkins. Please do not fret," he added, noting the concern on the poor man's face. "If she has not taken her leave by the time I return, I will personally see to it that she and that chit leave. She is not your problem, Elkins. Sadly," he added, his chest heaving as he let out a breath, "she is mine, and apparently she is insistent on choosing a wife for me."

Elkin's mouth rounded into an O.

"Indeed, Elkins. I quite agree with you."

Frustration fuelled Hunter's stride as he set off towards the stables, his mind a tangle of curses and condemnation towards his mother. *The absolute audacity of the woman to encroach on such an important decision as to that of the lady he would spend the rest of his life with,* he fumed inwardly. There was only one lady he wished to spend forever with, but she was currently dressed like a man and tending to his horses. Hunter stopped suddenly in his tracks, stunned by his own thoughts. He had only ever contemplated an outcome such as marriage to Audrey Whittemore briefly in passing, yet it had swiftly become a rather pleasant thought, he realised. *That*, he reminded himself as his thoughts quickly sidestepped the revelation, was a very good reason indeed to speak with Baldry. The man hadn't returned with any information on Whittemore or Gastrell yet, and it was damned well time his solicitor offered him something to work with.

Lord Gastrell, Baldry, Lady Carlisle, and Lady Vanessa simply vanished from Hunter's mind as he leaned against the doorjamb of the stable. Audrey Whittemore stood at the side of Galileo, oblivious to her employer's arrival, and reached up to run her slender fingers through the gelding's mane. Curls of rich, lustrous, mahogany hair cascaded down her back where the once neatly arranged pins had come loose, unwittingly freeing her glorious tresses. She either hadn't noticed, Hunter considered, or she simply did not care. "Good boy, Galileo," she sang as she rested her forehead against the side of the horse, then proceeded to pull an apple from her pocket. "We can share this," she whispered, taking a bite from the fruit, then handing the remainder to the horse. Galileo took it gratefully.

Hunter swallowed as his eyes trailed down Audrey's spine to the gentle curve of her bottom. His silent approach had gifted him a few moments to savour the sight before him. The woman was a breath of fresh air. Not only was her hair unbound but so were her feet, it seemed, for she had removed her boots, revealing her bare feet and petite ankles.

"You take too many risks, Audrey Whittemore," he drawled huskily.

Audrey jumped back, startled, her face flushed with panic.

"If I had been Lady Carlisle and had not known who Aubrey was all along," Hunter continued, as he moved slowly towards her, "then there would be no telling what my mother would have done. It was rather a dangerous situation to put yourself in, was it not?"

Audrey visibly swallowed. "You knew all along?" she whispered.

Her chest heaved with rapid breaths, drawing Hunter's eyes to her bosom. It seemed she had freed herself from the undergarment that had meant to disguise her femininity, and he was struggling to look away. "I did indeed. It is one of the reasons I offered you this position. That and I wanted a way to see you again. I saw you out there." Hunter pointed out of the stable door. "And I wondered how far you would take your disguise. I did not want you to seek work with anyone else." Hunter stroked his finger down the side of her face and trailed it along the line of her jaw, aware of the heat of unspent passion simmering beneath his skin.

"I wasn't going to," she rasped as she gazed assessingly at him. Her lips softly parted, trembling as she drank him in. Audrey's heart was pounding with trepidation and fettered curiosity, the beat growing louder in her ears with the uncertainty as to whether she wished to know if she had pleased or displeased him. "Do you wish for me to leave?" she queried breathlessly.

Hunter shook his head. "No," he drawled softly, his face inching closer to hers until he had closed the gap between them.

The brush of his lips on hers sent gentle, teasing sparks of pleasure prickling wildly over her lips, down her neck to the base of her throat, then spread over her chest, rushing into the tightened peaks of her nipples; her evident hunger for the man drawing her closer to him with a sigh.

The touch of her mouth on his and the soft sigh that escaped as she leaned into him seeped into Hunter like the sun's rays, warm and golden. Deepening the kiss, he pulled her against him, his hands sliding down her back and resting on the delectable curves of her backside. "I am very glad you are here," he groaned, reluctantly pulling away, before he could steal her virtue on the stable floor. He had never felt so utterly aroused from a simple kiss. "And I think you should stay, Miss Whittemore."

Audrey nodded, her eyelids heavy with desire and her lips swollen from their kiss. "I would like that," she replied, curling her hands around the lapels of his jacket, pulling Hunter closer until the tips of their noses touched and their breaths exchanged with an extraordinary sense of intimacy. When he had caught her out with the telltale signs of her identity, she had assumed he would have been furious and had asked her to leave, yet as he had wrapped himself around her, her entire being had begun to crave him. His touch and warmth fizzed over her skin, eliciting a quiver that coursed through the muscles of her thighs. The delectable tremble receded momentarily, then crashed over her again like the waves of an ocean upon a shore. Every part of her wanted to be closer to him, to feel him beneath her fingertips. The sensation had once been a stranger to her, but now that they were acquainted, she could not deny that it was delicious.

"I want you, Audrey," Hunter breathed in her ear, sending a ripple of delectation down her neck. His breath crept beneath her clothes, skimming over her nipples with delicate, invisible hands. "But I want to court you first."

"We both know that my father would never allow it. You are perhaps forgetting my predicament with Lord Gastrell. Surely such a wonderful thing as being courted by you is not possible?" she questioned, nervously running her hands down Hunter's chest, her touch pleading with him to tell her that she was wrong.

"Admittedly, it won't be how I would wish, but we can get to know each other here, can we not? And you needn't worry about Gastrell, I am making some enquiries." Hunter placed his hand gently over her trailing fingers, then kissed her again.

"What enquiries?" she queried between the soft, extremely pleasant and somewhat hungry nibbles he was inflicting upon her lower lip.

"Whatever I can find on him. Now, like I said, put that man out of your mind, Miss Whittemore," he growled, curling his arms around her waist and squeezing her bottom playfully with his large hands, "and tell me whether you will allow me to court you in this very stable?" Hunter grinned against the arch of her neck.

At the brush of his breath over her flesh, Audrey sighed dreamily. "I would indeed," she whispered, her neck slowly extending in an invitation that Hunter could not ignore. "*Oh, yes*," she groaned, "I believe I would like that very much."

Chapter Seventeen

Feeling a tad dishevelled in her appearance, not to mention rather emotionally dishevelled and somewhat exhilarated as she recalled Hunter's tantalising kisses upon her skin, Audrey scrunched a swatch of her skirts in her hand and hurried up the staircase towards her mother's bedchamber. She had not had the opportunity to speak with her since she had begun her position on the Carlisle estate, afraid that such conversations would have been too risky, what with the rather obvious danger of being overheard by her father.

Slipping into Marjorie Whittemore's bedchamber and closing the door quickly behind her, Audrey pressed her back against the door as though her body was some form of additional reinforcement to the already fitted catches on it. Satisfied that it was indeed closed, she pushed away from the door and straightened. "Hello, Mama," she beamed. *At last*, she mused, allowing her lips to curl into the burgeoning grin she had been suppressing since she had walked into the Whittemore residence. Delicately, she traced her finger over her lips with a soft sigh, every inch of her recalling

Hunter's touch.

"*Oh my,*" Marjorie Whittemore exclaimed quietly as she studied her daughter from afar, then simply smiled. "Why don't you come here, darling. I feel like it has been an age since I last saw you."

Audrey lowered her hand and ambled over to her mother, where she pressed a kiss into the soft grey curls of the lady's hair. "Apologies, Mama. It has indeed been an age. I did not wish to make Father any more suspicious than he already is by coming here, for he would never have allowed me any peace, but I hope you know that I have missed you."

"You are here now. That's all that matters, my darling. Although I am assuming you did not smile like that when he was anywhere in the vicinity."

"I do not know what you mean, Mama. I am simply happy to see you. I shan't hide that from Father," Audrey replied, her eyes glittering with the intensity of her new secret.

"Hmmm." Marjorie Whittemore narrowed her eyes playfully. "I shall not pry as long as you are careful, my dear."

"I promise I will tell you soon, but for now, what you do not know, Father cannot force you to reveal, and I do not want you to have to lie for me, Mama." Audrey discreetly plucked a short stalk of hay from a wayward strand of hair as it caught her attention in the corner of her eye.

"I look forward to hearing all about it, my

darling. And yes, your father will not stop until I reveal all. You do not get your strength from me, Audrey. I do not believe I would be with that buffoon if I had even so much as an ounce of it. Although," Audrey's mother added with emphasis, "I am rather hoping that your news will have something to do with that rather handsome Lord Carlisle."

Marjorie Wallace may as well have dipped her daughter's face in a pail of rouge, Audrey thought as the heat of a prominent blush rapidly crept over her skin, only to intensify when she noted the knowing gleam in her mother's pale green eyes.

"As we have agreed, you mustn't confirm nor deny anything, Audrey, but I will say this: I have eyes, and I know the look he had in his when he gazed at you over the dinner table. That is not a young man who thought of you as merely your father's daughter."

"He is not young, Mama," Audrey retorted, not knowing what else to say.

"He is to me."

"Besides," Audrey continued. "I will have to leave soon, will I not? What would be the purpose of getting close to him and caring for him now when it will only prove to make parting even more painful? It is unbearable that I must leave you and Flossie, Mama. How am I to bear leaving Hunter as well?" Audrey's chest tightened as she tried to inhale. It was a possibility, she realised, one that she had failed to consider when she had allowed herself to be thoroughly swept away by him. Of course, he said that he was making enquiries, but that did not mean he would find anything that would help her.

"Breathe, my darling," Marjorie Whittemore soothed, witnessing the alarm on Audrey's paling face and the tear slowly trickling over the soft contour of her cheek. "You mustn't panic." Marjorie clasped her daughter's hands gently, the soft skin of her thumbs slowly caressing over the back of them to comfort her. "You care very much for him, don't you?"

"Who?" Audrey responded with an effort to look perplexed at such a statement.

"Lord Carlisle," Marjorie whispered.

"I-"

"It is too late, Audrey," Marjorie protested kindly, "for you referred to him by his given name, and you cried at the very mention of him. If I am not mistaken, you are losing, or have already lost, your heart to him."

Wiping the tear away, Audrey angled her face to gaze at her mother. Anguish, gently crumpling her features. "That can't be possible, Mama, for I have not known him very long. Perhaps this ache in my chest is merely because he is everything Lord Gastrell is not; hence, he only serves to amplify all that I may never have."

"Perhaps, my dear," Marjorie crooned. "But do

not discard how you feel, for it does not take very long to care for another, or perhaps even to love them, my darling. The heart wants what the heart wants, I'm afraid."

Audrey's chest heaved as she lay her body over her mother's bed, placing her head on the lady's lap as she pushed the thread of hope that Hunter would save her out of her mind. She wouldn't be able to cope if he failed and her world came crashing down around her. "What am I to do, Mama? I wanted to find a way to escape a terrible marriage, not to find something or someone who would make me wish to remain here."

"The world can be a wicked place for us ladies, my darling, especially with regards to what is expected of us, not to mention the men we are all but forced to marry, but once in a while some of us find ourselves fortunate enough to find a gentleman that cares for us. Do you think that perhaps Lord Carlisle is a gentleman such as this?"

"I can't think about that, Mama. If I do, then I feel like I am losing control over my future again. I barely have a grasp on it as it is. Of course, I believe he cares, but a future with him is not something sufficiently substantial on which I can rely. If we were betrothed, or perhaps far away from Father and Lord Gastrell, then I would indeed place my faith in a future with him, but we are not either."

Marjorie stroked the side of her daughter's face, her thumb wiping away another tear at the corner of her eye. "I understand, my darling."

Both ladies let out a breath.

"I have every faith in you, Audrey," Marjorie whispered. "And a very good feeling about all of this, so please do not give up hope."

"Thank you, Mama, and I shall try not to."

"Good evening, Father, Lord Gastrell." Audrey walked briskly across the room, seating herself in the furthest position from both men as was indeed possible, merely so that the lecherous lord could not touch her again. After speaking with her mother and spilling her tears, all that remained was a simmering anger. It was a welcomed emotion, for it seeped into her every fibre, offering her a peculiar strength as she faced them, spine rigid and gaze determined.

Lord Gastrell licked his lips and started to rise from his chair to walk around the table towards her.

'That is quite close enough, thank you,' Audrey thought. Coughing delicately, she placed her gloved fingers over her mouth and feigned a look of surprise. "Oh, I do beg your pardon," she offered prettily. "I hope I have not caught anything terrible."

Lord Gastrell stopped suddenly, then returned to his seat.

Sometimes the carefully selected knowledge of a man's dislikes and foibles could be rather advantageous, Audrey considered, smiling secretly to herself. Had she not been aware that the lecherous oaf, currently salivating at the other end of the table, had a tendency to avoid all that may be deemed contagious, she would never have been able to have stopped him from approaching her. It was utterly brilliant.

"You had better not have, my girl," Wallace Whittemore snapped, glaring at her suspiciously. "We are to attend a ball tomorrow, and you will be there," he added.

"Oh, how wonderful," she lied. "I am sure I will be much better tomorrow, Father."

'Another evening where that odorous, sweat-ridden toad will insist that he dance a waltz with me. How terribly thrilling,' she seethed silently and quite sardonically. Clearing her throat and maintaining as polite an expression as she could, Audrey simply smiled, then turned to Lord Gastrell. "Will you be attending, my lord?" she enquired.

"I'm afraid that I must disappoint you, my dear," Gastrell began as he pressed a napkin to his forehead to dab at the sweat glistening in the folds of his skin.

The man dragged the cloth lower to his neck, where he continued to administer attention to the beads of perspiration pooling between the edge of his collar and his throat, all the while Audrey raised her own napkin to her slowly down turning mouth in an attempt to conceal the burgeoning grimace of disgust. One thing was certain, she mused, she had lost her appetite entirely. Even if she hadn't, she would not even so much as attempt to eat, simply for fear of casting up her accounts.

"Oh, that is a shame," she chirruped, bathing in the splendid warmth of relief as it trickled through her veins.

"Indeed, Miss Whittemore." Lord Gastrell's eyes dropped to her bosom. "I am afraid I will be away on business, for I have a little venture in London that needs tending to." The man licked his lips and returned his gaze to her face.

Audrey had never known that it was possible to despise someone as much as she did Lord Gastrell. He made her feel unclean with the way in which he looked at her, the words he said and the things he did. She wondered what fool would ever wish to work for a man like that. She certainly hoped that a woman would not be so naïve as to even consider working for him, no matter how desperate she may be for money. Although, she considered, she rather thought that the need for food and shelter may outweigh his unwelcome attention.

Audrey shuddered, yet she found herself wanting to know more of what he did. Perhaps she could offer Hunter some of the information he was apparently seeking. "You are in trade, my lord?" she queried.

"That is none of your business," her father spat.

Ah, yes, she had forgotten that one did not speak of these matters, apparently, for *trade* was considered distasteful.

"Apologies," she offered. "I meant no offence, my lord, for I was merely curious. I do not consider trade to be offensive."

"No offence taken, Miss Whittemore, and in answer to your query, yes, I am. But are you quite certain that it doesn't offend you?" Lord Gastrell's eyes darkened with venomous suspicion.

"Not in the least, my lord. In truth, I think it rather admirable." *'Of anyone else but you,'* she added silently. "May I ask what it is that you do?"

Lord Gastrell scowled. "Chits do not need to concern themselves with such matters," he sniffed.

Had she looked away, Audrey might have missed the glance exchanged between the two men. It was rushed yet filled with an air that was considerably darker than what one might refer to as a polite exchange. That, and the knowledge that Lord Gastrell was a man who was well known to pontificate about his achievements at length, seemed rather suspect, she mused. "Of course. I apologise, my lord," she replied, neatly storing the observation in the back of her mind to ponder later.

Lord Gastrell's obvious reluctance to divulge had unwittingly offered Audrey a shred of hope, for whatever his secret was, it may very well be enough to ruin him, she considered. The gentleman's ruination may be the very thing that would be ample to secure her way out of their betrothal, for her father would never wish to be associated with scandal. "If you will excuse me, gentlemen," she whispered, rising from her seat, offering another cough for emphasis of her apparent ailment. "I think I may need to rest for a while."

With her father's eyes narrowed with simmering outrage pointed in her direction, Audrey continued to cough as she walked towards the door, drowning out any objections he may wish to spout at her. She had a rather important missive to pen, and there was no time like the present. The sooner Hunter knew that she suspected Lord Gastrell of hiding something with regard to his business, as well as the suspicious exchange of looks between the oaf and her father, the better. In truth, to inform Hunter of her observations made her feel useful, for they could help him to obtain the information he was looking for. However, if it wasn't, she considered, her teeth scraping over her lower lip as she drifted towards the staircase, then it might be better if she simply request that he make enquiries on her behalf. Yes, that is exactly what she would do, she decided.

"You have correspondence, my lord," Elkins

announced, proffering a silver salver with a single folded piece of parchment at its centre.

Pinching the correspondence between his fingers, Hunter lifted it off the salver and held it in front of his face. The penmanship was not one he recognised, he noted, turning the missive over, yet the faint scent of orange blossoms drifting upwards made him rather curious. "Who delivered this, Elkins?"

"Ivy, my lord. One of Whittemore's maids. I have put the mail that arrived earlier on your desk in the study, my lord. Shall I bring them to you?"

"Yes, please, and thank you, Elkins." Hunter's voice trailed off as he turned away from the butler, his eyes caressing the curves of each letter. Surely, it would have been easier if she had simply spoken to him rather than go to all the trouble of sending a missive, he pondered, for a letter seemed a tad formal. A knot of dread formed at the centre of his stomach at the thought that she was simply and rather cowardly wanting him to know that she would no longer work for him. The idea that he may not get any time alone with her again was not one that he wanted to contemplate.

"Pull yourself together, Carlisle," he berated himself, shaking off the unwarranted thought and unfolding the parchment to reveal the mysterious contents. His eyes scanned every word. *Interesting*, he mused with a smile. It appeared that Audrey had her suspicions about Gastrell's dealings. "That reminds me," he muttered, picking up the pile of correspondence that Elkins had placed on his desk. "Bennett, Peterson, no, no. Lady Carlisle," he growled, slamming that particular letter on the mahogany wood with a tremendous thud. "And Baldry. That's the one I was looking for. Let me see whether the man has been as astute as Miss Whittemore, shall we?"

Flomping down into his chair, he opened the letter and began to read.

"I shall be out riding this morning, Elkins," Hunter called hurriedly as he rushed towards the entrance of Carlisle House. "Unless there is a sudden emergency or we receive any word from the Whittemores, I do not want to be disturbed. Is that understood?"

"As you wish, my lord. But don't forget you have Lady Peterson's ball to attend this evening."

"Thank you, Elkins," Hunter drawled, pulling on his riding gloves. "As much as I have avidly wished to forget it, I have not, but I thank you anyway."

The butler smiled. "Very welcome, my lord."

Overcast skies splashed with a somewhat dismal grey seemed rather like the perfect weather that one might wish to seek shelter in the stables,

Hunter considered. His grin dimpled his cheeks as his mind cast his body back to the sensation of Audrey beneath his fingers and her bosom pressed against his chest. After receiving her missive with pivotal information with regards to Gastrell, he had sent word to Baldry to dig deeper into the man's business dealings. The chit was intelligent and rather savvy, as well as everything else his body couldn't quite manage to express in words. Hunter shifted the fabric around the crotch of his breeches, noting they had embarrassingly become a tad more snug. Inhaling the cold, sharp air of the spring morning, he continued towards where he hoped Audrey would perhaps be waiting for him.

"Good morning, Hunter." Audrey's voice drifted on the breeze and tickled his ears enticingly.

Hunter turned to find the object of his desire wrapped carefully in her gentleman's clothes. They seemed to fit her a little better today, he thought as his eyes lingered on her waist, then rose slowly and admiringly to her lips. "I thought you might have changed your mind about working for me when I saw that you weren't here," Hunter whispered in a husky voice as he curled the loose strand of hair behind her ear. "That would have been very disappointing, to say the least." Grabbing Audrey by the hand, he tugged her through the door, pressed her against the wall and kissed her possessively. "After your missive, I had wondered whether you –"

"I wrote the missive because I thought it too

important to simply wait," she interjected, running her hands up over his chest and beneath his jacket. "Besides, when I am with you, I tend to lose all trail of thought," she added, reaching up on the tips of her toes and brushing her lips against his.

"As do I with you, Miss Whittemore, yet if we stay here, your virtue is not safe. Perhaps you might wish to join me for a morning ride across the fields? We might discuss what we will do with regards to –"

Unable to resist any longer, Hunter kissed her, trailing his lips and the tip of his tongue along the soft curve of her neck. She tilted her head invitingly, releasing a breathy moan. "Horse… ride…first?" she suggested.

Pulling himself with considerable reluctance away from the chit, Hunter placed both hands on the wall as he leaned over her. "Good idea," he rasped, then swallowed. "After you," he offered, pointing to the horses behind them. "As you are well acquainted with the horses now, I shall let you lead the way." Hunter did not wish to mention that if he so much as moved before she did, she would most definitely notice that his manhood was already leading the way, and that would never do.

Audrey was grinning as they followed the line of stalls and led the saddled horses out into the open. She was positively radiant, Hunter mused longingly. "I may be able to find you other work, if you prefer, Audrey, now that your secret is out," he offered. "I could find you work that will permit you to wear your gowns."

"I am happy here, Hunter," she replied. "And I have to confess that I am quite envious of you gentlemen to be able to feel so free in your clothing. Breeches and soft shirts are rather more enjoyable to wear," she stated as she placed her foot in the stirrup.

Hunter swallowed. A soft growl rumbled at the base of his throat, elicited in response to the delicious way her breeches tightened around the curve of her buttocks as she had lifted and bent her leg. Placing his hands on her waist, he lifted her up into the saddle. Up on the back of his brother's chestnut gelding, Ares, Audrey simply stole his breath.

"Thank you," she breathed. "Although I am quite capable, I must admit I was glad of the help. Ares is quite a bit bigger than Athena."

"Very welcome, Audrey," Hunter returned as he mounted Galileo. "Perhaps, if you enjoy our time together today, then tomorrow we can take a picnic?"

"That sounds lovely, but only if you are sure."

"I have never been more certain in my life, Miss Whittemore."

Audrey lowered herself down onto the grass, dismissing the possibility of dirtying her breeches. In the grand scheme of things, the state of her clothes hardly mattered at all. Besides, the day was far too beautiful to go unappreciated in such pleasant surroundings. The earlier grey clouds had shattered and dispersed, revealing an ice-blue blanket that added a sharp vibrancy to everything beneath it. The way in which the weather had turned was much like her life, she thought, for there were times when everything was grey and she did not want to so much as step outside, yet there were these rare times, she considered as she gazed at Hunter, when life offered her vividity and she wanted nothing more than to seize every moment of it.

"Your missive was rather helpful," Hunter announced as he positioned himself beside her. "I have asked my solicitor to dig a little deeper into that aspect of Gastrell's life in London."

Audrey inhaled the familiar scent of warm spice and coffee, allowing it to wash over her, her chest rising and falling with appreciation of how delightful it was, *how delightful he was*. Hunter had infused every part of her that was untouchable by the human hand, she realised, for he lived within her thoughts and had burrowed deep into her heart, so much so that she was petrified that she was falling in love with him. Turning away with a silent chastisement to the beating organ beneath her ribs, she hid her burgeoning tears behind the lids of her eyes as she closed them. "I wasn't entirely certain you would welcome it," she rasped, the emotions of her thoughts pinching at her throat. "After all that had happened—my deception by wearing gentlemen's clothing, the kiss..." Opening her eyes again and peering from beneath her lashes, Audrey tried to gauge his reaction to her words. He was smiling, she observed, relief rolling through her.

"I believe that I informed you that I wished to court you, Miss Whittemore, and one would think that such a declaration accompanied by the kiss you mentioned would be sufficient proof that I very much welcome your contact. Besides, I do believe I told you that I wish to help you with the matter of Lord Gastrell, did I not?"

Audrey nodded. "Yes, you did."

"Then that is all there is to it, Miss Whittemore. Oh, and by the by, I will have you know that I do not kiss a lady merely for the sake of kissing. You, Audrey, are a wonderful conundrum, and I am quite certain I care very much for you." Hunter's lips closed over hers, his teeth grazing her lower lip as she leaned in hungrily. Curling his hands to cup her face, he pulled away and rested his forehead on hers. "Kiss like that again, and I shall devour you."

"Oh." She giggled. "Really?"

Hunter's hand trailed slowly and teasingly up Audrey's leg, ruffling the fabric of her breeches as he dragged the tweed beneath his fingers, then released it, freeing his hand to tilt her chin upward so he could bask in the warmth and sensuous touch of her mouth upon his. "Yes, really. You are mine, Audrey Whittemore. I will not allow you to marry that old walrus."

"I do not wish for you to do anything you do not want to, my lord," she whispered, her mind distracted by the heated kisses trailing down her neck.

Hunter scraped his teeth over her sensitive skin, a rumble of pleasure vibrating from his lips and through her bones. "You know, I have never particularly enjoyed being referred to as *my lord,* but when you say it to me," he teased, his tongue flicking the lobe of her ear, sending a shiver down her spine, "I think I rather like it."

Audrey thought her heart would explode from her chest. Her entire body was shaking with trepidation and hunger. Hunger for Hunter. "We should stop," she muttered breathlessly.

Kissing her nose, Hunter put a little space between them. "Apologies. I overstepped."

"Believe me, you didn't. This is all very new to me. I am not used to how it makes me feel—*how you make me feel*. I have never felt like this." Witnessing the concern in his eyes urged Audrey to explain further. "I thought my heart was about to burst out of my chest," she added.

A lopsided grin brightened Hunter's features.

It wasn't seemly, she supposed, to confess

one's bodily reaction to a gentleman, but Audrey could not bear the thought of Hunter thinking she was uncertain of him and his attentions. To be close to him, in fact, was the one thing she desired most in the world.

"I am somewhat relieved, Audrey," he replied, lifting her hand to his lips and kissing the inside of her wrist. "For I have no intention of giving up on you."

Hunter held the solicitor's correspondence in his hands, absently waving it back and forth, mimicking the contemplation at war in his brain. He certainly didn't want to divulge such information about Lord Gastrell to Audrey, for it would petrify her. Damnation, he wasn't even a chit, and he could imagine how terrifying such a prospect would be to be marrying that perverse and distinctly putrid man.

Pacing the study floor, Hunter read the letter again. The bastard owned a house of ill repute, and Hunter was quite certain the man had no intention of being faithful to his supposed future wife when he had other women on tap, as it were. Taking a deep breath, he made his way over to the side table and poured himself a whisky, then returned to his desk, where he dropped into his seat.

He had hoped the alcohol would have warmed the cold dread running through his veins, but it was still there, sharpening into ice.

A knock sounded at the door.

"Come in." Hunter leaned back further in the wingback chair and closed his eyes.

"You required our services, Carlisle," a deep voice intoned, followed by several pairs of boots softly treading over the carpeted floor.

Hunter opened his eyes and nodded. "Have a seat, gentlemen, if you will," he encouraged.

Baldry positioned himself in the nearest chair with a sigh whilst Hobbs and Jackson both frowned.

"This sounds all a bit serious, Carlisle," Hobbs offered. "What's it all about?"

"Whisky?" Hunter enquired, proffering a filled glass to each of the gentleman.

Simple mumblings of gratitude filled the room as they accepted.

"I have a job for you gentlemen in London," he began. "Baldry here has all the details of where you must go, but I want ears to the ground and eyes open, gathering every scrap of information you can about Lord Gastrell. I believe his name is Lord Nicholas Gastrell, if that is required to clarify matters."

Baldry nodded. "It is," he muttered in agreement.

"Whilst you are there, I want you also to listen out for the name Wallace Whittemore. That information is important," Hunter added, taking a deep breath to stifle his anger.

"What is this place we have to go to?" Jackson enquired. "Of course, there is no question that we shall do as you ask, Carlisle, but I do not particularly enjoy surprises."

"Fair enough," Hunter conceded. "The place you are going to is a disorderly house. Baldry has the details of it. But if the information leads you to other addresses, I want you to follow it. Is that clear?"

All three men nodded.

"I thank you, Jackson, Hobbs, and Baldry. I would go myself, but I would like to keep an eye on things from here." He could not leave Audrey, Hunter had decided. It was far too much of a risk.

"Leave it to us, Carlisle," Hobbs returned.

As the gentlemen took their leave, Hunter settled back, once again, into the chair behind his desk. He needed to be one step ahead of whatever Gastrell and Whittemore had planned for Audrey at all times. Hell would freeze over before he allowed her to marry that scoundrel. The only man she would marry would be himself, Hunter grumbled as a low heat stirred within. However, there still remained the matter of her safety. He would have to do all he could to keep her out of their reach before the impending forced wedding.

"Elkins!"

"My lord?"

Hunter winced. *That damned title.* He only wanted to hear it from Audrey's sweet lips, not those of men and tittering maids. "First of all, it is Carlisle or sir, but please not 'my lord', Elkins," he requested.

"Yes, of course, sir."

"Thank you, Elkins."

"The other matter?"

"I beg your pardon?"

"You said '*first of all*,' so I assumed there was more than one request."

"Oh, yes, of course. Thank you, Elkins. Please, can you ensure that my deep blue cravat is clean for this evening? I would like to wear it."

"Very good, m—"

Hunter quirked a brow at the butler.

"Sir," Elkins finished. "Apologies."

"None needed, Elkins, and thank you."

Chapter Eighteen

The light from the chandeliers ran its fingers over the plum velvet of Audrey's gown as she descended the staircase. Cautiously, she stepped onto the ballroom floor and proceeded to follow the path around its perimeter between the array of tables and dancers. Her skirts sashayed about her legs, and, as the light caught the amethyst pendant upon a silver chain around her neck, she could not deny that she felt beautiful. A sense of personal power thrummed in her veins, for without the lecherous lord present, she had allowed herself a moment to be free, to discard any gown that would have covered every inch of her. This gown, she thought, with its daring neckline was utterly divine. Indeed, Lord and Lady Peterson's ball was the first event in so very many that she had not had to concern herself with the possibility of being subjected to the unwanted stares and indecent touches administered so often by Lord Gastrell.

Gazing into the throng of the ton, a ripple of excitement tickled at the centre of her chest. She could not quite believe her good fortune, and all at the suggestion of her father, no less. Perhaps he merely considered these her last moments of freedom, she mused. Whatever his reason, she certainly had no complaint, yet there was one more thing, or perhaps one should say *one more person,* who she knew would make the occasion rather more formidable indeed.

"Is something troubling you, my darling?" Marjorie Whittemore enquired as she stepped closer to her daughter's side, the hem of her emerald gown swishing around her ankles, teasing the tops of her matching satin slippers. "Or are you perhaps looking for a certain someone?"

"Mama," Audrey chastised mildly. "We must be discreet, or Father will hear. Besides, we have already discussed this, have we not? I cannot think about such possibilities." Audrey patted her mother's hand gently as it rested upon her arm. Hunter's promises, although rather splendid, were too fragile for her to lean upon, Audrey had reluctantly decided. Unless the gentleman offered her something more solid that could not be refuted, then she feared it would be too dangerous or perhaps too reckless for her to so much as rely on him, even a little.

"You know, if he is here…" Marjorie Whittemore halted her words, pressing her lips together as her daughter shot her a look of admonishment. The lady chuckled, inhaled deeply and then continued. "I was merely going to say that if he is here and wishes to dance with you, my darling, then I shall make it my duty to keep your father away. I may not be able to prevent your betrothal single-handedly, but I am quite certain that I can play a part, and what better way to do it than plying your father with enough spirits to soften his mood and keep his eyes averted – or perhaps one should say his vision remarkably distorted – for one evening."

Audrey giggled, pulling her mother a little closer as she hugged her arm. "Thank you, Mama. That is indeed very thoughtful and kind. Yet I do not know if Hunter is attending. Perhaps I should have enquired."

Audrey's reluctance to marry Lord Gastrell and her one momentous final and rather disorganised ongoing attempt to flee the hideous wedding looming in front of her had somehow stoked the cooling embers of the fight within her mother, for where Marjorie Whittemore had taken to her bed when initially confronted with the unspoken conflict within the household, the woman now stood as her daughter's ally, and rather stoically at her side. Whether her mother acted discreetly or openly, Audrey could not have been more appreciative or proud of her. Indeed, Marjorie Whittemore had reminded Audrey of who she truly was.

Audrey let out a breath.

"Audrey, dear, if you frown any deeper, I do believe your head will cave in," Marjorie quipped with a grin.

Audrey snorted as a chuckle burst from her lips. "Oh, Mama, you do make me laugh. My head will certainly not cave in. I was simply thinking about how wonderful you are."

Smiling, Marjorie curled her ink-black satin-gloved fingers gently around her daughter's hand. "Not as wonderful as you are, Audrey," she replied. "If I were so wonderful, then perhaps I would have done more to save you. I cannot tell you how sorry I am, my darling."

Tears glistened along the lower lids of Audrey's eyes as she gazed at her mother. "You mustn't think any of this is your fault, Mama. You know, as much as I despise admitting it, Father is a very cruel man. He has never kept that a secret from either of us. However, what bothers me the most is that when I leave, I will be leaving you behind." Audrey swallowed, then looked into her mother's eyes. "You know you could come with me, if you would like to?"

"Who will secretly do all they can to keep your father at bay if I should follow you, my darling?" Marjorie crooned, lifting her hand to cup her daughter's face affectionately. "Besides, you mustn't worry about me, for I think it is about time I pay my sister a visit, is it not? Once I know you are perfectly safe, of course."

Audrey nodded, taking a shuddering breath.

"Happy thoughts, my darling daughter,"

Marjorie encouraged. "Tonight is supposed to be a happy affair. And, *oh my.*"

Striding towards both ladies, in all his splendour, Hunter settled his ravenous gaze upon Audrey. His eyes were an ethereal blue much like the ocean, Audrey mused, noting the way they sparkled under the light overhead. They reminded her of rippling waves beneath the Mediterranean sun and indeed just as enticing. Jet black hair sharpened every angle of his face, drawing her eyes to his chiselled features and wonderfully wicked mouth. *Good lord.* All moisture vacated Audrey's mouth as her tongue peeked out between her lips in search of the tiniest drop. A glass of lemonade was placed in her hand as she vaguely noticed the familiar touch of her mother encouraging her to close her fingers around the vessel, but as Audrey brought the glass to her lips, she wasn't sure if she was even so much as breathing. As Hunter's eyes dipped to the low cut of Audrey's gown and slowly trailed back up to her lips, the hitch of her breath caught her by surprise.

"Good evening, ladies. Mrs Whittemore, Miss Whittemore." Hunter leaned over, kissing Marjorie's gloved knuckles, then grazed his lips over the tips of Audrey's fingers, trailing them over plum satin and very much lingering with considerably more attention than he had with her mother.

"Good evening, Lord Carlisle," Marjorie offered with a curtsy. "Please do not think me rude to rush off like this, but I believe I am being summoned by my husband." Marjorie excitedly flung her hand up in the air and waved it about. "I'm coming, Wallace, darling!" she sang, then with a quick, thrilled glance at her daughter, hurried off in the direction of Wallace Whittemore, who had not so much as looked at either of them, let alone waved.

Audrey was quite aware that her mother had been avoiding her father, and the man was evidently in the midst of guffawing and salivating over the sensibilities of outrageously opinionated members of the ton, simply so he could believe that they viewed him as their equal. However, Marjorie Whittemore had said that she would divert Wallace Whittemore's eagle-eyed attention from her if Hunter was present. She would thank her mother later, she reminded herself as she turned her full attention to the glorious man towering over her. "Good evening, my lord," she breathed, offering a small curtsy.

Hunter's lips twisted into a wolfish smile. "Minx. You do know I have had to ban anyone else referring to me as such. I cannot concentrate when I hear it anymore, for my imagination cannot help but wander towards that of you and how you feel in my arms."

A delicious shiver shattered the heat of the room as it slithered down her spine. She wasn't entirely sure what she should say, yet she was all too aware of what her body wanted to do. However, such actions would have been rather scandalous indeed, especially in the ballroom.

Hunter discreetly placed a finger over her full lips, observing the way Audrey's eyes danced to the rhythm of her thoughts. "Perhaps you can explain your thoughts by honouring me with a waltz, Miss Whittemore."

Audrey blushed. "I would be delighted, my lord. But I am not sure I have the words."

"You do not need words, Miss Whittemore. I consider dancing to be a universal language that requires no voice. Shall we?"

Delicately placing her petite fingers in Hunter's large, broad hand, Audrey allowed him to lead her and her inconveniently trembling legs onto the dance floor, twirling her into the first waltz of the evening. Warm spice and whisky, as his body pressed against her a little too keenly, set the temperature of her blood ablaze. She had never thought that to be within the presence of a gentleman could feel such a way, but it was as though his essence knew no bounds, wonderfully seeping through her flesh into her bones. Her heart pounded at the caress of his breath at the side of her face, and, once again, she listened as her heart told her that she cared deeply for him. *'One night, Audrey Whittemore,'* she silently told herself as she leaned in closer to him, basking in the heat of his body. *'You are allowed to have something for yourself for one blasted night of your life.'* Audrey turned her head a fraction to the side as a tear slipped from the corner of her eye and simply vanished into the satin of her glove where she discreetly brushed it away. It hurt to think that she may never have anything so wonderful ever again. Whether it be marriage to Lord Gastrell or simply running away that denied her the future she desperately wanted, Audrey was all too aware that she might have been dancing for the last time with Hunter. Mentally shaking her thoughts off, Audrey rather scandalously buried her head in the arc of Hunter's neck.

"What are you thinking, Audrey?" Hunter drawled in a whisper, placing a discreet kiss on the top of her head.

"I was thinking of you, actually," she replied, enjoying the way the heat of his hand trailed down her back, slowly lowering until it rested at the subtle curve at the base of her spine.

"Do tell."

"I was simply thinking that I shall miss you when I have to leave," she said, keeping her voice to merely a whisper, afraid that her plans would be heard.

"How can you miss me when I have no intention of leaving you?" he enquired with an elevated brow. "Did you think that I made the decision to kiss you so that I would simply let you leave me behind? I will have you know, Miss Whittemore, my intention of freeing you from Gastrell is purely selfish, for I want you." Gazing at the wavering hope in her eyes, he continued. "What would you say if I were to kiss you right here, right now, Audrey?"

Audrey opened her mouth to object. She did not want him to feel obliged to her in any way, but before she could speak, he placed a finger over her lips.

"Before you answer, Miss Whittemore," he added seriously, "I am perfectly aware of the ramifications of the act. However, you must know that it will ruin you."

Audrey's head was spinning, her breaths coming fast. "I don't know what to say. I think I need some air."

Guiding Audrey away from the dance floor and out of the ballroom, along a corridor, Hunter noted the way in which Audrey's body trembled with every step, all the while offering his arm to steady her. She certainly wasn't angry, yet there was an obvious element of concern etched across her features that would indeed need to be addressed.

"Once we find somewhere a little less public, I think I may need to explain myself a little better, for I appear to have frightened you," Hunter remarked as he led Audrey toward a room, tucked away just beyond the library.

"You haven't frightened me, Hunter," Audrey offered as she stepped inside. "It was unexpected, is all. I am afraid you will have to excuse me, for my mind is in quite a significant amount of turmoil, and it simply gets far more complex as I get closer to my…"

"Wedding to Lord Gastrell?" Hunter suggested, offering her a sympathetic look before he closed the door behind them and locked it.

A tear snaked down the side of Audrey's nose, but before it could kiss her top lip, she wiped it away. "Apologies, my lord. I seem to be quite the leaky vessel lately."

"You have no need to apologise. Perhaps I should explain my plan a little better. I overwhelmed you when you clearly have too much to cope with already." Hunter poured a little whisky into two glasses, handing one to Audrey, then settled in the chair, pulling her onto his lap. Audrey shifted to move, but he simply tightened his grip encouragingly. "Please stay," he pleaded, releasing her to give her a chance to refuse.

Audrey nodded, placing her untouched drink on the desk, then leaned her back against Hunter's hard chest.

"When I said that I knew the ramifications of such an action as kissing you, I meant it. I would marry you, Audrey." Hunter remained still, taking note of any changes in Audrey's body, but she did not tense at his words or touch, nor did she attempt to flee. She simply remained as she was.

"Although I appreciate your extremely kind

offer to save me," Audrey began, "I cannot allow you to tie your life to me out of some sense of chivalry, for you may look at me one day wishing you had never met me." Twisting her body, Audrey turned to face Hunter.

He smiled. "Is that what you think? As unromantic as it may sound to ruin you merely to force your father's hand so that we may be wed, I can assure you that where some may deem our marriage to be a price, I would deem it to be a glorious prize. Have you not been listening to me, Audrey? I want you. As much as you do not wish to marry that big bag of wind, Gastrell, I can promise you that I do not wish for you to marry him considerably more. There is only one lady whom I would wish to be my wife and to be the new Lady Carlisle, and she is you." Hunter gazed at the rows of tomes along the walls, trying to steady his heart that was pounding in the silence that stretched between them. It was dread, he realised, dread that she would refuse, dread that she would one day simply up and leave and he would never see her again. "Before you answer," he cut in before she could speak, although he wasn't sure she was going to. "I simply wish to say that I am quite aware that we have not known each other very long, and yes, I am perfectly sane."

Rising from his lap, Audrey walked toward the window, unaware that Hunter had crept up behind her. "Oh," she squeaked, "I thought you were still in the chair."

Sliding his hands over her hips and across the front of her waist, Hunter rested his chin gently on top of her head. "This could be us every day, Audrey, but at Carlisle estate or wherever you wish to live. When you give me your answer, please only think of yourself. All I want is for you to be happy."

That was the first time in Audrey's entire life that a man had ever considered her happiness. The declaration seemed to wrap itself around her heart and tenderly squeeze with the gentle warmth of summer. "If I agree to marry you, do you honestly believe that you will not have regrets, my lord?"

At the sound of his title upon her perfect lips, Hunter felt the rumble of his desire for her course up his centre and burst over every inch of his body. "No, Audrey, I do not simply believe that I will not have regrets, for I know without a shred of doubt that I will not have so much as a crumb of regret."

Turning the woman in his arms to face him, Hunter lowered his head and pressed his mouth to hers. He was slow and sensual as he slipped his tongue teasingly between her lips and deepened the kiss. A soft, sweet, arousing gasp bled from the back of her throat, tightening his abdomen and thighs around his evident lust. "You, Audrey Whittemore, are the only woman for me," he drawled breathlessly, pressing one last kiss to her throat before he raised his head to gaze into her pale green eyes.

"Are you quite certain?" she queried, her fingers tracing her kiss-swollen lips.

"I have never been more certain, so stop bloody teasing and say I have your permission to ruin you." Hunter grinned.

A squeal slipped from Audrey's throat as a smile spread across her face. "Then yes, ruin me, Hunter. I do indeed give you permission."

"Ah, another waltz. How very convenient." Hunter smiled wolfishly as he pulled Audrey into his arms and swept her into the very centre of the dance floor. "Trust me," he drawled seductively into her ear, noting the tremble of her hand in his. As his lips brushed her ear, he felt her shiver, then subsequently relax in his arms. "I promise you that you will never be alone again, Audrey."

Ribbons of soft music threaded through the throng of guests as it curled around them in pairs, pulling them into the centre of the room with the promise of a private moment within the embrace of another. "We have our audience," Hunter whispered. "So when you believe you are ready to change our lives for the better, Audrey, simply squeeze my shoulder."

Audrey nodded.

She could not simply reverse time and undo what they were about to do, Audrey reminded herself. Once their rather public display of affection caught the attention of the ton, all hell was bound to break loose, but, other than what Hunter himself thought of the plan and their future together, she did not care a whit for the opinion of others, she realised as she closed her eyes. Yes, her father would indeed be angry, but as for her mother, she knew she would be pleased. The idea of a life with Hunter, it seemed, thrilled Audrey to her bones.

Inhaling and exhaling three times to steady her nerves, Audrey squeezed Hunter's shoulder.

"Leave this to me," he offered, lacing his fingers with hers and drawing her forward, where he brushed her lips with his, his arm swooping around her waist until she was flush against his aching body. She softened in his arms as everything failed to exist other than the two of them. This was what it was supposed to be like, she thought as she combed her fingers through his hair.

Wide eyes and whispers cut through the magic as their kiss ended, yet the deep, velvety, baritone voice at her side smoothed the sharp edges of each critical blade. "I do beg your pardon," Hunter announced, bestowing an affectionate glance in her direction, "I believe I got quite carried away, for I have just asked Miss Audrey Whittemore to be my wife, and she has said yes."

Tittering and gossip twisted and coiled, ascending into applause and shouts of congratulations as the onlookers gathered a little closer. Had it not been for the pair of eyes that glowered from the corner of the room, she would have rejoiced. Crimson could not even describe the hue of her father's complexion above the stark white of his collar. Marjorie placed her hand on her husband's arm as if to restrain him. Guilt clawed at Audrey's insides. She had considered her mother's opinion but not what she would have to endure as a result of such a display. "I'm so sorry, Mama," she mouthed over the heads of strangers.

Marjorie Whittemore smiled, then winked as she placed her free hand over her heart. "Be happy, my
darling," she mouthed in return. "I love you."

Audrey swallowed the ball of emotion lodged in her throat as Hunter guided her away from the dance floor and towards her parents.

"Good evening, Mr and Mrs Whittemore. I apologise for not informing you before the entirety of the ton witnessed such a moment. However, it was entirely unintentional, I assure you. I simply got rather swept up in the joyful moment, as it were, for I was beyond elated that Audrey did me the honour of accepting my proposal."

Wallace Whittemore's teeth ground together as the muscles in his jaws twitched emphatically.

Pressing her lips together as her eyes sparkled with mischief, Marjorie Whittemore looked toward Hunter and then at Audrey, offering them a sly nod of comprehension. "Aren't you going to congratulate them, my dear?" she encouraged as she turned to her husband. "It is supposed to be a happy moment, is it not? Our daughter is going to marry a wonderful man."

Nostrils flaring and eyes darkening, Wallace Whittemore jutted out his chin. "Congratulations," he began, his eyes boring into Audrey's. "Congratulations on your very clever thinking. I believe I did not quite give you enough credit, my girl, for you are quite devious."

Audrey tightened her grasp on Hunter's arm.

"Mr Whittemore," Hunter seethed, stepping forward. "I insist that you do not speak to my betrothed in such a manner."

"Your betrothed? Pah," Wallace scoffed. "I do believe the chit is already spoken for. You may think it is too late, Lord Carlisle, but Lord Gastrell and I have an agreement."

Hunter loomed over Audrey's father, his shadow pushing the man further back. The scrape of wood on marble flooring cut through the tension as Wallace Whittemore's leg collided with a chair, his body scrambling for balance as Hunter backed him up further. "Audrey will marry whoever she wishes, Whittemore," he growled menacingly. "And what will you do now, when the entire ton has witnessed our happy occasion? It would be rather unseemly of you to interfere, would it not? For I believe I may have just ruined her reputation."

"Lord Carlisle," Marjorie interjected softly. "Please, you mustn't talk of my daughter that way." Marjorie's face quivered as she reached for Audrey.

"It is quite alright, Mama," Audrey replied as they both continued to observe the gentlemen at war with one another. "It was all part of the plan," she whispered, so her father could not hear.

"Oh, I see. How clever indeed. Your mama is rather proud, you know," Marjorie whispered, tittering as she kissed her daughter affectionately on the cheek.

"I apologise if I sounded rather coarse, Mrs Whittemore, but I care very much for your daughter, and there is nothing and nobody who will come between us," he added, turning his sharp eyes back to Audrey's father. "Is that understood?"

"How dare you lecture me, boy!" Wallace Whittemore roared. "Audrey is my daughter, and she will be dutiful to the needs of our family, which you are not, nor ever will be, a part of. Do I make myself clear?"

"Believe what you will, Whittemore," Hunter returned, "but Audrey *will* be Lady Carlisle, and you will either have to leave us be or swallow your greedy little pride so that we may welcome you into our lives. Your wife, on the other hand, is always welcome in the Carlisle household. Do I make *myself* clear?" Hunter turned on his heel, not giving the puce-hued prig another second to retaliate as he led

Audrey out into the gardens.

"Well, I think that went rather well," he drawled, his voice drenched in sarcasm as he pulled Audrey closer to his side.

She sighed. "I dread to think what he will be like to live with over the next few weeks. I do not relish the thought."

"I apologise, darling. I did not think he would react as such. I was hoping we would simply wedge him into a rather tight corner, as it were, so he would not be able to comment further. I never expected him to be quite so argumentative."

"No, it is I who should apologise." Audrey curled her fingers around the lapels of his jacket, pulling him lower as she pushed up onto the tips of her toes and kissed him. "I should have warned you of the kind of man he is," she added breathlessly as she twirled her fingers through the back of his hair. "I believe it might be for the best if I suggest that we leave early, then I can speak with my mother and father at home. I might be able to make him see sense."

"Shall I escort you?" Hunter offered. "I do not like the thought of leaving you at the mercy of your father." Hunter nuzzled into her neck, his arms curled around her waist, preventing her body from collapsing beneath the onslaught of pleasant shivers as the soft scratch of fine stubble tickled the arc of her neck.

"To the carriage perhaps," she breathed, leaning into him. "But if you continue, my lord, I do not believe I will be able to walk anywhere." Audrey giggled.

A low rumble of laughter vibrated through Audrey's flesh as Hunter released her and curled her arm into the crook of his elbow. "Then I best desist," he retorted with a devilish grin, leading her back into the ballroom to find her parents.

"Miss Whittemore."

Audrey turned at the sound of her name as Lady Peterson hurried towards her with a folded piece of parchment in her hand.

"Lady Peterson." Audrey smiled, offering the kindly lady a small curtsy. "Have you seen my mother and father?"

"That is the reason I wanted to speak with you, dear. Your mother left this note for you. I believe your father had a terrible headache, and so he insisted they leave."

Lady Peterson gazed at Audrey sympathetically, her kind words embellishing the truth so that it would be deemed rather less attractive to those who liked to gossip. It seemed that some of the guests, if not all, were quite aware of her father's displeasure with the announcement of her betrothal, and Audrey was grateful that the lady had sought not to inflame the matter further. "Thank you, Lady Peterson," she offered as she unfolded the parchment. Her mother had scribbled a quick apology and note of affection.

"Your mother suggested that your betrothed escort you home." Lady Peterson smiled. "I feel rather fortunate to have you announce your engagement at my ball," she whispered as though it was a secret. "I wish you both all the happiness in the world. There will be wonderful times ahead for you both, I just know it," she added with a quick but gentle squeeze of Audrey's hands.

"Thank you, Lady Peterson," Hunter drawled. "And you can be assured that I shall escort Miss Whittemore safely home."

Chapter Nineteen

The moon cast a translucent milky shadow over the Carlisle estate, blanketing the property in an ethereal lace as it bled across the land, then bent and stretched over every wall and rooftop in its path. The moonlight possessed the air of an unearthly spectre, Audrey mused, noting the way it enticed the scenery out of the darkness beneath its gentle glow. A hazy blue incandescent light softly kissed the tops of trees, hovering at the tips of leaves in a poised phantom mist, as Audrey and Hunter ventured further away from their homes. Every step the young couple took diminished the property and the ties that bound Audrey to her home. Back there, where the moon kept watch, were the shackles that tied her to her apparent duties as the daughter of Wallace Whittemore. It was that very thought that spurred her onwards, her eyes searching the night before her for the unmade path ahead, and her mind focusing solely on the warmth and touch of Hunter's hand clasped around hers. Like this, she thought, she could pretend that nothing and nobody else existed.

Hunter tucked Audrey possessively beneath his strong arm. The memory of her father's simmering temper fought to crease his brow as he considered whether Wallace Whittemore would do the right thing for his daughter simply by allowing her to marry the man she wished to. As much as he wanted to believe there was indeed such a possibility, Hunter was quite certain that Audrey's father was not the honourable man they hoped he would be, so much so that even such an event as a ruination wouldn't entice him from dragging his daughter to the altar and binding her to the groom of his choosing. The man was evidently an extremely selfish and arrogant father. Indeed, it was astoundingly clear that he gave not one whit for Audrey, which, of course, Hunter considered rather angrily, meant that it may take a miracle for that scoundrel to concede.

Dipping beneath the shadows of the trees, Hunter pulled Audrey into his arms and pressed her up against the trunk of a silver birch. Her gentle breaths brushing over the skin beneath his open collar. "My Audrey," he drawled, the tips of their noses touching as he teased her parted lips with the promise of a kiss. "Tell me you are mine, my love."

"I am yours, Hunter," she replied through short gasps. "I will only ever be yours."

A heated desirous groan bled from Hunter as he closed the distance between their lips. His tongue teased and danced with hers as she curled her arms around his neck, softly moaning with approval as she pressed her breasts against his hard chest.

"Promise you will never let your father win, Audrey," Hunter pleaded huskily, as his lips trailed her jaw and drifted seductively over her exposed collarbone.

Audrey's brain had positively melted. How was she supposed to have a conversation with the onslaught of pleasure doing terribly naughty things to her body? she mused as she tried to string a sentence together. "I …prom…ise… *oh my* …"

Hunter chuckled deeply. "That will do," he offered, then continued with his delicious torture as Audrey's brain practically oozed out of her ears with ecstasy.

'This will never do,' Audrey thought as she pressed the palms of her hands against Hunter's chest and gave a rather reluctant push. "You know, it is rather unfair to ask me questions when you are doing… well, you know… whatever you want to refer to it as."

"Kissing you?"

"Yes, I suppose that is one way of putting it. So, if you wish to discuss my father, then I would like my wits not on the verge of falling out of my ear in a puddle, if you don't mind," she teased.

Hunter straightened. "Perhaps we should discuss what may happen next. After all, your father did express his displeasure rather fervently."

Audrey hadn't meant to, but her mind had plucked out the word pleasure, quickly dismissing the three letters prior to it, causing her to shiver at the memory of his sensuous lips on her skin. *'You have butter for brains, Audrey Whittemore,'* she silently chided.

Daintily, she cleared her throat. "Yes, he was not a happy man at all. I have no doubt whatsoever that I shall be subjected to a bombardment of rather loud chastisement tomorrow. I shall have to rip the hem off an old petticoat and stick a piece in each ear to dull the volume," she jested with a wry smile as she tried to push her fear aside.

"Do you think I do not know what men like your father are capable of, Audrey?" Hunter grumbled. He hadn't meant to be angry, but he wanted her to take the matter seriously, for the suspicion that Wallace Whittemore would forbid her to marry him was as though the man was hanging off his back and wouldn't let go. It was a very probable response, and Audrey needed to be prepared.

The smile on Audrey's face faltered. "Apologies, I did not mean to make light of the situation. It is merely that I spend every day thinking about it, and I simply wanted tonight to be about us."

"I understand, Audrey, but I wish for you to know of what may come, or he will catch you off-guard, and you won't know how to react or what to do."

Audrey began to walk slowly away from the tree, her hand slipping gradually out of Hunter's as she put some distance between them. Hunter's gaze lowered to observe the way her hips enticingly undulated. He wanted to reach out and grab her, yet the way in which she moved spoke of contemplation, and hadn't that been what he wanted her to do? To contemplate what her father would do next? Of course, the urge to drag her back against the tree and explore every inch of her with his hands and lips was fighting him with considerable strength, but he would simply have to wait, he told himself, for they both should be certain of the other's intent.

"I have known my father four and twenty years," she began, turning back to face Hunter. Her lips curled in a soft, affectionate smile. "And yet he has managed to surprise me tonight."

Keeping his eyes on her, Hunter remained silent and attentive as he allowed Audrey to continue.

Audrey ran her fingers over the trunk of the tree, then casually dropped her hand by her side. "Although ruination was not a topic I had ever been familiar with before tonight," she continued, "I suppose I assumed, just as you had, that my father would simply concede and allow us to marry as we wish to. That was my wish, and I suppose it still is. I want you to know, though, that I do not intend to marry Lord Gastrell. I had not intended to before

I met you, and I do not intend to now, with much more vigour I might add, now that I *do* know you."

Hunter's shadow loomed over Audrey as he stepped up behind her, his warm hands sliding over her waist, heat transforming into delicate icy beads that rushed over her flesh in a delicious wave of approval. As stubble lightly scratched her sensitive skin, Audrey angled her neck giving him more room as she savoured the way his lips brushed upward then nibbled at the lobe of her ear. His hands followed, sliding up from her waist and cupping her breasts. Audrey gasped and arched her back towards him, feeling the strength of his desire through the layers of fabric that stood as the only barrier between them.

"If you ever feel like giving in, I need you to remember us, Audrey," Hunter breathed, as he spun her around to face him. "I need you to remember what we have and what we could have. Remember this."

Hunter pulled Audrey against him, carefully backing her up toward the tree. With every step he took, his mouth skilfully toyed and teased, following the sweet line of her jaw, tenderly kissing the lids of her softly closed eyes, and briefly brushing the tip of her nose until his attention returned hungrily to her soft parted lips. Every touch obscured Audrey's mind until the moment was faintly fractured by the familiar cold, uneven surface of the silver birch.

'*Remember us*'. Two simple words and the cold creeping dread that her father and Lord Gastrell had conjured into her heart and mind reared back like a frightened beast and fled into the night. Hunter's words, although simple, held considerable depth, the weight of them crashing through her doubts, shattering the last remnant of restraint she possessed as she leaned into his embrace, kissing him fiercely. Arms draped over his broad shoulders, Audrey's hands caressed the nape of his neck, her fingers splaying into the depths of his silky-soft hair as they explored.

The sultry sound of sincerity resonated from Hunter's body in a deep, knee-weakening rumble of approval. It vibrated between them, bleeding deep into Audrey's bones as her palms slid down his arms, then to his waist, where she curled her fingers into the cotton of his shirt and gently tugged, beckoning him closer still. "I could never forget you or us," she breathed.

"You have seared yourself into the very depths of my soul, Audrey." Hunter's voice was husky as his hand caressed up the side of her. His curious fingertips slipped between their bodies and trailed over the contours of her supple, soft skin, bordering the low neckline of her velvet gown. Thoroughly mesmerised by his wandering hands and the sensations fizzing through her body, Audrey found herself unable to look away from what he was doing, but as his lips captured hers again and his most inquisitive finger slipped beneath the fabric, teasingly skimming the peak of her nipple, she could not help but close her eyes.

Heat soared through Hunter's veins as his hands roamed Audrey's soft curves. The sweet gasps of her pleasure tightened his abdomen with a yearning ache that drifted between his muscular thighs. The woman would be his undoing, he realised, yet he was glad of it. Audrey Whittemore was the one, the woman he wanted to wake up to every morning and fall asleep beside every night. She was divine. Marriage had been such a feeble concept when he had spoken of it in passing to annoy his mother, but Audrey had given it substance. She had given it meaning. Indeed, Audrey had made it all make sense.

Thunder rolled across the night sky, propelling a magnificent army of raindrops down upon the earth. Tiny, watery soldiers dripped onto their heads and shoulders, creating rivulets that trickled over their skin, squeezing between their entangled bodies as the cool liquid attempted to stifle the heat simmering between them. A drop of rain trailed down the bridge of Audrey's nose, briefly settling in the delicate dip of her cupid's bow. As it spilled over, Hunter leaned in, capturing it between the soft clasp of his lips with a gentle tug, then turned his attention to her lower lip, nibbling delicately in time with the soft moans escaping with every one of her sweet sighs.

Water dripped from the rain-drenched strands of Hunter's hair and onto Audrey's bare shoulders, a temporary river, quickly disappearing between the hollow of her breasts as her fingers roved beneath his jacket, stretching and curling in intermittent grasps. Her fingers fumbled at the fabric between two buttons on his shirt, then flattened, gliding over the smooth contours of his chest beneath. The warmth of her skin on his sent crackles of fire blazing down his spine, tightening every muscle around his sudden overpowering surge of desire to make her his.

Careful not to dissuade Audrey from her evident need of him, Hunter pulled back to gaze down at her. "Perhaps we should take this somewhere a little more sheltered," he suggested, lifting a loose strand of her hair, the curl absent with the weight of the weather. Hunter restrained himself as another drop of rain wet her lips. Both he and she were drenched and sorely in need of shelter, yet one more touch of her lips and he knew he would have made love to her there in the rain under the moonlight.

Audrey nodded. "Perhaps we should," she rasped, offering him an enticing smile, then lifted the hem of her wet skirts to continue the walk.

"Oh, no, you don't, Miss Whittemore," Hunter drawled, scooping her up into his arms. "We are not finding another tree to stand under."

"I can't go into Carlisle House," Audrey protested. "If someone talks, my father will find out, and then you and I will never marry."

Hunter frowned. "Then where do you suggest, my love?" he queried, feigning an unsteady gait. "Hurry, Miss Whittemore, or I shall drop you," he teased.

"The stable."

Laughing in his velvety-rich tone, Hunter repositioned Audrey in his arms, basking in the way she curled into him. "Stable it is then, if you are certain?"

"More than certain, *my lord*." Audrey gazed up at Hunter beneath her lashes with a mischievous grin.

"Minx."

Slipping inside the stable, Hunter loosened his grasp on Audrey, her body slowly sliding down the front of him as her cheeks flushed with warmth. Pale green deepened into emerald, Hunter noted as he drank in the desirous glint in her eyes and savoured the sensation of her delicate fingers scribing unspeakable words upon the base of his throat. Hunter could not remember when his cravat had vanished, and he did not particularly care either, for the absence gave way to her presence, which he much preferred.

"Good God, you're beautiful, Audrey," Hunter

rumbled in her ear as he returned the favour by kissing the base of her throat. Her head fell backward at the touch of his lips, allowing him access to every inch of her exposed skin. Gripping the neckline of her gown with his teeth, he lowered it to reveal her breasts.

Audrey gasped as his lips brushed where her nipple peaked in approval, his touch coiling down her spine as warmth flooded between her thighs. With this and the sensual fragrance of warm spice and whisky that reminded her only of him, Audrey was quite afraid that she would perish on the spot. "Hunter," she breathed, her hands reaching down, following him as he lowered into a crouching position. From there his hands slid slowly up her bare legs. "What are you doing?" Her breath staggered.

Skirts up around her thighs, Hunter placed one of her slender legs over his right shoulder and then the other over his left. Standing slowly, the strength of his upper body and thighs sliding Audrey up against the timber as she curled her fingers loosely in his hair, Hunter never took his eyes off her. *Good lord*, he had never wanted a woman the way he wanted Audrey Whittemore, but tonight was about her, he'd decided as the sweet sounds of her gasps and sighs lingered in the air laced with the scent of orange blossoms. He could not deny that he wanted to claim her, to bury himself in her, but she deserved more than that, for the stables were not the place for a lady's first time, despite the ache she had conjured in his loins.

"Hunter?"

Hunter smiled at his future wife, the innocence in her eyes as she questioned what he would do next. "Do you not trust me?" He grinned wickedly.

"Well, yes, of course, but *oh, my*."

Hunter leaned in, silencing her with his wicked tongue.

Standing momentarily before the entrance of her home, Audrey inhaled, attempting several times to school her features. It appeared that Hunter had left her with a permanent smile that could very possibly hint at what they had been doing only moments ago. She wondered whether all it would take was one look and everyone would know what they had been up to in the stable. She blushed.

Knocking, she began to think of bland things such as paper, hay, gruel, Lady Pilkington's conversations, and her father. She assumed that would buy her some time to reach her bedchamber door without a ridiculous grin greedily hogging her features.

"Bernard," she offered. "I apologise for keeping you up so late."

"Not a problem, Miss Audrey."

"You are too good to me, Bernard," she said, smiling innocently as she made her way towards the staircase.

"Err, Miss Audrey. I am afraid your father is waiting for you in the drawing room."

Audrey paled. It seemed she did not need to think of bland things, for simply knowing what was to come next had wiped the smile off her face completely.

"I'm sorry, miss," Bernard rasped with regret.

"It is okay, Bernard. It is never anyone's fault but his," she whispered, returning to the butler and clasping his hand gently in reassurance. "I will see him now."

"Very good, Miss Audrey."

Audrey patted down her skirts, noting how quickly they had dried. "Thank heavens," she whispered to herself, for she did not know how she would explain a rain-drenched gown. Pushing the drawing room door open and deliberately leaving it that way in case she required a quick exit, Audrey stepped inside.

Wallace Whittemore faced the hearth, his hands clasped behind his back. The strength with which he held his own hands caught Audrey's attention. She swallowed. "You wished to see me, Father?"

"Did you think you would be able to simply

sneak into the house and avoid this conversation, girl?" he seethed.

"I had not even considered it, Father. I simply came home. I apologise if I am a bit late. It was because I needed to find a carriage and—"

"*A bit late*? Your mother and I have been home for two hours, and you are sopping wet!"

Audrey reached up to touch her hair. *Drat!* She hadn't even given it a thought.

Catching her father's eyes in the looking glass, Audrey cursed inwardly again. She had forgotten that the blasted sly looking glass had existed. Not that it would have made any difference because he would have eventually turned around to witness the apparent state of her anyway. "We got caught in the rain," she offered calmly. It wasn't a lie, per se, for they had indeed gotten caught in the downpour – well, not exactly caught but more that they simply stayed out in it – but she wasn't about to be utterly ridiculous by confessing where and what they had been doing.

Wallace Whittemore scoffed. "I am assuming you were with *him. Lord Carlisle?*"

Audrey inhaled at the pronunciation of Hunter's name. It rolled off her father's tongue as though Hunter was nothing more than dirt on the older man's boot. She was angry, she realised. This time the man's venom had been directed towards someone other than her, someone she cared deeply for. The truth wrapped its fingers around her heart and twisted into a burning desire to fight back. "Yes, Father. I was with Lord Carlisle. What was I supposed to do after you left me with little choice as to how I should travel home? Hunter kindly offered to escort me here." Audrey was shaking as her anger rolled across the room, colliding with the burgeoning tension conjured by her father's temper.

"Hunter is it, eh? Who knew my daughter would be the local whore?" her father snapped.

Audrey gasped. "I—"

"You have ruined everything. Did you and Carlisle plan this?"

"Plan what, Father?" Perhaps she should have admitted it, she thought, for her father was not exactly a fool, and she had not made any secret of her objection to the union between she and Gastrell, but this was *her* life, she reminded herself.

"You know exactly what I am referring to, girl," he roared, turning on his heel to face her. "You thought that your public display of indecency and the announcement of your betrothal would be ample to ruin my plans."

Audrey's jaw clenched, recognising the heat of her rage burning in her eyes as she fixed her gaze on Wallace Whittemore. "And there is the problem, Father," she spat. "They are *your* plans for me; they are not *my* plans for me. When were you going to ask me what I want to do with *my* life? What could possibly be so much more important to you that you would force your daughter to marry and bear children for such a hideous and odious man as Lord Gastrell? Was it money, Father? A fake title?"

Wallace Whittemore's knuckles slammed against his daughter's cheek, sending her tumbling to the floor.

Audrey rubbed the side of her face, dismissing the throbbing in her jaw. She knew all too well that he would have expected his action to quieten her, but it had only served to further stoke the flames of her fury. His disrespect for the people in his life had been like the bricks required for a wall. One by one they built up around his victims until one day said victim would tear down those walls simply because they could bear him no more. Wallace Whittemore had no idea that his continuous hatred for her and the rest of the household had practically eroded every molecule of love she had ever had for him. "Is that your answer, Father?" she ground out, shifting her jaw from side to side and giving it one last press with her fingers. "If it is, then I can only assume that it is a yes to one of the suggestions I have made." Slowly, pressing her palms on the seat of the chair behind her, Audrey forced herself up into a standing position to face him again. She would not cower in front of him anymore, nor would she allow him to lord over her when he did not have any respect for her at all.

"You, Audrey Whittemore, will marry Lord

Gastrell. You can forget any plans to marry that *baron*. That is my final decision." Wallace Whittemore walked back towards the hearth, his tone cool and collected as though he had never laid a finger upon his own child.

Curling her hands into fists as her eyes burned into her father's back, Audrey took a deep breath to still her nerves. "I will not marry Gastrell. I am marrying Lord Carlisle. The decision does not belong to you," she announced stoically.

Whittemore rushed towards her, halting within an inch of her face, his eyes obsidian as he pressed a finger to the middle of her forehead, pushing her backward into the chair behind her. "You will do as I say," he growled maniacally as he loomed over her crumpled form. "If you persist in your delusional thinking, there can only be one place for you. It would take just one word, and I would see to it that you would be the newest intake in Bedlam. So, pay attention, dear girl, when I tell you that you *cannot* and *will not* determine your own future. Is that clear?"

A knock sounded at the drawing room door, snapping Wallace Whittemore from his position as he turned and moved away from his daughter. "Who is it?" he called calmly as though he were a different man entirely.

Bernard peered around the door, his eyes filled with trepidation of what he might find. He swallowed as he looked at Audrey, his gaze softening with relief when he saw that she was alright. "I was wondering whether you need anything else before I retire, sir," he enquired.

"No, Bernard. That will be all."

"And what about you?" The butler queried, his eyes lingering on Audrey in sympathy. "Do you need anything?"

"Actually, Bernard, I do. Perhaps I might have a word?" Audrey replied, rising to her feet to join him. "I have a wedding to plan," she added, flicking a defiant glance back at her father. "Lord Carlisle and I are betrothed."

Out in the foyer, Audrey encouraged the butler away from the door and out of earshot from the man beyond it. "I think you may have just saved me a great deal of earache, Bernard. Thank you."

"Very welcome, Miss Audrey. I must admit, I did hear your father shouting, and it concerned me. I have never heard him quite so angry."

"Yes, indeed."

"Miss Audrey, may I speak freely?"

"Always. Say whatever you wish."

"I have worked for your father for a very long time, and in that time, I have not been naïve to his ways, as it were. I am rather pleased to hear that you have found a man who will care for you as you should be cared for, but the household is aware of his wish for you to marry that beast, Gastrell.

Be careful, miss. Insistence and persistence will not be the answer to overruling his wishes. He will do whatever is necessary to get what he wants." The butler patted Audrey's hand. "Please take care of yourself, miss, and might I suggest something for that?" he added, gesturing to the mark of her father's hand on her skin. She really hoped it wouldn't bruise.

"I'll see to it," she replied thoughtfully. The butler's words sent a chill trickling through her veins. He was older than her, and she was quite aware that he would have been privy to information that she had not. "And thank you, Bernard. I shall pay heed to your advice."

"Very good. Goodnight, Miss Audrey."

"Goodnight, my friend."

Up in the privacy of the bedchamber with a cool cloth pressed against Audrey's cheek, Ivy assisted the young lady in the removal of her gown, making light work of the feat as they replaced the heavy fabric with a light cotton nightgown.

"Do I have any clean and pressed gentlemen's attire in my closet, Ivy?" Audrey enquired, brushing her hair back off her face as she crawled beneath the coverlet of her bed.

"Yes, Miss Audrey. I managed to get them all cleaned, dried, and pressed this afternoon. Will you continue to use them, then, miss?"

"I think I might," she replied. "Now that my father knows of my wishes, I believe he will fight me all the way."

"It was a bit risky, miss, to ruin yourself in front of all them folks." The maid grinned. "But ever so romantic."

Audrey smiled. "How did you find out?"

"Your mother told me. She was so pleased, but she was also very worried about *him* downstairs."

"Who? Do you mean the devil?"

The maid giggled. "No, silly. I meant your father."

"Close enough, Ivy," Audrey teased. "I do believe that even Lucifer would be outdone by that man." She sighed, the smile fading on her lips. "I think Mama may have been right to worry, though. Nevertheless, despite Hunter and I being rather hasty with regards to our actions, tonight has given me something to fight for. I want a life with him, Ivy."

"Do you love him, Miss Audrey?"

"I have never been in love before, Ivy," she replied, "yet, if one was to be confident in their own heart, I would have to say that yes, I do… very much so."

The maid reached over and pecked Audrey lightly on the cheek. "Sorry, miss. I know it's not really my place, but, well, it is so lovely to see you happy and have something to hope for. I do believe that twinkle you once had has been restored by that neighbour of yours, and I'm very happy to see it."

"Thank you, Ivy. Now all I have to do is fight to keep it."

Chapter Twenty

"This is what her father had planned for her?" Hunter stared at the three men in front of him, an expression of incredulity darkening his eyes and creasing his brow.

"Indeed, Carlisle," Baldry replied with disgust at his own findings. "That man is… Well, he's…"

"I'll tell you what he is, Baldry," Hunter interjected, venom rising in his throat. "He's dead!" he roared, slamming his fist on the desk.

"Hold on." Baldry raised his hand. "I'm afraid there is more, Carlisle. Information I believe you should have."

Hunter rose to his feet, reeling at the information he already had. *Surely, Baldry could not have more when he could barely digest what he already knew.* Hunter's thoughts were loud and boisterous, echoing and resounding in his head, so much so he could hardly decipher what they were, albeit recognising the emotion that accompanied them. One thing was for certain, however, and that was that his main priority was to get Audrey away from her father.

"Sir!" Elkins called through the door.

"What is it, Elkins?" Hunter responded, his tone a little curt. "And come in for heaven's sake. I can barely hear you."

The butler gingerly pushed open the door. "Begging your pardon, sir, but Lady Carlisle and her friend arrived three minutes ago. What do you wish for me to do with them?"

That was all he needed, Hunter thought with exasperation. It seemed that his list of those he wished to be rid of was lengthening throughout the morning. "Let them wait in the foyer. If they arrive unannounced, then they shall have to make do. It is not your job to pander to them, Elkins, and I will not have them believe that it is."

Elkins nodded and began to retreat from the room.

"Elkins," Hunter called, stopping the man in his tracks. "That means that should they so much as request a cup of tea or a crumb to eat, you simply tell them that they will have to wait. They were not invited, and I am quite certain my mother is merely here in her umpteenth attempt to interfere. There is to be no hospitality whatsoever. I have more important matters to deal with, as I am sure you must have too."

"Very good, sir."

"And, Elkins."

The butler stopped again. "Yes, sir?"

"Thank you."

The butler smiled and nodded as he took his leave.

"Where were we?" Hunter queried with confusion. Trust that blasted woman to turn up again. She should be grateful he was busy, he considered, for if she thought he had been vexed with her before, then she would not like what he would have to offer her this time. Hunter was in no mood to deal with Lady Agatha Carlisle when his and Audrey's future hung in the balance.

"I was just saying that there is more to the story," Baldry offered.

"Ah, yes. Go on, please." Hunter rose and poured whisky into four glasses, then placed a vessel before each gentleman, keeping one for himself.

"Not only has Gastrell got plans for Miss Whittemore to be his latest attraction at the disorderly house, but there are also two more ladies he has already done this to."

Hunter's knuckles bled into white, his grip tightening furiously around the glass. "The man is the devil incarnate," he seethed.

Hobbs stepped forward. "Do you not see, Carlisle?"

"See what?" Hunter snapped, picturing Audrey helpless and trapped somewhere not even fit for the filth on his boots.

"The man is a bigamist," Hobbs replied with a sly grin.

"You mean to tell me that he married the other two ladies?"

All three men nodded. "You've got him bang to rights. Bigamy is illegal, which means that..."

"He could be facing years behind bars," Hunter offered in conclusion. "This is very good news indeed. Now, before I go wading in, what do we know about Whittemore?"

"We have copies of the deeds to the property," Baldry announced, pulling a rolled piece of parchment from his case. "It appears that Whittemore is a partner in Gastrell's business."

Lifting the roll of parchment from Baldry's fingers and unravelling it, Hunter scanned the deed. "This one looks as though it is out of date," Hunter queried, eyeing the solicitor for more information.

"That's because it is. It appears Whittemore got himself into a spot of financial bother, then sold his half of the business to Gastrell. But it didn't end there," he quickly added before Hunter could interrupt, "because it seems he wanted back in. The man I spoke to about these," Baldry said, gesturing to the deed copies, "said that this one here is a new contract recently signed stating that he would regain his half of the business once one Miss Audrey Whittemore was handed over and commenced her duties. It appears that Wallace Whittemore was also to gain a further ten thousand pounds for good measure."

"Good lord," Hunter exclaimed breathlessly as he slumped down into his chair. "Is there no end to the man's cruelty?"

Despite the news that would surely help him extract Audrey from such a terrifying future, Hunter could not help but think that it all seemed rather too easy. There was no doubt in his mind that Wallace Whittemore would deny the allegations. "Could I use those as proof, should I need to?" Hunter enquired, pointing to the deeds.

"For the disorderly house, yes, you can, sir. With regards to the bigamy, you will need the two young ladies, or at least one of them, to testify, but what would seal Gastrell's fate would be the marriage certificates."

Jackson remained quiet amidst all of the discussion, an intense frown furrowing his brow.

"I will need you to get those for me as soon as possible, but there is something that is bothering you, Jackson. What is it?" Hunter had never seen the man look so perplexed. His frown had deepened by the second since the moment he had arrived.

"Those ladies, Carlisle. Can't we help them? I hate leaving them there. Your lady doesn't deserve it, but neither do they," Jackson remarked thoughtfully.

"Then we have two more ladies that need to be rescued. Jackson, you and Hobbs retrieve the ladies from that dreadful place, and, Baldry, I will trust you to retrieve copies of the marriage certificates."

Dipping a quill into the inkpot on his desk, Hunter quickly scribbled an address on a piece of parchment and handed it to Jackson. "Take the ladies whom you can rescue from that place to this address. Make sure they have everything they need and will be comfortable before you leave them there. Tell the servants they are to treat them with respect."

Jackson nodded as Hunter began to write another missive, this time to Audrey. He needed to see her simply because he wanted to and because it was time he told her a little of what was going on. "As soon as you have everything, return here. Please be quick about it," Hunter encouraged, watching the gentlemen leave.

Audrey's eyes narrowed as they curiously roved over the fixtures and fittings of her bedchamber. There were no signs of anything amiss. Yet, she mused, pursing her lips, she had never witnessed the sun manage to filtrate the drapes with quite such vigour at an early hour before, and she was rather certain that Ivy would not have simply left her to sleep later than her usual time. The maid knew that it was the quiet of the early hours that had aided Audrey to sneak out if she so wished.

However, despite all of that, Audrey had the terrible feeling that she had quite overslept. *But why?*

Audrey sat bolt upright. "*Ivy,*" she breathed. *'What if the confrontation with her father had seen to it that the young woman had been dismissed?'* she panicked quietly, becoming a little terrified by the attention-seeking drumming of her heart at the base of her throat. "Dear lord, what have I done? No, no, no."

Swinging her legs out from beneath the coverlet, Audrey's feet hit the floor, making quick work of the distance between her bed and the bedchamber door. Curling her fingers tightly around the cold brass doorknob, she tugged.

Nothing.

She twisted.

Nothing.

A frustrated growl scratched the back of her throat as she rattled the door on its hinges, yet the dratted thing remained stoic and steady within its frame. "Ivy, are you there?" she called out. "Ivy, please answer me."

"*Ivy, please answer me,*" Wallace Whittemore mocked from beyond the door.

At the sound of her father's ridiculing voice, Audrey staggered backwards. She had never heard her father sound quite so petty. Enraged and hoping the action would free her, she threw herself with all the force she could muster at the door. The side of her arm ached with the impact, but she ignored it. "Please let me out, Father," she pleaded somewhat pleasantly through her gritted teeth. She should have held her tongue last night, she realised. What with her father's efforts to imprison her, she had evidently taken matters too far, and now, according to the stubborn door guarded by the man beyond it, she may never get to know the full extent of her dream.

"There is no use calling for your maid, and there is no use trying to sound so obedient now. Ivy works for me, and as for you, you had your chance, girl."

Closing her eyes, Audrey pressed her forehead against the wood. "Please, Papa."

"It's Papa now, is it? Oh dear, whenever will you learn? It must be the incompetence of the female mind," Wallace Whittemore drawled. "However, I am not an unfair man, so I shall explain. You see, everything belongs to me here—the house, the trinkets, the servants, the paintings, the rugs, and the flooring. Your mother as well, and of course, then there is *you*. You belong to me. Therefore, what I say is what will be. You may as well adjust your frail mind to the fact and have a rest because the next time you step out of your bedchamber, you will walk directly down the staircase and into an awaiting carriage. Lord Gastrell can deal with you until the marriage union so that I do not have to."

A chill touched Audrey's skin, tacky and

penetrating as it trickled through her veins. "Father, please!" she begged, slamming her fists against the door in desperation.

"Tsk, tsk, tsk. Temper, temper, Audrey. You should relax while you can, for I believe it will be quite an uncomfortable ride to London."

Audrey placed her back against the door, sliding lower until her bottom joined her feet on the solid floor, where she simply stared at everything yet at nothing at all. Her chest heaved in and out, though no breath seemed to be enough. It was as though the room was closing in on her, she panicked rather unhelpfully. Slowly, she began to count, each number a step upward towards what she hoped would be a calmer and more cooperative mind, for she felt as though she was on a crumbling precipice; one wrong move and her father would have his way. The man would quite willingly, she realised, place his hands on her back and push her into the depths of hell.

"Think, Audrey," she whispered. "You are not in that carriage yet." Wallace Whittemore did not have the right to have the final say for her future. That right was hers and hers alone, she reminded herself, and, unless memory served her incorrectly, then she was quite certain she was already betrothed to the rather handsome brooding baron next door. She would simply have to find another way to escape.

"There's a missive for Miss Audrey," a maid

announced, stepping closer to the door. "May I give it to her?" she enquired, sounding rather excited at the prospect of that one small task.

"No!"

The boom of her father's voice thumped against Audrey's door in time with her heart as the tormented organ slammed against the wall of her chest. What if the missive was from Flossie or even perhaps Hunter? she considered. If her father was this adamant to keep her prisoner, she was certain that he would not even allow her to leave with Lady Esme as had previously been planned. There was really only one way out of the room, she realised with a nervous gulp. She had to climb out of the window.

Donned in tweed breeches, waistcoat and cap, men's hessian boots that were a tad too large, and an ivory shirt, Audrey perched on the windowsill. "Breathe, you ninny," she chastised herself, trying to calm the tremble in her limbs. She had climbed trees her entire life so she could certainly climb down one more.

Audrey twisted her body, placing one foot on the branch directly below the window, then flung her arms around the trunk as though she were greeting a long-lost friend. Her breaths came hard and heavy as she closed her eyes, attempting to regain control of her nerves. Everything she was feeling – fear, anxiety, hurt, and even guilt over her current deception – thrummed in her veins.

"You can do this," she assured herself. Loosening her grasp on the rough bark, Audrey slowly but surely picked her way from branch to branch, feeling rather relieved that she did not have layers of petticoats and skirts to hinder her movements, and when she was as close to the ground as the tree's branches would take her, she dropped, landing abruptly on her feet.

Keeping low to the ground, out of sight of the windows, Audrey moved around the perimeter of the house towards the servants' side where, with the tilt of her cap over her pale green eyes and a gentle, practised swagger, she simply morphed into Aubrey.

Ivy's feet scrabbled over the uneven land as she hurried across Whittemore grounds towards the Carlisle estate. Still reeling from how her employer's despicable behaviour had escalated and witnessing how he had imprisoned dear Miss Audrey, she knew she could not allow it to continue. She had spent the entirety of her years under his employment keeping quiet and adhering to his demands, but when she knew that Audrey had found the wonderful opportunity of a happy marriage to Lord Carlisle instead of the repugnant Gastrell, she knew she would do anything—*risk anything*—to ensure that Miss Audrey would have her dream.

Panting, she knocked on the servants' door.

A tall, kindly looking gentleman answered.

"Please," she rasped, leaning over with one hand pressed into the soft flesh just above her knee as she tried to catch her breath. "Please give this to Lord Carlisle. It's very important."

"Of course. Can I say who it is from?"

"He won't know me, sir, but I come on behalf of a Miss Whittemore."

The gentleman nodded.

"When I say on behalf, what I mean is that she doesn't know, but he will want to see it, sir."

"Leave it with me, miss," Elkins smiled, perusing the folded missive.

"Much obliged, sir. Thank you."

As Ivy hurried away, back toward the Whittemore residency, Elkins pocketed the missive and headed back up the stairs. He had only come down to the servants' quarters to escape Lady Carlisle and that dreadful Lady Vanessa, and it seemed that it had been rather fortuitous, for he wondered who may have, or if indeed anyone would have, opened the door to the rather concerned maid.

Elkins had rather hoped that Lady Carlisle and her guffawing friend may have taken the hint and left by the time he returned to his usual spot in the house – he wouldn't have even minded if they had merely ventured to any other room in the property – but there they were as bold as brass, and now Lady Vanessa was apparently admiring a ring on her finger.

Elkins rolled his eyes and remained quiet.

Audrey stared up at the entrance of Carlisle House, wondering whether Hunter would be home or whether she would be turned away. This was the first time she had considered that her disguise as a stable hand may have had some flaws, and such thoughts served only to make her reluctant to knock. However, she realised that she had been left with very little option but to try.

At the third knock, the Carlisle butler slowly pulled open the door. "Yes?" he drawled, confusion settling in the lines of his face.

"I'm the new stable hand," Audrey explained, deepening her voice. "Lord Carlisle told me I should come to the front entrance," she added quickly, afraid that he would send her away.

"Very well, but I am afraid Lord Carlisle is in a meeting at the moment, and there are others who wish to see him." The butler eyed the two women, staring nosily at her with pinched lips. "Yet if you are happy to wait," he continued with a smile, "I am quite certain that Lord Carlisle would be content for you to remain here with the other guests."

Audrey noted the butler's sly expression of displeasure aimed at the two women before he turned to her with a wry smile and slightly elevated brows.

"I am happy to wait if you are certain that you do not mind, sir?" Audrey replied.

"Believe me," he whispered conspiratorially, "I will be glad of the sane company."

Audrey grinned.

Carlisle House was rather formidable, she thought as her eyes wandered up the walls. She had been trying to divert her attention, but the two ladies currently in the process of a rather vigorous discussion kept drawing her eyes back to them. The eldest lady shot a distasteful glance at Audrey. Pretending that she hadn't, she turned to the young, pretty woman at her side and smiled primly.

"Do you think so?" the older woman queried.

Audrey rather thought the woman had raised her voice an octave for her benefit.

"Oh, indeed. Hunter is a fine gentleman. A credit to you, as it were, Lady Carlisle," the pretty woman tittered in reply as she held her hand in front of her face and admired the ring on her finger.

The light caught the glint off the stone at its centre, and Audrey could not take her eyes off it other than to look at the young woman. If the older lady was Lady Carlisle, she ruminated, then who was the younger one? And why were they both waiting for Hunter?

"You, boy."

The sound of Lady Carlisle's voice snapped Audrey to attention. Realising she had been thoroughly staring at the younger lady, she began to worry her lower lip. "Me?" she queried nervously with a gentle press of her finger at the centre of her chest for emphasis.

"I do not see any other *boy* here, do you, Lady Vanessa?" The older lady scoffed in mockery, gently nudging the younger woman at her side.

"Apologies, my lady," Audrey ground out. The venom on Lady Carlisle's sharp, drawn features cast a dusting of understanding upon why Hunter found his mother so abysmal. Indeed, it seemed the woman was a female version of Audrey's father.

"Apology not accepted," Lady Carlisle spat, thrusting out her bosom and tilting her chin higher. "You," she continued, glaring down the bridge of her nose, "need to learn your place."

Quite unsure what Hunter's mother was referring to, Audrey simply glanced toward the butler. It appeared he preferred to rearrange trinkets on the sideboard rather than get involved, not that she blamed him, of course.

"Look at your betters when they are speaking," Lady Carlisle seethed.

"Apologies, Lady Carlisle," Audrey rasped with mortification. Had she been dressed as Audrey Whittemore, she perhaps would have retaliated, but her guise as Aubrey and what it offered her was too precious to risk so she turned her attention to the ladies, unwittingly permitting her eyes to dart from one to the other.

"And you can refrain from gawking at Lady Vanessa. It seems to me that you believe yourself far above your station, boy," Agatha Carlisle hissed. "Lady Vanessa is far too good for some lowly stable hand, and, besides, she is to be married."

Lady Vanessa smiled spitefully as she held up her gloved hand to reveal a glittering ruby ring in proof of Lady Carlisle's declaration.

"Congratulations," Audrey offered. Nausea began to creep up her insides and burn below her ribs.

"She doesn't need your congratulations, boy, when it is your employer whom she will marry. *My son.*"

Audrey's heart rattled in her chest. She could have sworn that she had heard it crack but then it seemed to plummet directly into her stomach. *She couldn't breathe*, she thought, flattening her palm over her bosom. *She had to leave.* "If you will excuse me," she whispered in short gasps as she backed out of the door. "I just remembered that I—" Before she could consider what it was that she should offer them as an excuse, Audrey turned on her heel and fled the manor.

As the sky mocked her mood, the blue bruised

by the burgeoning grey clouds, Audrey struggled to contemplate the vast divergency between the two scenarios. Last night she was certain that Hunter wished to marry her. After all, he had said it in front of everyone. Yet, now, it seemed that he was betrothed to the spiteful yet beautiful Lady Vanessa. Nothing made any sense at all. Nevertheless, she realised, there really was only one choice left for her that was at least somewhat palpable – she had to retrieve Athena from the stable and get as far as possible away from Whittemore estate.

After summoning the footman to deliver the carefully scribed missive to Audrey, Hunter had spent thirty more minutes confined to his study, simply in an attempt to avoid having to face his mother and the limpet of a lady who seemed permanently attached to the woman's side. It was never a good moment for Lady Carlisle to arrive, but she really had outdone herself this time.

"Sir." Elkins stepped into the room quickly. "I apologise for not knocking, but I think you should know that one of the Whittemore maids delivered this." The butler held out the folded parchment.

"When did this arrive, Elkins?" Hunter enquired as his eyes scanned the contents of the note. It appeared that the scoundrel Whittemore had locked Audrey in her bedchamber. Hunter's jaw tensed as fury towards the man slithered in poisonous paths through the very centre of his bones.

"I'm not quite sure, sir. It could have been an hour ago or perhaps two. I didn't want to disturb you, sir, as you were very busy. Was that wrong of me?"

Clamping his jaw around his desire to bellow at anyone and everyone, Hunter shook his head. "No, Elkins, you were correct in your assumption. I was indeed busy." *'Never too busy for this, though,'* he thought, giving the folded parchment a quick flap in the air and then sliding it into his pocket.

"Thank heavens." Elkins smiled and simply waited in the doorway, expectantly.

"Lady Carlisle is still here, isn't she?" Hunter groaned, running the palm of his hand down his face.

"I'm afraid so, sir. She and Lady Vanessa seem quite keen to see you."

"Thank you, Elkins. I will see to them now. Sadly, any attempts at avoidance will be rather pointless, for I shall have to pass them on my way over to the Whittemore's estate anyhow."

Rising from his chair, Hunter tugged on the hem of his jacket to straighten the fabric against his muscular frame. The simple action with the broadening of his shoulders made him appear as he had hoped, he noted as he caught his reflection in the window. Perfect. One can never appear too intimidating. In fact, he thought he looked somewhat terrifying. Of course, it was merely meant as a parting gift for his mother and the satin-swathed hyena. He did so hope that they would appreciate his efforts.

The heels of Hunter's boots clacked on the stone floor. "Are you still here, Lady Carlisle?" he drawled, pulling at the cuffs of his sleeves dismissively. "You know, I sometimes think you still believe that you live here," he added sardonically, peering down his nose at the pinched-faced woman.

She tittered. "He is always jesting. It is just as I said, Lady Vanessa. You and he are very similar."

Lady Vanessa batted her eyelashes. He supposed she was attempting to appear flirtatious and pretty, but it merely appeared to make her look as though she was being repetitively poked in both eyes.

"I have an errand to run. I assume you can see yourselves out." Without allowing them a moment to speak, Hunter strode towards and out of the door.

"Sir!"

"I will be back in a little while, Elkins," Hunter called back as he pressed on, wishing for the acidic temper towards his mother to remain merely so he could add it to his barrelling fury toward Wallace Whittemore. It was precisely what he required to clarify a few new rules with the blackguard. *Although*, he considered, he would have to keep control of a little of it, for he certainly could not burst in blurting out everything he knew of the snivelling weasel and Gastrell. Those cards, he decided, had to remain close to his chest. One slip of the tongue and he may end up rendering every detail he had sought on the man absolutely pointless. He wasn't much of a card player, but Hunter was quite certain that one should never show their hand until it was indeed the perfect time to do so.

"Oof!"

Hunter stepped back with surprise, bringing his hand to his chest as he looked down to see a rather breathless maid staring up at him. She was flapping her hand about in the air, short bursts of sound emanating from her throat as she breathlessly tried to compose herself.

"Audrey's maid?" Hunter queried, hoping he could assist the maid a little.

She nodded profusely. "Ivy," she gasped.

"Don't worry, I have your note here. I am on my way to have a word with Whittemore now."

"No, don't!" Ivy exclaimed. "There's no point."

"Of course, there is a point," he argued. "Miss Whittemore has been imprisoned in her chambers. I will not have her treated so poorly."

"She's not there anymore," Ivy practically squealed, then looked behind her and gestured for

Hunter to follow her back towards Carlisle House.

"I hope you are not doing this on behalf of your employer," Hunter said, narrowing his eyes at the maid. The thought that the young woman may be misleading him was perhaps a little unjust, yet he hadn't quite deciphered who he could trust and if indeed he wanted to trust anyone where Audrey was concerned. All he really wished for was to take her away from her despicable father so he could keep her safe in his care. He didn't give one whit for propriety, for, with the danger Audrey was in, propriety was exceedingly low on his list of what he should adhere to.

"Definitely not, sir," Ivy replied with an affronted expression. "I can't bear the way that pompous old windbag treats Miss Audrey."

"I am glad to hear it." As a drop of rain splashed beneath his eye, Hunter gestured towards the entrance. "Tell me everything, if you please."

Hunter ascended the front steps of Carlisle House, stepping inside and closing the door behind them as Ivy chatted nervously beside him.

"... so you see, there was nothing I could do because Mr Whittemore had taken the key to Audrey's room, but then when I lied and told him that she was casting up her accounts and he best see to it, he shoved the key in my hand and said that I was employed to see to such tasks and not him, which was exactly what I wanted him to do."

Hunter gazed down at the rambling maid with a gentle expression of impatience.

"Apologies, Lord Carlisle," she continued as they stopped in the middle of the foyer in front of the butler, Lady Carlisle, and Lady Vanessa.

Nodding to Elkins, Hunter turned his back on the other two ladies, allowing Ivy to continue.

"The point is, my Lord, Miss Audrey has gone," Ivy whispered, peering over his shoulder to ensure the ladies in the background weren't eavesdropping.

"Gone?"

"The window was open, my lord."

Hunter dragged his fingers through his dishevelled hair. *Why hadn't she come here?* he wondered. "Come with me," he beckoned to the maid.

"If I might have a word, sir?" Elkins interjected.

"Can it not wait, Elkins?" Hunter grumbled.

"I don't believe it can, sir." The butler shuffled closer, creating a small circle with his employer and the maid. "Someone called while you were in your study, sir. At first, I assumed they were one of your employees, but, despite their attire, I noted that the stable hand appeared a little feminine, shall we say? Could this be the missing young lady?"

Hunter and Ivy glanced at one another.

"Was she in a tweed suit and cap, sir?" the maid enquired.

"She was indeed."

"Where did she go, Elkins?"

"Well, Lady Carlisle decided to take it upon herself and accuse the young lady, who she assumed was a young man, of *gawking* at Lady Vanessa."

Hunter's eyes darkened as they flicked to his mother, throwing fiery darts of hatred at her back.

"You should also be aware, sir, that Lady Carlisle thought she would announce that you were betrothed to Lady Vanessa."

"What the—" Hunter broadened his shoulders, his eyes burning with rage as he turned fully towards the two ladies who were now tittering privately with one another.

"You haven't got time for that, sir," Ivy pleaded, grabbing Hunter's arm before he tore away from the small circle to spit fire at the woman behind him.

"You're absolutely right, Ivy," he admitted with a slow exhale. "You know, I can see why you are important to Audrey. Being aware of that and the fact that Whittemore will be furious when he finds out that you came here, I believe it is imperative for you to remain in this house with us."

Ivy's shoulders lowered with relief.

"I am going to look for her," he continued.

"Elkins, while I am gone, I want you to prepare one of the rooms upstairs for Ivy. Any clothes she may require, you will either need to source them from here or send the footman over to the Whittemore residence. I do not believe it would be safe for her to return now."

Elkins nodded. "Very good, sir."

"Word to the wise, Ivy," Hunter whispered conspiratorially. "If you value your sanity, I would suggest that you refrain from conversing with either of the two ladies behind us."

The maid chuckled. "Understood."

"Right, I don't know how long I will be, but I am going to find Miss Whittemore and bring her home to us where she will be safe. And, Elkins?"

"Yes, sir?"

"Lady Carlisle and Lady Vanessa better be gone before I get back."

Chapter Twenty One

"It's just us now, Athena," Audrey announced quietly as she secured the saddle, the tremble in her limbs being the only sign of the shock and disappointment prickling through every nerve in her body. "I warn you now, though, I have no idea where we should go nor where we will stay, but the coins I have pocketed will hopefully keep us fed and dry most of the way." A creak-like sound twisted at the back of Audrey's throat in her desperate attempt to swallow against the slow escalation of her emotions, ones that were enthusiastically threatening to rip her apart and make her drop to her knees. She had never experienced anything before that had made her heart ache with such ferocity.

"*Stop it,*" she grumbled to herself, pressing her knuckles into her breastbone. That pain wasn't what caring for someone was supposed to feel like, she thought. It couldn't be. If it were, then why would people even bother? Audrey would have walked away from Hunter the moment he approached her in Lady Chilcott's garden if she had known such a terrible fate awaited her, for only a self-inflicting sadist would have remained when in possession of such knowledge.

Mustering all the strength she could, Audrey placed her foot in the stirrup, pushing up and swinging her other leg over Athena until she was sitting comfortably in the saddle. It seemed her body was more willing to move than her heart was willing to allow itself a little dignity, for while the organ at the centre of her chest hid like a coward, nestled beneath her ribs, it was she who was taking great effort to rein in her tears and stop the dratted trembling that achieved nothing but to hinder her.

Audrey clenched her jaw and closed her eyes. *'Audrey Whittemore, you are an idiot,'* she inwardly chastised. Yet, as her mind pulled her back to the night before, mentally kicking and screaming at being reminded of what she would never have, Audrey couldn't help but wonder whether it had all been her fault. Had she really been so foolish to have believed what Hunter had said to her? Or perhaps she had misinterpreted a gallant gesture, an act, as it were, that had only been meant for a single night as a ruse? There was, of course, the possibility that caused her the most pain, and that was that Hunter had simply changed his mind about her. However, there was a small part of her – *oh, ok, perhaps it was a very large part if she were being honest* – that wanted to believe that the betrothal between the man who she cared deeply for and Lady Vanessa was all a lie and that Lady Carlisle was simply being malicious. Was Lady Carlisle that cruel? Yet, Audrey considered, the woman thought Audrey was a man, so then that theory was utterly null and void.

Audrey inhaled, drawing the air into her lungs in a staggered breath. Her mother had been right, she thought, swiping her hand over her cheek to wipe away a tear. She was in love with Hunter. She had had friends who had walked out of her life, and even though she had felt a little hurt, she had never felt like this. *This*, she mused, was utter agony.

"Come, Athena," Audrey announced bravely, pressing her legs gently at the sides of the mare. "We really cannot stay here any longer."

The horse brayed in apparent disagreement, then reluctantly trotted forward as though they were on a leisurely morning ride across the estate.

"Please Athena. If Father catches me, I may never see you again."

Athena's ears perked up as though she understood, then gently increased her speed, cantering towards the unmade path that led to the main road.

"That's it, my dear, but maybe a fraction faster, if you wouldn't mind," Audrey whispered soothingly.

Athena brayed once more, continuing her leisurely canter with a snort of defiance. Apparently, Audrey was merely talking to herself, she realised, twisting her lips into a small smile at her own madness. "You really do need to be faster than this, Athena," Audrey grumbled, shifting her bottom on the saddle with a hint of impatience. Her legs pressed again in the horse's sides as she clucked in encouragement.

Tangling her fingers in the reins, Audrey held on tight as her body was jolted backward, then quickly tugged on the thin leather ribbons to right herself. She leaned slightly forward, poised poetically over the long, sleek line of the horse's mane as Athena sped down the paths at a wind-defying gallop. "That's it, Athena. Good girl." Freedom filtered through Audrey's flesh and whipped in gusts of wind under the collar of her shirt. It billowed beneath the thin cotton and against her stays, then tunnelled down the sleeves, delicately ballooning the garment around her torso. The exhilarating moment was short-lived yet thoroughly intoxicating.

The fork in the road did not offer Audrey a wealth of choice of where she should go next, and with such a limited decision, she really did not need to take her time to consider her options. Instead, she simply steered Athena in the opposite direction from London. Her father had stated that Lord Gastrell had wished to take her there the moment she would be released from her bedchamber-cum-prison. She huffed at the thought, which was soon followed by an unexpected hiccup arriving on the tail ends of her silent, waning tears. The utter indignance at the very idea that she would travel so much as an inch in the direction of which her father and Gastrell wished her to, stiffened Audrey's spine and unwittingly offered her a little respite from what pained her the most.

The sound of Athena's hooves pounding the ground thrummed in time with Audrey's heart as she willed her rather unhelpful new habit to dwell to cease. She had lost track of the hours that had passed yet could quite easily say with considerable certainty that she had carried the weight of her troubles for the entire journey so far, and it was not helping at all. Indeed, dwelling evidently did not change a thing. It only seemed to have encouraged a terrible throb in her temples. Nevertheless, the unwanted image of Hunter with the beautiful golden-haired Lady Vanessa seemed to be seared at the forefront of her mind, forbidding Audrey to forget how she had lost everything she had begun to dream of. "It is done. Done, done, done, Audrey. Nothing you can do about it," she consoled herself quietly. Her breath faltered as her heart skipped a beat, but she quickly pushed the burgeoning revelation of memories aside before she began dissecting every detail of the night before and those of the day for what must have been the umpteenth time. *'What good would it do?'* she considered with a shake of her head.

A plump bead of rain dropped heavily onto the back of Audrey's bare hand. She watched it trail over her skin and disappear into the fabric of her breeches below, then lifted her gaze skyward. Despite the darkening, rain-threatening clouds overhead, there were at least a few more hours before nightfall, yet it wouldn't be wise to get caught out in *that* again, she contemplated begrudgingly. Heat drifted over her body as she shivered with the memory of Hunter licking the rain from her lips. "That's enough of that, Audrey Whittemore," she admonished herself.

As if the rain had simply been testing Audrey's reaction with a single drop and had come to the ridiculous notion that more would be welcome, the heavens tore open. Torrential showers of earth-scented water rained down, rapidly seeping through the ivory of Audrey's shirt and dripping slowly off the darkened strands of hair lingering at the sides of her face. Athena had halted; her only movement, the rise and fall of her flanks as she awaited her next command.

"Just a little further now, Athena," Audrey crooned with a cluck and gentle press on the horse's sides. She leaned forward, closer to the heat of the mare's body, shielding her face from the weather as she whispered in Athena's downturned ear. "There is an inn up ahead. I know you can see it. If you and I are discreet, I am sure we will find somewhere close by to shelter in and rest."

Of course, Audrey could have afforded a room, she supposed, but there were several reasons why she wouldn't – the first one being that she didn't trust anyone else with Athena. The second was that she wasn't *that* confident in her disguise. And the third was that her ivory shirt was somewhat drenched and translucent, and she did not even want to know what delights were on display for the entire world to gawp at.

Calmly, Audrey encouraged Athena onwards, stopping only once more as thunder rolled angrily across the sky, startling them both. "Shh, shh, shh. It's alright, my sweet Athena," she soothed. "Let's go this way," she added, leading the mare through a glaringly obvious gap in the tall hedgerow a few yards before the inn. The horse trotted willingly along the side of the property over the sticky soil and sporadically grass-covered earth while Audrey threw a quick glance into the open stable. They were, as she had assumed, occupied, and there certainly would not have been any place for her to hide.

"Just a bit further, Athena." Audrey settled her tired gaze on a rather wonky-looking shed, loitering to the left of a dense copse of trees. She scanned the area, ignoring the way in which her clothes clung to her body with the weight of the unrelenting rain. The weather puffed out its chest, battling forward, attacking the trees and bushes, sending an almighty gale careening toward the wonky shed, where it slapped the wooden walls of its rickety-looking frame. Unfazed, the rather deceptive, wonky building remained stoic and sturdy. It was rather perfect indeed, Audrey thought.

The timber door, set at a rather misguided angle upon its hinges, scraped through the earth as Audrey dragged it open. Hay whipped about her booted feet, agitated by an enthusiastic breeze stirring up the loose, golden stalks scattered over the wooden floor. As she ventured further inside, her eyes scrutinised the interior for any flaws. It was the soft bales of hay that eventually coaxed both she and Athena to the centre of the small shed. *Rather prickly, indeed,* Audrey considered with a sigh, yet, nevertheless, she had wished to rest on something at least a little soft to the touch, and at that very moment they looked deliciously soft to her and merely delicious to Athena.

Grateful for the meagre offering, Audrey closed the door behind them.

Hunter pulled on Galileo's reins as he faced the junction in the lonely road. With the tumult of theories as to what his betrothed must possibly think of him after his mother's lies, the very idea that Audrey had simply left without a word and could possibly have headed into London turned his stomach. It would not be safe for her there despite the apparent attire Elkins had said she had been wearing, for London was a beast to its uninvited guests. However, Hunter considered, Audrey was not some foolish chit, for she was indeed savvy enough to realise that her clothes would not blend in with the blacks and greys of the ton. It was perhaps that which inspired the belief in him that she had travelled in the opposite direction. Inhaling deeply as he sent up a prayer that his assumptions were correct, Hunter steered his gelding away from London, heading deeper into the countryside, toward its estates, quaint public houses, inns, and uneven roads.

Buttoning his thick overcoat at the top, Hunter stared up at the heavens, cursing as a heavy drop of rain flicked his eye. "Blast it," he fussed, wiping the unwanted moisture away. He was in no mood for anything, no matter how small, to add to his misery. The concern pressing at the centre of his chest for Audrey's safety was more than sufficient to contend with. It seemed the chit had had the power to pull him out into the blasted weather in a state of panic. He had never panicked over the absence of a woman before. It was rather strange indeed. "Where did you go?" he grumbled, scraping his fingers through his hair.

Wherever she was, Hunter thought, rolling his shoulders to ease the tension burying itself into his muscles, she was most likely drenched from the rain. It had been almost two hours for him—more for her, of course, he discerned, considering the time gap between her fleeing Carlisle House and his departure. She was probably at one of the inns, he considered carefully. Unease at her being alone in the company of so many men crawled over his skin. He had to hurry.

By the time Hunter reached the first inn, drenched is not quite the word one would use for the state of his attire. Perhaps *sopping wet* would be more apt, for he thoroughly dripped with every step. As he reached the bar of the inn's taproom, Hunter remained standing. If Audrey wasn't there, he had to keep looking.

"What can I do you for, my lord?" the innkeeper enquired, offering Hunter a broad smile as he draped a cloth over his shoulder.

"I'm looking for someone, and I am wondering whether you may have seen them," Hunter offered, ignoring the urge to peel the drenched fabric of his shirt away from his now clammy flesh. "But before I enquire further, I was wondering whether you had somewhere for my horse to rest for a while. It would be truly appreciated, for if the person I am looking for is not here, we will need to set off again soon."

The innkeeper's eyes roved over the throng of patrons. It seemed that everybody from near and far had gathered beneath the inn's roof and out of the rain. "The stable is full, my lord, I'm afraid. However," the innkeeper added thoughtfully, "if you don't mind somewhere a little less equipped, there is a small shed behind 'ere. I'll admit, it looks a little dishevelled, but looks can be deceiving, for that old contraption is as sturdy as the inn itself."

"Thank you, that is most appreciated," Hunter replied. "As for the person I am searching for," Hunter continued.

"Go on," the man encouraged.

"I wonder whether he may have been here or is still here. He is wearing tweed and, most likely, a flat cap, tilted at an angle like so," Hunter added, tipping his own hat in demonstration.

"Ain't seen anyone like that 'ere, my lord. Sorry. I'll keep a lookout for him, though." The innkeeper walked around behind the bar and proceeded to lift a glass. "Would you like a tot of brandy to warm you, my lord?"

"Perhaps once I have seen to my horse, sir, then I shall take you up on that. Thank you."

Hunter chewed the inside of his cheek as his mind sifted through the places he was acquainted with, ones he thought Audrey may have passed or, perhaps, if he was fortunate, may have stopped at. She wouldn't wander aimlessly, he was quite sure of that.

Hunter curled his body slightly away from the ghastly weather and slipped through the door-sized gap in the hedge, where he wandered towards the back of the building, exactly as the innkeeper had said to do. *'Good lord,'* he mused with a smirk, *'the man was not lying when he said it was dishevelled.'* Tilting his head awkwardly to the side, Hunter mimicked the angle of the rickety shed positioned by a dense copse of trees, wondering how or why the innkeeper had said that it was as sturdy as the inn itself. Perhaps he had misheard him, he considered as he continued his walk with Galileo towards the contraption, determined to inspect the wooden building before he simply left the poor gelding to his fate.

Athena snickered at the sound of hooves, whilst Audrey held her breath at the audible tread of boots. A horse she could contend with, but the thought of having to come face to face with a person? A strange man? *That* was what was making her heart gallop faster than Athena knew how to. "We have to be very quiet, Athena," she whispered as she slowly stepped backward against the wall, pressing her existence into the arms of the hungry shadows.

Tips of boot-covered masculine toes appeared in the narrow gap of the door. Audrey's heart slowed from a gallop, then began to punch and thud against her ribcage. Her breathing was oh so very loud, she noted, placing her hand over her mouth. She might as well have stayed where she was, she thought, for with her heavy breaths scraping the air, her effort to stay hidden was utterly hopeless.

"Come, Galileo. Don't be so stubborn. You need to rest so we can look for Miss Whittemore again. That's it... Athena?"

Familiar blue eyes roved the interior of the shed, halting abruptly on Audrey's feet. Apparently, she was ridiculously incompetent in the art of hiding. Not that it mattered anymore, she considered. All that was holding her feet firm on the ground was sheer willpower, for, in truth, she wanted to fling herself out of the shadows and wrap herself around Hunter. She wouldn't, she told herself, for he was marrying Lady Vanessa, and he was probably only standing there looking deliciously handsome and edible out of a sense of duty. She sighed.

The looming, formidable figure of the gentleman, who she could not seem to muster much anger towards, strode into the shed. A smile curling his lips. "There you are, Audrey," Hunter drawled. "You know, you may as well come out now. It is not as though I haven't seen you."

Audrey inched forward. She did not know what she was going to say to him. Not that it mattered, for the ache in her throat was warning her that if she so much as attempted a syllable, the tears would flow and there would be nothing she could do to stop the dreadful little telltales from falling.

Hunter frowned. "Please come out, Audrey," he pleaded. "You have nothing to fear from me."

Audrey remained still. She must look like a sulking child, she thought. Vulnerability – that was what it was – raw like an open wound. She cleared her throat. "You should go back to her," she whispered hoarsely, then quickly pressed her lips together around her anguish.

"I am assuming you mean that blonde chit my mother trails beside her like a pet wherever she goes?" he queried, stepping closer.

Audrey nodded. "You shouldn't say such things like that about the woman you are going to marry," she corrected. "Your mother told me. She told me that you are betrothed to Lady Vanessa. She is very beautiful. Congratulations. You will have such beautiful babies. I can see why you would choose her and not me, especially with how my father has been. Perhaps it is he that has deterred you from marrying someone like me."

Hunter captured her lips, silencing Audrey's nervous, frightened ramble. It was in that sweet moment that her first tear escaped in front of him, snaking silently from the corner of her eye. He kissed her tenderly, even between the quiet sobs, arms slipping around her waist and drawing her into the light where she belonged.

"Stop, please," she breathed, reluctantly pulling away. "Those should only be for your betrothed." Audrey shivered, turning away from him and out of his comforting embrace. It took but only seconds for the cold to seep back into her bones.

With a heavy sigh, Hunter stepped closer, sliding his hands around her waist, pulling her backside flush against his hips. "And you believe that Lady Vanessa is my betrothed, is that correct?"

"I do... I don't want to, but I have it on good

authority."

Warm lips and breath caressed the nape of her neck. "If you consider my mother as good authority, Miss Whittemore, then perhaps you are not quite as sensible as I had assumed. My mother has been trying to matchmake me with that woman ever since I returned, despite my constant refusal and rather blunt hints for her to leave me alone. I even put Lady Carlisle in my brother's property so I could keep her at arm's length. Alas, the woman seems to be a new species of leech, for she simply will not relinquish her grasp on me.

"Besides, I had assumed that *you* were my betrothed, Audrey," Hunter drawled, turning her slowly to face him. "Unless, of course, you have changed your mind and wish to live your life constantly travelling out of your father's reach whilst dressed in this," he added with a smirk, running his finger beneath the fabric at the open collar of her shirt. His free hand cupped the cheek of her bottom with a gentle squeeze, "And these wonderfully naughty little breeches. Is that how you were thinking of living the remainder of your life, Audrey, and without me by your side?"

Audrey shook her head. "No, I don't want to live like that, and there's nothing I want more than a life with you by my side. I should never have believed your mother," she offered timidly with a pale blush.

Hunter nodded. "I am glad to hear it, and

as far as my mother is concerned, please don't blame yourself. You have much to learn about Lady Carlisle, my love, and you shall have plenty of time to do so as my wife." Hunter affectionately brushed the tip of his nose against Audrey's as she closed her eyes with a soft smile. "However, for now, I believe we should get you dry and warm, and for that, we may need to outdo my mother by embarking on a little deception of our own."

"We are in need of a room," Hunter exclaimed, averting his gaze from the young woman in his arms and looking about the inn for the innkeeper.

Audrey, comfortably nestled in Hunter's warm spice and rain-scented, rather athletically built yet tender embrace, had adopted what she and Hunter had hoped to be a vulnerable position, one that would have any intrigued onlookers believing she was indeed unconscious and in great need of care. She silently giggled, caught between utter glee and mischief as her body stirred against his.

"Be still, young lady," Hunter chided quietly from the corner of his mouth, "or you will have us thrown back into that god-awful shed with Galileo and Athena."

Audrey blew teasingly against his neck, sending heat straight to his loins. Hunter stopped and inhaled through clenched teeth. The wriggling of her soft curves against his body had been trying indeed, but with the sweet caress of her breath on his skin, he was having great difficulty walking.

"Just you wait, Miss Whittemore. You won't be able to escape me in a minute or two," he growled playfully, before quickly schooling his features.

"Ah, there you are, my lord," the innkeeper exclaimed, his expression creasing into a frown of concern. "And who do we have 'ere?" he queried.

"This is the young man I had been searching for. He was in the shed you kindly offered to let me use for my horse. I am afraid I need to ask for another favour from you, for this young man needs a warm bed and rest."

"Of course, my lord. Anything you need." Flustered and apologetic, the innkeeper called for another man behind the bar. "Get that room upstairs open at once, Billy." Turning back to Hunter, he continued, "It's the only room I have left, my lord. Not very big, but it's clean."

"I thank you, sir. Perhaps you would send up warm water for a bath and some towels, for I am afraid he may catch a chill."

"Of course, my lord, right away."

Alone in the privacy of the room, Hunter lowered Audrey onto the bed, pressing his lips briefly to hers. His body fizzed torturously with the memory of her in his arms. "I can't believe I nearly lost you," he remarked as he regained his full height.

"I'm sorry, Hunter," Audrey offered. She didn't know what else to say.

"That is not what I meant, Audrey. I just need you to promise me that you will never leave me again." The fear stretching beneath his ribcage and applying pressure upon his heart surprised Hunter. The dread of losing the woman in front of him was somewhat consuming. He was in love with her, he realised.

"I promise I will never leave you again, Hunter," she whispered as she reached out and slipped her hand into his.

A knock startled them both, forcing Audrey into acting mode as she dropped her hand back onto the bed and feigned unconsciousness once more.

Hunter swallowed, then straightened his posture. "You may enter," he called.

"My lord?"

"Yes?"

"Would you mind opening the door for me?"

Embarrassed, Hunter rushed to the door and pulled it open. "Forgive me," he offered. "I did not think."

"No trouble at all. We will have this bath set up for the young m—" Billy's eyes narrowed assessingly at the figure on the bed, then offered a cheeky wink in Hunter's direction.

It was official, Hunter thought with a conceding smile and a finger to his lips, that Audrey's disguise was utterly diabolical when she was every inch the perfect specimen of femininity. He had believed that it was only he who had seen through it, for his mother hadn't, and neither had the innkeeper. Yet, he supposed, the innkeeper had only seen her curled in his arms, and as for his mother, it was hardly surprising, for she never paid any attention to any person whom she believed to be beneath her. In truth, he was rather glad of the woman's ignorance on this occasion, although not of her viperesque tongue.

"Your secret is safe with me," Billy grinned, heading for the door.

At the sound of the door clicking shut behind Billy, Audrey bit her lower lip and opened one eye. Hunter was gazing at her, one eyebrow arched in amusement. "It seems you cannot fool everyone, Miss Whittemore," he drawled, grinning wolfishly. "Now, where were we?"

Chapter Twenty-Two

Audrey gazed around the candlelit room, silently acknowledging the small table at the side of the bed and the thick drapes blocking out the remaining light beyond the window. The bath had been wonderfully warm, and Hunter had been the perfect gentleman by adhering to the expectation of privacy, but as they lay on the bed, side by side, she found herself immersed in quite the conundrum, for he had given her a rather important decision to make.

Pondering whether she did indeed want to know what else her father and Lord Gastrell had been embroiled in and how perhaps it would affect her, Audrey could physically feel the deepening of the frown upon her features. She quickly turned and proceeded to shield her expression beneath Hunter's chin, hiding the evidence of her contemplations against the hard muscles of his chest. Audrey curled her arm around his warm, solid body, shifting closer to breathe him in. The fragrance of warm spice had never really meant anything before, yet since she had met Hunter, it had become the scent she sought.

A delicious fragrance, offering comfort and a sense of protection – the latter of which she had never known before. Audrey released a soft sigh.

Kissing the top of her head, Hunter's arm gently scooped Audrey closer toward him. "What are you thinking?" he enquired.

His husky voice tickled Audrey's skin, syphoning the air out of her lungs and softening her voice to but a whisper. "I am not entirely certain I want to know the details of my father's plans for me," she replied softly. "Yet," she added, "there is a part of me that is all too aware that, if I do not know, my curiosity may very well crush me."

"Apologies, Audrey. I should have realised and perhaps not have said anything."

"No, we must have trust between us, Hunter." Audrey tilted her head to look up at him. "I am glad that you thought to tell me."

"Would you like me to distract you for a little while?"

Before she had any chance to answer, Hunter twisted his body over the top of her, lowering his head until his lips met her ear. Scraping his teeth gently over the lobe, he sent a deep rumble sliding amorously along the arc of her neck. Audrey's nipples pebbled in response to the tiny beads of rapture scattering over her skin. The warmth of his large hand on her breast mimicked the heat between her thighs, transforming Audrey's single breath into an inviting moan as her core tightened around the thrill of their intimacy.

"Well, that's...aw...ful...ly... cha...rita...ble... of... you," she responded, her breath hitching at the naughty things he was doing with his lips.

"I thought so too." Hunter's mouth curled into an evident grin as he chuckled, his lips skimming, breath whispering, and laughter vibrating as they wickedly tantalised her flesh.

The man was going to give her a heart attack, Audrey mused as the organ beat wildly within, every thump resounding through her body as her breathing became heavy with need. "Very char...it...able...indeed. *Oh.*"

The button of Audrey's breeches popped open at the flick of Hunter's fingers, or at least that was what it felt like, Audrey noted in the puddle that was now her brain. It seemed the man was rather a dab hand at it, for it had only taken a matter of seconds, and her shirt was wide open, revealing her thin shift peeking over the top of her stays. That was not all that was peeking over the top of her stays either, she realised as Hunter growled approvingly. *Good heavens.* She had never known that torture could be so exquisite, she considered breathlessly as he devoured her with warm spice scented kisses from her neck to her collarbone and then down toward where her breasts threatened to spill over the top of her undergarments. Audrey could not deny that his response to the sight of her beneath her clothes sent a soaring heat through her veins and to her fingertips and toes. Her hands itched to explore him with as much attention as he was now exploring her.

Without asking – fair is fair, after all – Audrey set to work peeling Hunter's clothes from his body, her fingers trembling with anticipation as she loosened his cravat. "I can't concentrate," she giggled as his mouth covered hers, his tongue slipping greedily between her lips as her brain danced between tending to the silk of his cravat and the silk of his tongue.

"Then I appear to be succeeding in what I intended to achieve," Hunter teased, kissing the corner of her mouth. His fingers caressed where his lips had once been, their tips trailing simultaneously down both sides of her neck.

Audrey's body stretched in response, her back arching away from the bed beneath them, offering more of herself to the beautiful man above her. Even though her eyes had closed in the grips of ecstasy, she could not ignore Hunter's gaze roving her body with a gentle heat, the vulnerable yet dangerously enticing moment punctuated with a masculine groan as he scooped her breast from inside her shift and bared it to the cold air.

She was positively on fire. Any more of this and she would surely turn to ash. More to the point, she was never going to see what lay beneath Hunter's shirt if he kept doing such sinful things to her, Audrey mused, raising her arms up until her hands met his chest. To her surprise his shirt was open, muscles bared and pectorals twitching beneath her wandering palms. The man was either a magician or an octopus, Audrey did not know, but, she realised, she really didn't care. His torso was magnificent, as was the rest of him. She wondered whether sculptors ever felt as intrigued as she was, for Hunter's physique was divine, as though it had been sculpted by the gods.

"Audrey," Hunter drawled.

Eyes hazy with lust, Audrey focused on the handsome face above her. "Hmmm?"

Hunter grinned wolfishly. "If you want me to stop, you must say so now." His voice was deep and husky. "I don't want you to do anything you do not wish to, but there is something rather important you should be made aware of."

"What is it?" she queried.

Carefully and very slowly, Hunter placed his large hand over the back of hers and placed it at his crotch.

"Oh, my. I see. You mean this?" she teased, slipping her hand out very slowly between his hand and his manhood.

Hunter's jaw muscles tightened and twitched. All he could manage was a nod.

"I've been aware of it this entire time." Audrey didn't know what had come over her, but she liked it very much indeed. There was something about being with Hunter that instilled confidence in her. She unbuttoned his breeches in a taunting manner, all the while biting her lower lip and keeping her eyes on his. Hunter was trembling. It was empowering to witness him react to her touch in the same way that she had to his. "And no, I do not want you to stop, Hunter."

Hunter released his breath. "Good lord, woman. You are a minx. An exquisite, sultry, delectable minx."

Audrey curled her toes, recognising the hunger hidden in the vibrancy of his blue eyes as the dark, undeniable desire burned at their centres. Just one look, and she found herself wishing to cling to him, to feel her skin against his. She wanted him with every morsel of her being. Indeed, she had never felt anything so demanding in her entire life.

When the final garment fell to the floor – or perhaps it may have been simply thrown across the room and currently hanging from a random piece of furniture – Audrey drank every inch of Hunter in, from very fine head to handsome toe. A bolt of unadulterated lust burned up her spine as she pulled him close, the press of his desire against her thigh, as she wrapped her now bare legs around his waist.

Hunter paused. He had to do this properly, he reminded himself – although making love to her prior to marriage was not perhaps proper, it was as proper as he could manage. She needed to know before he ravished her what he wished for. He certainly couldn't have her doubting the reason for why he wished to marry her.

"What is it?" she enquired quietly, placing her hand delicately over his heart.

"Audrey Whittemore, I have already announced that we are to marry, but I do not believe I have ever asked you in the correct manner."

Audrey pressed her lips together, stifling a giggle as her eyes flicked from his face downward to their naked forms paused in the midst of intimacy.

Hunter laughed. "Yes, well, perhaps you may have a point."

Audrey wriggled beneath him. "So do you," she teased.

"Not helping, Miss Whittemore," he ground out. "Please refrain from moving until I have said what I wish to say."

"Apologies. Please go on."

"I want to ask you again, but this time with no obligation forced on you by society."

"I have never felt obligated," she interjected.

"Perhaps that is true. But I would also want you to know that I want to marry you before I truly ruin you and not because of it. So, Miss Audrey Whittemore, would you please do me the very great honour of becoming my wife?"

Audrey sighed, love entwining with lust in

the tension of her body. "Yes, Hunter. I would be honoured to marry you and be your wife." A cacophony of sounds played in Audrey's ears as the thudding of her heart beat beneath the brush of her breath upon the air. She did not think he could have said anything more thoughtful or perhaps more romantic to her, other than, of course, the three usual words – ones that she wished to say to him as well, but that time, she assured herself, would come eventually. Why was it that three simple words were so terribly frightening to utter? she wondered. She could hardly fault him, though, for she could not even propel the three short syllables from the back of her own throat when she wished to either.

"I am very, very, very glad to hear it," he drawled, nudging her gently as he thrust his hips towards her with a growl.

Hunter grunted as Audrey lightly scored her fingers up the back of his thighs and over his backside, the muscles spasming delectably beneath her touch, bringing their bodies closer together.

"Where were we, *my lord*?" Audrey queried, biting her lower lip enticingly.

Hunter couldn't speak. No other woman had ever made him breathless the way she did, not simply with her beneath him but with her smile and the light in her eyes. *Those eyes*. Desire swirled in the innocence of them and something much brighter, wholesome perhaps. He wondered how he would ever be able to breathe without her. Now that Audrey Whittemore had become very much his world, he was not going to let her go.

With pale, velvet skin beneath his fingers and lips, Hunter explored her body, listening to the soft moans drifting into the room as he travelled from her collarbone, over her breasts, creating a divide with the heat of his fingers down the centre of her abdomen. Every touch, followed by his tongue and lips until they met the mound of soft curls between her thighs.

"Oh," she gasped.

Blowing upon her most intimate area, Hunter ran his fingers up her thighs, encouraging her to relax as a whimper bled from her throat. "I will be gentle, I promise," he whispered, positioning himself between her thighs, his manhood nudging her gently. "We can wait," he offered.

"No. I trust you, Hunter. I need you," Audrey insisted, cupping his face with her hands.

"Not as much as I need you, my love."

Audrey had never felt so deliciously sated. Perhaps brimming with utter bliss was more apt, she mused as she nestled in the curve of Hunter's body at her back. It was as if he was the last piece of the puzzle that was her life, for nothing had ever felt as right as it did when she was with him. Her mouth tugged at the corners with contentment.

"What are you thinking?" Hunter queried,

pressing a quick kiss to the back of her shoulder.

"Just how happy I am with you. Happy and safe." Audrey turned to face him, curling her arms in front of her chest as he pulled her closer, her head fitting neatly beneath the strong line of his exquisitely scratchy, unshaven jaw. "Perhaps I am ready to hear what it is that my father had intended for me," she added apprehensively.

"I will only tell you if you really believe that you wish to hear it. Although I know you are quite aware of your father's capabilities, as it were, *this*... this is something that is far beyond the imagination of any good father or even merely a respectable one. I am afraid he makes my late father seem timid." Hunter's eyes searched her face, afraid such hurtful news would ruin everything they had just experienced.

"I would rather hear it when I feel safe here with you, Hunter." Audrey did not care one whit about Lord Gastrell, but the uncertainty and hesitance on Hunter's face told her that she should prepare herself for just how underhanded her father really could be. Grateful as she was that the man lying beside her had given her the opportunity to remain ignorant, she was quite aware that if he did not tell her, she may very well be consumed by the very imaginings of what it could be.

Hunter had taken his time, carefully considering his words as he relayed the news of what Wallace Whittemore and Lord Gastrell's plan for Audrey had been, all the while holding the young lady – once again dressed in breeches and shirt, resuming her guise as Aubrey – close as though she were about to shatter into tiny pieces. Audrey had flinched, and Hunter had felt her frown against his chest, yet there had been no tears. It seemed that Wallace Whittemore had not hidden his cruelty but merely the truth of his intentions.

"I am not entirely certain what it is I am supposed to say to that," Audrey confessed as she pulled away from him and wandered toward the window. "Admittedly, I did not think he had arranged all of that for me, but that was probably because doing something so dreadful to someone, as he and Lord Gastrell had intended to subject me to, would never so much as cross my mind. However, I know my father, and it is not at all surprising."

"Then, my love, I shall make plans for us to return to Carlisle House." Hunter announced, feeling rather in awe of how incredibly strong she was. "Home."

"Home," Audrey muttered, unaware that she had spoken the word aloud.

"Yes. There should be a carriage outside the inn for when we are ready to leave here," Hunter drawled as he approached her from behind and wrapped his strong arms around her waist. "Your home is with me now, young lady. You will not have to see your father again."

Audrey could not deny that to hear such a statement was rather welcome and reassuring, to say the least, but amongst the relief and joy of it, there was the seed of growing fear as to the safety and well-being of her mother. "I do wish to stay with you," she began as she leaned back into his embrace.

"Then you shall," he soothed, curling his body around her.

"Yes, but what of my mother and of Ivy? Who will protect them?"

"Not you," Hunter replied swiftly, pressing a kiss to the top of her head. Slowly he stepped back, releasing her to pull out a chair for her to sit and eat.

Lowering herself into the offered chair, Audrey kept her eyes averted from him. "If I do not protect them, then I shall never feel truly happy, for my father will make their lives intolerable. When I am at Whittemore House, he focuses on me, which relieves them of his perversion to be cruel. *Oh.*" Audrey sniffed, placing her closed, trembling fingers over her mouth. "I have been so selfish."

Hunter reached across the table, closing his large hand comfortingly over her petite one. It seemed that what upset her about the circumstances was not concern for her own needs but for the needs of others. Audrey was the embodiment of kindness, he realised, bringing the underside of her wrist to his lips as he moved around the table and crouched before her. "Your maid is already safely residing at Carlisle House. I instructed Elkins to see to it. And, as for your mother, she is already alone with your father—"

Audrey gasped, realising her error.

"Do not fret, darling, for as soon as we return, I will ensure that your mother either resides with us or, if that displeases her, then Wallace Whittemore will not so much as think of upsetting her ever again. That is a promise, Audrey. You must trust me."

"I do, and thank you. You are indeed kind to me, even after I have caused so much bother," Audrey offered, turning her hand over until their palms touched and fingers entwined.

"You are not the cause of any of this." Hunter moved to sit on the edge of the bed whilst guiding Audrey off her chair and toward him until she settled into the warmth of his lap. "Besides," he added, capturing her mouth with his, "I have quickly come to realise that I would happily walk through fire for you, Miss Whittemore."

Audrey flushed raspberry pink. "I would never ask you to," she rasped, feeling quite overwhelmed by his declaration.

"And that is why I love you." Hunter held Audrey's gaze as he permitted her a moment or two to absorb the meaning of his words. He had known how he'd felt from the moment he had offered to ruin her at the Peterson ball, but he had not been as courageous as perhaps he should have been to openly admit it, for as he was coming to understand, within the quiet space between his declaration and her response, such words uttered by one conjured a certain rather uncomfortable sense of vulnerability within oneself.

Tears teetered on the lower lids of Audrey's eyes as she swallowed the sudden and rather unexpected urge to cry. It made absolutely no sense, she thought, for one was not supposed to cry when one was happy, were they? Yet there her body was, resolutely refuting her idea of what was correct at rather an important moment, and she was about to make Hunter's shirt rather soggy indeed.

"I did not expect to hear you say that," she choked out as she wiped a tear away and attempted to compose herself. "I thought it would be too soon, and that, Hunter, is the very reason I have kept perfectly quiet every time I have wanted to say the very same to you."

Curling his thick finger beneath her delicate chin, Hunter encouraged Audrey to look at him. "Never feel the need to hide how you feel, my love. Speak when you want to speak, for I want to know all of you."

"Then Hunter Carlisle," she whispered, her lips curling in a sensual smile, "I love you too."

"You do not know how wonderful that feels to hear you say it."

"You know, I am also learning how to demonstrate it," she muttered, blushing prettily.

"Are you indeed?" Hunter drawled, scooping her up into his arms as he stood to his magnificent height.

Audrey nodded. "Shall I show you?" She giggled, then kissed the base of his throat.

Hunter growled, leaning over her as he lowered her onto the bed. "Minx."

"Am I to assume everything has been prepared, Whittemore?" Lord Gastrell pulled his shoulders back as his chin multiplied over the tight, starchy white collar of his formal attire. "It pains me to point out that you are failing rather magnificently at upholding your side of the bargain."

Wallace Whittemore stepped forward, his face pale and his eyes wide. "I believe we have a problem, my lord," he snivelled.

The mere reference to his title narrowed Gastrell's eyes as he peered down his nose at the man who was causing him considerable grief. He could not understand how the buffoon could not control a chit. "Enlighten me, Whittemore, for I fail to see how all this could be any more of a problem than you have already caused me."

Swallowing, Whittemore stepped back to create a wider space between them. "As you are aware, Lord Carlisle announced his betrothal to Audrey—"

"Doesn't signify!" Gastrell snapped. "We have a contract."

"Indeed, but as you know, Audrey is rather argumentative and troublesome, so when I informed her of such, we fought."

"*We fought*," Lord Gastrell mimicked. "You sound like a chit, Whittemore. I don't enter into business with brainless chits. As a man and as her father, you do not argue, you simply demand, yet here you are telling me you had a *tiff* with a girl."

Wallace Whittemore curled his fingers into tight fists in his pockets. He wanted to pummel the condescending prig somewhere in the vicinity of his bulbous nose, he mused, unable to take his eyes off Gastrell's jiggling jowls as the man continued to question Whittemore's masculinity. Had it not been for the threats looming over his head, Whittemore was quite certain he would have taken great pleasure in loosening a few of the man's teeth. "I do not wish to discuss the relationship I have with my daughter, Gastrell," he seethed. "I merely wish to inform you that she has absconded."

"For your sake, Whittemore, you had better be

jesting," Gastrell retorted, his eyes piercing Wallace with promises of misfortune as he rocked back and forth on the heels of his highly polished shoes.

"As much as I wish that were true, it is not." Whittemore returned Gastrell's glare challengingly. "It seems that locking my daughter in her bedchamber in the hope she would remain there until you arrived to collect her was insufficient, for the chit succeeded in finding another way to escape me." Wallace turned away from Lord Gastrell, afraid his eyes would deceive him with the revelation of his concern. Audrey had ruined everything, he silently grumbled, mentally making a note to wring her neck when he caught up with her.

Gastrell remained silent, gathering his thoughts and words into a neat little pile inside his head rather than allowing the explosion of anger he had wanted to release to echo throughout Whittemore's residence. "I assume you have already issued instructions for her to be found and returned."

Whittemore nodded.

"That is something, I suppose."

As if on cue, two footmen entered through the front door. "We have news, sir," the tallest one announced, looking at both men as though he was unsure whether he should be discussing such matters in front of the guest.

"Well, get on with it," Whittemore spat,

growing rather irritable with all involved. *Why could he not, on just one occasion, have everything go according to plan?*

"We saw the Carlisle crested carriage outside an inn a few hours from here, sir."

"Ready the carriage then, *boy*. I think it is about time your employer had words with this Carlisle." Gastrell stared down his nose at Whittemore, daring him to argue.

"Yes, boy, ready the carriage," Wallace confirmed.

Audrey slipped out from beneath the sheets, wrapping Hunter's shirt around her naked feminine form, and tiptoed to the window. For the first time since she could remember, every muscle in her body felt at ease and in harmony with her mind. She gazed over at the gentleman sprawled across the mattress and sighed. How had her fortune changed so dramatically in such a short space of time? she wondered as her fingers tweaked the fabric and pulled the drapes a few inches apart to view the scenery beyond the cold glass panes. It seemed that Carlisle's servants had made good on their word, for there it was, the Carlisle crest emblazoned on the solid, glossy black surface of a carriage.

"Come back to bed," Hunter drawled, reaching out as though he could simply touch her from the distance where he lay.

"No," Audrey chuckled, turning her head back to peruse the comings and goings of patrons and staff.

"Then I shall come to you."

Hunter rose from the mattress in all his glory as Audrey's light green eyes widened at his god-like physique and evident arousal.

"You are wearing my shirt," he drawled, noting how the light filtered through the thin cotton of the garment, creating a silhouette of Audrey's body for his eyes to feast upon.

"Yes, I am, and that is because I have no idea where you discarded my clothes," she sniffed playfully. "I did not want to draw open the curtains and give the world outside a view of my person. That," she added, trailing a finger down his muscle-defined chest, "is only for you."

"I should hope so, my little minx," he growled, lifting her away from the window and carrying her towards the bed as he nuzzled into her neck.

Feeling rather splendidly ravished already, Audrey escaped his grasp to tend to her ablutions, then dressed in her breeches, shirt, and waistcoat, giving herself one last perusal in the looking glass as she tucked her defiant curls beneath her cap. "I should tend to Athena," she mused, peering over her shoulder at Hunter as he pulled on his boots. "She will wonder why I have left her in that ramshackle shed, not to mention with Galileo. If that gelding is anything like his rider, she will be blushing to her roots," she announced, grinning wickedly.

"Indeed," Hunter drawled, grabbing Audrey's hand and pulling her back onto the bed where she lay flush atop his body. Hunter wrapped his strong arms around her, laughter rumbling against her lips as he kissed her. "Athena will be utterly ruined. What will all the other mares say?"

Loud voices sounded outside the inn. Familiar ones, Audrey thought as she swallowed the rise of fear. How could her father know where she was?

Panicking, she turned abruptly, her forehead almost colliding with Hunter's chin as she scrambled off of him and stood. "They can't find me," she breathed, her hands curling around the tweed of her breeches and scrunching it nervously. *Air*. She needed air, she thought.

Hunter was standing only seconds later, and in one stride he was at the window. "Who and wh—" Staring through the thin pane of glass, Hunter caught sight of Whittemore and Gastrell. "Damn those men," he growled, pulling Audrey close to him. Curling his hands firmly, yet gently, around her upper arms, he placed the suddenly flustered Audrey in front of him. "You are not going anywhere with them. Do you understand?"

"Yes," she rasped, looking rather pale at the prospect of such a fate.

"Good. Now, you must stay here. Keep that disguise on and make sure none of those curls escape your hat," he ordered kindly. "I will see to them."

Watching Hunter walk out of their room, Audrey wondered whether getting rid of those two men would really be as simple as Hunter assumed it would be.

Chapter Twenty Three

Hunter had thought, *or perhaps rather he had hoped*, that Gastrell and Whittemore would have opted to have travelled the road to London, yet hearing them bickering outside the inn, as well as Audrey's name being batted back and forth from one man to the other, had enlightened Hunter to the fact that he had misjudged them entirely. Indeed, his misconception of the men had been a rather inconvenient error, for now he would need to get rid of them. Never mind, Hunter thought with a sigh. Wallace Whittemore may be somewhat of a pain in his backside, but, nevertheless, he was manageable, and as for Gastrell, he would have him running for the hills in no time, what with all the evidence he had against the man. Reputation ruination and the procurement of the four walls of a dark, dank cell as one's home for the foreseeable future were not exactly high up on a lord's list of priorities.

"Wait here," Hunter whispered with a gentle squeeze of Audrey's hand as he made his way out of the room, then descended the stairs. Taking a deep fortifying breath, he remained calm and focused as he headed into the taproom to seek out the innkeeper.

"Good morning, my lord," the innkeeper offered. "How's your friend? Hope he didn't suffer too much from the bad weather."

Ah, yes, the disguise. Hunter didn't know whether the innkeeper was playing along due to the need to be polite or whether Audrey had indeed fooled him. It was probably best for all if he simply stuck to the original lie, he thought, offering the man a smile. "He is much better, thank you." Hunter leaned slightly over the rough grey wooden bar with a conspiratorial air. Perhaps he could use this moment to gain an ally, for he needed someone to bar the way towards where Audrey waited for him. While he was out *discussing matters* with Whittemore and Gastrell, he wanted to know that she would be safe. "It seems," he continued in a low tone, "he needs our help."

The innkeeper's eyebrows twisted and dipped at the centre in confusion. "Go on," he encouraged.

Hunter's voice dropped to a whisper. "The young lad works for a neighbour of mine. For quite a while, I was oblivious to all the goings-on, but not so very long ago, *Aubrey* confided in me." Hunter shook his head, adding a flair of dramatics to lure the man further into the scenario he was embellishing quite nicely. "His employer runs a disorderly house and has ordered the boy to tend to the more risky and, of course, illegal errands for him, all so that he may keep his own hands clean. However, if Aubrey refuses, this man has promised to make his life, for lack of other words, hell."

The innkeeper looked horrified. "Bastard," he breathed angrily.

"Indeed, but he did not threaten merely that alone, for he also promised to use all of Aubrey's sisters as what he referred to as *attractions.* I believe we do not need to have it spelled out for us as to what he meant by that, now, do we?"

The innkeeper grunted with fury. "How can someone be so bloody cruel? Some of these toffs have no idea," he grumbled. "Excluding you, my lord, of course."

"Do not worry, good man. I do not think too highly of them myself."

The innkeeper smiled. "What I don't understand, though," he pondered, "is *why* he made such threats."

"Why does any man with power make threats?" Hunter retorted, giving the man time to mull it over. "Yet he did, and now the poor lad and his family have been forced to find dwellings far from here, simply so they may have a fresh start. He was on his way to meet his family when he became ill."

"Poor sod," the innkeeper sighed. "I will help him and you any way I can."

"Much obliged, sir, for it seems his employer

and his right-hand man are currently gathered outside this very building. I need you to send for the constabulary. Even though they may not perhaps listen to Audr... Aubrey-"

The innkeeper pressed his lips together as Hunter erred over Audrey's name, a spark of amusement crinkling the corners of the man's grey eyes. Hunter ignored it, yet he was quite certain either Billy had been talking, or the innkeeper hadn't been fooled by Audrey's disguise either and was merely playing along. Feeling slightly weary from all the pretence, Hunter couldn't help the thin veil of concession to the truth drifting over his own face. "I believe they will listen to me," he added.

Hunter was certain that, although the innkeeper knew Audrey was indeed Audrey and not Aubrey, the man had obviously sensed that what Hunter was telling him was a somewhat distorted version of the truth.

"I will send word at once, my lord. But what will you do until then?" the innkeeper queried, heading for the side door.

"There is only one thing I can do, and that is I must face them. It should buy us some time."

The innkeeper nodded. "I will make sure no one goes up those stairs," he said, pointing up towards the room where Audrey was waiting.

"Thank you."

Hunter's tall, broad figure filled the doorway

of the inn as he lifted his eyes to the sky. The weather had improved considerably, yet the two men lingering in the corner of his vision, utterly oblivious to his presence, syphoned any pleasure from it. Nonchalantly, Hunter pulled a cigar from his top pocket and leaned against the wall. Being someone who took no pleasure in smoking, he merely carried the things as a method of softening a conversation with a fellow businessman when required. Perhaps, he considered, he could make the conversation amicable, but as he caught two pairs of eyes glaring in his direction, he placed the cigar back into his pocket. *Perhaps not.*

"*You,*" Whittemore growled.

The man's gait was awkward, Hunter observed, his lip curling in displeasure. Had it not been for his own desire to throttle the man, he may have thought Whittemore's utterly pathetic attempt to intimidate him highly amusing, but all it served to do was irritate him further.

"Whittemore," Hunter offered in greeting, keeping his tone low so he would sound perhaps somewhat amiable. He had learned over the years that raising one's voice proved only to encourage an opponent to raise their voice higher than one's own. And, being thoroughly aware of what he wanted to say to Whittemore, Hunter knew that if he relayed it how he wanted to relay it, he was quite certain that the man would be positively squealing after the first sentence. So, instead, Hunter decided it would be best to keep his voice calm. "What brings you this way?" he drawled.

Wallace Whittemore halted, confusion flashing across his eyes as he faltered in his apparent mission. With a quick and rather audible clearing of his throat, the man flared his nostrils and puffed out his chest. "You know very well," he barked.

"Do I?" Hunter pushed away from the wall where he had been leaning and swaggered a few steps towards the men, his eyebrows raised and the corners of his lips tilted down in a puzzled expression. "I'm afraid you shall have to enlighten me." Reaching inside his coat pocket, he felt the cigar resting against the evidence of Whittemore and Gastrell's deeds. He pulled the cigar out – but not before giving the hidden folded parchment a gentle tap against his chest – then trailed it beneath his nose, pretending to savour the moment, as though he had all the time in the world. Yet beneath the surface, Hunter pulled back the beast that wanted to pounce on Audrey's father, for words of explanation hardly seemed apt for the anger he wanted to inflict on the man.

"Don't play games with me, boy. Where is she?"

"She? I do not believe I have been quite so fortunate for a long time, Whittemore. Besides, if you recall, I am betrothed to your daughter. However, if that is what has turned your flesh to the most terrifying shade of red, fear not, for I am loyal to my fiancée."

"She is not your fiancée!" Whittemore bellowed as the red of his skin deepened further.

Hunter wondered what other shades the man was capable of. Perhaps he should test it out, he mused. "That, Whittemore, is quite incorrect, is it not? I suppose if one is uncertain, they need only enquire amongst the ton, and I am quite sure they will all confirm my version of events."

Gastrell stood on the sideline, his dark, dilated pupils flitting from Whittemore to Hunter and back again.

"How dare you!" Whittemore bellowed, charging forward and knocking the cigar from Hunter's hand.

Hunter smirked. "My, my, we have a temper, do we not? You know, Whittemore, one cannot merely go around grunting and issuing accusations as and when one pleases and then not expect to have those accusations refuted. Nor can one expect to be liked when one is an utterly selfish tyrant of a father." Hunter rolled his shoulders, casually collected the cigar from the ground, then returned to his full height. "Do you not agree?"

Stepping back, regret, fear and confusion crossing Whittemore's features, the man stumbled, then quickly righted himself. "I know you have her," he stuttered. "You announced your fake betrothal so that you could simply bed the chit," he seethed, regaining some of his composure.

Gastrell placed one foot into the fray. "Perhaps we can make a deal, Lord Carlisle," he drawled. "After all, I am not a greedy man."

Hunter narrowed his eyes and curled his fists behind his back. He remained silent.

Mistaking his silence for interest, Gastrell continued. "From your intrigue, I believe you are very much like your father, the late Lord Carlisle. He, too, was a businessman. Well, perhaps he didn't dabble in trade as do you and I, yet one cannot deny that he was a very clever, cunning man. He knew what was good for him. It must run in the family."

Hunter wanted to bloody the man's nose.

"Yes, indeed," Gastrell continued. "My offer is simple. Once I marry this man's daughter, I will allow you to bed her. Test out the goods, as it were."

Hunter's fist flew with considerable force, colliding with Gastrell's chins, all six of them, taking both he and the oaf down to the ground, where he tightened his grasp around the repugnant lord's cravat. Hunter paused in an intense inward battle between common sense and animalistic urge as he fought valiantly to resist slamming the man's head back into the earth for good measure. That would never do. The last thing Audrey needed would be him in a prison cell unable to protect her.

Gastrell was trembling and whimpering. "Don't hurt me," he wailed.

Whittemore grabbed the fabric at the back of Hunter's jacket, but Hunter ignored the ridiculous man's feeble attempts to pull him off the lecherous beast. Instead, he leaned closer over the trembling lord and his jiggling jowls, allowing his eyes to burn into him. "Don't you ever speak of my wife-to-be like that or any other way. In fact, you never get to speak her name again." Hunter's voice was dangerously low. "Is that clear?"

Red blood against stark white skin, Lord Gastrell nodded profusely.

Hunter abruptly loosened his fingers from around the fabric of Gastrell's cravat, giving the oaf one last shove before he rose to his feet, then walked back to where he had originally been standing and simply glared at Wallace Whittemore. "What about you, Whittemore? You seem awfully quiet now for a man who had apparently come to rescue his daughter from me. I would have thought that your friend's words would have been enough to send any decent, loving father after the cad, merely to draw blood. Ah, yes," he continued, "I forget, for you are not a decent, loving father, and you didn't come here to rescue Audrey. You came here to ensure that you and the extremely poor excuse of a man at your side could continue with your little *arrangement.*"

"I have no idea what you are talking about, Carlisle," Whittemore said, somewhat flustered as he pulled on the ends of his coat to straighten the starchy black fabric. "Just hand over Audrey, and

Lord Gastrell and I will not have to resort to other measures."

Hunter snorted, then threw back his head, unable to contain a bark of laughter at the preposterousness of the man's threat. "Stop waving around threats you cannot reinforce, Whittemore." Hunter stepped forward. Anger darkened his gaze as he stood over Audrey's father. "You and Gastrell, here, have been misbehaving, have you not?" Hunter's lips curled at one corner. The anger inside him was delighting in seeing the man mentally shrivel and cower. However, it also enraged him that Audrey had a weak man for a father. She deserved people around her who would always protect her, those that would fall over themselves simply to ensure her happiness, but Whittemore… well, he was most certainly none of that. No indeed, he was the exact opposite.

In the background, Gastrell struggled to his feet but remained in the shadows, allowing Whittemore to continue the *negotiations*, not that Hunter would negotiate anything with either of them. They repulsed him.

"I will not ask you again, Carlisle. Where is my daughter?"

"I am here, Father." Audrey stepped out of the inn doorway. Her face was pale as she looked to Whittemore, then to Hunter.

Hunter cursed beneath his breath. He had

things he wanted to say to her father, yet he did not want to say them in front of her. He couldn't imagine how she would feel if she knew *every* detail of the kind of life Wallace Whittemore had no qualms subjecting her to. Hunter had explained, but he had skirted around the details, trying to protect her. It was evident, though, that she thought she did know every detail, he realised with a pang of guilt. Yet guilt or no, he did not want for her to know the truth of the men she would have had to deal with or how many she would have been expected to lie beneath.

Hunter blew out a breath. Witnessing Audrey standing there, brave and bold, undoubtedly ready to protect him, Hunter realised that she had no idea how incredibly beautiful and precious she was. "You should go inside where you are safe, Audrey," he whispered. The tips of his fingers tenderly brushed her cheek as he moved closer to her, enveloping her with the protective yet gentle side of his masculinity.

"I will, but I want to say something first, Hunter. Please?"

Green eyes that spoke a thousand words, with irises drowned in a pain that Hunter recognised, gazed up at him. He could see that this was important to her, and so he simply nodded. Unable to release her completely, he closed his large hand gently around her delicate fingers, then turned, revealing her to her father.

"Audrey, get in the carriage now," Whittemore demanded. "You are making a fool of yourself."

Hunter squeezed her hand for reassurance.

"No, Father. I am staying with Hunter," she declared, pursing her lips and gently jutting her chin out in defiance.

"You will do no such thing!"

Wallace Whittemore was forgetting their little discussion, Hunter thought irritably as he seized the man's wrist, preventing him from grabbing his daughter. "Have we not already had this conversation, Whittemore?" he drawled. "I would be terribly disappointed to think that you had not listened. Tsk, tsk, tsk, such terrible manners, especially from a man of your years. Perhaps you and Lord Jiggly-Jowls over there would like me to announce to everybody in the inn what you have been up to. Is that what you would like?"

The nervous amusement in response to Lord Gastrell being referred to as Lord Jiggly-Jowls died on Audrey's face as she noted the fury in Hunter's voice. Taking a deep breath, she stepped forward. She and Hunter were a team now. *She needed to say something*. He was, after all, doing this all for her. "It doesn't matter what you say, Father," she began curtly, "for I have made up my mind."

Hunter squeezed her hand and brought it to his lips, yet never once did he take his eyes off Whittemore. "Your father knows, my love, and I am certain he will not make any of us repeat it again. Now, please, *my heart,* for your own safety, go inside where these men cannot try anything underhanded."

Audrey's shoulders rose and fell with a great sigh. "Please be careful."

Hunter nodded. "I will not do anything to harm you, ever. Nor will I allow anyone else to."

"I meant you, Hunter. *I don't want anything to happen to you."* Lifting her hand up, Audrey cupped Hunter's face in a gentle caress.

Hunter kissed her fingers. "I shan't be long."

Audrey nodded. "I love you," she whispered, smiling, then with a last look at her father and a scathing glance at Lord Gastrell, she disappeared into the inn.

"Get back here, gal!" Whittemore shouted, spittle flying from his lips in rage. "I shall see that everyone knows that you are a –"

"A what?" Hunter interrupted, reminding the man of his presence. "If you were going to say what I think you were going to say, then I would find myself in a rather awkward predicament, Whittemore. You see, such a mistake on your behalf could be rather detrimental to your reputation."

"Don't say another word, Whittemore," Gastrell piped up from behind him. "This is all your fault as it is. Can't even control a chit," he grumbled.

Hunter's gaze sliced through the air, piercing Lord Gastrell with an unmistakable warning. "Ah, see," Hunter drawled. "Now, you are getting it."

Curiosity and a rather evident hope that they were incorrect played across the men's faces. There was a reason the ton thought that acting was beneath them, and it was simply because they were appalling at it. "Would you care for me to elaborate, gentlemen?"

"We are not interested in your absurd theories, Carlisle," Whittemore sniffed. "If the so-called knowledge you are implying that you have was indeed true, you would have spat it out by now, *and* you would have proof, and since you have neither, then I suggest you return my daughter, and we shall leave you in peace. After all, I would not take any pleasure in calling the constabulary to inform them of my daughter's kidnapping."

Wallace Whittemore clasped his hands behind his back as he turned his head to gaze sideways at Lord Gastrell, his face mirroring the smug, satisfied smile his partner in business wore.

"No need, gentlemen," Hunter began, dragging the sentence out simply to torment them a little longer.

"Glad to see you have seen sense," Gastrell boomed, stepping forward. "Perhaps I should merely go in and get the chit then."

Stretching his body lazily, Hunter leaned

across the door frame, filling it entirely and barring entry. "Oh, I apologise, Gastrell, and of course, to you too, Whittemore, for what I meant when I said that there was no need to call the constabulary was that I have already sent for them."

"What exactly is it that you think you have on us, Carlisle?" Lord Gastrell seethed, his face still bloodied from their earlier scuffle.

"Ah, finally!" Hunter exclaimed, straightening his spine and pulling his shoulders back. "I am so glad you asked. It took you long enough."

Gastrell stepped forward, a foolish amount of hot air emanating from his nostrils. He rather resembled a rhinoceros, Hunter considered as he flicked an invisible speck from his jacket. "I wouldn't if I were you, Gastrell. No indeed, for *if I were you*, I would do the sensible thing and pay attention to what I have to say. After all, you may not have time nor opportunity when you are being escorted to the gaol." Hunter shuddered for effect. "The very thought of spending years, let alone days, in such an environment sounds ghastly, does it not?"

Gastrell stepped away.

"Spit it out, Carlisle," Whittemore ground out.

"Patience, my good man. Such information and your response to it deserve to be savoured. They say that revenge is best served cold, but this version is rather delicious when it is hot. Now hush," he barked, startling them. "I shall explain.

"At first, when I had the displeasure of being introduced to you gentlemen, I have to admit that I found you… What is the word?" Hunter tapped his chin thoughtfully. "Ah, yes, that's it. I found you both rather *disturbing*."

"What is the meaning of this?" Gastrell raged, flailing his hands up in the air.

"Gastrell, believe me when I say that it is best that you do not interrupt me," Hunter warned.

Whittemore remained quite still, frozen perhaps, albeit his eyes that seemed to be scanning the area surrounding them, looking for a glimpse of an escape route, or perhaps he was simply curious as to whether Hunter was true to his word and thus looking for a constable.

"Your offence at my words has been noted," Hunter drawled, grinning to himself. "However, the introduction was merely that, simply an introduction. Although, if you will, please snuff out any hope that my opinion of you both has gotten any better, for you will be sorely disappointed, I feel. One does not like to disappoint in such matters." Hunter turned and paced in front of the inn.

"Go and get the chit, Whittemore. This boy does not have anything on us, and if he does, then he certainly does not possess any proof."

"I am afraid my solicitor and two other acquaintances may have to quite firmly disagree with you on that one, Gastrell."

Lord Gastrell froze.

"Very wise, Gastrell. I shall continue." Hunter paused and listened. The gentle sound of carriage wheels travelling over the unmade roads rumbled in his ears. "As I was saying... At my request, my solicitor did a thorough search into your life, past and present. And what he discovered and reiterated to me was rather interesting indeed."

The sound of carriage wheels grew louder, heightening Hunter's senses as one question seemed to be louder than all the others. *What would Audrey wish for Wallace Whittemore?* After all, he was her father. *Would she really wish for him to be incarcerated, or would she wish for something less harrowing?* Blast it, he grumbled silently; he should have asked her.

Squaring his shoulders, Hunter assured himself that there was still time. "Whittemore," he snapped, "go inside."

"I beg your pardon?" Whittemore huffed. "You owe us an explanation, boy!"

"He's got nothing on us, Whittemore. The boy is bluffing," Gastrell scoffed.

"If you know what is best for you, Whittemore, you will do as I say." Hunter shot the man with a warning glare, one, it seemed, he heeded. "Gastrell does not need you to hear his business, and you do not need him to hear yours," he added sharply.

The gravel beneath Whittemore's boots scraped the dusty earth as he turned his back reluctantly on both men.

"Before you go, you are to merely sit at a table and wait. Do not so much as attempt to speak with Audrey. Is that clear?" Hunter hoped that Audrey had had the sense to lock herself in their chambers.

Nodding, Whittemore disappeared through the inn doorway.

"Finally, that blithering idiot has gone. Now the *real* gentlemen can discuss matters."

Gastrell had morphed into pure arrogance, and it was rather obvious that he did not believe the constabulary had been alerted, Hunter concluded. How long he could remain that way was another matter entirely for which Hunter would receive the answer very shortly, indeed, if his ears were not deceiving him.

"Matters such as your disorderly house, Gastrell?" Hunter offered, wiping the smile off the man's face.

"I beg your pardon?" he stuttered, feigning outrage at such a suggestion.

"Come now, old boy. It is just you and I here." Hunter subtly peered over Gastrell's shoulder, noting the constable quietly step down from his vehicle and nod in his direction. The apparently rather astute or perhaps merely well-informed officer stopped quietly out of Gastrell's peripheral vision to simply listen.

Too het up with anger, Gastrell had not even noticed the constable's arrival but merely continued to quiver with rage as Hunter's revelation goaded him.

"You are very quiet, Gastrell. I shall have to assume that your silence is acceptance of your guilt in the matter. It is, after all, why you wished to marry Miss Whittemore, is it not?"

"Fine!" Gastrell snapped. "I own and run a business that satisfies a man's desires and needs. Men need satisfaction, after all," he grunted. "It is a service that is highly sought after, for half the gentlemen of the ton are married to washboards —women that are flat, unwilling, and thoroughly grate on a man's nerves. All I do is ensure that they can escape such monotony for a small fee. Miss Whittemore will be a fine addition. Indeed, every man will want to romp with her, as you are well aware, my boy."

Something far greater than anger simmered in every fibre of Hunter as his jaw clenched. He couldn't act on his urge to flatten the man as he had before, not with the eyes of the law upon him. If they escorted him away, he would have to tell them of Whittemore, for he wouldn't leave him anywhere near Audrey. Hunter shook his head, bringing his focus back to the matter at hand – *Gastrell.* "And is she aware of your plans for her?" he ground out, keeping his gaze to the floor so the wretched man would not notice the fire blazing in his eyes.

"The chit doesn't know what is good for her, so why on earth would I tell her anything?"

Hunter's short nails bit into the palms of his hands. "I had assumed you had merely wished for her to be your wife?"

"She will be that as well. Every gentleman knows that a successful businessman tests the goods first." Gastrell smirked.

Hunter lifted his head, his eyes settling on the arrogant lord. The man was enjoying himself, he realised as bile bit the back of his throat with its acidic fangs. "It is interesting you should admit you are willing to marry her and then house her in your establishment of ill repute, for I have it on good authority that she is not the first lady you have done this to."

"It hardly matters, Carlisle. Unless, of course —"

"Oh, on that account, I believe you to be highly mistaken, Gastrell," Hunter sneered, cutting the man off. "It seems that you intend for Audrey to be your *third* wife to enter and remain on the premises."

"What business is it of yours? Now step aside, and I shall retrieve Whittemore and that ridiculous daughter of his so we can be on our way. Time is money and all that."

Hunter could not believe the abhorrent arrogance of the man. It appeared that Gastrell was endeavouring to bluff his way through the never-ending trail of his misconduct. The buffoon did not even so much as possess a mere shred of decency. Truth be told, Hunter wondered whether Baldry had merely scratched the surface of Lord Gastrell's crimes.

Hunter dug his feet into the earth, refusing to put any distance between his body and the entrance to the inn. The constable's eyes were fixed on Gastrell, and time was indeed of the essence, for there was one more truth that needed to be spoken aloud. "I wonder what the law would say if they knew that your other two wives are still alive and are currently being forced to carry out *services* in your house of ill repute. I believe bigamy is highly frowned upon, Gastrell, and one might even say that it is illegal."

Hunter did not need to raise his eyes from Gastrell to know the constable had heard. The sudden rigidity of the man's posture in the corner of his eye informed him of the gentleman's disgust-induced yet carefully tempered rage.

"And who is going to tell them? You, I suppose? A mere baron," Gastrell mocked.

Hunter shook his head. "Oh, no, not me. Don't be ridiculous, old boy. I believe that has already been taken care of."

Gastrell narrowed his eyes.

"Yes, indeed," Hunter continued. "You, Lord Gastrell, saved me the job. Of course, I will claim a little of the glory, for I did help somewhat," he added, unable to keep the satisfaction and pleasure from his voice. "However, I applaud you, for your perfectly timed admission appears to have been the final nail in your coffin, as it were."

Gastrell swallowed as the constable's heavy hand pressed down hard on his shoulder. "This way, my lord," the constable snapped. "And to think if another lord hadn't reported you, you might have gotten away with it. I think the magistrate is going to be rather pleased with me. He ain't too keen on lords like you."

"It isn't just me!" Gastrell roared. "It was Whittemore as well."

Hand still clamped on the man's shoulder, the constable turned. "Is this true, my lord?" he queried, looking at Hunter for confirmation.

"Not that I have discovered, for it is only Gastrell's name on the deeds and, of course, the only name on several marriage certificates."

The constable nodded. "You don't deserve a title," the constable grumbled at the quivering Gastrell as he pushed him up into the back of the vehicle. "Blaming another man for the crimes you commit. Disgraceful, that's what you are."

"If I do discover anything else, constable,"

Hunter called, "I will be certain to inform you."

"Thank you, my lord. I wish all gentlemen were like you. England would be a much better country if they were, that's for sure."

Relieved and very much in need of a brandy, Hunter turned on his heel and headed back inside the inn. There was one more individual he had to deal with.

Eyeing the rather sheepish expression fixed to Wallace Whittemore's face, Hunter glided up to the table, promptly seating himself in the chair opposite the man. "How much of that did you hear?" he enquired as a single eyebrow rose, warning Audrey's father not to lie. The flash of a black suit as the man had hurried to the table, hoping Hunter wouldn't discover he had been eavesdropping at the window, hadn't been particularly easy to miss.

"Some," Whittemore mumbled. "I never knew that Gastrell was such a scoundrel."

"Save it for someone ridiculous enough to believe it," Hunter seethed, glaring at the gibbering fool. "Did you honestly believe that I did not find out that you and Gastrell were in all this together? Good God, man, you are a bigger idiot than you look."

"I knew nothing, I swear," Whittemore protested.

Hunter pulled several folded documents from his inside pocket and placed them on the table between them. "You can have these," he offered, pushing them toward Whittemore. "I have copies."

Wallace stared down at the offending documents. "What are they?" he queried, his hand shaking as it hovered over one of them.

"Why don't you take a look?" Hunter encouraged. "I think you will find them very interesting indeed." Hunter was becoming increasingly impatient. The sight of Wallace Whittemore was rapidly becoming beyond aggravating. He simply wanted all of this nonsense to end so that he could return to Audrey. He did not want to be away from her any longer than was absolutely necessary, and her father was wasting his time. "As you seem to be having some particular difficulties in picking up a simple document to read the first of them, then let me explain, in the simplest terms, what you will find in all three."

A snifter of brandy stopped suddenly beneath Hunter's nose as the innkeeper slid it towards him. "You deserve this," the man offered kindly and walked away. It seemed the innkeeper had heard everything.

"Thank you," Hunter mumbled, then quickly lifted the drinking vessel and tipped its contents down his throat for fortification, appreciating the comforting burn as it travelled lower into his body. "Where were we? Ah, yes."

Wallace Whittemore shifted in his seat, eyes flitting from Hunter to the innkeeper and back again. It seemed he had some level of intelligence then, Hunter deduced, as he noted the moment the man realised that whatever he knew of him, it was quite possible that the innkeeper did too.

"In these rather thick wads of folded parchment are documents that were due to be signed by you," Hunter began, lowering his tone so as not to cause a scene. "It states that *you*, the *father* of Audrey Whittemore, were willing to offer your daughter in payment for half of Gastrell's business. She was then to marry the blackguard and serve within said business." Hunter took a deep breath and sat back in his seat. "Can you imagine my surprise when I found out what sort of business you wanted to get your grubby little fingers on and, more to the point, the type of business you were willing to force your daughter to offer services for?"

If Hunter had thought Wallace Whittemore was pale before, he realised that the man's skin could indeed pale even further. "I can see that you are indeed very aware of what information I have on you."

Silence.

"Not very talkative all of a sudden, Whittemore. Very unlike you, I must say. Never mind because your silence will simply make it easier for me to tell you what you will do next."

Whittemore's eyes snapped to Hunter's in silent question, a flicker of fear sparking off them as he waited for Hunter to continue.

"Gastrell is currently on his way to prison with the understanding that this disorderly house was merely his and his alone. I believe I failed to mention your name, but believe me when I tell you that it was not for your sake; it was for Audrey's. You are still her father, and I do not want to be the man who puts you in prison."

The sudden shimmer of light in Whittemore's eyes was unnerving, Hunter thought, returning the man's expression with a scowl. "Do not get too comfortable, Whittemore, for if I get one tiny crumb of evidence that you so much as try to go near Audrey, I will *accidentally* let slip about your misconduct, and you will see yourself on trial at Gastrell's side. Of course, there is the possibility that your friend, Gastrell, will sing like a canary about you when questioned, so on that note, I would like to make you an offer."

Grey, Hunter mused. That was a new shade of skin tone. Not one he had seen before, but Whittemore was wearing it rather well.

"You will sign over the estate to your wife whilst I clear all of your debts, allowing that poor woman who has had to put up with you all these years to have a fresh start at life. You will also find yourself heading to Dover, where you will board the next boat out of England. I do not care where you go as long as you are so far away that it is impossible for you to harm Audrey."

"I will have nowhere to live," Whittemore objected quietly, running his hands through his thinning hair.

"I am not heartless, Whittemore. I will give you ten thousand pounds. That should be ample to see you settled on distant shores. Once you *are* settled, you will write to me, *and me only*, with your address so that should Audrey ever wish to see or speak with you again, then she will be able to contact you. Have I made myself clear?"

Whittemore nodded. "Perfectly."

Hunter stood. "Remember, Whittemore, this is for your benefit. If you defy me, do not think for one moment that I will not find out, and even if I didn't, I am quite certain Gastrell will send the constabulary after you, and there will be no boarding a boat then."

Whittemore nodded grimly. "I'll go."

"I am pleased to hear it. I will take care of everything," Hunter added, sliding a thick envelope across the table. "I brought this with me today, believing Audrey would need my assistance, but as the tables have turned, I will leave it with you."

Leaving the thick wad of money concealed in the envelope on the table, Hunter turned away from the rather crushed version of Wallace Whittemore and headed back up the stairs, pausing briefly as the door of the inn opened and then slammed shut.

"He's gone, my lord," the innkeeper called up

the stairs.

"Thank you, sir. I shall see you are rewarded for your help."

"No need, my lord. It has been my pleasure. May I suggest that you and your young lady have some breakfast?"

Hunter had been right, the man had known. "That would be wonderful," he called back, amusement lacing his voice. "Thank you. Oh, and apologies for twisting the truth. It was no reflection on you, I assure you."

"No need to explain, my lord. I probably would have done the same." The innkeeper chortled.

Audrey stepped back from the window. The familiar tone of dominance bent and shaped the fluctuation of male voices into words, yet as they drifted into the room through the thin glass window, they seemed to be nothing more than blurred, unrecognisable shapes to her ears. However, the things she did note were that the three men had dwindled to two, the arrival of a fourth voice – whom she had no clue as to their identity – met her ears, and Hunter had been marvellously in control of the situation the entire time. Finally, when there was only silence, she found that her stomach was in a knot and her head was positively spinning with it all. Sighing, she propped herself on the edge of the bed and waited.

The door to the room opened slowly. Audrey rose to her feet, apprehension roiling in her stomach as the floorboards creaked beneath her boots. Hunter was casually leaning against the doorframe in the stance she was beginning to know so very well. His well-defined body blocked the limited light from the landing as he dominated the doorway with the air of a protector. He was her protector, she realised as he strode in silent confidence into the room, closing the door behind him with a swift kick.

Wordlessly, he curled his large frame around her. "You are safe now," he rumbled into her soft, mahogany hair. "Gastrell has a one-way ticket to visit the magistrate and your father…"

Audrey noted Hunter's hesitance to speak of the man who had raised her. "You did not inform the constabulary of his part in it all, did you?" she whispered, pressing the side of her face against his hard chest.

"I did not."

Every muscle in his back and chest seemed to solidify to stone at the sound of his confession. *Did he think she would be disappointed in him?* she wondered. Loosening her hold around his waist, Audrey tilted her face upward. "Thank you," she whispered, pushing herself up on the tips of her toes and cupping his face with her hands – the tender moment born out of the need to simply brush her lips against his, to feel the sweet warmth of his breath mingling with hers. Audrey followed the first kiss with a second and then with a third, her soft lips teasing the delicately sweet act into something more sensual until it silently conveyed everything she wanted to say. She did not entirely understand the tear that slipped from the corner of her eye, but she was beyond certain that it was not born of sadness.

"I have promised to pay his debts and have given him enough blunt to ensure that he will be alright, on the proviso that he leaves England," Hunter explained. "It will not be safe for him to stay, for Gastrell is bound to speak of him with the constabulary, and your father will find himself in the one place we are trying to avoid for him. I have sent word to my solicitor to request that he travel to Dover in expectation of your father's arrival, and to ensure he will have all the relevant documents for him to sign. This will mean that your mother will have the entirety of the estate solely for herself and that you will be free to marry anyone you choose."

As silence ensued, Hunter cleared his throat.

Chuckling, Audrey tapped her chin with a slender finger. "Decisions, decisions," she teased. "There are so many handsome gentlemen to choose from."

Hunter scowled.

"I wonder if my neighbour will marry me?" she teased, her eyes twinkling as she delighted in the tightening of Hunter's arms around her.

"I have every faith that he w—"

"I mean, the butler *is* very handsome and smart."

"You leave Elkins out of this, Minx."

Hunter leaned in to kiss her neck as Audrey threw her head back with laughter. "I suppose I shall have to become Audrey Carlisle then," she sighed, enjoying every delicious touch.

"Oh, I believe you will be quite content, Miss Whittemore," he rumbled.

Chapter Twenty Four

The journey back towards Carlisle House was turning out to be quite the quiet one, Hunter thought as he watched the woman he was in love with gaze thoughtfully out of the carriage window. Her exhaustion from the prior days, and perhaps even weeks, seemed to have surfaced rapidly at the news of her father's departure.

"Penny for them, darling?"

"I would give them to you for free if I could decipher one thought from the other." Keeping her eyes on the view through the glass, Audrey reached out to her side, lacing her fingers with his.

Hunter lifted her hand to his lips. "I will take great care of you, Audrey," he promised. "So, please, if that is your concern, then you need not fret."

"My concerns are not about you, Hunter. Indeed, it is you who instills in me the little courage I have. My concerns are scattered from here to Dover."

"Your father, do you mean?"

"Yes. I know that he has behaved dreadfully, and he is very lucky that he has been given the opportunity to maintain his freedom, but I cannot help but worry for his safety." Audrey turned her eyes to meet Hunter, then shuffled a few inches across the seat, closing the distance between them. Even though their thighs touched, she inched just a tad closer still so that she could rest her head comfortably upon his shoulder. "I know I must sound ridiculous," she offered, quietly.

"Not at all. He is your father when all is said and done. Wallace Whittemore doesn't realise how incredibly lucky he is to have you." Hunter kissed the top of her head. "I did not mention it earlier," he continued, "but it may ease your mind a little."

Audrey shifted her position to look up at him. "What is it?" she queried.

"As part of the agreement with your father, I have requested that he write to us with his address as soon as he is settled. It will give you the chance to decide whether you wish to write to him or not. Whatever you decide to do is perfectly fine with me, Audrey. As long as you are happy, then so am I."

"Thank you. I think it will take time for me to forgive him, but it will be good to know that he is alright," she replied hoarsely, pressing the side of her face against Hunter's chest as she curled her arms around him.

"I don't know why," Audrey breathed as they

rolled into Carlisle estate, "but Carlisle House looks so much bigger than I remember." Audrey's eyes climbed to the top of the manor, then roamed the vast expanse of the property's exterior.

"Perhaps you are merely looking at everything in a new light, darling," Hunter drawled, alighting from the carriage and offering his hand to her. "Come. Let me show you your new home."

Audrey took Hunter's hand, her fingers tingling as though it were their first touch. This was real, she realised. The fear that had hung over her head for the past few months - a turbulent, vengeful cloud - had dissipated. She had fallen in love, and now she was on the path to spending the rest of her life with the most exquisite man she had ever had the fortune to lay her eyes upon. If Hunter had not been looking at her with such curiosity, she was quite certain that she would have pinched herself to ensure that it wasn't all some rather wonderful dream.

Blushing to the roots of her hair, Audrey smiled at each servant waiting patiently on the drive as Hunter made the necessary introductions. They were quite aware that she and Hunter were not yet married, but she supposed that having Ivy there with her as her maid and now companion, no one would so much as bat an eyelid at the situation. Yet, she mused, how they could not have their reservations and, perhaps more than that, suspicions of hers and Hunter's intimacy out of wedlock, especially with the way Hunter held her so possessively in front of them and bestowed kisses on her sporadically and entirely unabashedly, she would never know.

Audrey savoured the cool caress of a pleasurable shiver, the delicate spatter of delightful indulgence, kindled by the low rumble of Hunter's laughter as it tickled the tender lobe of her ear.

"Formality is something you must leave at the door here, Audrey," he offered, running the back of his finger along the remaining heat of her blush. "I run a rather different household than my mother."

"I believe I have met Lady Carlisle," she remarked, meeting the butler's eyes for the first time.

Elkins nodded and smiled knowingly.

"Correction, it was *Aubrey* who met Lady Carlisle," Hunter teased. "It seems I will need to straighten a few matters out with her. *That,* and, of course, the fact that she needs to cease interfering in my life. She has gone too far this time and I will not have her continuing with whatever it is she and that other chit, Lady Vanessa, are up to."

"Yes, indeed," Audrey retorted, her smile rather strained as she remembered the uncomfortable encounter with Lady Carlisle.

Hunter pulled her closer to his side as they continued the walk towards the house and up the granite steps.

"Good afternoon, Elkins, Gertie. I would like you to meet my betrothed, Miss Whittemore."

"Audrey, please," Audrey offered, her features brighter as she took in their kindly faces. "I apologise for the way in which I ran off the other day," she added as she turned her attention to the butler.

"There is no need to apologise, Miss Whittemore. I very much felt like running out as well." Elkins chuckled as he bent gently at the waist. "We are simply glad you are here with us now."

Audrey liked Elkins very much, she thought, as she softly cupped her hands over his and then repeated the action with the young lady at his side. "It is wonderful to meet you both," she assured them with a smile.

"Oh, and you, Miss Audrey. Isn't it, Elkins?" Gertie interrupted, nudging the butler as though his mind had wandered off in a completely different direction.

Elkins rolled his eyes playfully, all the while smiling and shaking his head in amusement. "It is indeed, dear Gertie. It is—"

"Oh, she ain't half pretty, sir," Gertie interrupted, her voice dripping with awe. "So glad you didn't choose that snooty mare, Lady Vanessa. Right one, she was."

Elkins cleared his throat as Hunter chuckled at Audrey's side. "Have you quite finished, Gertie?"

the butler chided.

The maid blushed. "Beg ya pardon, miss, sir. I get a bit carried away sometimes."

"No need to apologise, Gertie," Audrey replied. "It is lovely to be greeted with such kindness. And, as far as I am concerned, kindness is indeed always welcome."

"Your rooms have been prepared, Miss Audrey. Would you like me to show you to them?" Elkins offered, stepping forward.

"I shall see to that, Elkins, but thank you. I wonder, though, whether you could see to it that a bath is prepared," Hunter requested as he began to lead Audrey away, wanting to ensure that she would not become overwhelmed with it all.

"Of course, sir. All the lady's belongings arrived this morning and are in the designated closets and drawers."

"Thank you, my good man. We will see you all a little later, then."

"You will indeed, sir."

As soon as the door opened to her new bedchamber and her gaze fell on the lady in the room, Audrey hurried towards Ivy and flung her arms around her with the force and tenderness of her unwarranted guilt. "I'm so sorry I left you behind, Ivy," she expressed. "I didn't want to leave you. I was locked in, then Father told me that when I next left the house it would be with Lord Gastrell. I really didn't see any other way out of there."

"Shh, shh, shh, Miss Audrey," Ivy sang soothingly. "You mustn't fret. You are here now. See, there's no harm done. In truth, I would have done the same thing. Any sensible person would have." The maid tightened their embrace briefly, then, when she spotted Hunter behind her mistress, she uncurled her arms and turned her attention back to the chore of folding the remainder of the garments whilst stacking them neatly in the relevant drawers. Although Lord Carlisle seemed a very decent sort of gentleman, she hardly knew him and wasn't entirely certain whether he would find hers and Audrey's friendship somewhat unorthodox.

"I will leave you ladies to it," Hunter interrupted. "Ivy, should Audrey need anything, please do not hesitate to ask. And Audrey, my love, I will meet you in the dining room for dinner."

Audrey gazed affectionately at Hunter, allowing herself the time to absorb how her life was blossoming in the aftermath of the storm she had faced. "I shall be Audrey again by then," she returned playfully, gesturing to her attire. "I think I am quite ecstatic at the prospect."

Hunter crossed the room in one stride, scooping his arm around Audrey's waist and kissing her gently. "You have always been Audrey to me. *My Audrey,*" he assured her, then with a gentle squeeze of her bottom that made her squeak, he grinned and exited the room.

Contentedly, she sighed.

"Where is she?"

Audrey giggled, pleasantly surprised to see her best friend, as she sashayed down the staircase of Carlisle House. "You really do not need to be quite so loud, Flossie," she chided playfully, "for I am right here."

Golden curls bounced at the sides of Flossie's dainty-featured face as she unintentionally ignored Elkins, rushing past him with an obvious sense of urgency to embrace her closest friend. "I have been so very worried. Why did you not come to me?"

Brushing aside her friend's tickling curls from her face, Audrey loosened their embrace. "I cannot say that I was thinking very clearly at the time, Floss. Besides, it would not have been fair to your parents."

Flossie frowned. "Yes, perhaps you are right. Papa is rather apt at doing entirely the wrong thing when merely trying to do the right thing. Lovely, silly man," she tittered. "Oh, you have no idea how good it is to see you, Audrey."

"Come, let us have tea together," Audrey encouraged, stepping through the door of the parlour. She had been residing in Carlisle House for less than a day and had already managed to ascertain where a certain masculine bedchamber was, her bedchamber, the dining room, the main drawing room, the library, and the small parlour. There were so many rooms, she found herself wondering whether she would ever learn them all.

"Yes, please. That sounds wonderful," Flossie replied, unable to refrain from perusing their surroundings in the hope that she may catch sight of her friend's intended.

"Hopefully, you will meet Hunter soon," Audrey offered, recognising her best friend's inquisitiveness in her glances and the tapping of her fingers upon her knee. "He is quite busy, but I am sure we will see him if you stay a while."

"Gladly, Audrey. I want you to tell me everything." Flossie's cheeks dimpled.

"Elkins," Audrey called quietly, turning to catch the butler's attention, "please, may we have some tea and coffee and perhaps some biscuits?"

"Yes, of course, Miss Audrey."

"Thank you, Elkins."

"Very welcome, miss."

Warmth spread like a thick blanket over Audrey's heart as her eyes and mind basked in the ease and pleasantness of her new surroundings. She simply could not escape the gentle kiss of awe at everything new in her life.

"How is Lady Esme?" Audrey enquired as

Flossie rose from her chair and glided around the parlour. The young woman's eyes danced with excitement for her friend. "I hope she does not think badly of me for running off like that," Audrey added.

Lowering herself onto the settee, Flossie's blue eyes widened. "Oh, heavens, no, of course not, Audrey. You mustn't think that. I am quite certain that, had Aunt Esme been in the vicinity at the time, she would have helped you escape. We have all been so very worried about you, but never fear, for there is not one of us who thinks poorly of you."

"Oh, thank heavens." Audrey sighed. "I cannot tell you how much of a relief that is to hear." Audrey picked up the teapot, wondering whether her friend's words and understanding stretched to the impropriety of her new living situation. Of course, she indeed was quite happy, some may say thrilled, in fact, when Hunter had refused to relinquish her, but she was well aware of the frowns that such a sordidly viewed living arrangement could conjure from society. Mentally shrugging off the concern, she proffered the tea-filled cup to her friend, then picked up her coffee and sat further back in the chair. "A splash of milk and two sugars. I hope that was correct?"

"Yes, perfect. Thank you, Audrey."

"Lady Florence."

Both ladies turned as Hunter entered the parlour, sifting through the mail as he walked towards his betrothed and deposited a kiss on the top of her head. "Darling," he drawled.

"My lord," Flossie offered as she stood and curtsied.

Hunter grimaced at his title on another lady's lips, all the while noting the way Audrey stifled a giggle behind her cup of his best coffee. "Please call me either Carlisle or Hunter. I am not keen on the title, and I am merely a baron by default. It is something I have accrued forcefully and not by choice, I can assure you," he offered with a slight grumble.

"My apologies, Hunter. Please, I insist that you call me Flossie. We are all friends now, are we not?"

"Indeed. If you will excuse me, ladies, I am afraid this was merely a brief visit. It seems I will be in my study, for my time has suddenly found itself assigned to seeing to this nonsense." Hunter lifted the bundle of correspondence to emphasise what he was referring to, nodded politely, then exited the room.

"*Ding-dong,* Audrey," Flossie exclaimed as soon as Hunter closed the parlour door. Her eyes were wide, sparkling gems as she grinned mischievously with approval. "Your betrothed is even more handsome close up."

Relieved that she hadn't taken the sip of coffee she was thinking about, laughter burst from Audrey's lips. "He is rather, isn't he?"

"Excuse me, Miss Whittemore."

Audrey startled. In all the chatter, she had not noticed anyone else enter the room. Everyone seemed rather light-footed in Carlisle House, other than Ivy, who was trying very desperately to adhere to the sudden depreciation in noise. "Hello, Baldry."

Baldry swallowed as his eyes caught a rather prettily blushing Flossie. Intrigued, Audrey remained quiet in subtle observation of the two newly acquainted people and in her very best attempt to go unnoticed. Books often talked of love at first sight, but she had never thought it to be true. However, witnessing the instantaneous sparks fizzing across the room between Flossie and Baldry, she rather thought they were trying to prove to her that it was indeed possible. *Interesting*, she mused with a smile.

"Everything alright, Baldry?" Audrey interrupted when it all began to get a little awkward, her rather knowledgeable grin stifled by the pain her teeth were causing as they pressed into the inside of her cheek.

"Beg pardon?" Blushing profusely, Baldry gazed at Audrey with confusion.

"You were about to ask me something?"

"Ah, yes. My apologies. I seem to have lost Carlisle."

"He is in his study, sir."

"Thank you."

"Where are my manners?" Audrey exclaimed, her words halting the solicitor's exit. "Mr Baldry, I would like you to meet my very best friend, Florence Braithewaite. Florence, this is Mr Baldry. My apologies, Mr Baldry, for I am not familiar with your given name."

Bending gently at the waist, Mr Baldry lifted Flossie's hand. "Edward Baldry, my lady," he whispered, placing a kiss gently on the back of Flossie's satin-concealed fingers. "It is a pleasure to meet you."

"The pleasure is all mine," Flossie practically purred, standing, then offering the man a genteel curtsy. "Will you be at the wedding, Mr Baldry?" Flossie queried breathlessly as she rose to full height. She slowly retrieved her fingers from the man in front of her, merely out of a sense of propriety, it seemed, for at the speed their hands parted, it was quite evident that neither wished to let go.

"I will indeed. And, if you are attending the wedding also, then perhaps you will do me the honour of dancing a waltz with me this Saturday, Lady Florence?" the solicitor rasped, his face flushing a gentle pink.

"I would be honoured. I shall save it for you, Edward."

"*Oh, my,*" Audrey whispered as the door

closed behind the solicitor. "Perhaps I should run away more often, Floss, if this is what happens upon my return."

"Yes, indeed," Flossie replied with an air of wonderment laced in every syllable. A smile curled her lips as her eyes lingered on the door and her intrigue positively pinned itself upon the man beyond it. Shaking herself from her reverie, she turned her attention back to Audrey. "Anyhow, my dearest friend," she offered, determined not to get quite so carried away, "let us concentrate on you and Hunter. As I have said, I absolutely insist on all the details."

As if on a very poorly timed cue, the door to the parlour swung open with such incredible ferocity that Audrey's cup almost took flight. No longer able to narrate the edited, propriety-primped and preened version of her time with Hunter, Audrey simply stared in the direction of the door, mouth poised in an o, looking rather aghast. *Drat!* She had been quite looking forward to sharing her joy with Flossie, for one can only hold so much in before one would burst at the seams. However, as she rose to her feet, allowing her eyes to rove over the familiar woman standing in the doorway, all the desire to speak of such matters diminished.

"Where is my son?"

"I'm so sorry, Miss Audrey. I asked her to wait, but she wouldn't," Elkins panted, his grey eyes wide with sheer panic.

"It is perfectly alright, Elkins. It is not your fault at all," Audrey replied, shooting a mild look of disdain at Lady Carlisle.

"What are you apologising to her for?" Lady Carlisle spat spitefully at the butler.

Ignoring the woman, Audrey smiled kindly at Elkins, giving a gentle nod that he evidently understood, for he reciprocated the gesture and backed out of the parlour.

"Lady Carlisle, would you like to join us for tea? Or perhaps you would prefer coffee?"

"I am not here to visit my son's *strumpet*," she hissed, trilling the r in the word for emphasis. "I am here to see my son. His betrothed is very upset at the news of *your* unwelcome arrival." Lady Carlisle clasped her hands in front of her, then thrust out her bosom as she straightened her spine. She sniffed haughtily. "Get him at once, girl."

"Now, see here." Flossie abruptly rose to her feet, fury deepening into balls of fire where the once sweet pink of the apples of her cheeks sat.

Audrey raised her hand to calm her friend. "Do not worry, Floss. I have met Lady Carlisle before, and I am quite aware of her ability to fabricate, especially with regard to her son's apparent betrothal to Lady Vanessa."

Flossie flomped down into the seat with a huff to emphasise her disgust at the woman.

"*Fabricate?*" Lady Carlisle screeched. "You are simply his little plaything. Mark my words, girl, Lady Vanessa will be the next Lady Carlisle."

"I thought it was you." Hunter stood behind his mother with an expression that did not deny his utter disdain for the woman.

"Oh, Hunter, darling," Lady Carlisle crooned, turning to face him. "I was just explaining to this girl here that—"

"I know exactly what you were saying, Lady Carlisle. Once again you have been caught in your lies. In the fifteen years that I did not have to put up with your pitiful meddling, it seems that I had forgotten quite a bit of the venom that you always manage to combine with it, so I thank you, Lady Carlisle, for reminding me," Hunter seethed, his voice summoning the darkness into the glare he settled upon the woman.

"*Lies? Lies?*" Lady Carlisle practically screamed. "That little strumpet is the one who lies. Saying that I had told her before that you were engaged to Lady Vanessa. Pah! That is simply untrue. You see, it is *she* who is the liar."

"Wrong again, Lady Carlisle. You did indeed tell her that. You were the one who sent her running from this house in the belief that I may have betrayed her. I nearly lost the love of my life because of you," Hunter growled, pushing past Lady Carlisle and standing proudly at Audrey's side.

"Whatever—" Lady Carlisle began. Her voice slowly drifted into merely a thin whisper upon the air as realisation began to dawn upon her face.

"I see you are beginning to remember that you at least said such nonsense," Hunter stated with satisfaction.

"Perhaps I did, but that was to a boy, not her." Lady Carlisle ran her eyes over Audrey, her nose curling to one side. "It was you?"

Audrey nodded as she sidled closer to Hunter. "The disguise was needed," she protested, noting the hatred towards her as Lady Carlisle simply glared.

"Audrey," Hunter interjected, "you do not need to explain yourself to anyone. Make no mistake, Lady Carlisle is the one at fault."

"*I wish it had been you,*" Lady Carlisle hissed, anger rising in crimson upon her face as her eyes flitted in every direction, then drilled into Hunter. "I have been a good mother to you, and *this* is how you repay me. Argyle would never have done this to me. Your father should have ensured that you would never have had the opportunity to return. You bring shame on the family name."

Hunter yawned. "Have you quite finished, Lady Carlisle?"

Silence.

"Good. Now, let me reiterate what I have told you before, and let me be clear that this is the last time I will say it." Hunter released his grasp on Audrey and stalked towards his mother, placing his large frame between the two women. "You either go back to the home that I have permitted you to reside in, take the generous monthly allowance that I have ensured you will receive, and stay as far away from Audrey and I until I take leave of my senses and contact you again, *or, Mother dearest,* you will lose *everything*."

Lady Carlisle moved to step past him, her mouth opening to say something, Hunter assumed it was more distasteful words that had been meant for Audrey.

"Not another word," he growled. "*Leave. Now.*"

Audrey swallowed as she observed Hunter's mother storm out of the parlour, barely noticing the curl of Flossie's petite arm around her shoulders. "What a horrid woman," Flossie remarked quietly.

"That, Lady Florence, is an understatement," Hunter drawled. He exhaled. "Can I trust you to stay with Audrey for a little while longer?" he queried. Hunter's eyes were assessing Audrey despite him addressing her friend.

"Of course, Hunter. I shall let you know if I have to leave."

Audrey stepped forward and up onto the tip of her toes as she caressed the side of Hunter's face, enticing him lower until the tips of their noses softly touched. "I love you. I hope you know that," she whispered.

"And I love you, darling. More than I can ever put into words."

As Hunter returned to his study, he unclenched his fists. He had merely curled his fingers to still the fury surging through his veins and rattling his bones. He could not believe that his previous words had been that difficult for his mother to comprehend, but this time he had paid attention. It was as though a light had flared behind her eyes as his words fell upon her ears in crystal-clear sounds. Comprehension was apparently not as far from her reach as he had thought. She had indeed heard him this time. Having saved Audrey from her father, he had fallen in love with the one woman who had, unknowingly, saved *him* from his mother and the ties that bound him to his past. He was the most fortunate man to have walked the earth, he thought with a roguish and rather love-struck grin. Indeed, Saturday could not come soon enough.

Epilogue

As Audrey ran through the open fields, behaving very unlike the way in which a lady should, she squealed as her husband caught up with her, sweeping her up into his strong arms, then over his shoulder. "Lady Carlisle, the weather is frightful. I believe it is time we head inside so I can warm you up." Hunter ran his hands up the back of her legs. "Oh, how terribly scandalous, for I believe you have forgotten your petticoats again. It is an awfully wicked habit," he chided, continuing his hungry, light-fingered exploration all the way up to her thighs.

Audrey wriggled. "They are dreadful things. If you are so insistent that I wear them, then I dare *you* to wear them for at least a day under heavy skirts."

As they reached the stables, Hunter slowly lowered her to her feet, refusing the air an opportunity to invade and create a space between their drenched bodies. "I don't believe I said anything about you having to wear them, and if I did, I do not think I would ever be particularly insistent, for I rather like how I can do this." Hunter placed his large hands over her bottom and squeezed, all the while nuzzling into her neck.

After three years of marriage, the excitement that many ladies tittered about and had said often dwindled had only grown stronger between she and Hunter, Audrey noted breathlessly as shivers ran down her spine at the caress of his lips upon her skin. It was a vast difference between the life she had once believed she would have—the life her father would have forced her into—and she often found herself enthralled in a sense of wonderment at the world she and her husband had created together.

It took weeks for her mother to refurbish the Whittemore residence, and in doing so, Marjorie Whittemore had refurbished her entire life, it seemed. In fact, Audrey had to wonder why she had never realised just how incredibly unhappy her mother had been. Her childhood home now possessed the touch of summer with simple, refined décor and trinkets rather than the brash, overpriced statement pieces that she had come to loathe. Marjorie Whittemore had friends, friends who took the time to visit, who were not afraid that they would be turned away at the door. All of which only served to form a twinkle in her mother's eye and a pretty rouge upon her cheeks. Audrey thought her mother positively glowed. She wasn't the only one to notice either, she considered with a smile, for the woman had even caught the attention of a rather kindly duke.

As for Wallace Whittemore, his first letter arrived six months after the wedding. After a few weeks of waiting to see whether he would indeed keep to his word by writing to Hunter with his whereabouts, Audrey had begun to wonder whether her father's pride had gotten the better of him, or perhaps he did not care for her at all as she had already surmised. However, as she had read the apparent heartfelt apology along with details of his new address, she felt herself longing to give the man who had raised her the benefit of the doubt, thus luring pen to parchment and the steady flow of correspondence between them. Yet, even after three years, she maintained an unspoken distance within their relationship. He may have been in Italy, but words could be known to hold considerable power even in the written form. It was too dangerous. She simply wouldn't permit herself to forget that he was still the man who had tried to steal her future so that he could have his. No indeed, she was not willing to allow him close enough to destroy what she now had.

"Hunter Carlisle." Audrey grazed his lip with her teeth as she pulled away from him to conclude the rather heated kiss. "I do believe you promised to read our son his favourite book."

"I hardly think Theo would mind his papa being a little late," he drawled, leaning forward, suggestively nudging his hips towards her to remind her of the power she had over him. "Besides, the poor lad doesn't understand a word of Treasure Island, darling. Of that, I am quite sure."

"Be that as it may, *my lord,*" Audrey whispered, blowing the words softly against his ear, "I rather think he likes the sound of your voice. And then, of course, I have invited Flossie over for dinner. She and Edward will be arriving in just over an hour."

"You are a hard woman, Audrey Carlisle, and a tease," Hunter grumbled playfully, capturing her lips in a chaste kiss as he lowered her skirts, then pulled at the fabric of his breeches to ease the discomfort of his evident arousal.

Audrey gazed down at the evidence. "Oh dear," she giggled, wickedly sliding up against his body as though they were crammed into a tight space.

"Oh dear, indeed, Minx."

"I shall race you back to the house," she grinned. Audrey's eyes glittered playfully. "If you win, I shall make *it,*" she continued, gesturing to his nether regions, "up to you tonight.

"I will hold you to that."

A roar of laughter rocked Hunter's body as he stood beneath the portico of Carlisle House. The thought of his wife naked beneath him had been all he needed to fuel his determination to win. The rain had turned the soil sodden and slippery underfoot, guaranteeing his victory as Audrey slipped on her bottom, recovering quickly yet not quick enough as Hunter had beaten her to the finish line. The sight of a rather muddy version of his wife stalked towards him, a grin creasing her features and brightening her pale green eyes. "You win."

"Indeed, I do. In fact, I have been winning for the past three years, darling," he drawled, scooping her back into his arms and carrying her over the threshold and up the staircase as he gestured to a passing servant to prepare a bath.

The love in Hunter's eyes took Audrey's breath away as he lowered her drenched body, kissing her as her feet lingered only a few inches from the floor. "I adore you, Audrey Carlisle."

"And I you, my darling," she breathed. "So much more than I can ever explain."

Books By This Author

The Unanticipated Bride

Lady Lorelei Whitworth was quite content being an independent lady. Of course, some had referred to her originally as a 'Wallflower', which then quickly digressed to the rather derogatory title of 'Spinster', but that was no matter to her, for she would not allow herself to be party to conversations that referred to her as such. After all, she had her own home and was quite financially sufficient, so there really was no need to adhere to all the ton's unwritten rules and expectations, especially that of acquiring a husband. However, that did not mean that one did not, on the most odd occasions, feel a certain sense of loss, or perhaps it would be more suitable to say that it was a certain sense that something or someone was missing. It was quite troubling indeed, she thought, for she could not quite understand how one was to miss what they had never had.

Lord Maximilian Lazenby had already had one wife. Their marriage had been more of a business transaction between families rather than a love affair. As cruel as it may sound to those with sensitive ears and hearts, he did not even grieve for the woman when she passed but merely concentrated on his two daughters' struggle to come to terms with their loss. In truth, Max had often wondered whether he was capable of such a delicate emotion as love for a wife. Perhaps it was not meant for him, he had mused. Of course, he was not devoid of sight, for he was quite capable of appreciating the beauty of a woman, but he had never felt that something that others had often spoken of.

It seems that Lady Lorelei Whitworth may very well have been a spinster and set for a life on her own, and Lord Maximilian Lazenby did indeed believe that he was incapable of love, but when one does not consider puddles and pelisses, how is one ever to understand that fate has rather different plans?

Fictional Historical Romance set in 1800s with a little spice.

Guarding The Lady's Secret

Lady Clementine St. Clair had never been anyone's fool and where the matter of being tricked had been concerned, considered herself thoroughly immune. But it seemed that her heart would positively disagree with her rather splendid view of herself, for she soon finds herself on the brink of ruin.

Ezra Burrell made many a young lady and their mamas swoon, yet after his last attempt at love, he swore never to entertain the subject of romance ever again. However, despite his vow to steer clear of the female species, it appears there is one who he cannot avoid.

Thorn - Revised & Rewritten: Violet Hall

Violet Hall had never dared to dream, for she had always been informed that she would never amount to anything. They had been words, amongst many, that had been spat, screeched, and bellowed from her own grandmother's lips, so when the news of her grandmother's impromptu trip to London—leaving the young lady quite alone—whispered in her ear, Violet was rather glad of it, for it meant that she would be free to explore beyond the four corners of the land that had been her prison for twelve years.

Mrs Lavinia Bainbridge did not ask nor want to be burdened with her granddaughter. It was just typical that her daughter Kitty would be so selfish and die, thus leaving the chit in her care. It had been twelve years with that creature, weighing her down, and now that Violet's inheritance had dwindled, she needed another way to afford the lifestyle she desired. The girl herself, she'd decided, was indeed the answer.

Emil Merriweather was rather a fine specimen, according to the ladies of the ton. Indeed, he was often invited to soirees with the intention of the host to introduce him to some rather eligible young ladies, but to Emil, although the young ladies were indeed rather lovely, not one of them had the ability to make him want to court her, for he believed them all to be rather dull as well. However, it seems that his heart was not completely numb to the fairer sex, for Violet Hall was rather lovely indeed.

With Violet's need for freedom and her grandmother's need for wealth, will Violet ever find her happy ever after with Emil?
Dear reader, I certainly hope so.

Thorn is a fictional historical romance set in the 1800s with spice and very subtle fantasy.

Printed in Great Britain
by Amazon